DEADLY RENDEZVOUS

I took my keys out of the ignition, stepped out of the car and locked it. Even though it was a hot night I turned up the collar of my windbreaker and walked on the shadowy side of the lot, away from the building. I could see Shondra's Saturn under the trees. It was by itself and somewhat camouflaged in the shadows. I could not see Shondra in the driver's seat.

I did not see the other car until I was within fifteen yards of the Saturn. Then I heard its ignition switch on and saw its headlights flip up, and then it was rolling toward me very quickly, a big, quiet, smooth silver Olds sedan, and then I saw its rear window slide down as it turned, and the arm and the semiautomatic pistol-rifle with the silencer, and then I was diving behind the Saturn, hearing the quick, silenced thumps of the bullets smashing the asphalt. . . .

Also by William Jaspersohn

NATIVE ANGELS *(A Peter Boone Novel)*

LAKE EFFECT

A Peter Boone Novel

William Jaspersohn

BANTAM BOOKS
NEW YORK · TORONTO · LONDON · SYDNEY · AUCKLAND

This is a work of fiction. Names, characters, places, and incidents are the products of the author's imagination or are used fictitiously, and any resemblance to actual persons, living or dead, events or locales is entirely coincidental.

Special thanks to Joe McCarthy, Floyd Nease, and Henry Dunow.

LAKE EFFECT

A Bantam Crime Line Book / November 1996

CRIME LINE and the portrayal of a boxed "cl" are trademarks of Bantam Books, a division of Bantam Doubleday Dell Publishing Group, Inc.

ISBN 0-553-56993-7

Published simultaneously in the United States and Canada

Bantam Books are published by Bantam Books, a division of Bantam Doubleday Dell Publishing Group, Inc. Its trademark, consisting of the words "Bantam Books" and the portrayal of a rooster, is Registered in U.S. Patent and Trademark Office and in other countries. Marca Registrada. Bantam Books, 1540 Broadway, New York, New York 10036.

PRINTED IN THE UNITED STATES OF AMERICA

OPM   0 9 8 7 6 5 4 3 2 1

For Will Hopkins
and
Mary K. Baumann

lake effect n. The effect of any lake in modifying the weather in nearby areas.

LAKE EFFECT

1

"CAN YOU FIND HER?"

The lake lay low and flat through the wide window, its surface dark and thickly rippled near shore, but blue and sharply sparkling toward the middle. Beyond it, miles away, Jay Peak, humped and rounded like a green dome, stood above the lesser hills, its granite pale brown against the deep green, its tram towers tipped and craggy in the haze. Heat wave. Nan Holland and I had skied Jay a couple times last winter. Nan was a good skier who liked to lead down the black diamonds and whose legs absorbed the bumps with aqueous ease. Afterwards we would go to her place or sometimes mine, shower, cook a good meal, nuzzle over wine, and make love. Once, instead of dessert, we made love in her kitchen on the sliding seat of her rowing ergometer. A Concept III, we called it. Her oar puns to me thereafter had been raunchy and mischievous. They emboldened the two of us to make summer plans. That was in January. Then came mud season, season of suicides. In April she said she thought we needed time to cool off, rethink; perhaps see other people. I told her . . . it doesn't matter what I told her.

Now it was July. Now she was in Connecticut, at her mother's, hoping to finish her novel. I was in a house on Gatwick Lake, a big glacial artifact three hundred miles north of her, near a portion of Vermont called the Northeast Kingdom. The house's owner, a sad-eyed man in his forties named Arthur Cole, was standing near the window that framed the lake grinning at me. He was grinning in pain. He wore squashed boat shoes, a pair of baggy shorts, and, instead of a shirt, a canvas corset that pinched his chest, causing his nipples to protrude over its rough edge like fuzzy tubers. The hair on his head was dark and sparse; his build was thin but soft, his shoulders tufted. He told me the moment I stepped into the oversized old house not to mind the "flak jacket." He had injured his back two years before in a diving accident on the lake and was in almost constant pain. I commiserated; asked the obvious questions. Cole said he had tried every treatment: massage therapy, acupuncture, acupressure, chiropraxis, drugs. "All except surgery. The doctors say it wouldn't work. They say live with the pain. So I live with it." Grinning.

Tell me about pain, I thought.

He walked around the room, touching walls for balance, massaging his chafed tits as he talked. It was a big room, "the den" he called it, done to a sportsman's tastes in pine paneling, with worn leather furniture, ginger-jar lamps on old Shaker tables, a pine sink clogged with liquor bottles and, over a massive stone fireplace, a wall of North American trophy heads. There was an elk, a moose, a pronghorn, a caribou, and a black bear, all taxidermally gaping at something lost. On the floor were big, threadbare kilim rugs; on the walls were Remington gouaches and old Ettinger engravings and watercolors of hunting scenes. On a varnished powder keg was a Colt cavalry pistol and a brace of antique mallard decoys. Built-in shelves held books on cars, barns, guns, and sailboats. Near a Mitsubishi console was a glass case heavy with designer guns: Purdy, Beretta, Caprinus, Sauer.

"Quite the arsenal."

Cole flexed his lips into a pained smile. "Take 'em. They're props." He laughed sardonically. "Before the accident, my father-in-law used to drag me to Alaska to hunt with him." He limped to the fireplace and began fondling the moose's dewlap. "By his lights, I was somehow not worthy of living with his daughter in this house, which he gave to us let us remember, until I had bagged what you see here. And gone pigeon shooting with him in Mexico, duck hunting with him in Manitoba, turkey hunting with him in Texas. 'Make a man outta you yet,' he used to say."

"Looks like by his lights you've managed just fine." I gestured at the stunned heads.

"No, sir. By his lights, now that I've ruined my back, I'm a useless middle-aged fuck who can't put a gun to his shoulder. Mind you, I used to run his veneer mill in town. Now all I do is draw fat disability checks—off of *his policy,* lest we forget that, too." He grinned again, his pain and amusement intermingling.

I found myself thinking, why me. I had hoped not to work all summer, but instead go salmon fishing with Nan Holland on the Miramichi, trout fishing with her on the Battenkill, and striper fishing with her in Siasconset. She had said yes to all three after our first month's separation but then in June said no because of her book, although she still felt there was something between us and actually slept with me the night before she left for Connecticut. Multiple couplings on fresh sheets. Crawling away at dawn, exhausted and flensed. No commitments. At the door in her chamois bathrobe saying she'd stay in touch.

I couldn't see going solo to New Brunswick, Arlington, or Nantucket and so I had thrown myself back into work, a hazard of which was listening to this gimp's ramble.

"Hey, you want a drink or anything?" Arthur Cole said abruptly.

I glanced down at my watch. It wasn't quite eleven in the morning.

"I'll pass." I lifted my hand diplomatically. "But you . . ."

A look of gratitude flickered up from the sad, liquid eyes.

"I think I might. Pain's picking up." The lips flapping a stagy wince.

I watched him limp to the pine sink and build himself the mother of all vodkas. There was fresh ice in the leather-covered brass bucket and the lemon peels on the little cutting board looked freshly sliced for my arrival. Cole splashed a big dose of Stolichnaya into a toddy glass, took a pull on it, set it down, added more Stolly, then ice, then a lemon peel, then resumed his limping march around the room, nattering on about the fishing in the lake, how he thought it was coming back, how, a decade before, Reagan and that Larry Lightbulb, James Watt, had nearly decimated the lunkers. I watched him drink and half listened to him, figuring he would eventually get to the reason he had called. I gazed out the picture window at the ski mountain far away and thought of Nan. The coolness of her. My hand on her cool breasts. Her cool belly. The way she locked her legs around me. Her archings.

A zone of time passed.

"Well, can you?"

"Can I what . . ."

Arthur Cole was standing in my field of vision. The pliant mouth had somehow twisted into a worried pout. His glass was nearly empty. He looked at me with his poochy moist eyes and said accusingly, "You weren't listening."

"I'm sorry. My mind drifted. I'm very sorry."

"Did you hear what I said?"

"I did. After the part about Reagan you were saying . . ."

"Chelly and I were fishing—" He was eager to prompt.

"Chelly's your wife."

"Yes. C-h-e-l-l-y." He spelled it. "Pronounced 'shay' as in Canyon de Chelly in Arizona." He was swaying in front of me.

"I've been there. The petroglyphs. Very beautiful," I said.

"Her real name is Cheryl but she hated it and changed it to Chelly. Long before I met her, which was twenty years ago."

"You were starting to tell me . . ."

"That she uses her own last name, Killbride, instead of Cole and that, in the boat, in the middle of the lake, she said she was taking a day trip to Hanover, but that was three days ago and she hasn't returned and I guess I'm a little worried and I was asking you—"

"If I could find her."

"Yes!" His soft face was a pleading grimace. He drained the last gulp of Stolly, rattled the ice in the glass.

"Look, maybe I've made a mistake here. If you're not interested . . ."

"No, I'm interested."

"A friend of a friend at National Life told me you were the best . . ."

"Ernie Bellino?"

"Yes."

I smiled. Ernie Bellino was a first-generation Italian-American, the son of a Naples stonecutter who at age seventy still carved for Rock of Ages in Barre. Ernie was my catcher at Montpelier High—"a young Johnny Bench," the local sportswriters called him. He was touted as having a shot at the bigs but surprised everybody after high school by enlisting to catch the endgame in Vietnam. He was one of the last grunts out of Saigon, a lance corporal with shrapnel in his legs from a bog in Que Sanh and a Purple Heart and mass indifference awaiting him back home.

Ernie had a gym I used in Montpelier. When he wasn't pumping iron or hiring me to help him catch insurance cheats for National Life he studied religion and made himself available as my assistant.

"Does Bellino have it right, Boone? Are you the best?"

The trees on the lawn sweeping down to the lake were red oaks. A tree you saw a little but not that much in Vermont, Nan had said once. I squinted at Arthur Cole.

"Ernie's loyalties tend to be highly refined," I said.

Arthur Cole poured himself another snort of vodka and tottered back to me.

"Bellino said you'd find her and that you'd be discreet," he said peevishly. "That I wouldn't have to involve the police in any of this."

"Do you want them not involved?" A man saner than myself, I realized, would at least have gone alone to the Restigouche.

"I'd like to keep 'em out of it. Chelly's parents live just up from here, on the bluff. They're a big deal in this area. Lots of holdings. Big-frog prestige. They wouldn't like to pick up the papers and see, you know, their daughter the subject of a missing-person investigation."

"Win Killbride," I said.

"Hmm?"

"Win Killbride—he's your father-in-law, isn't he?"

"Right. Win and Claire. They don't know Chelly's gone. I'd like to keep it that way. Is that possible?"

The question had a nervous, charged ring to it. I decided, since I wouldn't be going fishing alone, that I owed it to the guy to play it straight.

"They don't have to know," I told him. "Nobody does."

Arthur Cole looked relieved. "Of course I'll pay whatever your fee is. An advance? Would that help?"

I shrugged. "Advance couldn't hurt." Adios, salmon, I thought. Moon-run stripers, adieu.

He asked me what my fee was. I told him. He didn't wince. He excused himself and went for his checkbook in the kitchen.

I shook my head. Win Killbride's daughter. What was I getting myself into? Win Killbride was more than just a big croaker on Gatwick Lake. He was known throughout the state as one of its biggest landowners. He was a timber dealer who owned several mills in the region and had spread his business interests into gravel, excavation, and concrete. Green-and-yellow dump trucks with "Killbride" stenciled on their doors were a commonplace in all the northern counties. Highways throughout New England were layered with gravel from Killbride pits. Killbride himself was frequently in Montpelier, seeking audiences with my friend the governor or testifying before subcommittees on the unconstitutionality of the state's environmental laws. He was an atavist millionaire, a postmodern resources baron. Word had it, he was dabbling in land development. Some said he even had the last Republican president's ear.

Win Killbride's invalid son-in-law, Arthur Cole, creaked back into the room and handed me a check for five thousand dollars.

"This is more than my fee."

"You'll have expenses," Arthur Cole said. "I just want to make sure you don't have to worry about money."

"I won't worry."

I folded the check in half and put it in my shirt pocket. When it was secure, Arthur Cole said, "Now I should tell you a few things."

I told him I was all ears and sighed at the realization of being employed again.

Arthur Cole did a flat-footed shuffle to the pine sink and gave his glass another hosing. I had been sitting the whole time in a leather wingback chair facing the big window. Cole gingerly lowered himself into a cane rocker across from me, the first time he had sat since I entered the house. His face looked slack and slightly complacent. The pain in the dark eyes seemed to have melted into easier regret.

"Cheryl—*Chelly*—" He tried to cross his hairless legs but gave up, masking his pain in a grunt—"is not a healthy woman."

"Go on," I said.

"She's on medication. Lithium and fluoxetine. Prozac. The doctors say she's low-grade manic-depressive. I think it's become more high-grade in recent years. On again, off again. Big mood swings. High as a kite one week. Down in the dumps the next. Was hospitalized for it. Five or six years ago. It stays more or less stable as long as she takes her medication."

"But sometimes she doesn't."

Cole nodded. "Sometimes she just stops and you don't notice until it's too late—she's either off the wall on one of her stratospheric ups or under a rock, thinking of slicing her wrists in a down."

"She ever act out?"

Arthur Cole torqued me an ironic smile. "Man knows the lingo." He laughed too hard. It was the vodka laughing. "Bellino said you were one smart fuck."

"Ernie's my herald," I said.

Arthur Cole resumed his manner of funereal earnestness. "She's tried a couple times. Once with Seconals, not a killing dose. Once in the garage with her car running. Once in the bathtub with my Sheetrock knife. Long cuts down both wrists." He raised his, as if to demonstrate.

"The real kind."

"But always when I've been in the house and able to

stop her." Cole drank. "This time I'm not there." The words echoed synthetically inside his glass.

"And you're worried."

"Yeah." He was. It was there in his face. Pain and worry.

"You know for a fact she's on a down?"

"No, I don't." Cole shook his head. "In fact, she may be way, way up. I can't be sure. She may have stopped her medication. I'm not sure of that either. For the past few days she's been borderline up."

"What's that like?"

"Borderline up? Big plans. Projects. She's gonna write a book. Win the Pulitzer Prize. Paint a picture series. Sculpt the greatest nudes since Michelangelo."

"She's an artist."

Cole laughed lightly. "She's got a studio out back if that qualifies. As far as selling her work goes—" He made an O with his thumbs and forefingers. A fat zero.

"You don't hang any of her paintings in the house?"

He laughed again, no more heartily. "We have an understanding. I get my den. Chelly gets everyplace else." Then he waved me off. "No. She hangs stuff where she wants to. I don't often object." He spread his hands helplessly as if I'd understand their marital dynamic.

"She ever been late coming back from anywhere before?"

"Yeah, but she's always called. Usually to say she'd be a couple hours or an extra day."

"From where?"

"Uh." He ruffled his sparse hair. "Boston. New York. Hanover . . ."

"What's she do in those places?"

"Shops. Goes to museums, galleries. Does research."

"On what?"

He made a boozy sigh. "You know, I can't honestly say? She says she's researching a book on different poets, so she'll go down to Hanover for a day, use the library there. Come home. Squirrel herself away in her studio until, I don't know, until she runs outta gas. Gets discouraged. Loses her way."

"I guess I know how that can be."

Cole gave me a throwaway smile, unconsciously scratched at a nipple. "She starts and abandons a lot of projects." His eyes went big. "A lot. Of projects." He rocked and sipped his drink and looked away from me, embarrassed for his wife. For himself.

"Was she going to do research at Baker down in Hanover?"

"I assume so. That's the Dartmouth library, right?"

"Right."

"I've never been there. I'm a city boy. Columbia."

I looked at him. He was perfect West End Avenue material. Upper seventies. "How'd you wind up here?"

He snickered. "Chelly cast a spell on me. At a Ginsberg reading. Ninety-second Street Y. Spirited me away from the city after business school. With Win's help I'd become a Natty Bumppo plutocrat. Chelly'd be Chelly in her studio. We'd all be one happy family here at the lake. Instead, she married my weak tendons."

I let the line die and Cole seemed grateful. I watched him take a long pull from his sweating glass. In a moment his mood lightened.

"Hey, I used to think the Dartmouth grads we ran into were a bunch of horny wackos."

"They are."

He laughed, and in his laughter one of his testicles worked its way from the folds of his shorts. He seemed not to notice.

I went for eye contact. "Does your wife have any acquaintances at Dartmouth? Anybody she visits or stays with?"

"No horny wackos, if that's what you mean." He grinned and shifted in his chair. Vanished the offending aggie. "No, the fact is, I've stayed out of Chelly's, call it what you will, creative life. I feel a little stupid here, Boone. I should be telling you more."

"You're telling me a lot. Are you sure you want me to go ahead? If I do find your wife, it may be in a way you're not going to like."

"You're saying she might be seeing someone?" His expression darkened.

"What do you think she's doing?"

"I don't know. I don't know where she is or what she's doing. That's why I called you. To find out."

"And why you want to leave the cops out of it?"

"It's mainly her parents." Arthur Cole held his hand limply near his stomach and made an alcoholic's threading gesture with it. "I really need to leave them out of this."

"Even if your wife is off her medication, suicidal, and the cops might be able to find her before she tries something?"

Arthur Cole rocked and sipped his drink and gave his fishy lips another workout. "I've got to risk that. I've got to have discretion on this one."

"Are you prepared for all forms of the worst?"

"What, that she's dead?" He looked at me, startled.

"That she's dead, she's left you, she's kidnapped, she's been deceiving you for longer than you'd care to know. I'm about to take this on, Mr. Cole. Not to sound like *film noir*, but the results might not be pleasant."

Arthur Cole blinked, clasped his hands around his glass, and kept rocking.

"All the same, I'd like you to find out where she is and bring her back," he said. "No matter what you find. If she's seeing someone I'd like to know about it. If she's not, I'd like her home. With me."

He sat there, sucking the last of his drink, sad eyes focused on the motes spinning in the sunlight near the window. I felt a sudden wave of pity for him. We were in the same boat. We both wanted our women back. Only he was worse off. Exiled.

Across the lake, over Jay, high clouds dappled the ski runs in shadow. A sailboat on the lake luffed in light air.

I said, "I'll see what I can do."

2

ARTHUR COLE LED ME FROM THE DEN THROUGH THE COOL house. The halls were dark and long, but I could see the wife's paintings on the walls. They did not look very good. The paint was laid on in thick gobs, and the colors were bright and unmixed. I saw poorly drawn nudes, garish still lifes, and lackluster landscapes, each signed in loopy brushstrokes with the one word "Chelly." The paintings were expensively framed, but no amount of gilt or molding could disguise their amateurishness.

Arthur Cole said nothing as we passed them. He led me down a short flight of stairs and through a screened storm door that opened onto a flagstone terrace.

It was cool on the terrace but not as cool as inside the house. In its center was a big, circular iron table painted green, with six cushioned iron chairs around it. A teak chaise lounge flecked with worm casings occupied a space near a stone retaining wall. As you crossed the patio you could see how the house was built into the hillside in three levels and how its substantial mass was hidden in front by the slope and the trees. It was a rambling, prewar house, green with shingle moss and bathed in deep shade, with big windows across the main level and a single shed dormer above. A flagstone path off the terrace led to a low dock on the lake a hundred yards away. Another path cut left at an angle toward a farther grove of oaks.

Cole took the path to the left. He carried his drink near his chest and walked with sclerotic unsteadiness. A pair of white Adirondack chairs sat on the green lawn halfway between the house and the lake. As we neared the grove I saw sculpture pieces among the gray trunks, and a large cabin deep in tree shadow.

The sculpture pieces were of welded iron and were perhaps not as bad as the paintings in the house. Zigzag shafts of reinforcing bar penetrated a huge, half-buried cog like primordial spermatozoa. A life-size sheet-iron maiden, her limbs angular, her mouth frozen in a tiny O, stood sentinel near the path beside a lumpy, prone mass. The Cosmic Egg, done in silhouette, cartoonishly hatched a sickle-bar question mark. The form nearest the cabin was a Tantric mandala, a monstrous web maybe ten feet square comprised of interwoven lengths of cable on crossed posts.

Cole looked back to see if I was coming, then fumbled a key out of his shorts pocket and unlocked the cabin which served as his wife's studio. He pushed the door back in a gesture of theatrical hospitality.

An odor of patchouli and linseed oil wafted toward me. The cabin was old and made of logs, and the outside walls were black with age and creosote. Through the door, though, it was light, and the log walls were honey-colored and chinked with white plaster. I held back on the path for a moment, feeling I had stumbled into an odd enchanted wood.

"Coming, Boone?" Cole swayed in the doorway.

I walked up the low worn wooden steps to the wide granite stoop and followed him inside. The cabin's honey-colored light came from skylights running the length of the rough-sawn board roof. There was only one room, with a river-stone fireplace in its center and work spaces in three of its four corners. In one far corner an empty easel stood by a table with painting implements on it. The floor was pine, except in the corner near the door where a concrete pad had been poured. On it sat a pile of rusted iron, an oxyacetylene tank, a torch, and a full-face welder's mask.

In the farthermost corner, partially hidden by the fire-place, was a writing space with bookshelves and a computer. In the other near corner, behind the door, was a bed, a reading chair, and a table. Navajo rugs and a row of plaster masks decorated the wall over the bed. The atmosphere of the spaces was comfortable, yet spartan.

"Welcome to Chez Chelly." Cole's words were slurred by drink. "Look around if you like."

From windows running along the cabin's front wall, I could see the lake glinting through the dark oaks. The trees dappled the light coming through the skylights.

"How does she get a big sculpture out of here once it's finished?"

"Double door on the back wall behind the chimney. You want to poke around, I'll wait outside."

"Thanks."

He shuffled out. I watched him walk to a reproduction park bench a few dozen yards up the path and gingerly lower himself onto its contoured slats. With his departure, a great stillness pressed down on the honey-colored room. I crossed quietly to the painting space and the scuffed pine floor creaked under my footsteps. There was a deep metal locker behind the chimney and in it, in vertical racks, were more canvases like those in the house. All were dated on the back in pencil; the oldest dated back almost twenty years ago; the youngest, five years. They showed no progression or advancement that I could detect, just the same penchant for slapping on paint in primary colors as thick as it would go.

There was maybe a year's worth of dust on the table of paints and brushes, and the paint on the easel was dry and cracked. On the wall behind the easel, postcards of Botticelli's "Primavera," van Gogh's "Sunflowers," and Michelangelo's "Delphic Sybil" shared space with prints of Shiva Maheshvara, Baba Ram Dass, the Egyptian fertility goddess, Isis, and a poster of the Grateful Dead. All were covered with dust, even Jerry Garcia, who grinned beyond mirth behind granny glasses and his emblematic beard.

The sculpting area showed equal disuse. Its iron was rusted scrap from old farm implements: gear parts, rake teeth, harrow disks, a plow. The inside of the welding mask contained a spider's web full of cluster fly carcasses. I brushed the oily dust from the face of the gauge on the oxyacetylene tank. The gauge read one hundred percent full.

The cabin was warm and stuffy from being locked up.

I was wearing khakis, a pair of Nike Airs, and a blue chambray fishing shirt now stuck to my back, no doubt making an interesting Rorschach blot of my sweat. My gun and a summerweight blazer were in the truck. Considering what my client was wearing I felt overdressed. Certainly, considering his physical condition, I was adequately armed.

I looked around the bed and reading chair. There were two hardcover books on a pine end table beside the bed: *The Shipping News* by E. Annie Proulx, and *The Complete Poems of Allen Ginsberg.* Both looked new and barely touched; the Proulx had a sales slip in it as well as a bookmark: Chassman & Bem, Church Street, Burlington, Vermont. Dated a week ago. On the hassock in front of the reading chair were magazines and newspapers: *Mother Earth News, Rolling Stone, The Village Voice, Holistic Health, The Nation, Spin,* and, for cultural balance, three back issues of *Vanity Fair.* The patchouli, an odor I thought I would never have to whiff again after the 1970's, was stored on a knicknack shelf behind the chair. A half-burned stick of the stuff sat in a small brass holder, a memento from the days of rolling papers and roach clips.

The white life masks on the walls were of three young men, an older man, and a much younger woman. With their eyes shut all looked weird and serene, a spooky human counterpoint to the animal heads back in the house. A worn slip of paper thumbtacked under the older man's mask had THE WORD written on it in faded calligraphic letters.

I went to the door. "Who are the people on the walls?"

Cole called painfully from the bench without turning around, "Friends of Chelly's from her hippie childhood."

"She in touch with them?"

"I rather doubt it. It's been over twenty years."

He sat on the bench the way a blind man would, cocking his head to listen for me.

"I'll just be a few more minutes," I told him.

"Take your time."

There was a mini refrigerator, a hot plate, and a double sink along a short counter between the bed-sitting

and writing spaces. A wooden dish rack in the sink held a
glass, a plate, a bowl, a fork, and a spoon. The refrigerator
contained an assortment of health foods and beverages.
There were half-used packages of tofu, bowls of brown
rice, Tupperware containers of *hommus* and three-bean
salad. A handmade stoneware pitcher was half full of stale
ginseng tea. A big bottle of Robert Mondavi Woodbridge
Sauvignon Blanc was nearly empty. The refrigerator gave
off a fecund odor of vegetarian neglect. I closed the door
gently to prevent more of the smell from wafting into the
room and ran my hands under the faucet in the sink to rid
them of unholy smells.

I dried my hands on a stiff dishrag lying on the
counter and walked past the stone fireplace into Chelly
Killbride's writing space. It was cozier and more intimate a
space than the others, with a long cherry writing table set
along the wall and tall bookshelves perpendicular to it,
serving to isolate the space from the back of the cabin. A
vintage Macintosh SE 30 with an ink-jet printer sat in the
center of the table; to the left was a telephone and a metal
accordion file jammed with manila folders. I removed the
folder nearest the computer. It contained poems, maybe
sixty pages worth, filled with penciled-in side notes, word
changes, and deletions, all in the same loopy handwriting
as the signature on the paintings.

I felt uneasy looking at what I supposed were Chelly
Killbride's innermost thoughts, and the poems were painful to read. Banal images in slapdash language skittered
down the pages in nervous blocks. There were many poems about life and death, nature and childbirth, all tending
to veer between angry abstraction and maudlin sentimen-
tality. The latest, written five days earlier according to the
date on it, was called "Breath" and began, "I suck you in /
but you do nought to please me/Fucker!!!/Why are you
everywhere /Are everything I breathe/And yet . . . /Are
nowhere for me?"

Good question, I thought. Another was, Why was I
already beginning to hate this case?

I closed the folder and put it back in the accordion
file. I riffled through every other folder there. A file of
rejection slips was the thickest one on the rack. Old Chelly

could not be faulted for neglecting to peddle her wares. There were rejections from *Partisan Review, Sewanee Review, Hudson Review, Kenyon Review, Paris Review, The New York Review of Books* and reviews I'd never heard of, including *Geedunk Review* and *The New Age Review of Wiccan Poetry*.

Great. I nodded. Suicidal. *And* a witch.

I read a note on cream-colored stationery dated a month earlier and signed by one Laurence Tetlow, Associate Poetry Editor, *The Algonquin* magazine. "Dear Ms. Killburn," it said. "Thank you for sending us your long poem, 'Cucumber Dreams.' We wish we could be the bearers of happier news about it, but the poem, with its autoerotic references and liberal use of four-letter words, does not adhere to our editorial standards. Nor, to us, does it meet the minimum requirements of economy and clarity. Rather, it sounds, to us, like a nervous person talking very quickly in a noisy, crowded room. We wish you luck in placing it elsewhere. Sincerely," etc.

At the bottom of the letter Chelly Killbride had written: "Laurence Tetlow is a short-dicked bag-licker. Fuck you, you fop!"

I put the folder back. She probably had a point. I finished going through the accordion file. In the second to the last folder I found the copy of a letter from Chelly to the editor in chief of Merrymount Publishers on Fifth Avenue in New York City. It began: "I am a poet and biographer living in Gatwick, Vermont," and went on to outline her idea for a critical study of a poet named Armen Karillian. "I am sure if you review the critical cannon [sic], as I have," she wrote, "you will agree that an opus on this great but neglected genius is long overdue." It ended, "I have already begun my research (fascinating, let me tell you!!!) and could have a finished manuscript ready for you in less than a year. If you wish to hear more about what I am positive will be a boffo best-seller, call me in my studio at the number below. I look forward to working with you in the months ahead. Yours in the exploration of a maestro! Chelly Killbride (Mrs. Arthur Cole.)"

For the second time that morning I felt pity—this time for the editor in chief of Merrymount Books.

I scanned the desk for anything else interesting. There was a small stack of computer disks with different labels on them—POEMS, STORIES, KARILLIAN BOOK, POEM IDEAS, STORY IDEAS. I decided I would be a bad detective and avoid the agony of looking through them; I put the disks back in their place and pretended they weren't there. I did look long and hard, however, at the photograph off to the right side of the computer. It was a snapshot in a silver frame among a cluster of desk objects: scissors, a tape dispenser, a crystal paperweight with some envelopes underneath it, and a stoneware dish of paper clips. The photo was taken on the stone terrace, and I recognized a slightly younger-looking Arthur in it, dressed in baggy brown shorts and a white T-shirt and grinning as always, though perhaps during a time in his life when he hadn't been in pain. He had one hand in a pocket and the other around the waist of an attractive dark-haired woman who had a hand draped over his shoulder and who appeared to be in her late thirties. She, too, was wearing shorts, though hers were blue canvas, and her shirt was coral-colored with white buttons and a simple spread collar and appeared to be made of linen or silk. Her hair was medium length and bounced thick and free off her shoulders. There was a red-and-black kerchief pushing it back off her forehead, and her face was frozen in a dazzling smile that showed her white teeth and her wide, slightly eager brown eyes. Her skin looked tan, clear and not unhealthy. Her nose was thin with nicely flaring nostrils and her lips seemed capable of forming an agreeable pout. She was not quite as tall as her husband but she wasn't petite either, and the body under the summer clothes looked well developed and fit, the legs smooth and tan. Only her earrings, which hung off her ears like miniature chandeliers, belied what I had begun to consider her bohemianism. The earrings were large—silver and Native American looking—festooned with turquoise and bits of downy feather. They forced you to look again into the eyes, and if you looked hard, you thought you could detect a faint I don't know thyroidal trace of manic independence bordering on dare I say it madness, though I wanted to be wrong.

I sat at the desk in Chelly Killbride's writing chair, a

comfortable combination of molded wood and leather, and studied the face in the silver-framed snapshot. Whoever she was, she was frightening her husband enough that he had called a private detective to go and find her and do it quickly and on the QT. The two of them apparently had no kids, only each other, and the quality of the wife's work suggested a psyche that might justifiably invite despair.

I put the photograph back where I found it. I lifted the paperweight off the stack of letters and went through Chelly Killbride's mail. There were form rejections of poems from *Antaeus Review* and *Salmagundi,* a dunning letter and card from The Poverty Law Center in Montgomery, Alabama, asking for the sixty dollars Chelly had pledged to them last winter, a two-week-old phone bill, a Miss Porter's School Alumnae Fund solicitation, the latest Body Shop catalogue, and a letter from Smith & Hawken explaining why her seed dibber and authentic chin-strap Panama would be delayed for six weeks.

I opened the phone bill. It was for forty-two dollars and eleven cents and the majority of the calls were to Hanover, New Hampshire, although a few were to numbers in Burlington, Vermont, and New York City.

I put the phone bill into the shirt pocket that held Cole's check and got up and looked at Chelly's bookshelf. There were many slender volumes of poetry in alphabetical order, some by names I recognized, many by those I did not. I looked on all the shelves for books by Armen Karillian but could find none, only an open space on a shelf of poetry, between Jarrell and Koch, which suggested that Karillian's books had been removed.

The rest of the books—desk references and art books—occupied the two lowest shelves. The only textual links to Chelly's youth were the complete works of Richard Brautigan, *The Dharma Bums* by Jack Kerouac, *The Electric Kool-Aid Acid Test* by Tom Wolfe, and a mildewed first edition of *The Whole Earth Catalogue.*

A Sony boom box atop of one of the bookshelves had a small collection of CD's beside it. Chelly's tastes ran the gamut from Bach to The Cranberries but the sixties weighed in heavily with albums by The Fugs, Janis Joplin,

The Youngbloods, Canned Heat, The Band, Paul Butterfield, and Country Joe and the Fish.

So Chelly liked poetry and vintage funk and couldn't write, paint, or weld her way out of a soggy sack. Interesting. As one who wrestled with the question himself, I wondered what it was exactly that sustained her.

Whatever it was, the husband didn't think it was enough. That's why I was here.

I walked across the wide-plank floor and out the cabin to Arthur Cole. He was no longer sitting on the bench. He was in the middle of the back lawn, near the Adirondack chairs, talking to an older man in khaki clothes. He spotted me and beckoned for me to join them. I hesitated on the path a moment. Then I left the shade of the oaks and walked across the grass into the sun.

3

"THIS IS KERR," ARTHUR COLE SAID, SWAYING, WHEN I GOT within a few yards of the two men. "He's the guy who keeps this place and my father-in-law's shipshape."

Arthur Cole slapped the older man on the shoulder. The man appeared not to notice the gesture. Instead, he gazed at me. He was wiry, quiet, and seventyish, with long, tobacco-stained teeth and a narrow simian face devoid of warmth or humor. Sinclair Lewis reincarnate, I thought. There was absolutely no question that Kerr would prefer to avoid a handshake, so I extended my hand and crinkled my eyes in amicable greeting. Kerr wore a Motorola beeper on his belt and his khaki clothes and black rubber boots lent him a nautical air.

"Who are you?" he said, proffering a bony hand. He gave me a Calvinist fish flap. The pale watery blue eyes did not cease their appraising gaze.

"This is Pete, a friend of mine passing through," Arthur Cole said. He grinned and winked and puffed his cheeks to stifle a burp.

Kerr's face was impassive. "Where you from?" The voice was native, flat, uninterested. The lined, gaping face exuded a weary guardedness.

I told him.

"What do you do?"

Arthur Cole shot me a glance.

I smiled. "A little of this and that. Consulting. Human resources management. I was just admiring Chelly's cabin studio. When was it built?"

"Cheryl around?" Kerr looked abruptly at Arthur Cole.

"She's away for a couple days. How 'bout it, Kerr? Remind me. When was the studio built? Early seventies, wasn't it?" The ice in Arthur Cole's glass tinkled as he moved his hand. He was soused.

"Fall of '69," Kerr said with some annoyance. "Win and I built it in a month."

"What did you build it for?" I asked.

Kerr looked at me as if it was none of my goddamn business.

"It was the fishing camp, right, Kerr?" Arthur Cole pumped as much wholesome enthusiasm into the question as his blood alcohol level would allow. "For Win and his buddies to roar in?" Cole winked at me and laughed.

"It was just a project," Kerr said. He began looking around as if to find a way to escape us.

"I hope you didn't mind our putting the skylights in." Arthur Cole's sad-eyed face was sweating and eager.

Kerr looked at Cole with unrestrained contempt. "Whatever I mind doesn't make a damned bit of difference, does it?"

"Oh, now, Kerr." The rubbery lips gave Kerr a joshing sneer. "You're not anti-Art, are you?"

"Art's fine, I suppose, for people who've got nothing better to do with their time. I'll be back to mow this afternoon."

The hired man turned on his heel and walked away from us without so much as a goodbye.

"Fun guy," I said when he was out of earshot.

Arthur Cole gave a disgusted wave. "He's just sore that Cheryl and I got the house. Before I came on the scene there was apparently talk that Win'd give him some land along the shore. But then Win and Claire moved out of here and built on what would have been his spot. They tried to make it up to him by buying a cottage farm down below. But he didn't want it. So fuck him, I say. *Fuck him!*" Arthur Cole shouted suddenly, but Kerr did not seem to hear.

The two of us watched the stiff-backed figure trudge toward a copse of distant trees. Beyond the trees, I could see a big house on a rocky rise above the lake. It looked younger in design than Cole's and there was a boathouse at the edge of the lake that looked new and baronial.

"Is that your father-in-law's place?"

From two hundred yards across the lawn, we could hear Kerr's beeper going off. The unpleasant old man plucked it from his belt and looked at it, then took what proved to be a folding cellular phone from his pocket. He punched a number into it and continued walking as he talked.

"That's Win's." Arthur Cole nodded. "The Eagle's Nest. Though there hasn't been a bald eagle seen on this lake in over forty years. He built it the year after Chelly and I were married. Then put us up here."

"Not a bad deal if you like your in-laws."

Cole laughed bitterly. "A lousy one if you don't."

We watched the hired man, Kerr, stalk off the lawn and onto a white stone path through the trees. The house on the rocky bluff had a big roof made of cedar shakes that glinted in the hot sun.

Arthur Cole shook his glass. There was nothing more in it to shake. He looked disappointed. "You find anything useful in there?"

"Some numbers on a phone bill I think I'll track down. I take it you two don't have any kids?"

Arthur Cole wiped his mouth with the back of his hand. "Not to say we didn't try. It may be a classically bad combination. My sperm count. Chelly's uterus."

I said nothing.

"She had so many D and C's as a kid, her insides are all scarred up. Doctors call it—uh." He contorted his face to wring his memory.

"Asherman's syndrome," I said quietly.

"That's it."

I knew about Asherman's syndrome. My wife and I had tried to make babies in the year before her death. Her doctor had concluded it was Asherman's syndrome that was making her sterile. We were going to try the new laser technology to clear the adhesions after I finished my first year pitching in the bigs. But that was another story.

"If I'm going to start my search I need to know what your wife is driving."

"A tan Range Rover. Or should I say"—he mimicked a New Canaanite with lockjaw—" 'Champagne Beige.' " Then gave me the Rover's year and the license number. I jotted them down on the phone bill. We started back toward the house.

"Is 'ere anything else before you get started, Boone?"

"I'd like to see her bedroom," I said.

Arthur Cole did not say anything. Our feet made quiet swishing noises through the grass.

"I could show it to you," he said. "The question is, do you want to see her bedroom or where she sleeps?"

He stopped and turned to me with a kind of drunken defiance. "Because if you want to see her bedroom, it's upstairs. But if you want to see where she sleeps, you just saw it."

"I see."

"Take your pick. Bedroom's up two flight of stairs and to the right. Sorry the bed's not made. Also sorry if I don't join you. I think I've had it with questions for the morning. I know I should be more of a man about this, but—" He grunted in pain. "There it is."

I let him stagger on ahead of me. He reached the terrace and let himself into the house alone. When I entered the back hall I could see his hairless legs retreating toward the den and the siren bottle.

I walked upstairs alone. There was beige carpeting on the stairs, so my footfalls were quiet, and the staircase had a hairpin turn in it with a landing in the middle before climbing six more steps to the top floor. Ahead of me was another long hall like the one on the main level but with more light in it and more garish paintings and four closed doors along it on the right and a long bank of six-over-six windows on the left letting in light. Through the windows I could see my truck parked in the curving asphalt drive and Cole's dark green Mercedes in front of the three-bay garage, and the private gravel road that ran in front of the house and the split rail fence with rambler roses on it that ran along the road. The road and fence disappeared a distance away into a wall of dark trees, and you could not see

anything beyond them, but I assumed the road led to Win
Killbride's big house. There were no other roads along the
lake.

I walked across the landing to the first door on the
right. I opened it and saw the unmade bed with the white
ladder quilt and piles of dirty clothes. The Coles' bedroom.
I stepped inside. The bank of windows looking out on the
lake was open, and I could see the roof of the cabin in the
oaks and the sweep of the great lawn below, and farther
out, the lake glittering long and wide and rimmed by shadowy hills with houses in them, a real deepwater glacial
lake with cold springs, and, maybe still, big fish.

I could also look north and see Win Killbride's house
better. It floated above the screen of trees and there was a
big deck that stretched over the edge of the bluff and a
massive stone chimney that anchored the house to the
bluff. A man on the deck was talking to a woman reclining
on a chaise lounge. He was in a shirt and slacks but she
was wearing a strapless single-piece bathing suit. He
walked around as he talked.

I turned away. The bed was a king without a head-
board, just two pine side tables with a brass lamp on each
and a big canvas by Chelly covering the back wall. The
canvas depicted a bride, a lake, a sun, and an angel done in
Marc Chagall colors but with a lumpy, sloppy technique.
It was signed CHELLY and dated twenty years ago.

I tried to imagine what looking at it every day of my
marriage would be like. I didn't like what I imagined.

Perhaps to blunt his view of the ugly thing, Arthur
Cole kept a clutch of liquor bottles on his side table along
with prescription bottles of Percocet, Dilaudid and other
edge blunters. Inside the table's one drawer was a tube of
K-Y jelly, a bottle of Body Shop massage oil, a half-empty
box of Trojan-enz prophylactics and a full-color suck-and-
fuck periodical called *Waitresses Wild*.

I sighed.

The table on the other side of the unmade bed was
bare except for the lamp. Its drawer contained a dia-
phragm in a swooping circular white box, a few Lake
Champlain chocolates with dust balls clinging to them, a
ten-year-old valentine from Arthur to Chelly that said

"Chelly My Dear, No matter what, I love you, A.," a wooden darning egg, needles and thread, the warranty to an electronic garage door opener, and a phallic-shaped vibrator, its three-speed switch powdery with corrosion, its batteries dead.

The room had pretty much been taken over by Arthur. The dirty clothes on the antique deacon's bench in front of the windows were his, and the stack of books at one end of it were male escapist: Len Deighton, Clive Cussler, Frederick Forsyth, and Tom Clancy. Chelly's clothes—shirts, shorts, jeans, sweaters, capes, scarves, shawls, dresses, and underwear—a mix of the practical and flamboyant—still occupied one closet and a bureau, and I concluded that if she didn't sleep in this room, she nonetheless got dressed here; there was a woman's blue silk kimono on a chair, and in the master bathroom near the closet I saw two toothbrushes in the rack and an array of women's beauty products near the sink.

So she was in the room but not of it. She was married to her sad, injured city boy but went about her business alone.

I went downstairs and looked in on Arthur in the den. He was passed out in a fetal tuck under the fireplace, the trophy heads looming above him on permanent alert.

I thought of waking him to tell him I was going but then thought better of it. I had his check and for the first time since I'd met him he looked comfortable.

"Take care of the guy," I murmured to the heads. None offered me so much as a wink of assurance. So I left.

4

THERE WERE TWO HIGH STONE GATEPOSTS MARKED
private at the end of the road to Arthur and Cheryl Cole's
house. There was no gate between them, and the gateposts
themselves were unfinished, as if whoever built them had
thought better of it and left them craggy and uncapped.
The road ran parallel to the lake, and beyond the gateposts
a half mile or so down the shore you could see a boarded-
up house and barn and an old cornfield, its brown soil
dotted with last year's stubble. Except for one or two summer houses further down along the lake, the shore was
undeveloped and exuded a pleasant wildness that made me
want to explore it.

A few hundred yards below the gate was a cement
bridge that crossed an inlet to the lake. A lone fisherman
with a rod and pail stood at the slack cable railing, bait-
casting into the little cove that led to the lake. As I approached in my truck, he turned and stepped into the road
and waved me down earnestly with one hand. I stopped.
He grinned at me from behind a closely cropped beard. He
was short and muscular, wearing Doc Martens boots,
jeans, and a plain cutoff T-shirt that displayed a weight-
lifter's physique.

He reeled in and walked over stiffly to the passenger
window of my truck.

"Hey, how ya doin'?" he said. He appeared about
thirty and spoke with a Boston accent. "Hey, you know
anything about what's in the lake?" I caught a hint of
earnest indignation behind the eager smile.

"Around here, perch," I told him.

"No lake trout?" The man's eyes were big and dark, his features chiseled and clean-cut beneath the cropped beard. The mannered movements of his upper body bespoke an inclination toward violence.

"Lakers are out in the middle, if there are any. This time of year you'd have to fish 'em deep."

"They never come in around here?"

"Not if they can help it."

"So I'd need a boat to catch a laker."

"Or a canoe."

"Damn!" The fisherman laughed at me and rubbed his bearded jaw with his thumb as if I'd given him baffling information. Then he began talking fast. "See, I come all the way up from Boston to catch a lake trout. Something I can hang on my wall, you know. But a boat, that fucks my budget, fucks it big time. What do I do, do I rent something like that around here?"

"I don't know. You'd have to check back in town."

"You're not from around here, then."

"No, I'm not."

The fisherman smiled at me boyishly through the truck window and shook his head. His arms were draped on the door and though his clothes looked clean his body odor wafted through the window. It was old and habitual-smelling, and the rattlesnake tattoo on his left forearm looked self-inflicted. I pegged him for an out-of-state early-releaser; I could see no car that he might have come in and he looked too old to be an AWOL.

"How 'bout the people up beyond the gate?" the fisherman asked.

"How 'bout 'em," I said.

"Maybe they'd know how I could get a boat?"

"Maybe."

"What's their names?"

"In the first house, Cole; in the second, Killbride."

"Cole and Killbride." The young man seemed to consider the names. "Them's new to me."

"Me, too."

"Wonder how long they been around here."

"I have no idea." I was anxious to get going. If I moved I could make it to Hanover by early afternoon.

"You know who owns that place down there?" He pointed to the abandoned farmhouse down the road.

"I don't."

"Pretty place. Shame it's gotta be all boarded up like that."

The young man grinned at me, then his eyes lit upon the checkered walnut stock of my Smith & Wesson nine. It was holstered and poking out from under my folded blazer on the seat.

"You a cop?"

"Nope."

"Security guy for the houses around here?"

"If I were, I'd have patted you down by now."

When he laughed, I could see that his back teeth had gone bad and his front teeth were blackening with decay. "Hey, you're a pretty tough guy," he said after he'd stopped laughing. "We ought to go fishing sometime together. Maybe you got a boat and we could fish for lakers. I'd also like to find me a woman up here. I'm Perry." He extended a hand. He was either the cream of the American gulag or an Ivy president slumming his way through a Sturges movie.

"I'm Dick," I said. We shook hands.

"I saw you coming down that road and I said to myself, 'This guy I gotta talk to.' Hey, Dick, do you know if they might be hiring up in those places, like somebody to do maintenance or that kinda thing?"

"Again, I have no idea."

"'Cuz I'm very proficient with hand tools," Perry said, "and places like the ones I guess are up that road, you gotta stay on top of or else they get ahead of you an' fall apart. Am I right?"

"I suppose you are."

"Yeah." The young man stretched and scratched his stomach. "I might just go up there and see about a job."

"Well, good luck."

"One last question." The young man stuck his head in the window as if he feared that the perch were eavesdropping. "You aren't holdin', are you, man?"

"Just the steering wheel."

He laughed hard and pushed back from the passenger window. "Right," he said, slapping a drumroll on his thighs. "No big keys in the dual air bags. See you later, man. Thanks for the hot fishing tips." He made a gun of his index finger and shot me with it. "Appreciate it."

When I was moving again, I briefly tried phoning Arthur Cole to warn him that he might have a visitor. But the bag phone in my truck got no answer, and I rationalized that Kerr and company were a sufficient deterrence to Perry. Anyway, I had to get going.

Near the abandoned farmhouse, the road forked left away from the lake and climbed back into the glacial highlands. The fields on either side of the road were planted with ryegrass and posted with signs forbidding hunting, fishing, trespassing, and other sins against God. I slowed so I could read God's name on one of the signs. It said W. KILLBRIDE, and the penalty for violating His Will was legal prosecution.

As I climbed the big hill away from the lake I looked back through the rearview and saw Perry or whatever the hell his name was walking with his rod and bait pail toward the twin stone gateposts. When I looked forward, I was cresting the hill and in front of me, where the road levelled, was a white prowl car, its blue bar lights flashing, its bulk broadside to the road and blocking it. Two cops in Ray-bans and S.W.A.T. gear were standing behind the car. One held a twelve-gauge Mossberg Persuader, the other an Ithaca Police Special, and both guns were aimed at my windshield. I stopped. The two cops sidestepped in opposite directions around the car and, with their guns raised, approached me.

I stuck my head out the side window.

"Is there a problem, officers?" I yelled.

By way of answer, the cop on the left turned his gun to the side, racked a load into the chamber and discharged it into the rye field. It made a hearty roar. I decided if there hadn't been a problem, there was one now. When the cop who had fired spoke into the microphone pinned to the shoulder of his flak jacket and his amplified voice from the prowl car said, "Step out of the vehicle," I decided to oblige.

The day was getting hotter. When I stepped onto the road, a hot breeze was blowing off the lake.

5

I LOOKED CLOSELY AT THE TWO POLICEMEN WALKING toward me. The one who had fired the Mossberg was big, sunburned, and bareheaded; his partner wore a S.W.A.T. baseball cap and was short and out of shape. They advanced with their weapons aimed at me, and their shiny black shoes made scuffing noises on the asphalt road.

"Step away from the vehicle and put your hands in the air," the big policeman said.

"What's this about?" I said.

"Raise your hands and step away from the vehicle or I'll blast you a new asshole." The big policeman racked another round in his gun and kept coming toward me.

"Would you mind telling me what's going on?" I stepped away from the truck but I did not raise my hands. The big policeman walked swiftly up to me.

"This—" He swung his gun back and brought the barrel forward swiftly to club me. I ducked and grabbed the barrel with my left hand and used the cop's momentum to wrench the gun away from him and send him somersaulting onto the road. He landed on his shoulder and rolled onto his hands and knees. I held his gun by the barrel with one hand off to the side. His partner aimed his Ithaca at my chest.

"You drop the gun right now or you're a dead man. Drop it!"

I looked at the partner. "What is this, an audition for *Top Cops*?" I set the Mossberg quietly on the road.

"Now raise your hands."

I did, to shoulder height. The big policeman picked

himself up off the road. The stout policeman walked closer to me and gestured with the gun. "Lie down on the ground."

"What for?"

The big policeman picked up his Mossberg, pulled his nightstick out of his Sam Browne belt, and walked behind me. An instant later I felt the force of the stick behind my knees like an electrical jolt. My legs buckled.

"The man said lie down," the big policeman roared. I felt the nightstick stab my spine. I reacted by landing a side kick to the big policeman's groin. The stout policeman acted confused—his partner was doubled over in his line of fire. The Ithaca wavered in his hands and he started to say something when the big policeman must have straightened and struck me across the back of my head. I saw stars and saw the ground coming up to me. There was the pain in my skull and then the two of them were on top of me. They handcuffed me from behind and the big cop pushed my face against the road and held the barrel of his Mossberg against my jaw.

"They don't call it the Persuader for nothing," the big policeman said.

"What's this about?" I said again.

"Just never you mind," the big policeman said. "Whattaya got, Bobby?"

The stout policeman was in my truck. I could hear him going through my possessions.

"Got a Smith and Wesson six-three-nine," Bobby shouted. "Loaded, in a nylon shoulder rig."

"What's a cunt like you doing with a nine-millimeter?" the big policeman said to me.

"Trying to protect myself from white-trash fascists like you."

The big policeman jabbed my jaw hard with the gun barrel.

"Aw, for god's sakes!" I said.

He jabbed me harder.

"Aw, fuck you, man!" I said.

"He's a P.I.!" the stout policeman shouted from the truck. "His name's Peter Boone, from in-state!"

"Boone," the big policeman said. "Boone. Seems I

heard that name somewhere before. Weren't you the bastard that broke that case down in Regis?"

"I might be."

"You fucked up the lives of some friends of mine." The big policeman had his face very close to my ear. "What were you doin' down there on the road with that lowlife?" The big policeman's breath smelled of clove Life Savers and stale coffee.

"What do you mean, what was I doing?"

"You were givin' him a blowjob, weren't you?"

"Oh, man."

"You were givin' him a blow job. Bobby and I witnessed it up here through our binoculars. We can pin a lewd-and-lascivious on you."

"Sure you can. And you can fuck a snake on a ladder."

A raven cawed and flew past my line of vision toward the lake.

I could feel the warm stickiness on the back of my skull where the stick had split my scalp. The right side of my face was pressed so hard against the pavement that my nose was bent sideways and my mouth disfigured.

High-pitched whoops suddenly emanated from the truck.

"What've we got here!" the stout policeman shouted. "Bingo, Chief! Big-time score!"

"What is it, Bobby?"

"Dried leaf product in a plastic bag in the glove compartment. Looks and smells like Mexican red."

I shut my eyes.

"That's echinacea, you asshole!" I shouted.

"Shut up." The big policeman jabbed me with the Mossberg.

Oh wait until I told Nan. She had given me the echinacea last winter as a preventative against colds. Two teaspoons in hot water twice a day, she'd said. She had tried getting me on a whole bunch of homeopathic powders. Echinacea had been the focus of some lively conversations between us. Now, apparently, it was about to send me away.

"How much in there, Bobby?"

"A lot. Maybe quarter of a pound."

"Ooh! A felonious amount." The big policeman knelt down next to me. "Which you were trying to distribute down there, weren't you, Mister Blow job?"

"You're gonna big-time regret this," I said quietly.

"From where I'm lookin', Peter *Boone*," the big policeman growled, "you're the one that's gonna have regrets. You're under arrest for possession with intent to sell. Bobby!"

"Yeah, Chief."

"Read him his rights."

Bobby came out of my truck. He pulled a laminated card out of his hat and read me my rights in a fast singsong, then they lifted me by the arms and pushed me into the back of the prowl car. The big policeman—the chief—drove the prowl car and Bobby followed behind in my truck. The chief didn't say anything and I decided to keep my mouth shut. We climbed through farmland away from the lake until we hit a narrow highway that paralleled the lake a mile away from it. There were houses along the highway, all of them likely built within the past twenty years, but none as big as Arthur Cole's and none with such a groomed, sweeping lawn or intimate views of the lake.

A couple miles and a turn or two later we were in an older, more densely zoned residential area with big trees and sidewalks, and finally in downtown Gatwick itself. There was a big stone Roman Catholic church on a hill behind the downtown and a few residential streets branching off its main street, which was very wide and built for diagonal parking. The downtown sat along the south end of the lake, and there was a causeway right at the end of the main street where people launched boats and fished. You could see up the length of the lake and the several small islands in it with spruce trees on them and the dark green hills on either side. I had always liked Gatwick when I fished north. There was a nice restaurant there with a high tin ceiling and ceiling fans and I liked to stop there for its *weisswurst* and sauerkraut and potato salad and beer. Afterwards, you would walk down to the causeway and talk to the anglers and look at the fish in their pails and watch the anglers take night crawlers out of paper buckets reminiscent of Chinese takeout and feel the sun on your back and the cool breeze in your face that you knew had come down from Hudson Bay.

I had always liked the way the main street rose away from the lake and how the stores and shops and businesses seemed to be surviving and the scale of the town was not so small that you felt noticed or out of place. Now I found myself rethinking my feelings about Gatwick as we drove through the main street and I watched the chief nod and wave at motorists and pedestrians we passed. The chief had a high-school-handsome profile gone soft with age, and I guessed him to be in his early forties. He drove smoothly without needless moves, and after a right and a left we were at the Gatwick police station, a single-story quasimodern prefab with a sign out in front and a big town garage and a salt shed behind it. Three road workers in front of a red sand truck watched the chief pull me out of the prowl car. They laughed and one of them shouted, "Whatcha got, Alden? Bank robber?"

"Don't you guys ever work?" the chief said.

An impounded motorcycle sat moldering in chains under a butternut tree near the back door. Bobby arrived in my truck, parked it next to the prowl car, and the two men walked me in through the back. I was taken past the dispatcher's cubicle and through a big office with three or four desks in it to a back room that served as the holding cell. There was an opaqued window covered with a metal grille, a gray built-in wooden bench under the window, and a pair of handcuffs attached to a short length of chain bolted to the concrete floor. A bare light bulb hung from the metal ceiling. The whole thing was about the size of a walk-in closet.

Bobby took the cuff off my right hand, thrust a freezer bag in front of me, and told me to empty my pockets. I did, but first I touched the base of my skull where the stick had split it. There was a good-sized lump there and my hair was matted with dried blood. The chief stood at the door with his nightstick and a can of mace in case I made trouble. When my pockets were empty, Bobby patted me down and walked me outside and fingerprinted me and did my mug shots with a Polaroid camera against a white wall. Then he took me back to the holding room and told me to take a seat. I sat on the bench and Bobby cuffed my hands in front of me, and clipped my cuffs to the pair on the chain.

"Do I get to make a phone call?" I said.

"You get to shut the fuck up," the chief said.

I was left alone. I could hear the chief and Bobby talking in the office but I could not make out what they were saying. Silence came and with it the pain in my head started up in earnest. I did my old shrink friend John McArrigal's trick of compacting the pain into a small glowing ball and moving the ball around in my body and sending it out my big toe. Over the next several hours I sent many small glowing balls out my toe. After a while the chief and Bobby came back.

"How you feel?" the chief asked.

"My head hurts."

The chief jerked his head. Bobby was wearing rubber surgical gloves. He came over to me and I let him examine the bruise.

"He's gonna need stitches," Bobby said.

I didn't say anything.

"Call Doc Nimick. Tell him we got a suture over here."

Bobby started to go. "I don't want a doctor," I said.

The chief looked at me. "What, you gonna be a hard case?"

"I don't want a doctor."

"You gonna go get some ACLU lawyer, smear your fabrications around this pretty town, put skull pictures in the local paper, is that your goddamn plan?"

"I'm not going to get a lawyer. I don't want a doctor."

"Because if it is, you're gonna be in deeper shit than you already are, my friend."

I told him again it wasn't my plan.

"What were you doing at Artie Cole's?" the chief said. He was in uniform now and I could read his name badge. Chief Alden Clapp.

"I wasn't doing anything," I said.

"There was a check of his for five thousand bucks in your pocket," Clapp said. "He hire you to do somethin'?"

"Maybe. Maybe not."

"Whud he hire you for?"

I didn't say anything.

"He hire you to go spyin' on his looney tune wife?"

I didn't speak. Years ago a Red Sox minor league blood who had served time for armed robbery had taught me The Look. Very useful, he said, when confronting The Man. I brought out my Look. Chief Alden Clapp did not like it.

"Shit!" He slitted his eyes, enraged. "You want me to paste you again? Artie Cole's a paranoid drunk worried every week his wife's gone coozin' with playboys. The whole family up there is nuts. Did Win Killbride call you to see Artie?"

I kept my mouth shut.

"Or Claire?" When I remained silent, the chief strutted in front of me, shaking his head. "Shit. You are in trouble if you take on Artie Cole's problems. Piece of advice? Professional courtesy? Stay away from the whole goddamn lot o' them. Win. Claire. Artie. Cheryl. They'll drag you down places *you don't want to go*."

I sat there without answering. Alden Clapp seemed suddenly very tired and disgusted with where he was.

"All right, Bobby. Outta here. I want to talk to this creep alone."

Bobby shot his chief a surprised look, but without a word he eased past him and stripped the rubber gloves off his hands and left the cell, quietly closing the door after himself.

When he was gone, the chief said to me, "You are truly in deep shit, you know that, don't you?"

When I didn't say anything the chief struck my face with the back of his hand. The blow hurt my nose. It began to bleed.

"I could bind you over to St. Johnsbury. I could make sure you're not given bail."

"This is Vermont," I said.

"It doesn't matter where it is, my friend. When it

comes to my word or yours, who do you think a jury of your peers is gonna believe?"

"What are you going to charge me with?"

"Anything. Take your pick. Murder. Arson. Robbery. Rape."

"You need a victim."

"I'm sure that won't be a problem." The chief leaned back against the wall opposite me and watched me bleed. The blood dripped from my nose and down my shirt.

We experienced a period of silence together.

"You want to cut a deal?" the chief said.

I shrugged without saying anything.

"If you want to keep me from closing your ear, fool, you'll speak up," the chief said.

I sighed, truly tired.

"What's the deal?" I said.

"I give you back your dope and send you on your way and you agree not to come back here, ever again."

"What if Arthur Cole wants to see me?"

"I'm telling you, even if I weren't kicking you out of town, which I am, to stay away from Artie Cole. Stay away from the Killbrides. Whatever business those people propose to you—it's bad business. You understand me?"

"You say so."

"Any speculation they offered me, I wouldn't touch with a Chinaman's dick."

A knock sounded and Bobby opened the door and stuck his head in. "Call on line one, Chief."

"Right." Alden Clapp pushed himself off the wall and stared at me as he talked to his officer. "Uncuff Mr. Boone and see him and his stash out the door, will you, Bobby?"

"Right, Chief."

"And get the poor man a wet towel."

He clucked his tongue at my dripping blood and strolled out.

I refused Bobby's towel after he released me and said nothing when he handed over my belongings. When I got outside, the sun had moved low in the western sky and the leaves on the trees around the station held its golden light. Traffic passed the station. From somewhere up the block, I could hear children's voices and the ring of bicycle bells.

The road crew was gone for the day and the big red doors on the corrugated garage were closed tight. It was a great afternoon in a beautiful, orderly little town.

I unlocked my truck and put my gun where it had been under my jacket. I put Nan's echinacea back in the glove compartment. Then I looked at my face. My blood had left a dry trail from my nostrils to my throat. I wiggled my nose a few times with my fingers. The bridge hurt but it wasn't broken.

I started my truck, backed it out of its slot, and crept in first gear to the mouth of the station's driveway. I was tired and sore and hungry. I went up Main Street, away from the lake and out of Gatwick. All the way up the hill that ran past the big stone church, children were playing on the sidewalks. I drove carefully and felt for the lump on my skull. It was hot and sticky.

6

I DECIDED TO HIT HANOVER THE FOLLOWING MORNING and drove over to John McArrigal's place, below St. Johnsbury. John's was a big white farmhouse on a bluff above the Connecticut River and it served as his home and his office for seeing clients. When I arrived at about six o'clock, he was cooking dinner, and his wife, Anny Artell, was cutting chives in her herb garden near the kitchen. Their two boys, Trey and Zachery, were in a side meadow bordered by a dark woods, shooting target arrows with handmade ash bows.

Anny Artell's mouth dropped when I walked toward her.

"Peter Boone, what happened to you, child?"

"Hello, Anny." I had wiped the blood off my mouth and neck but I still looked bad. "How ya doin'?"

"How'm *I* doin'? How'm *I* doin'? the man says."

Before I knew it, she had me sitting at their picnic table under an old maple, her strong nurse's hands probing the wound on my head, her slight, sibilant Texas drawl quietly clucking and sighing.

"Who did this to my baby?"

Anny Artell was five years my senior but somehow I was her baby. She was a lean, beautiful café-au-lait-skinned black woman who had worked as a registered nurse in Floydada, Texas, before John entered her life, a recent dropout from IBM and a Trappist monastery, and swept her off her feet.

I explained to her that I had slipped and fallen.

"Bullshit."

"What's bullshit?" John came out of the house, carrying a tray of crudités. He was wearing black jeans and a long-sleeved blue oxford cloth shirt open at the throat, and his gray hair was neatly combed and priestly looking. John had the kindest eyes of any man I knew, and to my recollection I had never seen him angry.

"So," he said, "I hear you've taken a vow of celibacy this summer."

"Who you been talking to?" I said.

He set the tray on the picnic table. I stood and we hugged each other. "What did you do to your head?" he said.

"He claims he fell, which is the worst bullshit I ever heard in my life." Anny Artell sulked.

"I did fall."

"Bullshit! I've seen enough popped heads from beer bottles and billy clubs to know when a patient's lying to me."

"OK, I was in a bar fight. I told a guy Catamount's a better-tasting ale than Magic Hat is. You know how those things go."

"They're both pretty good," John McArrigal said.

"It was a cop's nightstick and you know it," Anny said.

She went into the house and came out with towels, a bowl of hot water, and her suture kit. She washed and dried the split, hosed it with liquid antiseptic which stung like hell, and injected it with painkiller which stung worse. She shaved the hair around the split with a disposable razor, wiped the wet hair away, and sutured the wound, using a small, curved needle, forceps, and fine, black surgical thread. I could feel the tug of the thread through skull flesh and Anny's sensitive fingertips tying the fine knots. Anny had dropped out of Baylor as a premed to support her mother and four younger siblings and had managed to earn her RN on the side. She had been hospice nurse for both my parents; after they died she introduced me to John. For a time after my wife's death I had pretty much entrusted my soul to Anny and John. Zach, their youngest, the eight-year-old, was my godchild.

"Nan call here?" I cocked an eyebrow toward John.

He made faces as if being forced to reveal a secret, then grinned tiredly and nodded.

"In June before she left. She sounded quite determined and a little excited. Wanted to know if she could skip some of our sessions this summer. I gave my blessing."

"Thanks for not telling her to stay home," I said.

"Oh, listen to him sob, Anny. If a heart is determined to woo, Peter Boone, it'll not take 'I'm going to Connecticut' lying down."

"That's just it. I thought we were past wooing."

Anny slapped me smartly on the cheek.

"Ow! Hey, c'mon!" I yelped.

"How many times have I told you, baby, women ain't never past wooin'."

"Well, she had plans. She was firm about them. And they didn't include me."

John smirked and sprinkled salt on a cherry tomato and popped it into his mouth. "Well, that's good," he said, munching. "Though you may not like it, that's progress. She's stretching her wings."

"She's a lovely woman," Anny said. "It's a shame you don't appreciate her finer points."

"I appreciate her. I appreciated her all year. Then she goes and gets counseling from this quacksalver and ditches me for her Art."

"She hasn't ditched you," John said. "She took your crazy dogs with her, right?"

"Yeah, she's got Kai and Yeats for the summer while I work."

"Well, then, you two will have to see each other again, won't you?"

"I suppose."

"She's gotta do this," John continued. "Did you know that her ex was the only man she ever slept with before you came along? That's not counting some innocent stuff in high school."

"I love the way you maintain client confidentiality," I said. "No, I hadn't heard that. When'd she tell you?"

"At our first session."

"That's more than she told me at our first session."

"She was just discovering her independence when you came along."

"So I get blamed for curtailing her freedom, is that it?"

"No, you merely complicate and enrich a process she has yet to finish going through. That, in a way, she'll never finish going through."

Anny snipped the last suture and bandaged the wound with gauze and adhesive tape. Trey and Zachery wandered over to the table with their archery gear. Both were shirtless and shoeless, wearing only shorts and, on their chests and faces, Indian designs applied with red berry juice. The eleven-year-old, Trey, shook my hand. My godchild, Zach, hugged me. Both boys had coffee-colored skin, lean physiques, and beautiful, soft woolly hair like their mother's.

"What did you do to your head?" Zach asked me.

"He'll only tell you a lie," Anny said.

"I bumped it," I said.

"How many stitches?"

I looked at Anny.

"Seven," she said.

"Ugh!" Zachery looked at me as if I was Frankenstein. "Can Pete throw with us after supper?"

"If he feels well enough he can."

"Am I staying for supper?" I said.

"You're not gettin' your head stitched by me and *not* stayin' for supper," Anny said.

"Does that mean I get to spend the night?"

John cleared his throat. "Only if you agree to borrow some of my clothes and get out of those bloody rags."

"You drive a hard bargain. You got anything to drink?"

With Anny's permission I drank a Beam on the rocks, and we three adults drank and ate crudités and crackers under the maple while the boys played beer-can baseball near the garage. Beer-can baseball involved pitching beer cans to a batter who got invisible runners on base by hitting the cans into zones. The boys hit with a bat they called "shredded wheat" because of what the cans had done to its barrel. I had given the boys the bat and taught them the game, much to John's delight and Anny's frowning skepticism.

"How many stitches you suppose a child's face might need if it gets hit with one of them beer cans?" Anny asked.

"None if he puts a glove up or ducks," I said.

"Somebody should've reminded Herb Score," John said.

We watched the boys take turns hitting the beer cans and the sun got low behind the woods, spreading shadows across the lawn and sending pointillist splotches of light through the trees. When I turned my back to the sun I could look down off the bluff and across Route Five and see the river, wide and smooth-flowing and darkly silver. It was a tough river to fish because it was wide and deep, but John had shown me places where the Nulhegans debouched into it where you could stand and catch mighty fish. Nan had said she wanted to fish there. But that was last February.

"You may have a headache and experience double vision for a few days," Anny told me.

"He lacks focus to begin with," John said.

"Up yours, Padré." I flipped him the bird. He finger-wrestled it easily to the table.

Before supper, I tried phoning Nan. The phone rang six times, and I got an out-of-breath woman, who identified herself as Nan's mother.

"She's not in right now. Who's this?"

I gave her my name and identified myself as a friend.

"Well, Nan's out for the evening with an old high school classmate, Michael Waxman. Do you know Michael?"

"No, I don't."

"He's a nice boy. Produces rock videos. He did Sting's last video. And Michael Bolton's."

"Missed 'em."

"I know they were going into the city to see a play, and Nan said she might stay in there overnight to go to the Guggenheim tomorrow or the Met. I forgot which."

"I see."

"Is there any message?"

My insides fluttered with messages but I told Nan's mother there wasn't one and hung up without leaving a number. When I returned to the McArrigals' dinner table, John, Anny, and the boys were digging into platters of corn on the cob, marinated tomatoes, home-grown green collards, chive-sprinkled polenta cakes, and lemon-garlic chicken breasts. There was a pitcher of iced milk for the boys and two bottles of chilled Girgich Hill chardonnay that I had bought en route for us adults. There were lighted white candles, gold and blue napkins, big white china plates, and polished old silver. Playing on John's compact disc player was an album of jazz standards by Illinois Jacquette.

"You reach her?" John asked as I sat down.

"Out running an errand for her mother."

"If I were the beautiful Nan," said Anny, "I'd be out every night *on the town.*"

John's laughter echoed over the glowing saxophone music and my internal gloom.

After supper, I threw easily with the boys until the light was gone and Anny ordered them to get ready for bed. John took me out on the front porch, and we drank old port in small snifters and felt the day's heat rise from the highway and watched the fireflies come up in the field near the river.

"Trey's playing Little League this year. Did he tell you?"

"No," I said. "He's got a good arm. So does Zach. They're such good kids. Well done, Padré."

"Yeah, well. Anny's at least fifty percent responsible."

"I'd say more."

"You'd be right on that score. I thought that working out of the house would make me a more active father. It just means I work out of the house."

"It must also mean business is good."

"Business is always good."

John was a clinical psychologist with advanced degrees from Georgetown and Harvard. He specialized in hypnosis therapy but could pretty much do anything in the counselor's repertoire.

"It continues to amaze me," he went on, "that even here in Paradise people can be so screwed up."

"Paradise is where all the screwing up began," I said.

"Yes, but you'd think people would understand by now that we all have everything we need. Everything. Even the poor among us. It's all here." He tapped his chest. "It's here." He tapped his head and his balls. "It's out there. It's everywhere. Abundance. Try telling that to a poor stiff thinking of killing himself and his family because he got laid off. Or a woman coming off a decade of spousal abuse."

"Be a tough sell," I said.

"They come to me because they think I'll tell them what they want to hear. So I oblige them. Then I hypnotize the bastards and tell them something else."

We both laughed. A pair of big trucks roared south on the highway. We watched their red taillights grow smaller against the dark silhouettes of the mountains.

"Tell me about manic depression," I said.

John turned in the darkness and looked at me.

"You manic or depressed?" he said.

"Neither. A client's wife might be one or the other, or both."

"The same client who hit you on the head?"

"That was somebody else. This client's wife has run off and the client says she's manic-depressive."

"We big boys would say she suffers from bipolar affective disorder. Does her doctor say she's bipolar?"

"I don't know."

"Did her husband say she's on anything?"

"Lithium and fluoxetine. Only the balance hasn't been struck and she doesn't like taking them."

"Is she suicidal?"

"He said she's tried to kill herself three times in the past five years. But always when he's been around to save her."

"Right," said John. "Nick-of-time stuff. To send signals. Get attention."

We each took a pull from our snifters. The port was sweet, smooth and velvety on the tongue.

"So whaddya want to know?" John said.

"To begin with, what causes it."

He laughed. "If I knew the answer to that one I'd win the Nobel Prize for Medicine." His tone grew more serious. "Nobody really knows what causes manic depression. It involves neurotransmitters and neuroreceptors and these amines called norepinephrine and serotonin that influence mood. Some shrinks'll just tell their M-D patients they've got a chemical imbalance and then prescribe lithium and fluoxetine or other drugs just to try to reduce the breadth of the mood swings."

"But nobody knows where it comes from or how it begins . . ."

"No. It can be a system disorder—something you're born with that's genetic in nature—or it can be triggered by trauma or severe stress, or maybe it's a manifestation of post-trauma syndrome. Traumatized people can go through long periods in their life and get along okay. Then something happens that triggers the roller-coaster ride. Then, if you can, you try to regulate."

"But let me guess," I said. "Standing in the way of easy regulation are different obstacles."

"Right." John held up his last three fingers. "First, you've got to tailor the dose to the patient and that can be very time-consuming, extremely trial-and-error, and no two patients are going to respond in exactly the same way. Second, if the patient's in a manic state, *he don't want to come out of it.* He's having too good a time. He's up. He's euphoric. He's feeling great! Who wants to stop feeling great? I talked to a guy once who'd been up for seven days straight. No sleep. A furniture maker. Built ten Windsor chairs in seven days. We're talking bloody hands and blisters. Would not stop until we finally shot him up with Haldol, which knocked him down so we could regulate him."

"Jesus."

"I mean, it's a very serious mental illness."

I nodded. "What's the third thing that makes treatment hard?" I asked.

John lifted a hand and shook his head. "The very thing that makes this whole business hard in the first place. *Do I have the right diagnosis?*"

"I see."

"Is it really manic depression or is it something else? I mean, one shrink's diagnosis of bipolar affective can be another shrink's diagnosis of schizophrenia. Or a depressive patient can be psychotic—hearing voices, having hallucinations—and *appear* manic. So, diagnosis can be slippery. Plus, if it's a system disorder, you don't want to get too psychological with a patient. And if it's psychological—if some kind of trauma has brought about the manic depression—you don't want to just feed the patient drugs. Instead, you want to get at the trauma, see if you can clean it out."

"OK, but in either case, if my client's wife is manic-depressive, is there a chance she might kill herself?"

"Yes." John took a mouthful of port and swallowed it. "If she's the real thing and not on her medication—if she's been off it even for a short while—it depends, it depends on the patient. But yes, checking out's a very real scenario for a patient like that. And that's where you get families like this client of yours putting out all-points because he's scared shitless."

I nodded. Took more swallows of port.

"I better get to bed," I said after a while.

"Where do you start?" John asked quietly.

"Where she was headed. Hanover."

"You find her and you need any help with her, let me know."

"Thanks for not making me ask."

John hoisted his glass in a salute.

A few minutes later, Anny joined us on the porch. She came over to me and touched my bandaged head.

"Guest room bed's all made up. How we doin' here?"

I reached up and took her hand and laid it on my shoulder and kneaded the rough knuckles on the fine, long fingers.

"We're doin' fine," I said.

In bed a half hour later I thought about the day. It took me a long time to get to sleep.

7

DARTMOUTH HAD CHANGED IN THE NEARLY TWENTY years since I had been a student there. But then, what hadn't? I spent the morning driving through every parking lot in Hanover, looking for Chelly Killbride's Range Rover, but from the corner of my eye I noted the coeds, the new buildings, and the security locks on all the dormitories and began to feel weird. Time warp. The campus was still beautiful but I was a stranger in it. In the student parking lot out beyond the food co-op I came upon two attractive coeds in shorts and tank tops, leaning on a car, kissing each other. When they saw I had seen them they stuck out their tongues at me and fell over themselves laughing. I smiled and stuck out my tongue back. When they turned away, bored, and simultaneously mooned me without dropping their shorts, I not only felt strange, I felt rejected and old. Rip Van Winkle meets Sappho in *Brigadoon*.

There were two or three Range Rovers in Hanover, but none was Champagne Beige nor belonged to Chelly Killbride. As I drove around, my bandaged head began to throb. This was not going to be easy. From a pay phone in the Hanover Inn, I called the number on Chelly's phone bill and a woman's voice told me I had reached Professor Kenneth Hewlitt's extension in Sanborn House, the English department. The professor wasn't in, the voice said, but he was expected after lunch. I made an appointment to see Professor Hewlitt at two o'clock and the voice said that would be fine.

On an impulse I phoned Nan's mother's number in

Connecticut. I let it ring eight times before slamming the receiver down and stalking out of the inn, quietly cursing the name of Michael Waxman.

At a dark little restaurant on Main Street called Peter Christian's Tavern, I had a soft-shell crab sandwich and two steins of Sam Adams lager and tried not to think about Nan and Michael Waxman in New York together. Root canal surgery would have been easier not to think about. At ten minutes to two I strode up Main past the administration buildings and crossed to Sanborn House, diagonally in front of Baker Library. Before going inside I turned and saw the white buildings of Dartmouth Row across the green and the Hopkins Center at the far end of it. The sight of the campus filled my heart with unexpected longing.

Inside, Sanborn House was the same half-timbered reliquary that I remembered from studying there as an undergraduate. Hewlitt's office was on the top floor, and as I made my way up the stairs, students in baggy summer clothes brushed past me, their faces wearing earnest frowns still apparently nurtured on the English department's rarefied air.

A young woman at a desk on the top floor told me Professor Hewlitt was expecting me. She pointed me down a dark, half-timbered corridor that looked like part of Shakespeare's house, and I found Hewlitt sitting at a desk in the next-to-last office.

"Yes, Mr. Boone. Hello. Come in."

He rose and shut the heavy door after me as I entered. We shook hands. Hewlitt was a tall, angular man in an off-white linen suit, dark bow tie, and steel-rimmed Armani glasses that gave him a predatory Wall Streeter's air. His head was shaved and his eyes, magnified by the glasses, were shrewd and hawkish. I pegged his age at fifty-five, maybe a tad older. He invited me to sit in the office's leather easy chair and he sat at his desk.

"Wasn't expecting a private investigator," he said with a brisk click of the tongue.

"No one ever is."

On his desk were neat piles of papers, a pair of wooden lion carvings, and a multibladed African throwing knife. A window overlooked the green, and there were floor-to-ceiling shelves on two walls. The preponderance of books were either by or about Joseph Conrad, and a framed letter signed by the great writer and occupying a white wall near my head confirmed Hewlitt's specialty. As we settled down to talk, I noticed a yellowing elephant tusk in a corner behind Hewlitt's chair.

"Bought it from a game warden who'd taken it off a poacher in Zimbabwe," Hewlitt said.

"It's beautiful."

"I'd invite you to heft it but it weighs about eighty pounds." He ran a hand lovingly down the smooth yellowing surface.

"Heavy," I said, noncommittally.

"I'm afraid things in Africa are just as bad, if not worse, as when Kurtz was plundering it. It makes coming back here a slightly schizophrenic experience." He gestured toward the window, through which I could see undergraduates beginning to fill the green's intersecting walkways.

"I'll try not to aggravate your schizophrenia."

"You hope." Hewlitt grinned. "No, this is fine. I've got no more classes today. I just came in to review tomorrow's lecture notes."

"I told your secretary I was looking for someone you might be in communication with."

"Yes, when I got the message I began to wonder who it was I knew who'd have a private detective trailing after him."

"Her," I said. "Chelly—or Cheryl—Killbride."

Hewlitt's jovial demeanor quickly deflated.

"You know her," I said.

"Oh, yes." Hewlitt sighed. "Chelly's been something of a regular customer in recent months."

"How recent?"

"Ugh! It seems like forever. But in fact, since last February, early March? Sometime around then. She began phoning and coming by with what one might call wearying regularity." He smiled. Wearily.

"What was she coming around for?"

"Well, somehow she's gotten it in her mind that the

world needs a book about someone named Armen Karillian. Do you know who Armen Karillian is?"

I chose to play dumb. "Can't say as I do."

"My point to her three months ago. Nobody knows who the guy is, Chelly, so where's the book?"

"Who is he?"

"Karillian? He's a nobody. He's a schmuck. He's—I shouldn't say that." Hewlitt had his elbows on the arms of his desk chair and his hands were open as if he was indicating the length of a fish. "For one thing, I'll have my research assistant sore at me." He moved both hands as if he would drop the fish on his desk. "Karillian got a tenure-track lectureship here in the mid-sixties on the basis of two, in my opinion, very bad books of poetry, *Weasel Moon* and *Mambo for the Buckets of Dead*. Surely you've heard of *them* . . ."

I looked at him.

"'Moses, your Jewish cock is a burden I gladly bear?'" He recited with mock-quizzicality. "'Hebrew and gentile are marching on the Pentagon's vagina/O concrete donut, behold our massing lance/and quit thy juicy poison's flow on yellow innocence.'"

He paused.

"I missed that one," I said.

Hewlitt barked a guttural laugh. "Ain't it awful? It's that sixties shit that people seduced themselves into thinking was sirloin. His whole oeuvre's like that. Karillian thought of himself as the next big troubador, the natural successor to Whitman and Ginsberg. Trouble is, he got students around here actually believing him."

"When was he here? I don't remember him."

"Wait a minute, wait a minute. You were here . . . ?" Hewlitt said, blinking at me.

I nodded.

"When?"

I told him. The Conrad scholar leaned back in his chair, a little less glib.

"That was after Karillian had gone," Hewlitt said. "He left in '69." He suddenly leaned forward in his chair, whipped off his glasses, and squinted at me. "Wait a minute. Peter Boone." He flicked the glasses on again. "You were the pitcher here, weren't you?"

"That's right."

"You went on to pitch . . ."

"For the Red Sox. For a very short time."

"It's coming back to me, the news stories about you. Your wife was killed . . ."

"Mmm."

". . . and you found her killer and decided to chuck baseball for—"

I nodded. "Go ahead and say it. I don't mind."

"I'm sorry," Hewlitt said.

"For what? For what I do now?"

Hewlitt laughed nervously but could not ease beyond condolences.

"It must have been a tough decision, leaving baseball," he said.

"Not as hard as you might think."

"But still—" He searched for something more to say, couldn't find it. After a flustered silence he opened his hands to signal impasse. "What was your major here?" he asked finally.

"Comp lit. I don't think our paths crossed." But I was beginning to remember Professor Kenneth Hewlitt from my undergraduate days. He wasn't gray then, but he had kept his head shaved to a fine stubble. And I remembered he was one of the college's dollar-a-year men who didn't need the prof's salary but taught because he loved it or loved Hanover or maybe because he felt the work kept him out of mischief.

I seemed to recall that Hewlitt had an attractive wife, liked squash and rock climbing, and, when he wasn't retracing Conrad's footsteps in Europe, Africa, and the Far East, did consulting work for one of Washington's think tanks.

"I haven't done all that much over the years with the comp lit department, I'm afraid," Hewlitt said by way of apology. "Conrad's kept me busy enough."

"*Nostromo*'d keep anybody busy. You said Karillian left in '69. Where is he now?"

Hewlitt erupted in another sarcastic chortle. "A lot of

us around here would like to know the answer to that one." He tented his fingers, drew them toward his face and kissed his index fingernails. "Armen skipped out on his wife and kids in August of '69. Left everything. Word we got was he was either in Hanoi working for Ho Chi Minh's disinformation unit or in Bolivia with the remains of Che Guevara's guerilla force or in Havana as court poet to Fidel Castro."

"You're kidding."

"I am not." Hewlitt pursed his lips righteously. "Armen was that curious combination of charismatic crumb bum poet and erstwhile flaming anarchist. Call him a nineteenth-century hippie. Or the last pre-hippie beatnik. A hipster. Mailer's white negro. Only, there was this artsy-fartsy political aspect to Armen that was more polarizing than S.D.S."

I sighed. What was that supposed to mean?

"I don't follow," I said.

"What I mean is, that in the name of Art or some other goddamn icon he claimed willingness to do desperate things."

"Like what, become a revolutionary . . . ?"

"Oh," Hewlitt drawled. "Karillian already thought he was one of those. No, in so many ways he'd tell you he was prepared to do what one of those Conrad characters would do in *The Secret Agent*. Commit an outrage."

"What, he was going to set off bombs?"

Hewlitt smiled and shifted in his chair, obviously warming to the subject. "Armen could be very persuasive in providing a rationale for destroying any damned thing he pleased. But he always maintained a posture slightly above the fray. As an anarchist he distrusted any kind of politics, and yet he could go on and on about the corrosive effects of American culture—not just the war, which was going full tilt right then, remember—but everything. Blow it all up, he'd say. Bulldoze it all down. Start all over. There was this whole atavistic, anarchical slant to him. But with Armen it centered around art instead of—what? Raising goats and fabricating God's eyes. The trouble was, in the whole equation, the guy couldn't write!"

The green was full of students now. On the sidewalk

near Parkhurst Hall a young woman, walking backwards, was giving a tour to an edgy group of prospective students and their parents. Sullen suspicion beamed from the group like a toxin.

"You said he got students believing in him. A lot? A few?"

Hewlitt's grimace exuded tired pomposity. "Not all that many but—God, you're gonna get me going on this. Chelly's bad enough." Scratching an itch on the side of his grizzled skull, he resembled a lean, old dog. "All right." He sighed. "Up until he flaked out, Armen had his own little off-campus commune or salon. Call it what you will . . ."

"Where was that?"

"I knew you'd ask me. A lake over in Vermont, up north from here. I'm blanking on the name. What was it? Gowit. Gatwit—"

"Gatwick," I said.

Hewlitt snapped his fingers.

"Bingo."

A thrill of discovery radiated throughout my body. The room seemed to go suddenly silent. Hewlitt picked up on my attentiveness.

"Has Chelly Killbride ever told you she lives up there?" I asked.

Kenneth Hewlitt slowly cocked his head and stared at me. "She's never told me anything about where she lives."

I looked at Hewlitt until he had to look away. He picked up the throwing knife lying on a sheaf of papers on his desk and began turning it over in his hands. "She never told me any of that at all," he said. His long fingers caressed the dull iron blades. "That's very interesting."

"Go on," I said quietly. "About the commune."

"Well, it wasn't really a commune." Hewlitt placed the knife back on the papers. "I'm not sure what it was. A house on the lake, I was told. He shuttled students up there and they'd do whatever they did, I don't know. Three of 'em, I remember, produced a book of poems with Armen. I've got a copy, if you'd like to see it."

"I would."

Hewlett rose from his chair and went over to the

bookshelf. From a top shelf he plucked a small, saddle-stitched chapbook with a blue cover bearing a splotchy woodcut illustration of a nude woman lying on a bare mattress. He placed the volume in my hands. Its title was *Rapture Mama*. It appeared to have been hand-printed.

"I missed this one, too," I said.

"Take it with you." Hewlitt, seating himself, made a dismissive gesture.

I opened the book. Its three contributors, according to the title page, were John Spoonacre, Tom Jessup, and Duncan Keel.

"Spoonacre, Jessup, and Keel," I said. "Sounds like a white-shoe law firm."

"Ah, yes, the Poetry Gang," Hewlitt said with expansive humor. "I think that was Armen's tag for them."

There was a photograph of the trio printed on the inside back cover. They were long-haired, bearded, and bare-chested, in headbands and jeans—three jolly amigos in three different sizes, from big to small, standing with stoned insouciance near a beat-up Volkswagen bus covered with peace signs. The Poetry Gang.

"Does Chelly know about these guys?" I flipped through some of the poems. Lines of verse reminiscent of Ginsberg and Corso fluttered up from the pages.

Hewlett shrugged. "I don't know. I don't recall showing that to her."

Some of the poems weren't bad if you didn't mind high-flown emotion mixed with low-down images; others, like those I'd seen of Chelly's, were dreadful. Grocery lists from cerebral landfills.

"How is it Chelly came to you," I said, "if your specialty is Conrad and her interest is Karillian?"

Hewlitt cleared his throat with practiced self-importance. "Besides teaching the honors section on Conrad, I'm also the department person in charge of overseeing Karillian's papers, among others. They came to us a while back through his wife."

"Where's she?"

Hewlitt emitted a small sigh. "Dead," he said. "She committed suicide some years ago. Her estate was tied up in the courts for eons. We finally wound up with the papers last year."

"Any chance Karillian himself'll come back to claim them?"

"I rather doubt that. Contrary to the hagiography I told you earlier, it's my belief Armen went underground in 1969 to avoid federal prosecution. On what, I'm not sure. Income tax evasion? Weapons charges? Some kind of problem up in Gatwick? There were a lot of theories floating around campus at the time. None of them, to my knowledge, substantiated. But. With Armen any of 'em would fit."

"I see."

"As a matter of fact, the FBI was here last fall, going through the whole collection. They didn't take anything. But they sure spent a helluva lot of time looking at it."

"What's the status of the papers now?"

With an index finger, Hewlitt pushed his Armanis back on the bridge of his nose. "I've got a young woman going through them, computerizing everything so we can make sense of the collection, though I use the term loosely with Armen's work. You might want to talk to her about Chelly. Her name's Taylor Swimm. She's actually been letting Chelly help her with the papers."

"I'd like to meet her," I said.

Hewlitt looked at his watch, a gold Cartier tank with a thin leather strap. "She'll probably be by in a few minutes. How are we doing on questions here?"

He gave me a cranky grin that managed to mix impatience with gentlemanly unflappability.

"Just a few more," I said. "Do you know where"— I read from the chapbook —"Spoonacre, Jessup and Keel can be found?"

"I have no idea," Hewlitt replied. "I never knew them. Registrar might be able to help you, though they'll probably tell you they can't."

"Alumni confidentiality," I said.

"Unless you're the alumni fund." He barked his laugh again.

"Could you help me get their addresses?"

Hewlitt didn't care for the question but I didn't care. After a pause he said, "I suppose I could."

"By this afternoon?"

"Sure." His mouth twitched between amicability and annoyance.

"When was the last time you saw Chelly Killbride?" I asked.

Hewlitt peered out the window and murmured, "I think I see Taylor coming," then stretched his arms over his head and seemed to consider my question. "When was it?" he said. "Probably a week ago. Maybe a little longer. Week to ten days. I barely spoke to her, thank God. She and Taylor went off to the library to sort out more Armen together."

"How did she seem when you saw her last?"

"The way she always seems: engaging, charming, enthusiastic, and—you'll have to forgive me Mr. Boone—a royal pain in the ass."

As if recognizing for the first time what he'd been enduring about Chelly all these months, he erupted into loud, sustained laughter.

"You'll have to excuse me," he said, collecting himself. "I find, the longer I sit in this room, the more I feel like Marlowe waiting for the darkness to come to him!" He opened his hands in a gesture of ironical befuddlement. "I mean, I think I'm a good citizen. I vote. I pay my taxes. So why should I be accosted by an early-middle-aged woman eager to discuss a subject that holds so little interest for me?"

"Nature abhors a vacuum," I said.

He appeared not to have heard me. "It's just—she's so—sweet and earnest—and persistent—that I can't turn her away. It's as if, by taking on Armen's papers, I've become a magnet to these—these nut cakes!"

There was a knock on the door.

"Come in," Hewlitt said.

The door opened and suddenly standing before us was one of the loveliest young women I had seen in many a month. She was tall, trim, and creamy-skinned, with dark hair flowing down to her shoulders and a Botticelli face framing sparkling brown eyes and an expressive full-lipped smile. She wore leather sandals, a calf-length paisley skirt, and a sleeveless denim vest. On her shoulder was a green nylon book bag.

"Hi, Kenneth," she said to Hewlitt, then looked at me.

Hewlitt rose from his desk with elaborate courtesy. "Taylor. Nice to see you. I've got a visitor I'd like you to meet."

I stood up.

"Taylor Swimm, my research assistant and curator nonpareil, this is Peter Boone. Mr. Boone's a private detective, Taylor."

She nodded and her smile turned quizzical and fascinated.

"I've never met a private detective before," she said.

"Happy to be your first." We shook hands. Hers was warm, strong, and slender.

"Mr. Boone's conducting a search," Hewlitt said, turning the corners of his mouth down to indicate seriousness. "He's looking for Chelly Killbride."

Taylor Swimm's expression went from fascinated to bewildered to shocked. "She's missing?" she said.

"For three days," I said. "Her husband has me looking for her. You haven't seen her recently, have you?"

Taylor shook her head and looked at Hewlitt. "Not since last week when she was here to help with the papers. This is terrible! Is she all right?"

"Let's assume for now that no news is good news," I said. "But I'm looking for leads to her whereabouts. Professor Hewlitt says that you've been spending a fair amount of time with her."

"Yes, when she comes to Hanover," Taylor Swimm said. "She's been helping me go through the papers of this poet she's interested in."

"Armen Karillian."

"Yes." The shocked expression was giving way to intent concern.

"Had she been seeing anyone else when she came here?" I asked both of them.

Hewlitt pursed his lips and shook his head. Taylor said, "I don't know. I don't think so."

"Had either of you expected to see her three days ago?"

"You mean, was she scheduled to come in?" Taylor looked at Hewlitt for an answer. He shook his head again.

"Can't recall that she was," he said. He touched his assistant's bare elbow. "Taylor, Mr. Boone probably wouldn't mind asking you questions alone about Mrs. Killbride and, for that matter, good old Armen. What's your plan of attack for this afternoon?"

The cords of Taylor Swimm's tanned neck tensed as she grimaced and sucked in air. "I have to meet with some of the archives people to talk about storing and microfilming the Karillian stuff. I'm going to be tied up all afternoon." Her hands waved expressively in front of her face and she bobbed on her toes. The helpless, wanting-to-be-helpful research assistant.

"Would you be free this evening?" I said. "We could have dinner together, my client's treat? Professor Hewlitt, you're welcome to join us."

"You staying in Hanover for the night, Boone? Stay out at my place," Hewlitt said. "That's where Taylor's staying. Well, she's in the garage apartment. I'll put you in the guest bedroom. We could all have dinner at my place."

I thought about the idea for a split second.

"That'd be very nice," I said.

"As a matter of fact, what I can do is get those addresses for you from the registrar, have them for you tonight. Taylor, what you could do, if it's no trouble, is pull together some of the material you and Chelly have been working on and maybe walk Mr. Boone through it this evening."

"That'd be fine," Taylor said, turning her full-lipped smile on me and looking into my face. "I'll be at the house by six. I could pick up things for supper."

"That won't be necessary, Taylor. I'll throw some dinner together." Hewlitt looked at me. "Something light. On the grill, perhaps. I assume you like wine and aren't a vegetarian, Boone?"

I thought about Nan's efforts to make me eat tofu. "Not yet on the vegetarian part," I said. "And wine'd be terrific."

Hewlitt gave me his copies of *Weasel Moon* and *Mambo for the Buckets of Dead,* and I accompanied Taylor Swimm downstairs to the tunnellike corridor that connected Sanborn to Baker. As she apologized again for not being able to talk to me, I could not avoid noticing how developed her arms and shoulders were and how well her chest filled the denim vest, apparently without the help of undergarments.

"What will you do for the rest of the afternoon?" she asked me outside the corridor.

"Read Karillian and look around some more."

"Chelly's a nice woman. I feel awful thinking she's missing. I'm sorry you have to do this."

"So am I."

"Well, see you this evening."

I nodded and heard a door slam behind us and looked around.

"What did you do to your head?" Taylor Swimm said.

"Made contact with something I shouldn't have."

"Ouch!" She gave me a sympathetic smile and turned me around and touched Anny's bandage with her fingertips. "You should be more careful where you put your head."

"Right." I twisted around to see her full-lipped smile again. "That's one I'm learning all over again."

8

I WENT BACK INTO SANBORN AND FOUND MYSELF AN empty alcove in the English department library. Hushed and sepulchral, it appeared not to have changed at all since two decades before when I had curled up there with a booking board and a heavily annotated edition of *Paradise Lost*. The few undergraduates in the room paid me little notice. I settled into the overstuffed easy chair and told myself I'd give the poetry of Armen Karillian an hour of my undivided attention.

Five minutes later, I wanted to wing *Weasel Moon* and *Mambo for the Buckets of Dead* the length of the room. What was it with these people that they wrote so badly? *Weasel Moon* and *Mambo* were essentially the nightmare ravings of a narcissistic verbal diarrhetic. America was the target, or, more precisely, the punching bag of Karillian's warped and all-encompassing rage. Every line was an indictment; every word, the flap copy proclaimed, "demonstrates the angry sensitivity of one of America's modern seminal poets, the passionate vision of one who truly feels . . ."

Angry sensitivity? I muttered to myself, reading a poem called "Zombie Dorks." This is angry sensitivity?

Black man chain to big ole tree and crawlin' with
   whiplash maggots
while you, Uhmurkah, with your Marlboro man
smoke the brand that burned his body
and zombie dorks among you glom Leave It To Beaver

*and fill June Cleaver's de Milo tits with toilet plunger
    thoughts
of sterile lust . . .*

Sure. And I suppose the poem called "Mommy Fucks"
demonstrated the passionate vision of one who truly feels.

*Mommy fucks milkman fucks paperboy fucks plumber
    fucks farmer
fucks doctor fucks lawyer fucks Emmett Kelly
fucks Mickey Mantle til he hurts his leg
fucks Fidel Castro with his pussy-tendril beard
fucks Cuban cigars fucks plastic Ken and Barbie
fucks Julius Caeser fucks Sid Ceaser fucks Caesar salad
fucks Fabian at Caesar's Palace
fucks Annette fucks Cubby fucks Jimmy fucks Roy . . .*

I quit at Roy. The thought of Mommy going at it with the
big Mousketeer truly depressed me.

My least favorite poem, aptly titled "This Is What I
Vomit," included a graphic description of the poet up-
chucking a naked Dwight D. Eisenhower ("Up my gullet
Ike's legs slide/attached to his hairless sagging ass/his bristling balls/his bulbous cock . . .").

The taste of soft-shell crab rose in my own gullet.

Nausea, thanks to Armen, would never be the same
for me.

I flipped to the author's photo on the back jacket of
Weasel Moon and glowered at the crackpot face of Armen
Karillian. It was a big face with a bald pate, a long, thick
nose, and heavy, rubbery lips and ears. It reminded me of
pictures I'd seen of old-timer clowns out of makeup, sitting
outside their circus wagons, jackpotting—shooting the
shit. Karillian was sitting on a beach by the sea, holding a
cigarette and staring soulfully into the camera as a small
child built a sand castle at his feet. He was dressed in a
white T-shirt, black high-top sneakers, and khakis, and
there was a white watch-strap line on his otherwise tanned
and very hairy left wrist. The author's bio said:

Poet **Armen Karillian,** one of the finest voices to emerge from the so-called "Beat" generation, was born in New York City, in 1932, the son of Armenian emigrants. He briefly attended the famed Black Mountain College in North Carolina, before embarking on a ten-year odyssey across America that would provide the material for *Weasel Moon.* He has taught creative writing at Bard, City College, and San Francisco State. His poems and political writings have appeared in numerous underground journals.

Armen Karillian lives with his wife, the actress Cora Goltz, and their son, Mikah, on Manhattan's lower East Side.

The bio upset me. I wanted to know if Karillian's mommy was the poem's mommy who fucked.

I left Sanborn in a fog of vague sullenness and walked back downtown to the Nugget Theater, behind which I had parked my truck. The Nugget was a duplex now, but I was in no mood to feel nostalgic for the loss of its big screen or for the loss of a store next to it called Edith's, condom outfitter to generations of Big Greeners.

I drove around Hanover once more, sweeping the lots for Chelly's car, and as I did, I tried to beam Nan's mother's place on my bag phone.

Nan's mother answered on the second ring.

"Nan never came home this morning," she announced into my reddening ear. "She called to say she's staying in New York at Michael's again tonight. Is there a message?"

I went silent. In front of Topliff Hall a heterosexual couple was smooching and another was walking shoulder to shoulder, heads down, smiles on their faces, toward the Hop.

I managed to peep, "How are the dogs doing?"

"They're doing fine. They follow me wherever I go around the yard and push at me with their noses. They're quite the little herders. Are they your dogs, Mister . . . ?"

"Boone. Yes, they are."

"Well, when Nan told me she was bringing dogs with

her, I thought, 'Oh, no!' But they're proving to be very good company."

"I'm glad to hear that."

"Yes. Now, tell me again, what is your relationship to Nan, Mr. Boone?"

She's the second love of my life, I wanted to scream.

"She's a friend," I said.

"Yes. And I take it from what she said, you're the gentleman who gave her some help last summer in dealing with her ex-husband."

"I guess I did."

"Well, as her mother, I'm grateful. Greydon was just hideous to Nan. Having gotten to know your dogs, I'd like to meet you someday, Mr. Boone."

"And I'd like to meet you, Mrs. Holland."

"Nan and Michael are due back tomorrow. Shall I have her call you?"

Yes. Have her explain to me why she's seeing Michael Waxman and messing my mind!

"That's okay." I tried to sound sunny. "I'm on the road for a few days."

"Well, I hope you're not having the hot weather we're having in Connecticut."

"It's been heating up here, too," I said, thinking of the people I had met in the past twenty-four hours.

Mrs. Holland clucked. "I guess we all have to suffer," she said.

"Yes." I nodded to myself. "I guess we do."

9

I WAS STANDING NEAR THE PITCHER'S MOUND AT MEMO-rial Field, looking in at home plate sixty feet away. It was late afternoon and I was due at Kenneth Hewlitt's in half an hour. Memorial Field had a low chain link fence around it and two brick dugouts and a bunch of big evergreen shrubs fringing part of the outfield. Behind the backstop I could see the red brick varsity house where, as an undergraduate, I had changed into my uniform. When I turned toward the outfield, I saw, just beyond it, Leverone Field House where the baseball team took spring training. The football bleachers, looming behind the home team dugout, cast long shadows across the baseball field. I was alone and Chelly Killbride's Range Rover was nowhere in sight.

I stepped up onto the mound. Always like climbing a little mountain. The good ones always felt so firm and solid they left you winded climbing them. I did not know what I was doing on the mound. Yes, I did. Harvard had a big sophomore pitcher my senior year, and one Saturday afternoon in mid-May we dueled on this mound for nine innings, both of us pitching beautiful shutouts until I came to bat with a man on first and hit a triple off the smug lout and won my own ball game. My teammates actually carried me off the field that day. My wife-to-be was in the stands that afternoon, and after a good dinner that night at the Hanover Inn, we walked back down to the field, and in a darkness smelling of wet spring grass, I spread my jacket for a blanket and we made love quietly and hungrily on the pitcher's mound.

Now I thought about the woman I was searching for, who was about the age of my wife if my wife were still alive. Somehow Cheryl Killbride was drawn to Armen Karillian, even though he wrote like a septic pipe and even though the picture in *Weasel Moon* made him look like a fifth-rate poseur.

"Well, maybe you're wrong about that," I thought aloud, though I doubted it. I scraped the toe of my right shoe in the dirt in front of the rubber the way you did when you wanted a good plant. Maybe I was being a little too harsh. Maybe Karillian was the best thing to come down the pike since William Butler Yeats and Wallace Stevens and Dylan Thomas and Emily Dickinson combined. Maybe Chelly Killbride had holed herself in a room somewhere to unearth the hidden meaning of *Weasel Moon* and would be back soon to show Hewlitt and me the error of our critical ways. Yes, and maybe soon there'd be peace on earth and the Red Sox would win the World Series.

Anger at Nan and jealousy and envy had driven me to the pitcher's mound and now the mound was calming me down and firing me up in a kind of balancing act of emotions the way it always had. You knew there was pressure but being on the mound helped you blot it out and if you were any good you took that with you off the mound and used it in other parts of your life. It had been a long time since I had had to think, consciously, about blotting it out but now standing on the mound was helping me do that and I started to feel I could take it with me. Nan was a fine woman. Michael Waxman was doubtless a fine man. They had each other, it seemed. For how long, who knew? But it was none of my business. And if I wanted to keep functioning I would have to forget about it or not think about it, but only think of what I had to do.

I had to start allowing that my dogs might be the only ones coming back to me from Connecticut and that that would have to be all right with me. No, it would not have to be. But that's the way it could happen and if it did, then I had to say, as my wife used to say, Well, there it is.

So, what I had to do for now was forget about Nan and go about my business of looking for Chelly and see what tomorrow'd bring. I wasn't happy with what I had to do but it sure beat howling at the moon.

"Ow-oooh!" I bayed quietly as I walked off the pitcher's mound.

My howl needed work.

10

PROFESSOR KENNETH HEWLITT'S PLACE WAS A CONVERTED barn at the end of a dirt road off Route 10, south of Hanover. It was built on a high promontory, and, below it, through the hemlocks, you could see the Connecticut River flowing south toward Long Island Sound, two hundred miles away. There was a long driveway through a hemlock grove that opened onto the house, and next to the house was a big, double-bay garage with dormers in the roof and a pair of big windows above the bays. Both structures were sided with vertical barnboards that had been stained to a rustic antique brown. An old forest-green Volvo station wagon with Vermont plates occupied the space in front of one bay. The other bay door was open, and inside I could see a shiny red 1953 right-hand-drive MG convertible that appeared to be superbly restored. The car fit the landscape perfectly. Kenneth Hewlitt's place had the well-groomed, slightly unlived-in appearance of a gentleman's country retreat.

I parked my truck behind the Volvo and grabbed my blazer as I stepped out onto the drive. Not knowing when I'd be returning home, I had treated myself before going to the ball field to a spending spree at the Hanover Gap. I was wearing a new pair of jeans, a black drop-shoulder T-shirt, and a much-needed change of underwear and socks. I also carried three bottles of Clos du Cailleret that I had bought at the Hanover Food Co-op.

As I walked up the flagstone path toward the house, a pale brown Siamese cat darted from the bushes in front of me and beat me to the front door. When I reached the front stoop and rang the doorbell, the cat began vigorously rubbing its arched back against my legs.

"If you want to stay alive another minute, you'll stop that."

The cat paid me no heed.

I was about to launch it into the shrubbery with the side of my left foot when the doorlatch rattled. I managed to give the cat a little nudge with my ankle before the door opened and Taylor Swimm was in front of me again. "Hello!" she said with her full-lipped smile.

The cat darted past her legs and into the house.

Taylor Swimm's hair was up and she was dressed like a J. Crew model in an untucked sage green silk shirt, baggy blue cotton shorts, and blue deck sneakers. The shirt showed the delicious outline of her nipples, her teeth were perfectly straight and white, her legs were long and curved in all the right places, and she wore no makeup, only a lavender scent that wafted toward me the moment she opened the door. The sight of her made my throat go dry.

"How are you?" I croaked, lifting the bottles from under my arm. "Kenneth said dinner would be something light."

"So you brought light." Her smile with its beautiful teeth radiated across her face, then in an instant turned crestfallen. "Unfortunately, Kenneth's not going to be here tonight," she said.

"He's not . . ."

"No. He was called away on family business in Massachusetts and had to leave this afternoon. He left about an hour ago. But he gave me those addresses you were looking for and he said, by all means, his invitation to stay here still stands."

"Well, look." I shifted the wine bottles against my chest. "I could still get a room back in Hanover or up the road at the Chieftain or—what—what is it?"

She was reaching with both hands toward my chest. She lifted two of the wine bottles out of my arms. "It's silly to pay money for a room, don't you think?" She smiled at me. Even when she didn't smile she was beautiful. "Besides, the Hanover Inn is so expensive."

"Well." I gestured with my free hand. "Uh, let me at

least take us out to dinner. I mean, you and Kenneth weren't expecting me, I take up all his time this afternoon, and here I am showing up with little advance notice—"

"Are you through?" The look on her face mingled exasperation and amusement.

"I don't know. Am I?"

"I've got the grill going out back, Kenneth bought us two Norwegian salmon fillets, I'm making wild rice, steamed vegetables, and a salad. And you're staying. OK?"

I hesitated. "OK."

"Good. Come on in."

I did. Hewlitt's house was open and spacious. There was a row of windows and a set of French doors leading onto a deck that overlooked the treetops and the river. There was a living room area with comfortable couches and chairs and ottomans in tan muslin, a brick corner fireplace, a green Oriental rug with red and gold highlights, floor-to-ceiling bookshelves, and track lighting on exposed oak beams. Tucked behind a wide staircase was a dining area with dark Windsor chairs and a bird's-eye maple drop-leaf table and silver candlesticks. Near the dining area was the kitchen, an open space with gray slate countertops, cherry cabinets, a huge refrigerator, and a Viking gas stove. A saucepan of wild rice bubbled on the stove, and the countertop near the sink was strewn with salad fixings. I felt as if I had stepped into the back pages of *Architectural Digest*.

"Nice place."

"Isn't it?" Taylor Swimm walked the wine into the kitchen and put it in the refrigerator. "When I came to Dartmouth I didn't know anybody and I couldn't really afford a town apartment. So Kenneth offered me the garage apartment for practically nothing. It's been perfect."

"Excuse me for asking, but isn't Kenneth married?"

"No." Taylor rolled her eyes and shook her head. "I know what people must think. But Kenneth and I . . . it's strictly a working relationship."

I nodded agreeably. "But wasn't he married?"

"I think so." She moved around the kitchen, taking plates and wine glasses from cupboards as she talked. "I think he and his wife divorced a long time ago, like back in the seventies. I was moving some of his stuff around in the attic above the garage and I came upon this photograph of him and a woman. You went here, right?"

"Right."

"Do you remember his having a wife?"

"I thought I did but they were, like, separated or something?"

"The woman in the photo had dark hair. Short. Sort of a patricianlike quality about her? Pearl earrings, even tan?"

"That qualifies for patricianlike." We both laughed. "Yeah, it sounds like her. So, I take it she's left Hanover and Kenneth stayed on."

"I guess." Taylor shrugged. "Kenneth's all business. He doesn't talk much about his private life. Can I get you something to drink? How's your head?"

"My head's hanging in there. What are you offering?"

I was leaning against a counter at the edge of the kitchen and it was nice to watch her move. She opened a cabinet beside the refrigerator to reveal a well-stocked liquor shelf. "As we might've guessed, Kenneth's got it all," she said.

"How 'bout I build something for the two of us." I took off my jacket.

"That'd be great." Taylor's eyes took in my chest and arms.

At her request I made her a Bombay gin and tonic with a wedge of fresh lime, and the gin smelled so good I made one for myself. I handed her her glass and watched her take the two slabs of salmon from the refrigerator. The fish was lean, fresh, and pink and it exuded an oceanic smell that made my mouth water.

"Do you know anything about grilling salmon?" Taylor asked me.

"I do."

"Good. You're in charge of grilling these while I make the salad."

"It's not going to take very long if the fire's hot. What do you say we both make the salad and get the vegetable going and then we can go out on the deck and grill-watch."

"Excellent." She hoisted her glass. "To dinner."

"To dinner."

Together, we built a hefty salad of watercress, romaine lettuce, tomatoes, mushrooms, and cucumbers, and Taylor put native string beans and broccoli on to steam, and I put the salmon on the grill. It was a handmade, welded-iron grill and the coals were mesquite and very hot and the slabs of fish began sizzling the moment I put them on.

Watching me, Taylor said, "By the way, I've brought some of the Karillian papers home if you'd like to see them."

"'Like's' not a word I'd use to describe my feelings toward Karillian's work. But I should look at them."

"You read the books of poems, then . . ."

"Tried to."

"You found them difficult?"

"'Difficult' would be putting it mildly." I shrugged. "What can I say? I think the guy's second-rate. I don't think he can write. The stuff he does write I find ugly and banal. Should I go on or am I offending you?"

"You're not offending me." She stood beside me and watched as I lifted each piece of salmon with a spatula and rotated it forty-five degrees and set it down. "I hardly think Armen's the greatest poet in the world," she said, "but I do find his papers interesting. And he does provide this different take on what was going on in the late fifties and the sixties."

"Yeah, but there's no insight." I pressed the salmon with the spatula. "I've heard the complaints. I don't like complaining. Ginsberg does it better, and even Ginsberg wears thin after a while."

Taylor laughed engagingly.

"What? What is it?"

"Nothing," she said. "I just find it odd to be talking to a private detective who also reads poetry and cooks."

"I also recite," I said. " 'Beauty and cooking are truth. And truth, beauty and cooking. That is all I know on earth and all I need to know.' "

"Beauty and cooking and baseball, according to Kenneth."

"Right. And a whole bunch of other things not worth going into." I flipped the salmon and was pleased to see the diamond grill pattern on both fillets. "We'll give these another two minutes."

Taylor watched me rub a little butter on the fillets and then sprinkle dill and salt on them.

"You from around here?" I said.

"You come here very often? Have I seen you before?" Taylor laughed, then said, "New York. But I've lived in a lot of other places."

"What brought you to Kenneth?"

"Oh." She took a long swallow from her glass. I enjoyed watching her throat work. "I'd been bopping around from job to job. I decided what I really wanted to do, at age twenty-six, was go back to school and get an advanced degree in literature. Which, I'll grant, for my generation is a little anomalous . . ."

"Why anomalous?"

She looked at me as if I was a New Guinea bushman.

"Generation X?" she said, as if that explained everything.

"Ah, yes. The angst-ridden generation. The one that whines all day and listens to Pearl Jam."

"That's the one." A kind of mellow anger simmered beneath her engaging smile. "Raised by single moms and MTV. Taught life is hard and getting harder. National gravy train downsized and derailed. Too many people chasing too few bucks . . ."

"That is all ye know on earth and all ye need to know . . ."

She sighed. "If I sided with my generation I'd either be on Wall Street analyzing leveraged buy-out opportunities or flipping burgers at McDonald's. I've done both. Hated—*despised* both."

"So here you are."

"Here I am." She toasted her new existence. "Researching the Beats, working for Kenneth, and applying to grad schools. Kenneth's been great rounding up references for me."

"These are done."

I took the fillets off the grill and carried them inside

on their wooden board. While Taylor opened a bottle of
the Clos and put it on ice, I made a quick dipping sauce for
the salmon of chopped onion, grated horseradish, dill, and
sour cream. We heaped our plates with food, our glasses
with wine and carried them to a small, rustic twig table on
the deck. There, we ate and drank and enjoyed the broken
view through the hemlocks to the river.

"You and Chelly ever talk about anything other than
Karillian?" The smoke-tinged salmon and cool, flinty wine
mingled well on the tongue. I briefly wondered what Nan
was having for dinner. Was the food and setting and company as nice as this?

"You mean, does she confide in me?" Taylor sat at an
angle from me and I could look at her casually between
forkfuls of salmon and glimpses of the dark, silvery river.
She was beautiful company after days of getting clubbed
on the head and left, it seemed, for a guy named Michael.

"I mean, does she say anything to you other than
what a great poet Karillian is?"

Taylor nodded. "She's real nice. A little flaky but at
the same time down-to-earth. She tells me about her husband. How he's sweet and all, but how he just doesn't get
what she's about. I guess he drinks a lot."

I nodded. "She ever say anything to you that might
make you think she's seeing somebody other than her husband?"

"No, but she did talk to me recently about wanting to
get in touch with one of the guys on your list." She dug a
folded piece of paper out of the hip pocket of her shorts,
opened it, and laid it beside my plate. On the sheet were
three addresses:

Thomas Jessup, c/o Mr. Lon Jessup, Birch Creek
Hollow, Lebanon, N.H.

Duncan Keel, Pettigrew & Keel, Ltd., Battery
Street, Burlington, Vt.

John Spoonacre, Esq., Couchman, Spoonacre,
Roebuck & Dunn, 7 Pine Street, Burlington, Vt.

"It's Tom Jessup. She said he was an old friend and knew Armen well and might be able to help her with her book."

"So she knew Jessup . . ."

"That's what she said."

"Did she say she knew Spoonacre and Keel?"

Taylor considered the question a moment. "No. At least not that I remember."

"How recently did she mention wanting to see Jessup?"

Taylor shrugged. "Last couple of weeks."

"Did she ever tell you that she was from Gatwick Lake in Vermont and that Karillian once had a place over there?"

"I knew that already. From Armen's papers."

"But did she say anything about it, or about knowing Karillian himself?"

"No, but that's interesting, isn't it? Her living over there, too."

It was interesting. "Do Karillian's papers say anything about this place, like where exactly it was located?"

"I'm not sure. Armen called it Villa Poetica, but it sounds in his notes more like a run-down farm."

"Is any of that in the notes?"

She smiled. "I knew you'd ask. What I brought home is stuff from that last summer on the lake. It's kind of cryptic and it's not a lot. Armen didn't go in much for notebooks and diaries. I can let you look at the stuff tonight but I've got to bring it back to the library tomorrow."

"No problem."

It got dark and we finished supper and brought our plates and glasses inside just as the mosquitoes came out in force. Taylor said they were the one drawback to the place. She switched on a bank of track lights in the kitchen, and I helped her rinse the plates and put away the leftover food. When everything was picked up she opened another bottle of Clos and said, "I don't know if you want to read that stuff now, but if you don't, I could show you Kenneth's recreation room downstairs. No visit is complete, et cetera."

"Sounds diverting. Lead on."

She smiled and we picked up the bottle and our wine glasses and she led me to a door behind the stairs. The Siamese intercepted us, with a dead gray mouse in its jaws. It dropped the mouse at my feet.

"Pip Pirrip makes a propitiation," Taylor said.

"Pip Pirrip?"

The cat rubbed my leg, very pleased with itself.

11

KENNETH HEWLITT'S BASEMENT WAS A FITNESS ADDICT'S Shangri-la. The space was big and open, and Hewlitt or Jack La Lanne had divided it into different recreation areas. Across the front of the basement, along a row of French doors that opened out under the deck toward the river, was a lap pool, smooth and inviting. Sunken next to it, framed in redwood, was a Jacuzzi big enough for four people. Along a side wall was a sauna and a tiled shower stall, and to the back of the room was an array of body-building equipment and aerobics machines. There was a stair treader, a stationary bicycle, a treadmill, a cross-country machine, and a rowing ergometer. There was a Nautilus for the pecs, a Universal for the traps, delts and lats, a Cam II for the quads and hams, and free weights and inclined benches for every muscle in between.

In the center of the room under a hooded bank of lights sat a heavy, regulation-size billiard table, its slate top covered in blue felt. A wet bar was tucked alongside the stairs. Dividing the weight area from the aerobics machines was a couch, an easy chair, and a big, space-age Sony console.

"What, no jukebox? No pinball machines?" I turned to Taylor.

"Yeah, it's disappointing, isn't it." She put her fists on her hips and puckered her lips to one side of her face and squinted at everything.

"No Ping-Pong table, no shuffleboard. No basketball court. No pistol range. *No darts!* That's it. I'm leaving . . ." I started for the door.

"There's darts!" Taylor grabbed me with two hands around my bicep, spun me around, pushed her palms against my back, and walked me to a classic English-pub-style dart board hanging on the wall behind the stairs.

"Do you play?" I asked.

"Yeah, I play."

We played. She had a kind of earnest determination about playing that made me abandon any thought of coaching her. She swore at herself when she missed and crowed when she hit the bull's-eye. The wine seemed to make her audaciously competitive. Between tosses, she'd say things like "I'm gonna clean your clock, Boone!" and "Pack it in, mister!" and "Send the pitcher to the showers!"

She was fun to look at, and, as I paid her more and more attention, she beat me handily. I really didn't care. We drank wine and threw darts and she beat me four games out of seven.

"What can I say?" I bowed to her. "The Red Sox never win the big one."

"Excuses, excuses." She swigged more wine and patted my stomach and swayed a little. "God, your stomach is hard!" She laughed and her eyes went big.

"I work out here when Kenneth's not looking."

We were both a little drunk. I suggested a game of billiards. She let me break and when I missed my third shot and it was her turn, it became apparent that either she was more than just a little drunk or she didn't know the first thing about holding a billiard cue. I let her scratch and curse before saying, "You want a pointer?"

"No." She rubbed an itch on her nose with her fingers. "Yes." She was stretched over the table, her shirt loose and hanging forward, her hair half undone, wisps of it touching her shoulders. I placed the cue ball back where it had been and went around to her and put my left hand in front of hers on the cue.

"Depending on the shot, there are a couple different finger positions for the front hand," I said.

She turned her face up toward mine and looked at me. "No shit."

Her eyes were dark and glowed under the lights, and

her smile danced between amusement and avidity. I bent down and kissed the full lips. We both let go of the cue and kissed each other hard and greedily. Before long, we had rolled onto the table and were pulling at each other's clothes and knocking billiard balls out of the way with our hands and forearms. I ended up penetrating her wearing only my white socks and a condom that had been in my wallet since God knows when and she wearing only her blue sneakers. She dug her nails into my back and squeezed her thighs against my hips. The first time she came, it was with a series of cool, high, predatory cries that transmitted her sexual hunger like electricity through my groin and up my spine.

Over the next two hundred minutes we had sex on the billiard table, the couch, the pecs Nautilus, an inclined bench, and the wet bar. After some sessions we would swim for a while in the lap pool, soak in the warm bubbling surf of the Jacuzzi, and find ourselves revived and ready to go again. I was surprised by my appetite for simple, animal sex and amazed by Taylor's, which was ferocious. Once when we were standing together in the pool she put her hands on my shoulders and her legs around me and did pullups against my flayed groin until she came. Afterwards, she looked into my face and smiled at me for a long while.

"Strange interlude," she said, catching her breath.

"You got that right."

"But nice."

"You got that right, too."

"Is there another woman in your life right now, Peter Boone?"

"Was. Is, maybe. We're 'seeing other people.' " I made quotation marks with my first and second fingers.

Taylor's chlorine-reddened eyes widened with droll disbelief. "Tell her for me she's crazy. Tell her she's missing the best sex in the Western Hemisphere."

"I wouldn't go that far."

"I would."

Later, we placed the couch in front of the lap pool and the French doors. Naked and facing each other on the couch, we slowly drank the third bottle of Clos together.

"I'm such a tramp," Taylor said with a satisfied smile. "I hope you don't mind my being a tramp with you."

"I don't mind at all."

"Do you feel guilty about this?"

"No."

"I must have surprised you—the straitlaced graduate student?"

"There's not a straitlaced bone in your body."

"I wanted this to happen the minute I saw you in Kenneth's office. The nanosecond."

"Well, you got it."

She moved her foot between my legs and began gently pressing my groin with her toes. Naked, she was wholly amoral. "And you?" she said.

"I found you instantly desirable, too."

"And yet we scarcely know each other."

"Right."

"For all I know, you may be a serial killer. For all you know, I may be a robber on the lam."

"Serial killing's not one of my fortes," I said.

She set her glass on the floor and moved on top of me again.

"Fucking is," she said.

Hours later, in the guest bedroom Hewlitt had made up for me, we rutted like dogs on one of the twin beds and afterwards Taylor plopped forward on her stomach and fell asleep. Kneeling above her, I could not bring myself to think of the two of us as sex maniacs. I felt unbelievably calm and cleansed. Through the guest room window I could see the river's dark outline and the lights of a few houses on its Vermont side. It pained me to think I had to go out into that world again tomorrow.

"Boone," Taylor murmured without opening her eyes.

"Hmm?"

"Don't hold any of this against me, okay?"

I patted her on the ass. "No sweat," I said.

"I'm not really a nymphomaniac," she said.

"I never thought otherwise."

"I'm not."

"What are you?"

"I'm just a poor little girl alone in the big bad world," she said.

I lay down beside her and stroked the back of her head.

"Woulda fooled me," I said.

12

TAYLOR SWIMM WAS NOT IN BED BESIDE ME WHEN I AWOKE the next morning at eight. Story of my life. My sutures itched under Anny's now-wet dressing and I was pretty hung over. I found my clothes neatly folded on a chair at the foot of the bed; a manila envelope sporting a Post-It lay on top of them. The Post-It said, "Boone, An amazing night. Thank you. I'm sorry to cut out on you so early. Read the stuff in the envelope here. If you need more, call me at the number below. Call me anyway. Keep me posted on Chelly. I stole one of your business cards from your wallet. I may call you! Who said the party's over? Yours in lust, T."

The note was almost enough to cure my headache. But not quite. I stumbled into the guest bathroom, found a bottle of cheap aspirin, popped four and chased them with a half quart of water. Then I padded downstairs in the nude and looked out the door. Pip Pirrip was stalking robins on the lawn, but Taylor's Volvo was gone. Alack. I went down into the rec room. The couch was back in its place, and there were no signs of the previous night's debauch. Back in the kitchen I started a pot of coffee and drank some orange juice and tried not to think of Taylor and me in that room. It wasn't easy. I took a shower, changed the sodden bandage on my head with one I found in Hewlitt's medicine chest, got dressed, and read through the contents of the envelope as I drank coffee and ate a plateful of corn muffins that Taylor had left for me.

There wasn't much in the envelope, just photocopies of some typewritten notes and the drafts of three more god-awful Karillian poems. The notes covered the period from June to August 1969, and didn't say much that wasn't already said in *Weasel Moon* and *Mambo for the Buckets of Dead*. I gathered from them that Karillian hated authority, was suspicious of the FBI wiretapping his telephone, despised the draft and Richard Nixon, advocated free love and the mind-liberating benefits of hallucinogens, believed in the feasibility of a utopian community of artists, suffered money problems, had hemorrhoids, and fancied himself God's gift to women. "For the first time ever in our two-year relationship, X spent the entire night with me at V. Poetica," he wrote on July 6, 1969. "She couldn't keep up with me. Marriage, we agreed, was an antiquated façade that inhibited healthy sexual expression. With me, she said she felt freer than she had ever felt in her life."

"X," I said aloud. "Who's that?"

July 11, 1969: Mix sodium and chlorine and what do you get? Sodium chloride. Salt! The fundamental compound of life. I am now figuratively swimming every night in salt. I'm in a bliss state unequaled since my nine months in Mama Karillian's womb.

July 17, 1969: Salt and now carbon. The oldest/youngest building block. I am on a sexual carousel, only the horses are alive and all too willing to buck.

July 24, 1969: A red-letter day, with sweet rounds of salty carbonation and no one the wiser. Is there a long poem to be written from all this ecstasy? Maybe. If so, move over Henry Miller!

July 31, 1969: Big dose of salt today. In garage. In cornfield, giggling, as storm troopers drove by.

August 4, 1969: Consuming horse sometimes consumes my appetite for my pretty horses. Ah, well.

August 8, 1969: Merde meets moving fan blades.

August 10, 1969: Compound still tasty!
August 11, 1969: Element, too!
August 12, 1969: Armen, mind your P's &
Q's!

That was Karillian's last entry. I flipped through the
remaining four or five pages but found only revisions of
poems I had read in *Weasel Moon*. The revisions weren't
helping at all. I put everything back in the envelope and
found paper in one of the kitchen drawers. I wrote a note
to Hewlitt, thanking him for his hospitality, and another
to Taylor, telling her she was pretty amazing herself, and
that I'd call. I put Hewlitt's note on the dining room table
where he couldn't miss it and stuck Taylor's, with the envelope, under the locked door that led to her apartment
over the garage. Standing there, I knew it was time to put
away my fantasies for a while. The thought so depressed
me that when Pip Pirrip took another go at my leg, I made
like Quasimodo and treed the fucker.

By nine o'clock I was in my truck, barreling down
Route 10 toward Lebanon. Tourist traffic heading north
from Connecticut and Massachusetts was steady. At the
parking lot near Wilder Dam, I asked a lineman in an
orange truck for directions to Birch Creek Hollow. He
pointed me south, then east a few miles into the hills. The
day was warm but not as humid as when I had met Arthur
Cole, and the lineman's directions were good. After a few
miles I was in Birch Creek Hollow on a dirt road that
wound up the side of a small wooded mountain. Here and
there, I saw ugly open spaces with brown skidder marks
and strewn tops where sloppy logging operations were underway. I saw other lots with shacks or trailers on them
that reminded me of places I'd seen in Appalachia. Heavy
electrical lines dipped umbilically into the openings off of
creosoted poles. The road petered into a muddy turnaround and Lon Jessup's was the last place on it.

Parked in the rutted driveway was an old, mud-split-
tered Dodge sedan with scaly fiberglass bodywork under
its doors. I parked behind it and walked across the
grassless yard to the trailer's front door. A sign on its
screen said OXYGEN IN USE and showed a cigarette in a red

circle with a slash through it. A handlettered sign in the window said BAIT.

I hesitated before knocking. A television somewhere within was tuned to a morning talk show. In lubricious Australian accents, the host was chastizing someone as the audience howled its approval.

"You only wanted sex!" the host crowed. "And look what it cost you—your job, your wife, your kids, your house, your car!" An odor of failing septic system carried on the morning breeze. I knocked on the door.

A short, heavy old woman appeared at the screen. "Can I help you?" she said between dry coughs.

"I'm an old friend of Tom Jessup's. I'm looking for him. Does he live here?"

"No." She coughed again. "And you're about the fourth old friend that's visited here in the past month."

"Is that right?" I tried not to look surprised.

The woman nodded. "First a woman, then two men. Woman sayin' she knew Tommy goin' way back, wanted to have a reunion or somethin'. Men sayin' they was his friends an' needed to talk to um. I don't know. Lon talked to the guys. I wasn't here. Lon said they seemed mighty anxious about somethin'."

"You're Tom's mother, aren't you?"

"That's right. Who did you say you were again?"

"I'm Peter Swimm."

The woman uttered a grunt.

"You're screwed!" the Australian TV announcer howled.

"Did you and Tommy go to Dartmouth together?" the woman asked.

"Yeah, but we were in different classes." I thought quickly. "Listen, if Tom—uh, Tommy isn't here, would you mind if I asked you and your husband some questions about him? I'm with alumni records. We're doing this survey . . ."

The woman emitted a bitter chuckle. "I don't remember the college ever bein' *this* aggressive." But she opened the screen door.

Entering, I saw a kitchenette with tiny appliances and a fake-maple dining table covered with prescription bot-

tles. The TV was in a living area dominated by a hospital
bed and a brown metal oxygen converter. A thin old man
with an oxygen clip in his nose was sitting up in the bed.
He was wearing a blue pajama top and a plaid woolen
bathrobe. His legs were white and his toenails curved like
primal claws over his knobbed toes. When he noticed me,
he said in a gasping voice, "I've already got—two policies.
When are you crooks—gonna leave us alone?"

"This ain't the insurance man. He's a friend of
Tommy's!" the woman shouted with faint annoyance.

The man blinked. "Tommy ain't—here."

"I told him that!"

"We haven't seen him—in two years. Before that—we
hadn't seen him—*in twenty!*"

"This fella's from the College, Lon. He just wants to
ask us a few questions!"

"Don't you feel a shred of remorse?" the TV voice
cried. The old man lifted a remote control, aimed it with a
wavering hand at the screen, and fired.

The TV went mute. Behind its silence, the sound of
the oxygen unit became audible. It made a sound like fat
intermittantly spattering on hot coals.

"I'm curious," I said, emanating as much affability as
I could muster for both of them. "Was the woman who
came here looking for Tommy dark haired, good looking,
in her late thirties?"

"I'd say she was pretty," Mrs. Jessup said.

"Did she say her name?"

Mrs. Jessup was wearing a housedress with no collar,
and clusters of moles were prominent on her thick neck
and shoulders. She squeezed at a clump of them on her
collarbone. "Oh. Lon, what was the name o' that woman
come by?"

With long fingers Lon patted the lapels of his bathrobe as he thought. "I don't remember. Didn't she tell
you?"

"Oh . . ." Mrs. Jessup closed her eyes.

"Did she call herself Chelly Killbride?" I said.

"That's the one." Mrs. Jessup slapped her short-fin-
gered hands decisively, shaking the flesh on her arms.

"Drove one of them expensive Range Rovers. Said she knew Tommy from when he was at Dartmouth."

"And you say she wanted to stage a reunion or something?"

"Somethin' like that. Said she and Tommy took courses together at Dartmouth an' they were in this writing club and she was curious how he was doin' and wanted to see um and have this little get-together."

"But you don't know where Tommy is, you say . . ."

"Waal, I know he's over in Burlington someplace. He just don't come by, that's all. And with Lon bein' sick, we don't get out 'cept for me goin' to the store."

"It's rough." I squinched my face sympathetically. "Who were the other guys?"

"Lon saw them. Lon—" We turned to the old man in time to see him slowly inflate his cheeks and hawk a great glob of green phlegm into a plastic cup. When he looked up I noticed for the first time how slow his glassy eyes tracked when he moved his head.

Sister morphine. Advanced use.

"Lon, what were the names of the two guys who said they was friends of Tommy's?"

"Oh. Them two." The old man stared ahead.

"What was their names?"

"Were their last names Spoonacre and Keel?" I said.

"Spoonacre's a lawyer over in Burlington," Mrs. Jessup said. "Lon knows Spoonacre. He came by here last year."

"Did he?" I said.

"It wasn't—him," Lon tiredly gasped. "These were—city fellas. One of 'em—big and blond—white-blond. Other one—bald—looked like—a wrestler. Drove a Lexus—dark blue. Pretty car." Lon's eyes widened with chemical remembrance.

"Did they say why they wanted to see Tommy?"

"No." Lon shook his head. "Only that they—was friends," he said after a while.

"Did they leave a number or anything?"

"No. No number." Lon slowly blinked.

"And you don't have Tommy's address," I said to Mrs. Jessup.

"When he was here two years ago, he said he was livin' in Burlington," Mrs. Jessup said. "But he never left an address for us. *I* would've liked to have it so I could send him his junk mail. Here, look at this . . ."

She led me through the living area down a dark hall to a tiny room. It was filled with mail—stacks of *Dartmouth Alumni Magazines,* Publisher's Clearing House solicitations, coupon giveways, credit card applications, catalogues, come-ons—two decades of postal detritus in twenty-plus boxes stacked three high.

"Amazing," I said.

"I mean, does he want me to keep it for him or throw it away. Same with his shell collection. Lookit here—"

With surprising agility she was suddenly on her hands and knees, pulling a sweater box out from under a daybed. I helped her put it on the bed. A clattering sound arose when we jostled it open. The box was filled with snapping turtle shells.

There were dozens of them loosely wrapped in tissue paper, in sizes ranging from six to sixteen inches across. They were brown and smooth and heavy with varnish; some showed entry holes made by a .22.

They reminded me of military canteens from long-forgotten wars.

"Tommy shot these when he was in junior high," Mrs. Jessup said with some pride. "There's a pond down below, at the edge of the woods. Tommy and his friends liked to swim there. Waal, one day, one of the boys got bit by a snapper. It was that one—" She held up one of the larger shells, a fifteen-incher. The shell was housed in a wood-and-glass case that Mrs. Jessup said Tommy had built especially for it in eighth-grade shop class. "I wish you coulda seen what this snapper did to that boy's leg. Ripped a chunk out of it, size of a golf ball."

She reached down and grabbed her own doughy leg below the calf.

"Lon said if Tommy was gonna swim there anymore, he'd have to clean 'em out. So Tommy got Lon to buy um an old double-action Colt pistol, and Tommy went to work on 'em through the summer.

"He was always a good shot, Tommy. But with that

pistol he got so he could put a bullet through a turtle's eye at twenty feet and hit the brainpan. He'd kill a turtle, bury it, dig it up the next summer—all 'ud be left was the shell, which he'd varnish. Tommy buried lotsa turtles that first summer."

"Did he clean out the pond?"

"Oh, yes. For a while. But you know snappin' turtles. They're like weeds. You kill one and two spring up in its place. Soon as Tommy stopped shootin' 'em, they come back. Now, I imagine the pond's teemin' with 'em, though I can't be sure. I ain't been down there for thirty years."

I put the box back for her and let her give me the rest of her tour. A narrow closet still contained some of Tommy's old sixties rigs: Caribbean drug-runner suits and Jimi Hendrix shirts and a fur-fringed sheepskin vest. From a bureau drawer she pulled out his high school and Dartmouth diplomas, both framed and under glass. She rubbed the dust off the glass with her palm.

"Lon worked as a janitor at the College for thirty-eight years. Tommy was always a good student. Lon thought the College'd be good for um."

"What about you? Are you happy he went to Dartmouth?"

She scoffed. "I don't know what good it did him, except to make him a more educated bum."

She showed me his high school graduation picture. It looked like any graduation picture taken before 1965. Neat haircut. Jacket and necktie. Pleasant smile with a look of earnest determination to it.

"Doesn't look like a bum there."

"When Tommy was little, I used to take him with me when I'd go off and do housekeeping summers. He was a good little worker right up through high school. Then everything changed." Bitterness consumed her voice. "All that sixties crap."

"I remember."

I studied the earnest face for a while. A face on the verge of Aquarian induction.

When ripeness was all.

"You have any pictures of Tommy taken recently?" I asked.

"Just one. Not very good of um."

She led me back into the living area, where Lon was now upright against the edge of the bed, urinating into a hospital flask. He held the flask in both hands. His eyes gazed at it tenderly.

Mrs. Jessup went around his bed to the side table. She rummaged among his effects until she found a snapshot.

"What are you doin'?" Lon turned his head but kept the flask pressed against his crotch.

"Showin' Mr. Swimm Tommy's picture!" She wiped it on her breast and walked it back to me. "This is two years ago," she said.

The figure in the photo was lean, vulpine, and sporting a few days' growth of dark beard. Its grin was crooked, its thick, combed-back hair black but going to gray, and the dark eyes radiated uneasy, amused suspicion. The crooked-grinning face seemed to be saying, What? You wanna take *my* picture? *Me?*

The figure was wearing faded jeans and a beat-up black T-shirt with the word BURTON on it. The face was a far cry from the one in the graduation picture.

"You mind if I borrow this?" I asked Mrs. Jessup. I fabricated a story about alumni records compiling a memory book for nostalgic old Big Greeners.

I thought it an innocent lie.

"Go ahead." The old woman waved her arm disgustedly toward her husband. "*He* won't miss it."

"I need a shot," Lon Jessup said. The flask was at his side. His penis was exposed; in its nest of iron-colored pubic hair, it looked like a small, skinned animal.

Taking the flask from his hand, Mrs. Jessup drew the folds of the bathrobe over his groin. "It's early yet!" she shouted in his face.

Lon Jessup appeared to sulk.

"Oh, all right. Mr. Swimm, could you help him back in while I . . ." She hoisted the flask.

"Sure."

It was not a new experience for me. Like every terminal patient, Lon Jessup was heavier than he appeared, as if his weight had been compressed into the very marrow of his bones. I lifted him back onto his bed and his wife returned from the bathroom with the rinsed flask and took a fresh syringe of morphine from the little refrigerator. She had me roll him to his side; at the last moment she grunted and began painfully flexing her thick-fingered right hand.

"Wouldn'tcha know it, my fingers gotta be bad today." She added in an alarmed voice—"He can't wait for the hospice nurse."

"Here, let me do it." I pried the syringe from her fingers.

"You done this before?"

"Yeah."

"Hospice nurse ain't in until two. I want to set him up on an I.V. drip but she won't do it!"

I slipped the plastic cover off the syringe. "Maybe you should talk to his doctor."

The needle marks from past injections had left ugly bruises on his sunken hip. I found a clear spot, swabbed it with alcohol and stuck the needle there. He coughed quietly when I sent the dose home. I withdrew the needle, pressed the gauze over the new puncture and gave the needle back to Mrs. Jessup. Her hands shook as she recapped it.

"We turned down chemo and radiation because we felt it'd kill him," she said. "It's in his lungs and they can't operate. We felt the quality of life would be better this way."

"I'm sure it is." I touched her arm.

"This is cleanin' us out!"

She began to sob. I put my arms around her. It was not what I expected to be doing.

"We thought, when Tommy come back when this first started, that maybe he'd help out and we'd see more of him," she sniffed. "But we ain't seen shit of um. Not shit of um. Whaddya gonna do?"

"Is Tommy here?" Lon Jessup said without turning toward us.

"No, Lon." Mrs. Jessup's voice revealed a steady affection.

"Huh?"

"No!" Her face flushed with fury.

We rolled him over on his back. The underwater eyes found mine.

"I never thought—I'd get—this tired." The wasted face looked into mine.

"Twenty years of split shifts and migrant housekeeping," Mrs. Jessup clucked. "So our kid could be a god-damn *bum*."

The oxygenator made its spattering hiss. I heard it in my head the rest of the day.

13

AT THE SUNOCO STATION NEAR I-89 IN WEST LEBANON, I patched a phone call from my truck to the offices of Couchman, Spoonacre, Roebuck & Dunn in Burlington. John Spoonacre's assistant told me he was in court for the morning and was tied up with meetings all afternoon. I told her I needed to see her boss on a life-or-death matter, that I'd only need a few minutes of his time, and that if I knew John Spoonacre, he would not be happy to learn that his old buddy Boone called and had not been fitted into his schedule.

"You're a friend, then . . ."

"Yeah, well, you know how it is with us Dartmouth guys." I gritted my teeth at having to play the college card.

From her guffaw I could tell she knew exactly how it was.

"Hold on a moment," she said.

I waited, thinking about Chelly and the two guys in the Lexus and Spoonacre visiting the Jessups, and about Tom Jessup suddenly being on Spoonacre's and the Lexus guys' popularity lists. Then I thought about Taylor Swimm and Nan. That thought was pleasurable and confusing, with a lot of bodies moving around in it.

The assistant came back on the line.

"Yes, Mr. Boone, I can fit you in after lunch but only for five minutes. Mr. Spoonacre's schedule is jammed."

"Wah hoo wah," I said.

"I beg your pardon?"

"That's Big Greener lingo for 'Wonderful,' " I said.

She laughed. "Can you come by a few minutes before two?"

"With bells on," I said and hung up.

At the McDonald's up the street I bought a cup of coffee and realized that if I spilled it on my crotch, I could sue and collect a lot of money and not have to think about Chelly or Tom or Armen and the Poetry Gang ever again. Right. Instead, I'd have third degree burns where it matters most and be free to think about Taylor and Nan full time.

"Yikes," I said aloud.

I pried the tab off the coffee lid as far away from my crotch as I could.

The drive from West Lebanon to Burlington takes about ninety minutes on I-89, but less if you have the right electronics and know the speed traps. I made it to the Pine Street parking garage in seventy minutes, with time enough before my meeting with Spoonacre to do sushi at Sakura on Church Street. I bought a *New York Times* at Chassman & Bem and ate *maguro, hamachi, ikura,* salmon-skin hand-roll, and scallion-laced *tekka-maki* at the bar while I read All the News That's Fit To Print and watched the chefs perform their cutting magic in front of me. I drank two bottles of Kirin beer, checked the sports pages to see how the Red Sox were doing (no pitching this year, except Clemens, so not so hot), paid my bill, left a tip, and walked down Church Street for my appointment at one fifty-five.

Since the early eighties, Church Street has been a walking street, closed to traffic, and the pedestrian areas on this sunny day were jammed with shoppers and with vendors hawking their wares. As I wove my way past skateboarders, stroller-pushers, college kids, and Rastafarians, I waved to my friend the Hot Dog Lady, nodded to the silversmith, said "Hi" to the woman selling Vermont-Only T-shirts, and watched a blind banjo player near Leunig's restaurant beguile a small crowd with his instrumental version of "American Pie."

I made it to 7 Pine Street with two minutes to spare. Seven Pine is an eight-story office building built above the Porteous store and a parking garage on the backside of downtown Burlington. The pavement in front of the door was hot, and the security kid at the desk was sweating and watching a soap opera on a miniature television.

"Help you?"

"Couchman, Spoonacre," I said.

"Eighth floor."

The lobby was dead. I rode the elevator alone. At the eighth floor, it opened into a carpeted area with a receptionist's desk in the middle of it. The receptionist, an ash-blond woman in a plaid summer suit, was smiling at me as I stepped from the car.

"May I help you?" The voice conveyed an officiousness I associated with parts of Chittenden County.

"Are you from Shelburne?" I asked.

"Why, yes." The woman dipped her head and clutched at the pearls around her throat.

Score one for the P.I. "I'm here to see John Spoonacre."

"Do you have an appointment, Mr. . . . ?"

"Boone. I do."

"Won't you have a seat, then, Mr. Boone. I'll tell Mr. Spoonacre's assistant you're here."

She picked up the phone receiver and nodded me to the waiting area near her desk. I sat in a leather wingback. The reception area of Couchman, Spoonacre, Roebuck & Dunn was decorated, like its receptionist, in plaid, with touches of mahogany and brass to soften its institutional quality. I could hear the murmur of businesslike voices emanating from the offices along the outer walls. Through a door behind the receptionist I saw a conference room with views through wide smoked windows of Lake Champlain and the Adirondacks. I could see sailboats on the lake; they moved behind the smoked glass as if in a lucid dream. The magazines on the mahogany coffee table in front of me were English; the prints on the walls depicted horses and manors. The ventilation system hummed; the air was pleasantly chilled. It was all halfheartedly Anglophilic. At any moment I expected to see Alistair Cooke.

Instead, the elevator doors slid open and a big man emerged gripping a leather briefcase. He was dark-haired and strapping, wearing a celery-colored silk tweed sports jacket, tan worsted slacks, a red bow tie, and a starched white oxford shirt, and he moved past the reception area with a quick, big-handed earnestness. His face was red and sweating, and patches of sweat were wilting his crisp, white shirt, but he moved as if he was going to strip the shirt off anyway and leap out the window in cape and tights.

He disappeared into a far corner office, trailing a scent of cigars and bay rum.

"Good afternoon, Mr. Spoonacre," the receptionist said in a quiet voice to his residue of churned air.

A moment later, an attractive strawberry-blonde in a blue paisley-print dress and low navy heels emerged from the office near Spoonacre's and walked over to me.

"Mr. Boone?" She had freckles and nice green eyes and her hair cascaded to her shoulders in loose ringlets.

"That's right."

"Why don't you go in now."

"Thanks for fitting me in," I said.

"Wah hoo wah." She flashed me a conspiratorial grin. I gave her a wink, rose from my chair, and strode into Spoonacre's office before she could change her mind about me.

"Yes?" John Spoonacre, standing at his desk, one arm in his briefcase, looked up, startled, when I walked through his door.

"You don't remember me?"

Spoonacre stammered. "Ah-am I supposed to?"

I turned to his assistant, who was standing in her doorway, expecting to see a sweet reunion of old class-mates. I opened my hands. "He doesn't remember me."

She returned the gesture with a smile and a shrug.

I made a face. "But he will." And shut the door on her.

"Look, I'm very busy," Spoonacre said with weary restraint. "If you wouldn't mind telling me who you are, if I'm supposed to know you, and what this is about . . ."

He had thick slightly drooping lips and eyes and a prep school drawl. A dandy. Soft but strapping. Fancied himself tough-minded. And leery of anything uninvited.

I stepped toward him.

"My name's Boone." I tossed him my license. "I'm looking for a woman you know. Chelly Killbride."

He gave me an amused frown. "Chelly Killbride. *Cheryl* Killbride? Little Chelly Killbride from Gatwick Lake?"

"That's the one."

He studied my license and shook his head. Chuckled to himself. "This is weird."

"What, the likeness?"

"No, no!" Spoonacre chortled, handing the license back to me. "I haven't seen Chelly Killbride in, Christ, it must be twenty-five years."

"She hasn't been in touch with you recently?"

"No!" He laughed at the outrageousness of such an idea. "At least not that I know of. I could check with Trish and see if she's called here. But I haven't seen her."

"Mind if I ask you a few questions anyway?"

He laughed again. "I don't mind."

Spoonacre was big, clean-cut, and very fit for a guy in his forties: a sort of middle-aged Clark Kent and a far cry from the scruffy wordsmith on the inside back cover of *Rapture Mama*. He lifted his briefcase off his desk, took a handkerchief out of his jacket pocket, and, wiping his face, invited me to sit in one of the two client's chairs near his desk.

He said, "I've only got a couple minutes, though."

"That's okay. I've only got a couple questions."

He pulled off his jacket, hung it on a heavy brass coatrack behind me, returned to his desk, and sat, too. The desk was reproduction Georgian with a big leather-tipped green blotter, brass banker's lamp, and piles of legal documents on it. Behind Spoonacre was a credenza covered with family photos in silver frames. There were snapshots and studio portraits of an attractive woman and four girls ranging in age from about fifteen to seven. The snapshots were all taken at a tropical beach somewhere. Shelves along the side wall were filled with tan volumes of Vermont statutes. The view of the lake and waterfront was sweeping.

"So you've had no contact with her in twenty-five years."

"No. What can I say?" Spoonacre bent and opened the desk's bottom drawer and rested his foot on it. An office reflex. "I graduated from Dartmouth in '69 and basically never looked back. I got a four-F for a bum knee that summer. Went to Harvard Law School in '70. Graduated from there in '73. Set up practice here in '74. Got married in '78. Have a wife, four kids, and a humongous mortgage in Charlotte. I haven't been in touch with Chelly Killbride or, for that matter, the class of '69 since I left."

"Duncan Keel?"

Spoonacre looked surprised. "Oh, Dunc. Sure. Dunc's in town. I bump into Dunc from time to time."

"So that's one classmate."

"True. That's one."

"And Tom Jessup?"

"Where are you pulling out these names?" Spoonacre grinned and made a supplicating gesture toward the ceiling.

"Didn't the three of you write *Rapture Mama* together?"

"Oh, Jesus!" Spoonacre clapped his hand over one eye and winced. "You *have* been doing your homework, haven't you?"

"I try."

"Tom Jessup I haven't seen in I don't know how long. Eons. In fact, I sometimes wonder about that boy."

"Is that why you visited his parents not long ago?"

Spoonacre stopped grinning. He gave me a sizing-up look. "That's right. I've wondered how he is. I wanted to see the guy."

"You didn't know he was living somewhere in Burlington?"

"No. I mean, I'd heard rumors but it took going through his parents to discover that he was here."

"Did you find him?"

"No. That is to say, I haven't looked very hard. He's not in the phone book, I can tell you that."

"So you don't have an address for him."

"No."

"Do you have any idea why Chelly Killbride might be looking for him?"

Spoonacre shrugged. "Unless she's getting nostalgic in her middle age like the rest of us, I have no idea." He looked at his watch. "You're gonna have to excuse me. I've got a meeting in the conference room. If I can be of any further help in your search for Cheryl—Chelly—please let me know."

We exchanged business cards.

"Just one last question," I said, slipping his into my blazer pocket and standing. "Do you still write poetry?"

"No! God! That was just a phase." Spoonacre shook his head and blew air through his lips as he stood. "It was the sixties. I was just a kid. You grew your hair long. Wore beads. Smoked dope. We were all delusional. I wrote poetry, or thought I did. Now? I'm a lawyer, not a poet. Frankly—" He came around his desk and walked me to the door—"the sixties were a corrupting time that I'd just as soon forget. Art? Me?" He slapped a hand on his chest. "I was never an artist. I leave that to somebody else."

He opened the door for me. I studied his face. The years had completely transformed him.

"So Armen Karillian no longer holds sway over you."

Spoonacre pinched the bridge of his nose and sighed.

"Armen Karillian was a crackpot," he said emphatically. "No matter what you hear to the contrary, he ruined lives."

"He certainly ruined the language."

Spoonacre's manner became lofty and stern. "Make no mistake: The man was a fraud."

He waved at his clients gathering in the conference room.

"Karillian was crazy," he concluded. "What can I tell you? I was glad when he took off."

14

SPOONACRE WAS RIGHT; TOM JESSUP WASN'T IN THE BUR-
lington phone book, and statewide information didn't
have a listing either. From a pay phone across from Victoria's Secret in the Burlington Square Mall, I had an easy
walk to Battery Street three blocks away, and the offices of
Pettigrew & Keel, Limited.

Battery Street runs along the lake, and Pettigrew &
Keel occupied the second floor of a newly gentrified brick
building across the street from a popular restaurant called
The Ice House. It had no reception area, just a long, polished wooden counter at the front of an open room where
six worktables sat, each with a big computer on it. Five of
the tables were vacant. At the one farthest from the
counter sat a young man dressed in black. A CD player on
a shelf beside him jingled the latest mosh music at low
volume. I waited as long as I could stand it.

"Excuse me?"

The kid eventually looked up. He had a ponytail and
a goatee. He pointed to himself.

"No, your sister," I murmured.

"Could you help me?" I said in a normal voice.

The kid held up one finger, tapped a few keys on his
keyboard, studied the results a moment, then rose and
sauntered up to the other side of the counter. He was
wearing expensive black cowboy boots, black jeans, a sil-
ver-tipped black belt, and a black silk shirt buttoned at the
neck. In his left earlobe was a tiny gold ring; in his left
nostril was a tiny diamond. He didn't speak; merely lifted
his chin in my direction.

"I'm looking for Duncan Keel," I said.

"Back office."

"What's the deal? Can I go back there or do you announce me?"

"You can go back there."

The kid turned and sauntered back to his desk.

"A talky one," I said aloud.

There were hardwood floors, white walls, a black ceiling, and track lights. Along the left wall were two heavy steel doors. I went to the first.

"This one?" I turned to the kid. "You can nod. You don't have to speak."

Without a word, the kid pointed me to the next door down. I went to it. Knocked and looked over at the kid. He appeared to be snickering to himself.

There was the sound of metal hardware being manipulated and then the door opened and a gnomic, silver-haired man was looking up at me. He wore a white guayabara shirt over white linen slacks and had icy, pale blue eyes and a tanned face crosshatched with fine wrinkles. He looked like a transplanted Iberian poet or a specialist in Mediterranean antiquities. He did not look like a middle-aged ex-hippie Dartmouth grad.

"Duncan Keel?"

"Yes." He gave me a small-toothed, pleasant grin.

"I wonder if I could speak to you a moment. I'm a private detective."

"You are?"

"Who is it, Duncan? We've got a lot of ground to cover."

Keel opened the door wider to reveal a thickset woman with flowing gray hair, sitting at a large oak desk. Her face was doughy and she was scowling. The streaked black caftan she wore made her look like a sybilline judge.

"Who are you?" she asked me.

"My name's Boone. Who are you?"

"This is my wife, Hepzibah," Keel said with his elfin smile. "We were just starting a business meeting."

"I'm sorry," I said. "I was told I could come back here."

Keel looked past me to the kid. He was playing a CD-

ROM game on his computer. When he saw us looking at
him, he punched up the volume of the CD player and
leered inwardly at the monitor.

"He's waiting for his check. This is his last day," Keel
said.

"Where is the king? Find the king," the computer was
saying.

"I need a moment of your time," I said. "A woman's
missing."

"What's he saying, Duncan? We need to get started,"
Hepzibah Keel said.

Her office walls were dark green and decorated with
blowups of greeting cards. The covers were photographs
of Vermont landscapes; the insides conveyed banal senti-
ments in singsong rhyme. One with a snowscape began:

> *"I heard you were ill,*
> *so I just had to write*
> *and show you these hills*
> *all snowy and white . . ."*

"I can come back later," I said.

"No," Duncan Keel said in a low voice. "Why don't
we do this now. Do you need to speak to both of us?"

"Just you," I said.

Hepzibah Keel called from her desk, "Can we get
started, please, Duncan Ratfuck Keel?"

Keel turned to her. "I'm going to talk to Mr. Boone a
minute," he said in his airy voice. "Then we'll get started."

Hepzibah Keel slapped her hand on the desk and
looked out her window. Her view consisted of a dead oak
and a white brick wall.

Keel shut his wife's door and led me into his office. It
was neat, white, small, and spartan, and looked to me like
a painter's studio minus the easel. There was a white
worktable on black plastic sawhorses, a modernistic black
plastic swivel chair, and a kitchen chair of brushed aluminum. On the table was a Macintosh PowerBook, a legal
pad, a big Mont Blanc Meisterstück pen, and a copy of
The Synonym Finder by J. I. Rodale. Along one wall were
a few shelves of poetry books and boxes of greeting cards.

Behind the desk was a framed poster of a painting by Jacob van Ruisdael, titled "View of Alkmaar."

Keel whisked a small carton of birthday cards off the kitchen chair and gestured for me to sit. He sat in the desk chair and placed his arms on the chair's arms and crossed his legs at the ankles. On his feet was a pair of tan canvas espadrilles with rubber-covered jute soles. His hands were small. His ankles were thin and white.

"Who you looking for?" he asked in his quiet voice.

"Chelly Killbride," I said.

"Oh, no. Chelly." He put his hand to his mouth.

"Have you seen her?"

"No. Not for some months."

"But you have seen her in the past year."

"Yes." Keel clasped his hands and rested them in his lap. "From time to time when she comes into town we have lunch together. Nothing special. This is unhappy news." He rubbed his hands like they needed washing. "Where do you suppose Chelly's gone?"

"I don't know. That's why I'm here."

"Well, if there's any way I can help. I mean, damn. Chelly's a buddy."

"Is your wife a buddy of Chelly's also?"

"No. She hardly knows her."

"Did she ever come with you on any of your lunch meetings?"

Duncan Keel's upper lip curled in amusement. "Hepzibah, Mr. Boone, doesn't come with me much on anything these days." He reached out and stroked the keys on his small computer the way you would stroke a cat.

"What kinds of things did you and Chelly talk about when you had lunch together?"

"Oh." He tipped his head back. "We'd talk about writing since we're both nominally writers. She'd show me poems she'd been working on. I'd comment on them. She doesn't write well but she's a good heart, and also doesn't seem to have very many people to talk to."

"So you fill a need."

He shrugged. "Her husband doesn't seem to do so. Maybe Chelly and I fit the definition of 'co-dependents.' "

"Are you anything else?"

"You mean, are we lovers?" Keel gave me a silky look. "I've known Chelly a long time but I can assure you, Mr. Boone, I am not fucking her."

"How 'bout Tom Jessup?"

"What? Am I fucking him?" Keel burst out laughing. "Have you seen him? For that matter, is he fucking her?"

"Why do you want to know about Jessup?"

I lifted a hand. "I have reason to believe Chelly is looking for him. She might be desperate enough to want to kill herself. Finding Jessup might help me find her."

Duncan Keel released a grim sigh.

"The last time I saw Tom Jessup," he said, "was late last summer at Eastern Mountain Sports. He was chatting up one of the shop girls. They were touching hands. It was typical Don Juan Jessup stuff. Passionate looks in front of the freeze-drieds. Outrageous." Keel smiled at the memory, then added, "The girl's name was Pippa. Pippa the Campa. Tall. Braided red hair."

"Do you know where Jessup lives around here?"

"I have no idea." Keel shook his head. "He lived in Essex but that was a long time ago. I've bumped into him a few times over the years but he's very secretive about his permanent residence. 'Southwest' was all he'd say to me, as if he was afraid I'd come crashing in to stay with him."

"What about John Spoonacre? You ever see him?"

"I see John here in town all the time."

I nodded. "Has Chelly ever talked about wanting to get in touch with Jessup?"

"No. Not directly. She's asked me a few times if I knew what he was up to, if I ever saw him, but that was about it."

"No urgent statement that she had to see him, that kind of thing?"

Keel pushed his lower lip out and shook his head again. "No. Chelly can sound urgent about a lot of things but I don't remember Jessup being one of them."

I nodded some more. I'd check out Pippa but this was getting discouraging.

"Tell me," I said, "where was the farm on Gatwick Lake that Armen Karillian kept in the late sixties?"

"Armen Karillian?" Keel sounded mildly surprised. "How do you know about Armen Karillian?"

"I've seen his poetry," I said. "I've seen yours. You, Spoonacre, and Jessup were members of Karillian's Poetry Gang."

"That's right." Keel smiled his elfin smile. "Though I haven't heard the words 'Poetry Gang' in about twenty-five years."

"Where was the farm?"

"Do you know Gatwick?"

I said I did.

"The farm was on the eastern side of the lake," Keel said. "In fact, it was right down the road from Chelly's parents' place."

"Where the road T's," I said.

Keel nodded. "Chelly spent a lot of time with us at Armen's. But you probably knew that already, right?"

I didn't but it fit. I nodded. "How old was she back then?"

"Chelly?" Keel squinted, remembering. "She couldn't have been more than fourteen or fifteen."

"And you guys were all how old?"

"We were juniors and seniors. Twenty? Twenty-one?"

"What did all of you do at the farm back in those days?"

The same white brick wall visible through Hepzibah's window was visible through Keel's. His chunk of white wall had a window in it; through the window I could see four or five women in leotards and spandex tights stepping in unison on and off inverted plastic boxes.

"What did we do, what did we do?" Keel rubbed his left eye and yawned as he repeated the question to himself. "I suppose," he said, "that what we really did was played at being cool hippies. But what we thought we were doing was being serious artists."

"With Karillian as your mentor."

"With Armen as our mentor."

"Did you do drugs?"

"Does the proverbial bear defecate in the proverbial woods?" Keel laughed. "We did a lot of things twenty-year-olds did back then."

"What drugs did you do?"

Keel fidgeted, then shrugged. "Grass, acid, peyote buttons, mescaline, psilocybin. Whatever blew the mind."

"Any minds get blown?"

"There were bad trips. Chelly had a couple. We all did. Part of the scene."

"Anybody do heroin?"

"Armen did. But not a lot. We all tried it. Lived to tell the tale."

"Needles?"

Keel shrugged again. "The works."

"What's your theory on what happened to Karillian? He disappeared, right?"

The woman nearest the window in the white wall was attractive and going at it hard. She wore pink leggings and a lowcut floral print leotard. Her healthy determination reminded me of Taylor's.

"I don't know what Armen did. Skipped out, I guess you'd say. Why he skipped out, I have no idea. You'd have to ask him."

"That'd be tough," I said.

"Armen, you understand, was enigmatic," Keel said. "I mean, he took us in, he encouraged us. But it wasn't like we were allowed access to his innermost thoughts."

"The poet as cipher," I said.

"If you wish."

Our interview was interrupted by a loud pounding noise on the office wall. "Duncan Ratfuck Keel!" Hepzibah's muffled voice shouted threateningly.

Keel offered me a benign smile and stood. "I think I'd better go," he said, "before she does her full-tilt version of Roseanne meets Mighty Joe Young."

"What is it the two of you do together?" I asked.

"What do we do?" Keel said brightly. "Why, we produce greeting cards, of course. She's Pettigrew. I'm Keel. I write 'em, she markets 'em. We make our own images on computer from stock shots. Ship disks and layouts to the printer's. Distribute nationally through independent reps and card shops."

"Sounds slick," I said.

"It is. Only business is a little off right now and Hepzibah is rather anxious."

The pounding sounded on the wall again.

"It seems a long way from writing poetry as a twenty-year-old." I stood.

"Oh, I still keep at it—the poetry." Keel opened the door. He was sweating and his smile was strained.

Hepzibah was waiting for him outside her door. Her size was formidable.

"If you don't get in here I'm going to have your balls for breakfast," she said.

"Can I get a check here, please?" The kid in black spoke in a bored singsong.

"One minute, Gary," Keel said evenly.

"Write him his goddamn check, then get your ass in here," Hepzibah said.

"Gary, first I want the Misty Morning files," Keel said. "They have my verses in them."

"Misty Morning's dead," Hepzibah said. "Your verses are Pablum."

"You seem to forget, my verses have helped you double your weight in a decade, Hepzibah, my darling."

"Your verses are taking us down the toilet!"

"Get him the check yourself if you want him to have it so bad." Keel stormed into his own office and slammed the door after him.

Hepzibah put a hand on her huge waist and bent forward.

"Bloody testicle strings flapping in the breeze!" she taunted.

I left on that note.

As I walked downstairs I could hear the serious shouting start. The words "money," "bitch," "ha," and "failure" seemed to dominate the Keels' marital vocabulary. Something big and electronic-sounding with glass in it crashed against a wall. I kept walking. I could hear their shouting all the way down the block.

15

FROM THE SAME PAY PHONE OUTSIDE VICTORIA'S SECRET, I
called an editor friend named Toomey at the *Burlington
Free Press* and asked him for any news items dating back
to 1969 on Spoonacre, Jessup, Keel or, for that matter,
Armen Karillian in Gatwick. Toomey, a thick-voiced Bos-
ton-Irish expatriate from Dorchester, said the paper's li-
brarian had just quit and a search like that could take
weeks. I told him the Red Sox would love to have him and
his twelve-year-old son as its guests the next weekend the
Yanks came to Fenway, and Toomey suddenly thought he
might have something for me in a couple days.

"By the way, if it's the Spoonacre I think it is, he's in
the news all the time these days," Toomey said. "Does
legal work and fundraising for the state Republican
party."

"It's the same guy," I said.

My truck was a furnace when I opened it. I drove up
the hill past the university and the Sheraton to EMS. EMS,
or Eastern Mountain Sports, is located on a thoroughfare
called Dorset Street, on the other side of route 89. There
are fine views of Camel's Hump and Mt. Mansfield as you
make your way toward it down from the university, but
these disappear when you cross the highway overpass, and
once you see the Howard Johnson's and the dry cleaner's
and the big mall down from the little one that EMS is in,
you know you're in sprawl.

I parked in the little mall's lot and walked past the
other storefronts to EMS. Several were vacant, including a
bookstore I had liked that had been run out of business by

a discount bookstore. I thought about that, and about how when you were in a mall you couldn't tell where you were in America anymore because all the malls and merchandise looked the same.

Pippa the Campa was easy to find. She was tall and redheaded, as Keel had said, and she wore her long coppery hair in a thick braid that hung down her back. She was freckled, pretty, athletic, and looked to be in her late twenties. When I walked in, she was in the shoe department, fitting a portly Thoreauvian with a pair of hiking boots. The Thoreauvian could not make up his mind. Pippa sat on her little stool with the man's black-stockinged foot between her legs and many boxes of hiking boots around her.

"I don't know what else I can show you," she said.

The fat man, who wore canvas walking shorts and had stubby, thick-muscled legs, said with a lisp, "My feet don't like those lasts."

Pippa said nothing. I stood near the camp stoves, feigning interest in a Primus. Finally, with a sigh, the man put on his sandals and without a word of thanks waddled away from the wreckage he had caused.

Pippa began swiftly closing boxes. I waited a moment before going over and sitting in the fat man's chair.

"You'll have to wait a moment, sir." She spoke in a sharp voice before looking up. Then we made eye contact.

"Pippa?"

"Yes."

I told her who I was and flipped open my license for her. "I'm looking for someone you know. Tom Jessup?"

The eyes, green like those of Spoonacre's assistant, but prettier, went from somewhat inviting to cold, hostile, and sullen.

"Haven't seen him."

"But you know him."

"I guess. Who are you?"

I told her again. "Could I talk to you for a few minutes? See, this woman is missing and I'm looking for her and Tom Jessup may know her whereabouts."

Pippa the Campa snorted. "I'll bet he does."

"Let me guess," I said. "You two have split up."

"That's one way to put it." She reached for a box of boots and slammed the lid on it.

"Look, I know you're working but this'll only take a few minutes, and the fact is, this woman I'm looking for may be suicidal and I'd like to get to her before"— I waved my hand over the floor —"you know . . ."

Pippa said, "Anybody'd be suicidal if they hung around that creep." Then her eyes narrowed with a sudden thought. "Did Tom send you here?"

"No."

"Who did then?"

I gave her Keel's name. She did not appear to know it. "Again," I said quietly, "you might help keep a woman alive."

"Yeah, yeah." She looked around her at the many boxes, then stopped another young female clerk as she barged out of the back room with an armload of cotton sweaters. "Melanie, I'm gonna clean up this stuff and then take my break."

Melanie looked at the two of us; her face lit up in joy for her colleague.

"Leave it, Pippa. I'll do it."

"You sure?"

"Yeah. Definitely. Go." She smiled and winked. "He's gorgeous."

Melanie strode away with her sweaters, proffering me a mischievous leer.

When she was gone, Pippa looked at me. "Don't mind her. Ever since Jessup, the whole store's been trying to matchmake for me."

"What are friends for?"

She smiled wearily. "You want to talk here, or outside, or . . ."

"You got time for a coffee next door?"

"Yeah. Let me see that ID again?"

I showed her my license and gave her one of my cards. She studied both carefully. "Hmp." She kept the card and handed me back my license. "Wanna go?"

She had an athlete's body and an athlete's rangy way of walking. She was wearing Teva sandals, gray shorts, and a white blouse with a green tag on the left pocket that said her name: PIPPA LOCKE. She gave Melanie a bored wave and did not smile when Melanie, at the sweater bin, returned an enthusiastic thumbs-up.

The restaurant next door, the Cork & Board, had an angled glass roof and a glass front wall like a greenhouse. It was late afternoon and the restaurant was nearly empty. Pippa and I took a table along the front wall and ordered *latte* and *biscotti*. The waitress brought them quickly.

"So who's this woman?" Pippa, all business, said, picking up a chocolate-covered biscuit and dipping it into the coffee.

I explained to her a little about Chelly: her manic depression, her suicidal tendencies, her agitation to produce a book on Karillian, her apparent search for Jessup.

"She sounds worse off than me." The possibility of such a thing greatly amused her.

"Jessup ever talk to you about Chelly?" I pushed the milk foam on top of my *latte* with my spoon, trying to keep the mood casual.

"No." Pippa shook her head. "Tom never mentioned her. But then, he didn't talk much about anybody."

"He ever talk about his parents?"

"No."

"Keel? John Spoonacre? Armen Karillian?"

"Negative. Wait a second. Who was the second one?"

"John Spoonacre."

"He's a lawyer in town, right?"

I nodded.

"He's been in the store once or twice in the past month. Asking for Tom."

"Did he say why?"

"No."

"What did you tell him?"

Pippa looked annoyed. "I told him if he wanted to find Tom he should find Shondra Maine."

"Who's Shondra Maine?"

Sunlight streamed down on us through the ceiling windows; though there were blinds over the windows and the air-conditioning was icy, the sun and the hot coffee raised a light film of sweat on both our foreheads.

Pippa shook her head, both hands around the coffee cup.

"Boy, I don't know if I want to talk about this," she said.

"Take your time."

But when she started talking, there was no stopping her.

"See, for the past couple years since college I've been having my problems with men," she said. "Like, two years ago there was this guy, Jake, a photographer? And we start a relationship and he's just getting his career under-way. And I have a loft off Church Street, so naturally I let him move in with me and use my loft as his studio. And naturally, I'm the one bringing in a steady paycheck and he's not. So naturally I buy him this beautiful used Sinar and like six incredible lenses—it costs me eight thousand bucks. And he and I are talking like, if not marriage, some-thing permanent, right? So what does Jake do? A month after I buy him the stuff he splits with it for Los Angeles—doesn't even tell me he's going!"

I said nothing.

"I have to go home and discover that the bastard's walked out on me." She sulked.

"I'm sorry you went through that," I said.

Pippa took a pull of *latte*. "So, d'you think I learned my lesson and would never let a man pull that shit on me again?"

"You tell me."

"Of course not!" She set the cup on the saucer and laughed at her own folly. "A month after Jake splits, Jes-sup walks into the store and I let the son of a bitch sweep me off my goddamn feet."

"How'd he do that?"

Pippa made her eyes big and puffed air out of her mouth. The answer, to her, was obvious. "He's a poet. He's a con man. He came on to me like this big sensitive outdoorsman. He took me to dinner. Showed me some of his poems. I fell for his act like a dumb duck. Within two weeks he was living in my apartment."

I murmured my sympathies. "Where was he living be-fore he met you?"

"In his truck!" Pippa's words lashed out of her like an indictment. "He has this '49 Chevy he's fitted out with this trailer, like. He was living on the lake near the boatyards. Wherever he could sponge. The guy's a leech."

"How long did he stay with you?"

"Ten months." Pippa took another pull of coffee. "From last June to this March. Don't get me wrong. We had good times. He wasn't completely insolvent. We'd go places in my car. He'd pay. I let him set up a little work area in the studio. He'd write. I'd come home. Cook dinner for him. Be the good little poet's housewife."

With her lower lip she grimly wiped away the milk mustache.

"We had these plans. We were gonna drive cross-country in my car. Go south across Texas and tour the southwest. I've never been there. He said he spent a lot of time out there. Knew all the sights. Said there was this place he had in Winslow. A cabin. We'd use it as a base. Go off and hike the canyons, y'know?"

"Sure."

"I really wanted to see Arizona and hike the Grand Canyon. He talked about it like it was a done deal." She shook her head, eyes glaring in recollection.

"What happened?"

Pippa hesitated before emitting an enormous sigh.

"One day in March I came home early and found him in my bed with Shondra Maine." Her chin quivered. "I'm not a prude, but how am I supposed to feel when I catch my boyfriend in bed, naked, with another woman and he's been living with me?"

I shrugged. "I suppose you feel disappointed."

"Disappointed? . . ." She looked away from me with rekindling rage.

"What did you do?" I asked after a while.

"I kicked them both out. I threw out all his stuff. I told him I never wanted to see him again."

"Has that happened? Not seeing him?"

"No. This town's so fucking small, it's like, every time I walk down Church Street, there they are, the two of them, going at it, practically humping each other in public."

I was running out of sympathetic nods and noises.

"Not to dwell on the unpleasant," I said, "but do you know where Shondra Maine lives?"

"*No.*" Her expression was steely.

"Can you describe what she looks like?"

"Oh, sure." Pippa flipped her hand dismissively. "She's tall, dark haired, trim, beautiful. And black."

"She's black?"

"Medium brown, yes. But not Caucasian. She dresses like a fashion model. The girls in the store say she dresses like a slut."

The waitress asked us if we wanted more coffee. Both of us said no. I asked for the check.

"How recently have you seen Jessup and Shondra in public?" I asked Pippa.

"Is it important?"

"It might be."

Pippa looked away, miserably. "I saw them last week at the Vermont Pasta Company restaurant. I walked in with a couple of friends and had to walk out again."

"Did Jessup see you?"

"Oh, yeah. He just gave his big, shit-eating, surprised-to-see-me grin and went back to talking to her."

"Sounds like a great guy."

"He's a fucking weasel. If I had my way I'd . . . I don't know what I'd do. Castrate him."

"You're the second woman I've met today who'd like to do that to her man."

"Well? . . . What the fuck?" Pippa made a gesture of reasonableness with her hand. "You guys ask for it."

I didn't bother to disagree with her. Deep down, I wanted to get away from her as quickly as I could. It was interesting, though, that as a victim she was attracted to Jessup. Maybe Jessup brought out the victim in every woman. In Chelly. Who knew?

"Let me walk you back to the kayaks and camp-stoves."

"You don't have to," she said. "In fact, if you don't mind, I'd like to sit here by myself for a while."

"No problem." I thanked her for her time. I paid the bill at the register. When I got in my truck and looked back, she was still sitting there, hunched over her cup, bathed in misery.

"Pippa the Whina," I murmured. And drove away.

16

FINDING SHONDRA MAINE'S ADDRESS PROVED TO BE A LOT easier than hearing about Pippa Locke's love life.

The address was listed in a brand-new Burlington phone book that I found at a pay phone in the lobby of the Burlington Sheraton. It was 237 1/2 Pine Street, just a block east from Keel's office and a few blocks south of Spoonacre's.

Two thirty-seven and a half Pine proved to be a row of furnished apartment units built off an old three-story house in a tree-shaded residential district. A sign on the house said PINE STREET APART-MENTS——FURNISHED——WEEK——MONTH——LONG-TERM. There was parking off the street, but for TENANTS ONLY. Sure enough, as soon as I pulled into one of the spaces, an elderly woman was out the back door of the house, her arm raised.

"You can't park there!" she screeched.

I switched off the truck's engine and stepped out of the cab.

"I just need a minute of your time."

"If you think you're going to leave that rig and go shopping, you've got another thing coming." The woman stormed to within a yard of me. "I'll have the police down here *and* a tow truck. This is not a public lot. You people think you can walk all over me because I'm eighty years old, but you'll pay the tow charge. I can assure you of that."

I raised my hands in a gesture of placation. "I'm not

here to go shopping. I'm not here to chisel a parking spot. I just came by to ask a question . . ."

She appeared ready to spring at my throat. She was small and gray, sharp and wiry. The pale skin of her fine-featured face was finely etched and liver-spotted.

"For whom did you have a question, then?" she demanded.

"For you!"

"Oh."

Her head jerked and her eyebrows moved up and down. She was wearing a pleated blue skirt, a white blouse with a gold lodge pin on the collar, and a pair of black low-cut Chuck Taylor All-Stars. A gray panther if ever there was one.

"Does Shondra Maine live here?" I asked.

"Not anymore!" The gray panther's eyes flashed angrily. "She cleared out of here five days ago."

"Did she?"

"And good riddance, I say."

"Why do you say that?"

"Augh!" She flung her arm skyward and soliloquized to the driveway stones. "Her and that lowlife boyfriend of hers. Up all hours. Going at each other like a pair of sex-starved alley cats. You could hear them all hours doing things with their bodies that decent people shouldn't have to hear!"

"Uh-huh!"

"Plus, look at the facts." She slapped the fingers of one hand into the palm of the other. "They're of two different races! I mean, come on! And he's pawin' her *poitrine* every time they come out the door, and she's all over him, hand down his fly? Tuh! Why I say good riddance. And may they never come back!"

"You know where they've gone?" (I calculated. Left five days ago. Same number of days since Chelly disappeared.)

Gray Panther's eyes narrowed. "Why do you wish to know? Are you a friend?"

"No." I spoke honestly. "In fact, I'm not looking for them so much as I am for a missing woman. But they might know where she is."

Gray Panther cocked her head from side to side, now the Gray Rooster.

"You a plainclothes detective or something?"

"Plainclothes and private," I said. "Hired by the missing woman's family." I gave her my card. I'd given out quite a few that day.

She read it with the aid of rhinestone glasses hanging by a chain from her thin neck.

"Well." She started to hand the card back to me. "You're not the first person come looking for Miss Maine since she left, Mister"— lifting the card —"*Boone!*"

"I'm not?"

"No. Two nights ago, two hurly-burlies in a slick blue car parked right where your truck is and demanded that I tell them where Shondra Maine was."

"What did you tell them?"

"I told them I hadn't the slightest idea and that they could move their car or I'd have the police here in less than five minutes. Well, you should've heard the language they used then, but I held firm. They left. But not before they'd called me every cursed name in the dictionary. Ooh! I'd like to put lye soap into those mouths." Her clawlike hands pried invisible jaws open as her own teeth clenched with the effort.

"You wouldn't remember what the two guys looked like, would you?" I tried not to sound too interested.

"Wouldn't I! Big lugs, both of them. One bald, the other blond. Big strutting know-it-alls who think they can bully little old ladies like me. Well, I scared 'em off. They didn't get what they wanted from me!"

Her eyes glittered and her head twitched. I worked my mouth in a series of frowning puckers so as not to laugh.

"Could you have told them what they wanted?" I asked when I had regained control of my facial muscles.

"About Shondra?" Gray Panther squinted. "Of course I could have, but they weren't polite to me."

"Would you tell me, if I were polite?"

"Well, you *are* polite! Anyone can see that."

"Well then, would you tell me where she went?" I looked into the fine-boned face. "Please?"

She fidgeted for a moment with the glasses around her

neck, then sucked her teeth. They were her teeth, straight and gray, and she worked her lips and tongue around them, making squeaking noises.

"Come inside, please." She looked around the empty court as if afraid of being observed, then led me into the back of the house.

There was a little office just inside the door, its walls dominated by a crucifix and framed photographs of John Kennedy and the current pope. Gray Panther opened a black ledger lying on the office's desk. There were neat entries done in fountain pen on the pages and Gray Panther had no trouble finding the page she wanted.

"I don't have one of those photocopiers. So when I receive a check, I write its information down." Rhinestones on her nose, she scanned the page. "Here we are. Miss Maine checked into apartment one on March fifteenth. Paid thirty days rent in advance. Personal check number—well, you don't need that, do you? Drawn to the Bank of Groton."

"Connecticut?"

"Yes. That's where Miss Maine said she came from, and that's her address on the check. Twenty Riverside, Groton, Connecticut. Told me she was going back there and asked if I could forward her mail to that address."

I copied the address into my notebook. My mind churned with questions.

"Did her male friend go with her?"

"You mean that low-life Jessup?" Gray Panther spat the name. "He blew out of here the day before she did. Went in that stupid truck of his. You seen it? Always hogging two spaces because of that idiotic camper on the back. I don't think those two are still together. In fact, I think *she* left because *he* split up with her. I say that because I heard 'em arguing, and then he was out the door."

"Did you hear what they were arguing about?"

"I didn't. But it wasn't the usual noise that came out of their place, I can tell you that!"

"So let me get this straight. They moved in together in March, and then he walked out on her six days ago."

"*No!*" Gray Panther shook her head impatiently. "*She* moved in *alone* in March and a week later *she* showed up with *Mister Low-life* on her *leash*. But she paid the extra, and she paid every month on time. So . . ." She made a what-are-you-gonna-do gesture with her hand.

"Do you know if either of them worked?"

Gray Panther's mouth congealed into a rictus of sarcastic mirth. "Work!" She rolled her eyes and wobbled her head from side to side, chortling. "I don't think there was a day when either of them got out of bed before noon. And when they'd leave here, it wasn't in any rush to punch a time clock. No, if you want my view of them: She's a whore and he's a skirt-chasing bum."

"And you don't think they're still together . . ."

"No." The thin-skinned head shook fiercely. The office smelled of rectitude and urine.

Back in my truck as I cruised down Route 7 toward the Interstate, I thought about all the people I had talked to during the day and felt no closer to finding Chelly Killbride than I had twenty-four hours earlier. Almost as bad: I was hungry and my stitches itched. It was early evening and I debated whether to drive to Connecticut that night or go home and start fresh in the morning.

Before I had gone far on the Interstate, the decision was made for me. The truck phone chirped. It was Arthur Cole. He sounded a little drunk and more than a little upset.

"Can you come up here, Boone? Right away? Two things awful have happened."

"What are they?" I had to shout. The signal was weak.

Arthur Cole sounded almost hysterical.

"My in-laws know Chelly's gone. And—"

Static garbled his next words.

"And?" I shouted. "Repeat?"

Cole's voice shouted back. "And"—above a shrieking crackle—*"we've had a break-in!"*

17

I DECIDED I DIDN'T WANT ANOTHER ENCOUNTER WITH AL-
den Clapp's nightstick, and that the best way to avoid one
was to switch vehicles. Fifty miles north, at my house in
the hills, there was an '85 black Saab Turbo and a '79 blue
Ford panel truck gassed and ready in my garage. Both had
rust, dents, and Florida-tinted windows. Either would
make me invisible.

I picked up the Saab an hour after Cole's call, built
myself a ham and Swiss with Bibb lettuce and honey mus-
tard on Lilydale sourdough rye, pulled two Sam Adams
lagers from the refrigerator, and was in Cole's driveway an
hour later. The green Mercedes hadn't moved in three
days; there were three days' worth of *Burlington Free
Press*es on the front doorstep, and a copy of the *Watchtower* inside the screen door. The house was dark. The
Watchtower was stained and crinkly. Apparently it had
not gotten its chance yet to save Cole's soul.

I knocked on the door a few times. No answer. I tried
the brass latch. Locked. The big willows off the driveway
swayed silently in the evening breeze. From somewhere far
down on the lake a dog barked.

I went around back and tried the back door off the
patio. It was locked, too. The lights were off in the back of
the house and the windows in the upstairs bedrooms were
shut. It was dusk. The lake reflected the whiteness of the
dusk sky, and the lawn was dark and silent as in a dream.

I took the flagstone path across the lawn and into the
grove of darkening oaks. It was so dark in the grove that I
could not at first see the cabin. Then I saw it and walked

quickly to it past the sentrylike sculptures to the wooden steps. The cabin door was unlocked. I lifted the iron latch and pushed the door open and stepped inside.

A polished shucking noise sounded from within.

The quavering voice of Arthur Cole said, "Don't move, or I'll blow your fucking head off."

"Arthur, it's me, Boone."

The cabin was dark and shadowy. From behind the chimney's dark mass, Arthur Cole stepped forward. He was holding a gun and I guessed from the shucking sound that it was one of his custom pumps. The Beretta.

Arthur Cole looked at me a long moment, then lowered the gun. "You find her?"

"No."

"Any leads?"

"Maybe."

"You alone?"

"Yeah."

"Anybody see you drive in?"

"Not that I noticed. Can we turn a light on in here? And can you turn that thing away before you kill me?"

Arthur Cole pointed the shotgun toward the window. "Close the door first."

"Fine. You got your finger off that trigger?"

"It's off."

I shut the door. Cole hugged the shotgun against his chest.

"You carrying a gun?" His voice was husky with shot nerves. He sounded as if he had been drinking.

"I am."

"Thank God!" He set the shotgun, butt down, on the hearth and fumbled on the mantel. There came a sound of match scraping stone and a flame flared up in Cole's wavering hand. He lit a single hurricane lamp on the mantel, and, grunting, wobbled the lamp's mantel into place. The glass and lamp tines made a fragile sound together, like a clock mechanism.

In the lamplight, Cole's eyes were big and white and his face was shiny with nervous sweat. He was wearing the same dirty canvas shorts and squashed shoes he had worn three days earlier. His corset's straps dangled below the tails of a soiled gray Ralph Lauren polo shirt. He wiped his face with a shaky hand. His lips did not stop moving.

"Could you handle the lamp and keep it away from the window?" he said.

"Sure."

He walked from the mantel, closing his eyes and pressing his palms into the small of his back. I took the lamp off the mantel and turned the light into the middle of the room. As soon as I did, I could see what had happened. The room had been tossed. It had not been a violent tossing—nothing appeared to have been broken—but virtually everything in every corner of the room was out of place. I walked over to the five plaster masks that now were scattered facedown on the bed. I turned each of them over. I knew who each of them was now. By process of elimination I assumed that the unknown face was Jessup's.

I turned to see Cole pressed against the front wall, peeking like a character in a Bergman film toward the lake from the leftmost front window.

"Are you sure nobody saw you?" He did not take his eyes off the lake.

"Yes, I'm sure. When did this happen?"

"I don't know. Everything was all right when I checked last night at about eight. Then I didn't check again til about five this afternoon. So, what's that? Sometime in the past twenty-one hours."

"You notice any vehicles during that time?"

"No." Cole shook his head. "That is, I haven't been paying much attention. This afternoon I took a nap." He made a weak gesture with his hands.

I could picture Cole taking one of his naps. Then I thought about Perry at the landing.

"Did a guy come by the house here the morning I left?" I asked.

"Yeah." Cole nodded. "He stunk something wicked. He said he was looking for work." His face registered suspicion. "You think it was him did this?"

"I don't know. What did you tell him?"

"I didn't tell him anything. He asked for work. I said I didn't have anything for him. He said he was gonna try Win's. I said I doubted there was anything up there either and that it was all private property. He thanked me and left."

"Did he see the cabin?"

"I don't know. He knocked on the back door. From the patio he could've seen the cabin."

"You ever seen him before?"

"No."

"He say his name?"

Cole thought a moment. "No." And moved toward me. "Jesus, Boone, you think he was scopin' out the place?"

"He could've been. You never know. Unless my judgment's slipping, he's done time within the past year."

"You mean, *prison*?" Cole shuffled a few steps sideways. "How do you know that?"

"My P.I. intuition." I grimaced. "Let's see if he or whoever it was took anything."

I made for Chelly's writing area because that seemed the most disordered. There were papers, computer disks, and books on the floor, and the stack of letters that had sat under the crystal paperweight were scattered over the desktop.

I set the lamp on the desk and squatted next to the heap of material on the floor. There were a great many papers. The metal accordian file was empty and the contents of each manila folder had been dumped and pawed through. It would be impossible for me to inventory the papers—even Chelly, I thought, would have trouble doing it. I collected all the computer disks I could find among the papers and counted them. There were eleven. I couldn't remember the number in the stack from the other day. The boom box was still on the bookshelf; the CD's were untouched. It wasn't a straightforward boost, I thought. The intruder had taken the place apart in search of something. Or Cole and I were being sent a message.

"I don't think anything's missing over here," Cole called from the painting area.

"Same over here." I was pawing through the pile of books.

"Of course, I'm not entirely familiar with everything in here."

"Neither am I, but this ain't no robbery." I straightened and rubbed the dust off my hands onto my jeans.

"What do you think it is?" Cole shuffled into view from around the fireplace and stood in front of me. His expression was blank with fear.

"I'd say it was a research expedition. Whoever came in here was looking for something. My guess is they didn't find it."

"What makes you say that?"

"Place has been taken apart too thoroughly. Either that, or they found what they wanted and masked it by tossing everything."

Arthur Cole appeared ready to drop through the floor from pure dread. "Do you think they'll come here again?"

"They could, but I doubt it. They've lost the element of surprise. They know you'll be laying for them. Does Chelly keep any of her paperwork in the house?"

"No." Cole shook his head. "But that's where they might go next, isn't it? If they didn't find what they wanted here?"

"Not if you turn on some lights up there they won't. How long you been down here?"

"Since five. I discovered the mess, went back to the house, got a gun, and came back."

"Well, now it's time to go back to the house and stay there. And put some lights on."

"Should I keep the gun with me in the bedroom?"

"If it makes you feel better. But do me a favor: Unload it, put the shells on the night table and don't bring the gun in bed with you."

"Right." Cole swallowed and his lips pushed out and then in. The thought of him handling a gun at all made me uncomfortable.

"You learn anything about Chelly?" he asked.

"Just that at around the time of her disappearance she might have been looking for a guy named Tom Jessup. You know who he is?"

Cole shook his head. "No."

"Chelly ever mention his name to you?"

"Not that I recall."

"How 'bout John Spoonacre and Duncan Keel?"

"Never mentioned them either."

I nodded. More and more Chelly's past appeared to be a dark chasm between them.

"You mentioned on the phone her parents know Chelly's missing. How'd they find out?"

"I don't know!" Cole's eyes twitched. "Claire called me this morning and said, 'You don't know where she is, do you?' She'd like to meet you. So would Win."

I looked at him. "How do they know about me?"

Cole looked down at the floor and chewed his lip. "I told them." He quickly raised his hands. "I'm sorry. What was I supposed to do? They're my in-laws, for crissakes. They're worried about their daughter."

I shrugged. "It doesn't matter either way," I told him.

"They don't know about the break-in. Look, when you go up there, if you wouldn't mind telling them you think I did the right thing by hiring you. You know? So they don't think I'm a complete asshole?"

"They wanna see me now?"

"Uh-huh."

I stepped away from the pile of books.

I went over to Cole and put my hand on his shoulder. It was soft, spongy almost, as if its bones floated beneath the skin.

"Don't worry," I said. "I'll tell 'em you're the best thing since beer in cans."

Cole looked genuinely grateful.

I took Cole's shotgun off the hearth, unloaded it, and handed it to him. We left the cabin as it was, locked it, and made our way through the trees back to the house. Cole unlocked the back door with a set of keys in his shorts and I noticed in the dying light how his hand shook and how the keys jingled in the stillness. He locked and bolted the back door after us and turned on the back floodlights. The near back lawn and patio were bathed in light. He did the same at the front door and, giving him the .12 gauge's shells, I said I'd better be going. To my surprise, he took my hand in both of his and would not let it go.

"I'm counting on you, Boone. Thanks for coming up."

"You gonna be all right?"

"I'll be fine." He swallowed. "Don't worry about me."

"I'm not worried. Get some rest." I disengaged my hand.

He called out to me as I walked to my car.

"Don't let my in-laws scare you. They're actually nice people."

When I drove off, he was still leaning in the doorway, his hand upraised in farewell.

18

THE ROAD FROM ARTHUR COLE'S CURVED AND CLIMBED and came out upon a big, cedar-shingled house surrounded by old trees. Its lights were on in expectation of visitors and its smooth, crushed-stone driveway curved around a big, groomed lawn and looped back on itself near the front door. There were sunken lights near the shrubs and flower beds, and a polished cube of white marble sat in the lawn's center illuminated by a pair of low spotlights. Three cars were parked in the driveway: a new oyster-white Cadillac de Ville, a silver '85 Greenwood Corvette, and a new maroon Chevy Corsica. A wide brick walkway led to a set of double doors. I parked behind the Corsica and crunched my way over the driveway and up the walk to the doors. I pressed the doorbell. A loud chiming noise sounded within. There were two teak benches flanking the entry and a lattice roof extension like a pergola over the walk. Morning glories grew up the posts to the lattice. I could look through the perpendicular slats and see the stars.

The door opened. A lean, fortyish woman in jeans and a work shirt stood before me. There were paint splotches on the shirttails and her dark hair was uncombed and her feet were bare.

"Yes?"

A slight lifting of the thin nose. An appraising gaze from the dark hazel eyes.

"I'm here to see Mr. and Mrs. Killbride. Their son-in-law Arthur Cole sent me."

"And your name?"

"Peter Boone."

"Come inside, Mr. Boone. I'll tell them you're here."

I followed her into a foyer dominated by a big painting on a white wall. The painting consisted of a large brown rectangle floating over a smaller rose-colored one. I was no connoisseur of modern art but this was a Rothko, one of the good ones, probably worth hundreds of thousands if not millions of dollars.

The woman vanished down a hall and came back a half minute later, smiling loftily.

"Come this way."

She led me in the opposite direction from where she had just come. It was an extension off the foyer and it led left through a doorway into an enormous white living room. The living room had a white cathedral ceiling, and the front wall was glass and overlooked the lake, but the side and back walls were white except for a set of glass doors leading to a deck, and there were many other modern paintings on the walls. I could easily identify a half dozen paintings and drawings by Picasso, two Matisses, a Dufy, a Modigliani, a Pollock, a Kandinsky, and a Bonnard. I was less sure about the Motherwell, the Rauschenburg, and the Lichtenstein, but the big mobile hanging from the cathedral ceiling on slender black rods was definitely a Calder. On that I would stake my investigator's license.

"Mr. Boone?"

I turned from the mobile to see a trim, elegant grayhaired woman enter from a doorway in the back of the living room. She was wearing a cool black silk tunic, white linen slacks, and sandals, and her hair was clipped and permed to sculptural, backswept perfection. She did not exactly sweep into the room, but she did not slouch either and she was at me fast, extending a strong, slender hand and smiling at me with beautiful teeth. "Claire Killbride. How do you do?"

She invited me to sit in the room's central grouping of off-white linen couches and genuine antique Stickley chairs.

"Care for a drink?" Her voice a melodic ring to it.

"Sure. What are you offering?"

"Beer. Wine. Something harder, perhaps."

"Beer sounds fine."

She rang a bell on a dark seventeenth-century English table behind the central couch, then sat diagonally across from me in one of the Stickleys. A Latino maid in a gray housedress and white apron appeared from the back doorway.

"Beatrice, a beer for Mr. Boone and a sweet Cinzano on the rocks for me," said Claire Killbride.

The maid nodded and left the room. Claire Killbride smiled at me, revealing her beautiful teeth again.

"So you're the private investigator."

I nodded.

"My husband is swimming his evening laps. He'll join us in a moment."

She gestured toward the set of side doors and I saw, sunken into the big deck, a floodlit lap pool where a lone male figure in goggles and rubber cap toiled at his crawl.

"Beautiful house. Beautiful collection," I said.

"Do you like it?" She gestured with pride. "The four big Picassos are going up in the Guggenheim in a few weeks. They span each decade of his work from 1900 to 1930. The oldest painting, that one from his café period, goes up in the top spiral. I'm very pleased. Of course, I'll remain anonymous, but it's a splendid affirmation of the work's historic and aesthetic value, don't you think?"

"I suppose it is."

"Do you know modern art, Mr. Boone?"

"Not personally."

The woman who had answered the door materialized at the back of the room.

"Oh, Becky, come here! I'd like you to meet someone!" Claire Killbride arched her spine and made a beckoning gesture.

The woman joined us. I stood.

"Mr. Boone, this is Becky Lightfoot, our artist-in-residence. Becky, this is Peter Boone."

"I know." Becky Lightfoot made a sniffing noise in my direction.

"Mr. Boone is a private investigator, Becky."

Becky Lightfoot looked at me with a cool, closed-lipped smile.

"Does that mean you wear a gun and shoot bad guys?" she said.

"Only if they try to shoot me first."

"It sounds like such a phallic enterprise," Becky Lightfoot said.

"How so?"

"Like little boys comparing penises to see whose is longer." She made a fluttering gesture with the back of her hand.

"Actually," I said, "we compare the breast sizes of dark-haired women we know."

I watched her face. From her chair Claire Killbride coughed.

"Becky is on the verge of becoming one of her generation's most successful nonrepresentational artists," Claire Killbride said.

"Is she?"

"Yes. That's her painting on the far wall."

She pointed to a moderately big canvas hanging between a Chagall and an Albers. It consisted of smears of red, orange and black paint on a rough, putty white background.

I looked at it for a while.

"What do you think, Mr. Boone?"

"It's certainly on the verge," I said.

"Do you like it?"

"To be honest, I like your daughter's paintings better."

Claire Killbride coughed again. Becky Lightfoot made a noise that sounded like "wha!"

"You can't be serious," Claire Killbride said. "Cheryl is a rank amateur compared to Becky."

"Woulda fooled me."

I stood there. A palpable angry silence radiated like heat from the resident painter.

"I don't have to stand here and listen to this," Becky Lightfoot said. "Good-bye," she said to Claire Killbride, then looked at me.

"I know." I looked at her coolly. "You're searching

for a killer comeback but you're nonrepresentational and thus words fail you."

"You are an ass!" Becky Lightfoot spat. Then turned on her heel and stalked from the room.

"Write it. The man is an ass." I scribbled the air with pinched fingers.

"Really, Mr. Boone. There's no need for insolence here," Claire Killbride said.

"Her insolent manner invites it."

Claire Killbride crossed her legs at the knee and smoothed the edges of her black silk tunic. "I didn't ask Arthur to ask you to stop by so that you and Becky could trade insults."

"Then Becky should learn she's better off keeping her eyes open and her mouth shut."

Claire Killbride cleared her throat but said nothing.

The drinks came on a silver tray. Claire's Cinzano was set atop a cork coaster on a side table at her right hand. My beer, a Long Trail lager, was sloshed, a foot in front of my nose, into a frosted crystal stein. It was all I could do to keep from shouting "Gimme that" at the maid and snatching the bottle from her.

The head she poured was easily four inches high.

"Cheers," Claire Killbride said. "To Cheryl's safe return."

I hoisted the stein and sullenly sucked off some foam. "To Cheryl."

Claire Killbride lowered her glass from her lips. "We are quite worried, Mr. Boone. That's why we asked to see you. Have you learned anything?"

"Not really." I set the stein on the floor; I could've taken a bubble bath in the suds. "Arthur may have told you Chelly'd been down to Hanover recently. But nobody who knows her there has seen her in the past three days. She may be looking for a guy named Tom Jessup. Ever heard of him?"

She pursed her lips and furrowed the skin on her fine-lined forehead. "No."

"Twenty-five years ago he hung out down the road with a poet named Armen Karillian."

"Oh, that oaf!" Claire Killbride turned her head and slapped her hand below her throat.

"You know him?"

"One could not live within a mile of that cretin and not know him," she said.

"What was he like?"

"He was an overbearing lout. A noisy, destructive, devious, malicious . . . snake."

"Sounds like fun."

"Augh! The parties and noise and filth that emanated from that farm while that man was its resident. Appalling. The drugs. Young people wacked out on LSD. Peyote. Psilocybin—whatever those hallucinogens are. Couples fornicating in the fields. Whenever I went in to town I practically had to drive blindfolded, it was so disgusting. Garbage and prurience everywhere."

She leaned backward, rubbing her forehead. "Every day we watched as everything we knew and loved here seemed to be heading south."

"From what I gather, it sounds as if Karillian headed south instead."

"Wherever he went, good riddance." Claire Killbride snapped. "He was *so loathesome*. He was destroying everything!" She closed her eyes in revulsion.

The foam in the stein had dropped an inch. I sipped through it.

"Chelly hung out down there for a while though, didn't she?"

"Hmm? What?" Claire Killbride peered at me blankly over the rim of her glass.

"Cheryl hung out with Karillian. Right? That's how she would've known Jessup."

"Is it?"

"Jessup was one of Karillian's students. He hung out there, too," I said.

Claire Killbride sipped at her drink, then pushed her lower jaw forward as if reflecting on something.

"Cheryl was—how shall I put it—wild in her youth," she said. "Win and I would impose limits. She'd overstep them. We forbade her to go to that farm. She went anyway. Now, you say, she might be trying to contact one of

Karillian's disciples. Well, that seems so . . . foolish to
me and so unlike the grownup Cheryl I know. She's far
more settled down."

"Is she . . ."

"Yes. But if this search of hers, for Jessup or whomever, is what you claim you've unearthed . . ."

"I don't claim to have unearthed much of anything," I
said.

Claire Killbride shook her head and emitted a small
patrician sigh. "Oh, Cheryl." She drank, then had a
thought. "But surely she'll turn up again, won't she? I
mean, if she's only out looking for this Jessup fellow?"

"There might be other things working against her," I
said.

She cocked her head at me.

"Her mental state?" I said.

Claire Killbride sighed again and shook her head wearily. "I see Arthur's been downloading his own neuroses
on you, Mr. Boone."

"He said she's suicidal."

Claire Killbride waved my words away. "Arthur's
such a baby. Cheryl's the picture of health. The two of us
go swimming together all the time. Where Arthur gets
these *ideas* about *suicide* . . ."

"He says she's tried two or three times."

"Yes, Mr. Boone. I've heard Arthur's stories. Let's see:
There was the Seconal episode—it turned out Cheryl'd
taken two; she told me. Then there was the garage episode.
He said she left the motor running—it turns out she just
plain hadn't. Then there were the wrist cuts in the bathroom—made, it turns out, by the Sheetrock knife that
slipped from her hand as she was putting up wallpaper.
There were no suicide cuts, Mr. Boone. Cheryl showed me
the nick. It was all a clumsy accident."

"Then why would her husband say otherwise?" I
asked.

Claire Killbride closed her eyes and pinched the
bridge of her nose as if this was all too much for her.

"One word." She raised her head; fixed her eyes on
me. "Pity."

"Pity," I repeated.

"That's all Arthur wants. For himself. For Cheryl. For the two of them. They can't have children. Pity. He hurt his back. Pity. She can't do art to save her soul. Pity. 'No one pities us?' Arthur says, in effect. 'Well then, let's embroider. Look at me. I'm an alcoholic. Look at Cheryl. She's suicidal.' "

"Manic-depressive, Arthur said."

"Cheryl is no more manic-depressive than you or I, Mr. Boone. Cheryl herself knows she's not manic-depressive."

"That's not what Arthur says."

"Let me please make something clear to you now." Claire Killbride swayed her head from side to side. *"Arthur . . . lies."* She leaned forward in her chair. "He's a weak man for whom life hasn't unfolded as he's wished. I sometimes think his lying is deeply pathological, but then *I* don't want to be guilty of embroidering."

"Embroidering what?" a voice said.

Claire Killbride looked up and smiled her radiant smile. "Oh, hello, darling."

I turned to see the dripping figure of Win Killbride in the side doorway. He was barefoot in a white terry cloth robe, and water dripped from his muscular thick calves onto the varnished oak floor. He walked toward us, wiping water from his iron-gray hair with a white towel.

"You're Boone. Don't get up." He extended a thick hand. "Win Killbride." The handshake was hard; the hand, callused and meaty and thick. The voice was unaccented but native; and deep and violently raspy. "You find Cheryl?"

"No."

"I'll fill you in on details later, darling." His wife spoke coolly. "It appears that Arthur's been up to his old embellishing tricks with Mr. Boone."

"That asshole!" Win Killbride had a ruddy, creased face and handsome pale blue eyes that were slightly bloodshot. He looked like a retired successful heavyweight prizefighter. He looked like he took shit from no one. "I ought to go down there and fix it so he can't walk."

"Now, darling. Be calm. Mr. Boone says Cheryl might be looking for someone. Named . . . who again?"

"Tom Jessup," I said.

"Who the hell's that?"

"A disciple of—hold on to your hat, darling—Armen Karillian."

"That creep?" Win Killbride's face started to boil. "I thought he skipped the country."

"He did," Claire Killbride said. "But one of his disciples apparently didn't."

"What in hell's she want to see an associate of Armen Karillian for?" Win Killbride squinted at me as if I had the answer.

"I have no idea," I said. "It's only a lead."

"Well, it doesn't make sense to me." Win Killbride slapped the chest pocket of his robe. He produced a crumpled pack of Merits and lighted one with a butane lighter. He dragged deeply on the cigarette and spoke, exhaling explosively. "If I was Arthur—no offense—I'd save my money and let Cheryl come home on her own."

"Arthur says she might not make it on her own."

"Claire must've told you: Arthur's full of shit." He took another long, deep drag. "What are you costing him, anyway? Couple grand a week?"

"That's between him and me," I said.

Win Killbride guffawed in genuine mirth. Smoke blew from his compressed lips as if from a lidded kettle. "Well, it's your time and his dough. But from where I sit, it sure looks like a boondoggle to me."

"Does that make him . . . Peter Boondoggle, darling?" Claire Killbride tittered at her lame pun.

I glanced at my beer. It was still ungodly foamy. "Either of you got anything else on your daughter?"

Win Killbride turned down the corners of his mouth and shrugged. "I don't have anything. D'you, Claire?"

Claire Killbride gave me her sadly suffering Nancy Reagan smile. "Just don't believe everything Arthur tells you, right?"

"Who am I supposed to believe?"

"Just not Arthur, say, fifty percent of the time?"

"I'll try to remember that."

"Good. One more thing." Claire Killbride sitting in the Stickley exuded a kind of ice-maiden regality. "Arthur did tell us you were discreet. Can we all at least believe *that* from him?"

"I don't see why not," I said.

"Good. The last thing this collection needs as it goes to the Guggenheim is *indiscretion*."

I made my farewells. Win Killbride shook my hand hard again, said to let him know if there was anything he could do to help, and his wife stood and tilted her head in my direction like a tall, stately species of lakeside bird. The two of them moved closer together as I left the room, a pair of opposites deeply attracted to each other.

Outside, I could see Becky Lightfoot through one of the house's side windows, staring at a canvas on an easel. The canvas was blank, the room brightly white under recessed spotlights. A tape deck wafted something familiar by Vivaldi.

With a housepainter's brush Becky Lightfoot made a wide black smear across the canvas, then stepped back and examined her work. What she saw caused her to dance a brief flamenco.

I wanted to walk under the window and blow her a lip-fart but a noise near the cars made me turn instead. A figure was walking around from behind my car. He saw me and started to change direction and in the shadowy light I saw who it was.

It was Kerr, the hired man. He was still in khaki work clothes and he walked quickly away from me, with a lot of elbow action.

"Kerr, wait!" I called in a friendly voice.

He froze and turned to face me. I walked over to him, giving him a friendly smile. He had something in his hand that he put in his flapped shirt pocket. He buttoned the flap. His face was ugly and implacable.

"How are you?" I said.

The face gave me no hint of amicability. "Evenin'." The voice was deep and nasal.

"What are you doing here?"

"I work here."

"No, I mean, what were you doing around my car?"

"Wasn't doin nothin'. What are *you* doin' here?"

"I was invited. You been down to Arthur's lately?"

The cold eyes slitted and the mouth puckered like an anus. "Can't say as I have."

"Been down to Mrs. Cole's writing cabin?"

"Why would I do that?"

"You work around there, don't you?"

"There's fifty acres along this shore I'm responsible for. I work around a lot of places." The simian jaw thrust upward in Yankee defiance.

I smiled at him for a bit of time. "Nice talking to you, Kerr."

"Hmp." The unpleasant old man turned and walked away from me, into the darkness. His boots made swishing noises over the freshly cut grass.

Thinking about Arthur Cole and his in-laws and their art collection and Chelly and her paintings and cabin and the Poetry Gang and Perry and Kerr, I drove down the darkened road. There was a lot to think about. In the hot July night, the dark fields sparkled with fireflies. Their light seemed pure and oddly providential to me. They lit the roadsides all the way back to my house.

19

I LEFT FOR CONNECTICUT AT DAWN. THERE WAS LITTLE traffic on Route 89, and Route 91 I could practically drive blindfolded. The hills along the Connecticut River were green, but the fields that had been cut for hay a few weeks earlier were very yellow and the lawns of the farmhouses not shaded by trees along the river were burned brown. The radio talked of drought now. I was not at my house much but I had been checking my spring these past few weeks, sliding its heavy tile cover off with a board and then sticking the board end first down into the cool darkness, holding it steady so it would not float loose in my hands and pushing it, floating, to the bottom for a measurement. The board always came up dripping cool and stained with the cool spring water, but over the past few weeks the level had dropped and now I worried like everyone else in the state about rain.

I drove fast because I did not know how hard it would be to find Shondra Maine, and I did not want to waste any more time than I had to if I couldn't find her. I was in the Saab because it was faster than the truck, and I ate meatloaf sandwiches I had made that morning and drank coffee from a metal thermos and listened to Walter Parker on the radio and then a religious talk station and then golden oldies.

In this way I passed from the brown hills of Vermont through the brown river valleys of Massachusetts and into Connecticut. By noon I was crossing at the mouth of the Thames River and exiting in the blue salt haze of Long Island Sound for downtown Groton.

I asked directions to 20 Riverside at a clam shack on Route 12. It turned out Shondra Maine lived in former Navy housing a mile or so east of the submarine base. The neighborhood was a series of circular turnoffs around which dilapidated bungalows were clustered. Scruffy kids rode rusted monkey bikes on the potholed entry road. I parked more or less out of sight near a forsythia bush at the edge of the circle marked "Twenty Riverside" on a chain link fence and looked in. There were six bungalows, each with a little porch in the front, and each a faded white and badly in need of paint. They stood about fifty feet apart, one from the next, and the little grass lots between them were weedy and burned dry. Something about the forlornness of the place made me decide I should keep a low investigative profile. I put on a pair of mirrored Vuarnet sidewalls and a dumb porkpie hat with the brim turned down that I kept in the glove compartment for moments like these, and I pulled a clipboard with a lined yellow pad clipped to it from under the passenger seat. From the passenger door pouch I removed a vinyl pocket saver filled with pens. I tucked the pocket saver in the breast pocket of my shirt, and across the top of the yellow pad I wrote Shondra Maine's name and address. Then I checked myself out in the rearview mirror. Not a pretty sight. I looked like the chief suspect in a federal office bombing.

I stepped out of the Saab and locked it. Cars were parked in the first two lots and a kids' water mat called a Slip 'n Slide was stretched in the weeds near the road. It was covered with dust and bird shit, and a kid's tricycle lay smashed and overturned beside it in the scorched weeds.

A skinny, shirtless man was waxing the car in the second driveway. Through the window of the little house I could hear a television playing and see the dark silhouettes of children's heads passively watching it. The man was young, mustached, tanned, and missing teeth. His hair, brown and thick, cascaded to his shoulders like a French courtier's wig, and he was rubbing Turtle Wax with a yellow chamois cloth onto the hood of a vintage blue

Plymouth Duster. The sweet smell of recently smoked marijuana hung in the salty haze.

"Hello." I thickened my voice so I sounded like Jimmy Stewart's lost cousin. "I wonder if you can help me. I'm looking for someone who lives around here?" I made a pretence of peering down at my clipboard and reading from it. "Is it—Sh—Shondra Maine?"

"Yeah, Shondra." The hemp gave the young man's voice a lazy drawl. He leered at me through sleepy, reddened eyes and cocked his head on one skinny shoulder. "You here for a roll?" His upper teeth stuck out when he grinned.

"Beg pardon?"

The kid chuckled at me. "Nothin'." He sized me up before going on. "I figured you might be one of Shondra's 'clients,' if you catch my drift."

"Clients? Oh, no no no. I-I'm not one of those." I gave him my best Jimmy stammer. "W-why? Does Ms. Maine have a lot of clients?"

The kid shrugged, mellow with amusement. "Let's just say Shondra's massage business is doin' real good. Hell, if I wasn't tied down I might be contributing to Miss Shondra's upkeep myself." He tittered limp-wristedly at the thought. He was one stoned puppy.

"So this is the right place." I gestured at the compound. "She's here . . ."

"Last place down. Only you won't find her there right now."

"I won't . . ."

"Nah." The kid rolled his eyes. "Miss Shondra's got a straight job." He tittered again.

"She does . . ."

"Yeah. She serves drinks up at Foxwoods. You been up there yet?"

"No."

He spit. "I won two hundred bucks there last night, playin' baccarat."

"Congratulations."

"Eeyayuh!" He shifted air gears with his scrawny fists. Then he sobered up. "Foxwoods is where she'll be on

Thursday. Workin' the afternoon shift. Whudja say you wanted to see her for?"

I took a deep breath. "Roaches?" The kid looked at me. I plunged on. "I got a call on my beeper, either from her or somebody else, to come by and check out the cockroach situation."

"You're an exterminator?" The goofy teeth protruded in another grin.

"Yeah, well. In the trade we call it pest control. But yeah, part-time. Moonlight sort of thing." I did a little Jimmy toe-scuff to indicate modesty. "I was just driving by, thought I'd spec out the job. Come back tomorrow with my spray rigs. I'm Ethan Allen. Live down Mystic way. You're?"

"Corky Gullet." We shook hands. His Adam's apple bobbed agreeably. He seemed to be buying my act. "You got any stuff to zap the deer ticks around here, you'd do us all a service."

"They bad around here?" I compressed my mouth in an earnest frown. Any more earnestness and I'd be baptizing this yahoo in the Thames.

"Oh, they're bad all right!" Corky Gullet shivered with firsthand knowledge. "One bit my girlfriend in the ass ten days ago, now she's laid up inside with that Lyme disease. Fever? Weak? Aches all over. Looks like shit. We don't let her kids out 'cept to play in the park." He looked at his groin. "I hafta wear pants out here in the heat and they still crawl up my legs. I had a wood tick on my pecker. Got um before he bit me."

"*Great*! Um, d'you mind?" I jerked a thumb across the way. "I just want to get a handle on the size of the job at Ms. Maine's? Glance through the windows, see what attachments I'll need to bring tomorrow."

"Yeah, shit. Go inside if you want." Corky Gullet flapped a lazy hand. "Key's under the mat. I looked after the place while Shondra was gone this spring."

"She was gone?"

"Yeah, said she had a job outta state someplace. Never said where or what. Waitressin' or whorin', I suppose." He chuckled into his chest. "Just come home a week or so ago."

"Roaches probably came while she was away," I said.

"I suppose. I know *she's* had 'em." He nodded toward his girlfriend's house. "Only I ain't seen none since I moved in."

I thanked him, saying I'd only be a minute. Corky Gullet kept talking.

"I tell Shondra when she's lyin' out on her porch in one of her thong bikinis, she'd better watch out. Someday she'll have more than ticks crawling up her butt. Go on!" He shooed me off good-naturedly.

I thought I did a pretty good job of fumbling with my clipboard and touching my hat brim. I ambled through the thick grass, stumbling a little bit, sizing up the other bungalows as if I'd moonlighted in pest control for years. Maybe I had. Corky Gullet resumed waxing his car, and I walked to the front corner of Shondra Maine's bungalow. I lined my heels up with the edge of the wall, then paced to the other front corner, stopped and made a big deal out of writing the number of paces on my pad. I did the same thing along the side of the house, returning to the front corner so Corky Gullet could see me write down that figure, too, then multiplying the two lengths and tapping my pen on the clipboard and frowning as I walked up the rotting front steps and stopped at Shondra Maine's front door. I lifted the mat, found the key.

I turned. Corky Gullet looked up at me from his waxing.

I raised the key and an index finger to indicate the one minute. Corky Gullet gave me the peace sign. I unlocked the door.

Shondra Maine's apartment was shabby but neat. It had a small living-dining area with a sprung couch, coffee table, and stuffed chair facing a TV with a cable box on top of it, and there was a kitchen table set with two white plastic chairs and ceramic salt and pepper shakers molded in the shape of little cupids. There were cheap posters on the walls of cute puppies, kittens, and rabbits. The reading matter on the coffee table—*National Enquirer, Star, Soap Opera Digest*—was straight from a 7 Eleven's impulse rack.

I took off my sunglasses, slid them into my shirt pocket, and made for the kitchen.

The kitchen, lucky for me, did have roaches—not a plague of them, but enough to warrant calling a mountain man turned pest control expert. I opened cupboards with my fingernails, noted the *cucarachas* playing bumper car in the breadbox and under the sink. I also checked out Shondra Maine's refrigerator. Its top two shelves were stocked for a giant happy hour with many bottles of Mumm champagne, Schweppes tonic, Canada Dry ginger ale, and Polar club soda, and many cans of Coke, Diet Coke, Sprite, Heineken, Bud, Bud Light, Molson's and Miller's. The bottom two shelves held jars of olives, capers, cheese spreads, lumpfish caviar, and pickled herring. There were tubs of potato salad from a deli in Groton; there were plates of cold cuts, sliced cheeses and fancy boiled shrimp. The booze was in gallon jugs, in two cases under the window. There was Wild Turkey bourbon, Johnny Walker Red scotch, Tanqueray gin, Absolut vodka, Mount Gay rum, Canadian Club whisky and Don Pepe tequila. There were two-liter bottles of Gallo blush chablis and Sutter Mill cabernet sauvignon. There were big cans of cranberry juice, pineapple juice, lime juice, V-8 juice and clam juice. There was Noilly Prat vermouth, Peychaud bitters, Rémy Martin brandy and Uncle Dave's Bloody Mary mix. There were enough alcoholic variants to satisfy forty dipsomaniacs, their spouses and their next of kin, and all of it, according to the cases, had come from the state liquor store in Lebanon, New Hampshire.

It was hot enough and I was tired enough from the drive that I would have loved to mix myself a gin and tonic and call it a day. Instead, I went into Shondra Maine's bedroom.

That woke me up. The bedroom had a big Fedders air conditioner going full blast, and the windows were covered with louvered shutters so that it was chilly and dark there. I switched on a wall light with my shoulder and was greeted by the sight of my own image staring at a big bed covered in hot red satin. My image was reflected in a mirror behind the bed, and there were mirrors on the other walls and the ceiling. Welcome to my parlor. The closet next to the bed was partially open and in it I could see filmy negligees and strappy little costumes in leather, rubber, and brass that weren't so filmy, and a row of sleek, expensive high-heeled shoes, and little dresses made of lace and silk, and a rack of whips, cuffs, clips, and collars for inflicting pain, pleasure, or both, depending on the inflictee. On a cheap Danish modern bureau were six blue glass bottles of Caswell-Massey massage oil in all the flavors, a mink mitt, and a footsie roller. There was a CD player and a stack of new-age CD's on a bedside table. All that was missing was a pimp and the peep slots.

I did not quite know what I was looking for and I knew I did not have much time before suspicion would cloud Corky Gullet's mellow high, so I quickly fingernailed open the top drawer of Shondra Maine's bureau to see what I could find.

What I found was nowhere near what I expected. On a pile of crotchless underpants, beneath a box of ribbed prophylactics and a red double-ended Chinese dildo that looked like a boomerang on steroids was a cigar box containing a small manila envelope. I took the envelope from the box. Opened it. For reasons I can never quite figure at times like these, my heart started pounding.

Inside the envelope, each in its own glassine slipcover, was a small stack of Polaroid snapshots. When I shuffled through them and looked at them through their glassines, I could see only the hazy outline of two figures on a bed together. But when I slid a shot out of its glassine I saw that the two figures were women, attractive women, one a light-skinned black with an oiled, muscular, sinuously curving body, cropped black pubic hair, and firm, conical breasts, the other a dark-haired Caucasian, her body more ample and very white, yet hardly less firm and sinuous. On a bed with a hot red satin spread, in a room without mirrors, they were making love to each other. In the shot I studied, the two were in profile and the hair of the light-skinned black woman was drawn tight into a sleek black bun, her fingers were splayed against the other woman's open crotch, and her tongue was touching the woman's upturned breast. Her free hand seemed to be holding a chrome plunger attached to a shiny black wire that disappeared from the frame. The other woman's face in profile was partially obscured by her own free-flowing, wildly wisping brown hair, but it was not so obscured that I could not make out the fine nose and an earring that dangled from her ear like a miniature turquoise-and-silver chandelier.

The other woman in the picture was Chelly Killbride.

A quick riffle through the stack told me she was in all the pictures, and by the last she and the black woman, with the help of the double-ended dildo, were bringing each other to what looked like a seismic orgasm.

I didn't like what I saw. I didn't have time to give the room a proper tossing. I put the pictures in the envelope, stuffed the envelope in my pants pocket, closed the top drawer with my elbows, shut the light off with my shoulder and closed the door with my fingernails. I looked into the bathroom on my way down the hall. It could have been a bathroom in any scruffy bungalow. Only the big cardboard box of disposable douches near the toilet seemed out of the ordinary.

I stole one of Shondra's Kleenex from the back of the john, took my sunglasses from my shirt pocket, and began wiping the lenses. I strolled out of the house, onto the front porch, keeping my head down as I wiped the lenses. I put the glasses on, looked up, saw Corky Gullet looking at me, and tossed him a salute. He waved back. I closed the door and blocked his view as I wiped the knob with the tissue and turned the key in the lock. I wiped the key with the tissue, palmed the two together and put the key back under the mat, careful not to touch it with my bare fingers.

I scribbled numbers on my clipboard and walked back toward Corky Gullet.

"See any roaches?"

"Yeah, yeah," I said, rediscovering Jimmy Stewart behind my adenoids. "In the kitchen. It's loaded with them."

"You see the bedroom?" Gullet wiggled his eyebrows and made slobbering noises.

"I didn't." He looked at me. I feigned an uncomfortable shrug. "You know, she's not home. I don't want to go traipsing all over her house. Besides, you don't usually see roaches in bedrooms."

Corky Gullet slithered his tongue over his lips and said, "Ooh-la-la! Mr. Allen, in that bedroom you see . . . *everything*!"

20

IT WAS LATE AFTERNOON BY THE TIME I EXITED ROUTE 95 and drove Route 2 north to Ledyard.

The Foxwoods Resort Casino looms like a piece of Oz on land in eastern Connecticut belonging to the Mashantucket Pequot Indian tribe. The land is very beautiful, with woods and high rocky outcroppings and crows and hawks in the air, and the casino floats on a rise above the trees, its roof a bright blue with flagstaffs against the sky, its walls big, tan and smooth with many black windows and blue gables. A few years earlier, the Pequots had built the casino, the first and only in New England, and now the tribe was earning millions by it, raking in money, buying up nearby real estate, trying through the courts to annex it to their nation, and in the process alarming their non-Pequot neighbors who feared they would soon be dispossessed. I did not go out of my way to follow the heated issue, but I did feel a certain delicious glee over the Indians' erecting a gambling establishment, plying the white man with his own firewater, seducing him with his own coarse ideas of entertainment and dining, then legitimately separating him from his cash with his own potshot games and buying up his land at an alarming rate. I drove up Route 2 in the thick late afternoon heat and thought of Custer, Sherman, Sheridan, and all the other dead Indian fighters and wondered what they would make of Foxwoods. I had to laugh. The Indians were beating the white man at his own game.

There were many acres of paved parking lots surrounding Foxwoods and all of them looked full when I reached the casino. Two high school kids in sweat-stained blue shirts near the turnaround in front of the hotel directed me around back to the parking garage. I drove around back, under a big glass pedestrian bridge, past a long fleet of junket buses, under high windowed walls and overhead arrows, and followed signs to the garage where I found a space in a corner on level two. The air was fetid with anticipation and trapped exhaust. I trailed four older women through a set of double doors to a bank of open elevators. The elevators were new, plush and big as downstairs bathrooms. The women knew their way around. One of them punched a button, the door closed and all the women whooped a little bit. They were there to play the slots. They had four hundred dollars among them and they told me they intended to triple their money, then quit while they were ahead. Their husbands were all dead. They each played a hundred dollars a month from their Social Security checks. They said they needed to win whatever they could to make ends meet. I wished them luck. It was a hell of a thing. I tried not to think about what I'd be doing when I got older.

When we got upstairs, I said good-bye to the ladies, used the men's room, tipped the attendant fifty cents for a paper towel and a slug of mouthwash, and strolled down the wide carpeted hall past the entertainment theater, the shops, and the restaurants to the first casino. It was hopping in there. There was a big room full of slot machines, and at least three quarters of them were being played. The noise of electronic bells and *ka-chunking* bandit arms and clinking slot wheels was very high. You made quiet sounds with your voice and you could not hear yourself. That was part of the idea. I saw the women I had ridden up with fanning out to play the dollar slots. They had been to the cashier's window. They each had a white plastic bucket in one hand and a roll of dollar slugs in the other. Their faces looked radiant and eager. They could have been anybody's mothers. They did not notice me when I walked past. I strolled the aisles, looking at the slot players, noting the baccarat tables in a distant corner of the room, and checking out the cocktail waitresses I passed. The cocktail waitresses were dressed in moccasins, flesh-colored tights with seams running up the back of the legs, and skimpy low-cut costumes meant to depict Indian dresses. They wore head-bands with feathers stuck in them and carried big trays of assorted drinks. Few of the cocktail waitresses looked like Mashantucket Pequots to me. The costumes, however, looked like punishment for years of thoughtless cultural abuse. They looked demeaning and silly. Maybe that was part of the idea, too. To make white people understand that Cleveland Indian and Washington Redskin and Mil-waukee Brave and Tonto and Little Beaver and Chief Knockahoma didn't sit well with them. Who knew?—maybe the Pequots were going to adopt a cute little white man for their mascot. Dress him in a business suit. Show his little legs flailing to catch a commuter train. Call their team the Westchester Whiteys. What the hell. The wait-resses' costumes made you think things like that.

I did not see Shondra Maine near the slot machines, nor did I find her anywhere near the baccarat tables or the horse track machines. The lobby had many shops and an artificial waterfall and an enormous crystal sculpture of a Pequot aiming his bow and arrow toward a skylight. A low roller in a windbreaker and powder blue slacks was passed out on a bench near the sculpture. His mouth was open and his false teeth had fallen loose and he was snor-ing. He looked dead. I watched two security men in blue blazers lift him by the armpits and walk him to a door behind a newsstand. Then I crossed down another wide corridor to the second big casino room. It was even more packed than the first. There were many roulette, craps, and blackjack tables. The poker tables were downstairs. There was also a big space for slot machines, and that's where I spotted Shondra Maine. She was dressed in a skimpy tan waitress's dress and there were two red feathers in her straight, pulled-back hair, and her arm muscles flexed tautly under the weight of her tray of drinks.

"Beverages!" she sang brightly as she sashayed past a row of slot players. "Beverages!"

I went to the cashier's window and bought a twenty-dollar roll of dollar slugs. I took a white bucket off the counter and walked up behind Shondra Maine.

"Beverages!"

"Excuse me. Could I get a beer, please?"

She turned. She set the tray on an empty padded stool near a slot machine and looked up. We made eye contact. She was not as good-looking as her photographs because the photographs did not show the thick scar on the left side of her face. The scar was short, thick, and straight and ran from the front edge of her cheek to the edge of her upper lip. It pulled her face and distorted it. When she smiled, though, the scar flattened and she looked beautiful.

"Haven't I seen you before?"

"I beg your pardon, sir?"

"Haven't I seen you?"

"If you come here often enough, I suppose you have."

She had a saddle of tan freckles across her nose and cheeks, and her lips were full and her eyes were brown and very bright under the big false eyelashes she wore.

"You're Shondra Maine," I said in a friendly voice.

"Now how'd you know my name?"

"I learned it from a friend. I'd like to talk to you."

"About what? I can't talk now. I'm working." She smiled.

"I know that. I'd like to talk to you after you get off."

"Where would you like to do that?" Her smile got friendlier.

"Any place you like. Here? Someplace else?"

"Hafta be someplace else, honey. This place is crawlin' with supervisors."

"Then someplace else. You name it. We'll go there."

She gave me an amused frown. "You a cop?"

"No. Do I look like a cop?"

"You do have a certain coplike quality about you, yes."

"I'm private, not public."

"I beg pardon?" She tilted her ear toward me and still smiled.

"I'm a private cop. I'm looking for Chelly Killbride. I'd like to talk to you about her and your friend Tom Jessup."

The smile flicked off like a sixty-watt bulb, and she bent and picked up her tray.

"I'm sorry we don't have the beverage you wish, sir."

"I'll take that beer," I said in a loud voice, pointing to

a stein of flat suds. She had to set the tray down to hand it to me.

"Both Chelly and Jessup could be in trouble. I need to talk to you bad, Shondra. I'm willing to pay—"

"That's three dollars for the beer, sir."

"Please—"

"Three dollars. Right." Then in a lower voice. "You're gonna get me fired, you bastard. My supervisor's standing not twenty feet away."

I fumbled in my pocket for some cash, feeling the envelope of Polaroids there. "I know you know them both," I said, handing her a ten and taking the beer off a tray.

She jammed the ten into her apron and made change. Her hand shook, extending the bills to me. "I don't know what you're talkin' about," she said.

"Did your relationship with Chelly start before Jessup or after him?" I clutched her extended hand.

"I don't know what you're talkin' about." She tried to hand me my money. I squeezed her fist.

"I've got the Polaroids, Shondra. And the dildo." I gave her my most knowing wink. "Keep the change." I watched her mouth drop open, patted her hand, took a sip of beer, and strolled off down the row of slot machines until I found one I liked. I did not look back at her. I put the bucket on the shelf beside the machine and began slipping dollar slugs into it. I preferred pulling the arm to pushing the button to make the machine go. The machine was called "Lucky Sevens." I won a few slugs and lost a few more than I won. I liked being deliberate about slipping the slug in, pulling the handle forward, releasing it and watching the drums spin. It was wrong to rush it. I did not get excited when I won a few dollars and I did not get anxious when I was down to my last slug. I merely picked up my beer and walked to the cashier's window and bought another roll of slugs and went back to the same machine and kept going. I did not see Shondra anywhere near me but I sensed she was not far away. I blew through the second roll of slugs and bought a third. I was down to my last two slugs and my last sip of beer when I felt her presence near my side, smiling her stretched-mouth smile and talking in her musical, singsong voice.

"Another beer for the gentleman?"

"That'd be very nice."

She lowered the tray and I looked over the assortment of drinks and chose the freshest-looking stein of beer, which did not look too fresh.

"You're trying to get me into trouble, honey," she murmured through her friendly, cocktail waitress's smile.

"No, I'm not." I put the fresh beer on the counter and the used stein on the tray. "Just want to talk."

"How long?"

"Long enough to hear about you, Jessup, and Chelly."

I reached into my pocket and pulled out another ten so she'd have to make change.

"There's nothin' to hear," she said, taking the ten dollars and breaking it.

"Let me ask the questions and we'll see," I said.

"What's in it for me?" She was still smiling and handed me my change.

"Maybe I'll give you your pictures back."

I plucked the bills from her hand. She looked at me. She was not smiling.

"Where'd you get 'em?"

"Sources."

"How do I know you got 'em?"

"Because I can describe every pubic hair on your and Chelly's bodies and I can run the pictures' sequence for you all the way to orgasm."

She said nothing but her breathing got very hard and fast and her nostrils flared.

"You bastard!" she hissed.

"Now I neither approve nor disapprove of what you and Chelly are doing in those photos, but I do need to talk to you. And if you don't want to talk to me, maybe I hand the goods over to your supervisor there. Or the cops. Or the newspapers. Or all three. In your line of moonlighting I don't expect you need that kind of publicity, now do you?"

She was speechless for a second or two. Then she remembered where she was and cranked up her artificial smile.

"Sure, I'll be glad to come by when you finish that beer, sir," she said in a louder voice. "Will you be staying here at this machine?"

"I'll be here."

"Great!" She smiled, then picked up her tray and murmured in my ear as she passed, "I'll be back, you motherfucker."

I'll give her credit. She was a cool customer. She made me wait. I waited an hour. It wasn't until my ass had gone numb on the stool and I had lost nearly two hundred dollars at the same machine that she came by and gave me a smile.

"There's a tavern south of here on Route Two called the Black Swan," she said in a low voice. "You know it?"

"I think I remember passing it."

"About six miles down from here on the right."

"That's the one."

"Be there at nine-thirty, sharp," she said. "In the back parking lot. We'll talk there."

"What kind of car you drive?"

"Cute little red Saturn," she said. Her smile was smooth and demure. "And when you get there, don't try anything funny 'cuz I'll be armed."

"I wouldn't doubt it," I said.

"You gonna bring me my pictures?" she said.

"Not necessarily. Being armed, you might put a bullet in me and take them."

"I wouldn't do that." Her grin was rough silk. "But I'd like 'em back."

"I'll bet you would. I'll tell you what. We'll talk first. If I like what you say, you get 'em back. Maybe. If I don't, you don't."

"What's this 'maybe' shit?" Smiling had become an effort for her.

"It is what it is."

"How can I believe you won't feed 'em to the cops anyway?"

"You don't. You're working on faith. Way I see it, that's all you got."

"Shi-it! The last time I trusted a white man I got fucked over," Shondra said. "Who are you?"

"Not saying."

Her smile was completely gone now, as was any pretence at being friendly.

"Nine-thirty," she said, finally. "And bring the fucking pictures."

"I'll think about it," I said, and toasted her with the warm, flat beer.

21

I LEFT THE ROOM WHERE SHONDRA WORKED BUT HUNG around Foxwoods until nine o'clock that night. I played more slot machines and won back the two hundred I had lost, then cashed out and treated myself to steak, salad, and beer at a restaurant across from the first gaming room. Sitting in the restaurant I could see the people streaming through the halls and it didn't take much to spot the high rollers. They were all business and did not wait in the credit lines; nor did they play the slots, preferring poker, roulette, or craps instead. I spotted a couple cheeses I knew from Atlantic City but did not say hello, deciding not to make my presence known. On the way to my car, I saw their Cadillacs and Lincolns out back, their parking lights on, their black-liveried drivers standing in clusters, smoking and talking in the evening heat.

It was nearly dark and the Black Swan Inn was busy when I pulled off the highway and into the parking lot. The Black Swan was one of those fake half-timber watering holes you see a lot of in Jersey and Connecticut. There was a sign out front with the name of the place and the words COCKTAILS LOBSTER STEAK RIBS ENTERTAINMENT and the image of a dark swan outlined in red and blue neon. There was a front parking lot by the road and a side lot that stretched deep around back as Shondra had said. A few couples coming from the casino were yukking it up over the money they had won. With my car window rolled down I could hear the sound of a live country band inside. I swung down along the side lot, saw Shondra's Saturn in a vacant, shadowy space in the back corner under some trees, did a U-turn when I was thirty yards from her, and found a parking space back up near the road.

In the car I put on a dark windbreaker I carried in the back seat and a plain black baseball cap and the sunglasses, and in the pocket of the windbreaker I put a Smith & Wesson .38 Bodyguard I kept stashed in the glove compartment.

I took my keys out of the ignition, stepped out of the car, and locked it. Even though it was a hot night I turned up the collar of my windbreaker and walked on the shadowy side of the lot, away from the building. I could see Shondra's car under the trees. It was by itself and somewhat camouflaged in the shadows. I could not see Shondra in the driver's seat. Maybe, I thought, she had gone inside. It was very quiet out there in the back lot and very shadowy and I did not see the other car until I was within fifteen yards of the Saturn. Then I heard its ignition switch on and saw its headlights flip up, and then it was rolling toward me very quickly, a big, quiet, smooth silver Olds sedan, and then I saw its rear window slide down as it turned, and the arm and the semiautomatic pistol-rifle with the silencer. And then I was diving behind the Saturn, hearing the quick, silenced thumps of the bullets smashing the asphalt and whistling through the trees, fifteen or twenty silenced shots striking behind me, and then the big, smooth Olds picking up speed and sliding out of there, up the parking lot, out on Route 2 heading south and into the night before I could count heads or read its tag.

I was off an embankment behind Shondra's car, dizzy from diving and somersaulting, feeling the hot burn in one knee and in the heels of both hands, but knowing even before I moved that I wasn't hit. The hole in the right knee of my jeans was the size of a half-dollar and my right knee stung and was hot and wet, but I wasn't hit. My palms stung and were gritty with pieces of pavement but I was OK. I could move and I moved my trunk. I felt no pain there. I moved my neck, arms, and legs. The shooter car was gone. I stood up but stayed low and walked to the driver's side of Shondra's car. There were no bullet holes in the car body but that didn't mean much of anything. I took a handkerchief out of my windbreaker pocket, wrapped it over my hand, and opened the door. I didn't open it far. I didn't have to. Shondra Maine, in white short shorts and a strapless white elasticized tube top, was lying across the Saturn's console, her forehead pushed against the front left corner of the passenger seat, her arms tucked under her torso, her legs twisted under the car pedals. The bun in her straight, pulled-back hair was undisturbed, but below it, at the point where her neck intersected with the base of her skull, dangled an ugly wooden handle at a steep upward angle. The handle was part of an ice pick whose point was lodged several inches into Shondra Maine's cerebellum. There was a great deal of blood. The wound had sent a heavy flow of it off both sides of her neck and left a dark, thick pool of it on the gray seat, and more blood had flowed from her ears, nose and mouth. A foul septic odor of urine and excrement mingled with the blood smell and both had seeped obscenely over the inside of the body's legs.

I shut the car door. I touched nothing with my bare skin. I took some deep breaths, sidestepped away from the car, and walked deep into the shadows behind the parking lot to see if anyone had seen me. Cars were coming and going way up front. Small knots of people moved along the walkway near the front door. A few yards directly behind the building was a Dumpster, and as I stood in the darkness a screen door creaked and a bartender in a white shirt and black vest came out into the night, carrying a pail of garbage. I didn't move. He was forty yards away and I could only hope he couldn't see me. He set the pail down, lifted the lid of the Dumpster, and emptied the contents of the pail into it. My legs were numb. My heart was beating fast. The bartender tapped the pail a few times, closed the Dumpster and, turning to go back inside, noticed Shondra's car. He stared at it. I didn't like the way he was staring. He tilted his head to one side, and, to my dismay, began walking toward it. He was walking toward me. I didn't move. I was deep amongst the trees, near the trunk of an old oak, and all I could do was hope he couldn't see me. He was looking at Shondra's car. He walked up to it, looked in the driver's side window, opened the door, saw what I had seen, smelled what I had smelled, and muttered the words, "Holy shit!" He closed the door and backed away from the car and spun on the balls of his feet and started running. He ran to the back door. I heard the screen door open, saw him run inside, heard the door slap shut, and as soon as he was in there, I bolted toward the front of the lot. I stayed in the shadows. The area off the lot was steeply banked, its border planted with junipers, and I stayed low, using its height and the bushes for cover. It took maybe twenty seconds for me to come up behind my car which was bathed in lamplight. I did not wait for a lull in pedestrian or car traffic but instead popped up alongside my car, casually took the keys from my pants pocket, unlocked the driver's door, and nodded to the drunk taking a leak in the high juniper bushes at the corner.

"Just bleedin' my tweeter," he said with alcoholic camaraderie.

I gave him the thumb's up. At the other end of the lot, about eighty yards away, I could see the bartender leading three or four others to Shondra's car. It was now or never. I got into my car, closed the door quietly, inserted the key into the ignition, took a deep breath, and started the engine. Ten or so spaces down from me another car whose occupants, I told myself, couldn't have seen me, began backing out.

Go.

I slipped the parking brake, slid the gearshift into reverse, and backed out in synch with the other car. When I was out, I looked in the rearview mirror and saw the group opening Shondra's car door. At that moment, I shifted into first, smoothly released the clutch, and rolled out of the lot. For a hundred yards or so, I drove down Route 2, feeling I had lost my night vision. Then I remembered. I switched on the headlights. Took off the sunglasses. I did three miles, heading south, before I saw the cop cars coming up the road in the other direction. There were three of them. Their lights were on and they were coming fast. They passed me and I kept my speed steady.

22

A WAXY HALF-MOON HUNG IN THE NIGHT HAZE OVER Groton when I exited the interstate and retraced my steps up Route 12. It was past eleven and against my better judgment I was driving back to Shondra Maine's. Call it a hunch, call it lunacy, but I felt I needed to see her house one more time, to see if the people in the Olds had been there since the afternoon.

It turned out I needn't have wasted the gas. Two miles before the turn to 20 Riverside I saw the orange light above the electrical lights against the hazy black sky, and at the turn I could smell the smoke seeping through the Saab's air-conditioning and see the red lights flashing and hear the pumps whooping in the American La France pumpers. There were police barricades where I had parked that afternoon, and the fire fighters had just arrived and were working three yellow pumpers but they were too late. Shondra Maine's place was an inferno. Great sheets of orange flame billowed like silk above the dark roof, sending sparks high into the sky, while flames flapped like wild curtains from the windows. Twenty or thirty rubberneckers stood behind the barricade, among them Corky Gullet and what I supposed were his girlfriend and her four little kids. Corky was still in his jeans, the woman and kids were in nightclothes, and Corky was grabbing his head and gesturing toward the blaze like a wild man. I did not want him to see me. There were enough people along the road and enough cars between me and the barricade that I was able to back up, do a Y-turn, and get out of there. But Shondra Maine was dead and her house, with its liquor, food, and sex toys, was gone. That gave me something to think about. So did being shot at with a silenced weapon by a wet-job artist in a smooth, quiet Olds.

I thought about each of those things all the way down the interstate through the craggy industrial blight of southern Connecticut and into the bigger blight of New York City. I took the Hutchinson River Parkway over the Bronx Whitestone Bridge, followed the Whitestone Expressway to the Grand Central Parkway, and turned off it into the maze of ramps leading to LaGuardia Airport. It was two-fifteen in the morning. My body was tired but my head was very much awake. I parked the Saab in the garage, took a canvas overnight bag with a few clothes in it out of the trunk, put the gun in the wheel well under the spare tire because I didn't have a carry permit for it for where I was going, locked the bag, locked the car, hoped I wouldn't need the gun, and walked across the bridge into the terminal.

It was dead in there. I walked down to the American terminal. There was one attendant, a young woman, at the long counter and a middle-aged baggage guy was keeping her company. I asked her when the next flight to Albuquerque left and how much it cost and she told me it left at six that morning and that for twelve hundred seventy-eight dollars she could sell me an unrestricted round-trip ticket. I bought one, paying cash.

There was a lounge on the way to the gate and I bought a black coffee there and a hot sausage in a Portuguese roll. I sat by myself at a circular table and read a *Daily News* that someone had left there and ate and sipped coffee and tried to stay awake. The canned music played and the cops patrolled the hallways and homeless people on blankets slept near the exits, but very few travelers moved through the terminal and time seemed to stand still.

I ended up drinking two more cups of coffee and reading every story in the newspaper and when I looked at my watch it was five o'clock and the sky outside the big windows in front of me had turned lavender. I picked up my bag, walked to a phone booth, shut myself in, and called Nan's mother's house.

Nan was still in bed when she answered the phone.

"You're up awfully early," she said in a sleepy voice.

"I'm in New York," I said. "I'm on business. I thought I'd call and say hello."

"Hello."

"You're not in New York," I said.

"No," she said. "I was there."

"I know. Your mother told me."

"Yes. She also told me she told you about Michael."

"Yes."

"I'm sorry, Boone."

"There's nothing to be sorry about. Really."

"Well, I'm sorry anyway. It's not exactly what I expected to have happen here."

"Me neither, but that's the way these things go sometimes."

"I guess. Did the news upset you?"

"That doesn't really matter," I said.

"Michael's a nice man, Boone."

"I never thought otherwise."

"I sort of feel I need to see where this one is leading," she said.

I said nothing.

"I still miss you," she said.

"I miss you, but that's the way it is on that one, too."

"I guess."

We didn't speak for a moment.

"How are the dogs?" I asked.

"They're great. Do you want them back right away?"

"Not if you can hang on to them for a while."

"Are you pretty busy these days?"

"I've been away from the house a lot. The dogs are a lot better off with you right now than they are with me."

"My mother loves them. We're having such a good time together, Mom and me. I never thought I'd ever say that."

"Things change," I said.

"I may get her a Border collie for her birthday, my mother."

"Get a pair, a husband and wife. They're happier that way."

"I'll remember that." Then she said, "Are you in New

York for a while? Could you come out here for a day or anything?"

"I'm leaving today. I'm on kind of a tight schedule. But thanks for the invite."

"I'm making progress on the novel. Did Mom tell you?"

"She didn't. That's good."

"I never thought I'd be creative in the house where I grew up but it's working out."

"I'm happy for you, kiddo."

"I may be done before Labor Day. Then I'll be heading home."

"It'd be nice to see you again."

"I wish you could stop by here," she said. "I'd like to show you my childhood home. And I'd love you to meet my mother who'd love to meet you."

"I've enjoyed talking to her."

"She's become a sweetie in her old age," Nan said. "I feel blessed."

"Maybe I'll come by some other time," I said.

"You sound tired, Boone."

"I am."

A voice on the public address system announced my flight to Albuquerque.

"Where are you?" Nan asked.

"Airport," I said. "I gotta go."

"You all right?" Nan said.

"I'm fine. Just a little tired. You?"

"I'm all right, too. Take care of yourself, OK, Boone?"

"Sure," I said. "I always do."

I hung up and took a deep breath. The sky outside the windows was turning pink. It was an effort to breathe and I felt like I was moving underwater. I opened the door to the phone booth. A decent-sized crowd had materialized at the gate for the plane to Albuquerque. Many of the passengers were men who wore western hats and light suits with dark piping and western boots. None seemed to notice me or to be carrying a weapon. Still, you never knew.

I showed my boarding pass. Got on the plane.

I was asleep before takeoff.

23

I SKIPPED THE PLANE'S PITIFUL EXCUSE FOR A BREAKFAST, slept through the layover in Dallas, and awakened as we touched down in Albuquerque, feeling like a sack of dead cats. It was a feeling I remembered from my Red Sox days. The good old days. The main terminal at Albuquerque International was pinkish brown and looked like a big loaf of Art Deco adobe, and the air outside was hot, dry, and clear. My sinuses started shrivelling. The brightness of the sky hurt my eyes. I put on my Vuarnets. Across the city to the east I could see an undulant chain of mountains called the Sandias, where I had heard nice cutthroats swam in the drainages.

I rented a basic white Ford with air-conditioning, threw my bag in its trunk, and by eleven mountain time was away from the airport, crossing the wide Rio Grande with its cottonwood bosques and small flocks of ducks, and heading west at a good clip on Route 40.

Within a few miles the city stopped cold, and I was in desert, brown and pink, and fringing the horizon far to the west was a chain of low mountains. Route 40 overruns much of Old Route 66, the road made famous by the Bobby Troup song and the first chunk of blacktop linking the eastern U.S. to the west coast. There are still remnants of the 66 mystique on the frontage roads that parallel 40, but you have to get off on the business loops if you want to savor the old diners, the tacky motels, the cement-teepee motor courts, and the curio shops.

I didn't have time. I was still looking for a missing woman. I thought I could get a lead on her out here.

There were many RV's and cars pulling trailers on 40. Some families had stencilled their names on their vehicles. I passed Mel, Dee, and Deb from Pennsylvania, the Rizzos from Kentucky, and Babe and Barb Ploof from Fort Meyers, Florida. Along the road billboards advertised franchises hundreds of miles away, as if there was nothing else worth looking at between the billboard and what it advertised. A sign in ten-foot-high letters on a smooth sandstone bluff said LIVE BUFFALO FOLKS, WELCOME! I passed through towns with names like Casa Blanca, Grants, Bluewater, and Prewett, and then the land got greener and the great wall of rock called the Continental Divide loomed before me, its presence a natural line of demarcation, its string of ridges, cliffs, and mesas a huge geological sculpture curving north.

Just west of the Divide, near a town called Thoreau, I took a break at a truck stop near a railroad track. I bought a bowl of chili, some bread, salad, and a beer and after I had finished sopping up the last of the chili and washing it down with the beer, I called my answering machine back in Vermont and swept its messages. There was only one, from my buddy, Toomey, at the *Burlington Free Press*.

I phoned him.

"Yeah," Toomey said. I could picture his jowls jiggling as he talked. "I ran down our Gatwick clips going back to '69. Found a few items I thought might be of interest. Where are you? I could fax 'em to you."

"That's all right. I'm on the road today. Photocopy and Fed Ex 'em to my account number. I should be back in a day or two. What did you find?"

"Well, it seems back in the summer of '69 some local kid OD'd on heroin at Karillian's farm, and Karillian and, what's their names, Spoonacre, Jessup, and Keel were implicated in the kid's death."

I grew very quiet.

"You there, Boone?"

"Yeah, I'm here."

"Both the state's attorney and the U.S. attorney got investigations underway. There was talk of Karillian being arrested. Then Karillian skipped town—hell, skipped the country for all anyone knows—and the other three weren't charged with anything."

"Nothing?"

"Nada. The investigation was dropped. Coulda been very ugly. The kid who died was retarded and a minor. And apparently, a female minor was there when it happened, too."

"You have names for them?"

"OD victim's name was Leathers, Jerry Leathers. Local kid. Only child. Lived with his parents in Gatwick. Female minor's unidentified in the story. I don't think I'll be able to find the background records. Otherwise, I'd cough you up her moniker."

I scribbled the name "Leathers" in my pocket notebook.

"Interesting, ain't it?" Toomey said, "Spoonacre where he is now, in spite of what he did then?"

"Maybe he didn't inhale," I said.

"No, but a couple other old-timers at the paper seem to remember scuttlebutt that Spoonacre's print may have been on the works that killed Leathers. That never came out officially."

"Narcs find any drugs besides what went into Leathers?"

"No. And that was one of the things that had the state attorney pissed: that Karillian and his kids had probably cleaned up the crime scene before the cops got there."

A vulture circling in the thermals near the highway suddenly glided out of sight into a canyon. Late lunch?

"I owe you box seats, Tooms."

"You owe me more than that," Toomey said. "There's more."

"Whoa!"

"I kept going up the ladder because I wanted to check if my own memory was correct. It was."

"Let's have it."

"Well, it turns out, in an unrelated story, fifteen years later, in the summer of 1984, Karillian's kid, Mikah— that's with a *k* and an *h*—was tried and convicted for burning down a house on Gatwick Lake."

I felt my hand grip the receiver hard.

"Is that right," I said after a cold pause.

"He was eighteen years old at the time. Corrections moved him out of state to Massachusetts because he was stirring up the inmates at Windsor too much."

"How much time did he get?"

"Twelve years. But the likely stretch according to the '84 clip was six up the river, four years monitored parole."

"So he could be out and free now."

"He could be, but I didn't find any clips on it."

"That's OK, Tooms."

"I done good?"

"Yeah, you done good. Whose house was it?"

"What? That the Karillian kid torched?"

"Yeah."

"Wait a minute, I've got it right here. Yeah, belonged to a—here it is, belonged to a Dartmouth prof by the name of Hewlitt."

"Kenneth Hewlitt?"

"That's the one."

"Kenneth Hewlitt had a place on Gatwick Lake?"

"That's what it says. South of Karillian's farm about a mile. You sound a little stunned, Pete. Did I still do good?"

I watched a Santa Fe freight train slide along the rails behind the station. I felt as if it was running through my head.

"Pete? You there?"

"Yeah, I'm here, Tooms. Yeah, you still done good. As always, Tooms. Good stuff."

He made a joke about how I owed him a World Series pennant now but I was hardly listening. The freight train cars moved along with heavy, deliberate speed.

"I'll have the press office send you those Yankee tickets, Tooms."

"You're the tops, Pete. My kid'll call me a hero."

We rang off. I stood in the phone booth, my head on the glass door, trying to absorb everything Toomey had just said. I couldn't quite do it. I got back into the car and shut down my mind for a while and started driving. In forty-five minutes I had crossed out of New Mexico into Arizona, and for the next hour and a half, until I reached Winslow, I tried to make sense of what I knew. It seemed

Karillian was more than just a crackpot poet. The atmosphere he created, if not the scag he proffered, had killed a kid. And his son, whose name I remembered from the back jacket of *Weasel Moon,* was either a chip off the old block or harboring some kind of grudge against Hewlitt.

Hewlitt.

That grizzle-headed fuck hadn't leveled with me. Neither had Keel. Nor Spoonacre.

And Taylor Swimm. Did she know more about her boss than she let on?

At a speed one-sixth of Mach one, I blew across eastern Arizona. By late afternoon I had turned off 40 into Winslow, a dark and bristling oasis on the desert plain. It was strange to have traveled on a road made famous by a song and be driving into a town made famous by another one. Downtown Winslow was all straight streets and brick and clapboard buildings with frontier facades and railroad yards and fast-food franchises and cottonwood shade trees and heat. There was a mix of tourists and locals on the sidewalks, the latter distinguishable by their Stetson hats, silver belt buckles, and cowboy boots. There were a few Navajo Indians on some of the benches along the sidewalks, and there were many pickup trucks with rifles hung in their rear windows.

I smiled to myself. The rifles made me feel right at home.

At the phone booth outside the bus station, I skimmed the local directory for Jessups. There were two over in Holbrook, the county seat, but neither was named Tom. I began to worry that Pippa Locke had given me a bad lead.

But she hadn't. I found the city hall in the center of town and walked into the town clerk's office. The office was cool and dark, and the clerk's assistant, a Navajo woman with straight black hair, crinkly brown skin, and a large mole on her forehead, like a third eye, was quiet and obliging. I asked her if a Tom Jessup lived in the Winslow area, and she said she'd have to check a deed book and see. She went into a back room with a vault door on it and was gone for quite a while. When she came out she handed me an address on a slip of paper neatly printed with the name FRISKETT'S MOTEL.

"He's about fifteen miles south of town, off ninety-nine, on the road that leads to Clear Creek. Turn right about a mile after the Double D sheep ranch. The road's dirt. There's a sign. Follow it to the end. About seven miles. That's where he'll be."

I pocketed the slip of paper and thanked the woman. "You make it sound simple."

The woman's smile was enigmatic and serene.

In deep afternoon light I found Route 99, the sheep ranch, and the turn. There was a rusted well-drilling rig for sale at the turn and the land was a washed, pale sandy green and the greasewood clumps held jackrabbits, small hawks, and phainopeplas. A fine range of mountains capped with snow loomed in the distance beyond the pale hills. The empty highway spooled south in a long, unbroken ribbon. The sheep farm was abandoned and made me feel alone.

A long spume of tan dust trailed the car as I bumped down the dirt road toward Jessup's. About a mile in, along a wash that bordered the road, I spotted the first of several wrecked trucks. Their wheels were gone, their windows shot out, and their frames were rusted to a dark orange. I counted four of them. On the door of the fourth, an old Studebaker pickup, a bullet-pocked signboard read: I AM NOT THE WAY.

On another sign, a mile further, beneath a smoke tree: FORGIVE ME MY TRESPASSES.

And a mile beyond that: NO ROOM AT THE POSADA.

Over the next three miles, in quarter-mile increments, the signs resembled old Burma-Shave billboards:

WHEN THE SNOW IS GONE
AND THE GRASS IS RIZ
THIS IS WHERE
SALVATION IS.

YOU CAN TAKE THE POT
OFF THE POET
BUT YOU CAN'T TAKE THE POET
OFF THE POT.

ALL THE WORLD'S A STAGE
BUT NONE OF ITS PEOPLE
CAN ACT
WORTH SHIT.

In the last mile, the road climbed past stands of pi-
ñons, then dropped toward a band of blue water rippling
through a basin of yellow earth and scrubby vegetation.
The car rattled over a cattle guard that spanned a small
arroyo. Near the creek bed, under a clump of green willows, sat a neat, compact, darkly stained shack. Yellow
boulders the size of automobiles lay scattered behind it.
Parked beside the shack was an old Chevy pickup with a
high, homemade wooden cap on its bed and white New
Hampshire license plates.

I parked behind the Chevy and thought of my gun
back at LaGuardia. A double door in the rear of the cap
was open and a duffel bag, an uninflated air mattress, and
several dunnage boxes lay strewn on the ground.

I got out of the car. I had changed into khakis on the
plane and the wind whipped their fabric against my legs. A
mandala nailed to the door of the shack vibrated steadily
in the hot wind.

Through a window beside the shack I could see many
kitchen implements and a table with a book on it. Nothing
more.

The boards comprising the shack were black with
golden streaks like hair and whorls like fingerprints running through them. I knocked. No one answered. I lifted
the clawlike latch. Entered.

"Hello?"

The shack, a single room smelling of garlic and old
sweat, was like a dwelling preserved from a nameless
fable. To one end was a kitchen with a Magic Chef gas
stove and a Servel gas refrigerator; in the middle was the
table set with two chairs; to the other end was a bed, a
washstand and a bookshelf.

Jack London's southwest pied-à-terre. I smiled to myself.

I did not close the door, nor did I step very far into the
room before I felt the knife point against my rib and

smelled the cheap whiskey on the breath that said, "Don't move."

"Jessup?"

"Shut up."

"Can I talk?"

"Put your hands up."

I did.

"Can I talk?"

"You do or you try anything dumb and you're dead."

It was a nervous voice, a nasal and slightly slurred voice. I didn't say anything. The knife point poked me.

"Move."

I took a step into the shack. The knife point moved with me. I felt its pressure against my flesh. I didn't like that.

24

AS I TOOK MY SECOND STEP, I SPUN FROM THE KNIFE POINT and swung my right arm sideways from the shoulder and clubbed the knifeman across the side of the head with the heel of my stiffened hand. The blow made a sound like a dead fish slapping marble. With my right foot I drove a flick kick to the knifeman's left shin, and when he lunged at me with the knife, an ugly Navy S.E.A.L.S. job, I chopped down on his forearm with my right hand, causing him to drop it, seized his wrist with my left, kicked the knife under the bed, pushed the hand back behind him, kneed him in the groin, and, as he compressed in pain, struck him with a left cross to the neck and a right upper- cut to the chin. The second punch lifted him off his toes and sent him flying against the table, upending it.

He lay in a heap of upthrust table legs and overturned chairs. I bent and picked up the knife, feeling the old after- surge of adrenaline course down my arms and legs.

"You Jessup?" I stood over the sprawled figure.

He nodded.

"Get up." I kicked the sole of his cowboy boot. When he didn't move fast enough, I reached down and grabbed him by his black pocket T-shirt, yanked him to his feet, and hurled him outside on the dusty ground. He landed on his stomach. At first he didn't move. Then he moved like a sick man trying to get comfortable on a dusty bed. His hair was oily, dark, and long; his entire body from face to feet now was powdered in yellow dust. A dark spot of blood glowed through the dust on his lip where I had clipped him. His mouth hung loose and his eyes were half shut.

I stood near his head.

"I didn't come three thousand miles to get gut-stuck by some goddamn jackleg," I said.

"Point taken." Jessup spoke in a grunted whisper. "Who are you?"

I told him. I showed him my license. I squatted down next to him and flipped him over. In pain, he lay sideways, his knees drawn to his chest.

"I'm looking for Chelly Killbride," I said. "I have reason to believe she's been looking for you. Have you seen her?"

Jessup didn't answer fast enough.

"Have you seen her?" I gave him a short, straight punch on the flesh leaf of his right ear.

"No!"

"You're lying!"

"I'm not!" He grabbed his ear and cringed. "Please! I'm not lying!"

"Why would she want to see you?"

"I don't know—"

"Why would she want to see you?"

"I don't knowpleasedon'thitme!"

"You goddamn fuck." I started landing punches on his face, arms and head. Jessup covered up, squealing, but I tore his arms away from his head and slapped his face hard three times. *"Answer me!"*

"All right!" Jessup's hands were tensed like a craven peasant's pleading to the *commandante* for mercy. His head bobbed up and down. His eyes rolled back in his head. I saw their whites. His body shook. He had been drunk when he pulled the knife on me. Now he wasn't so drunk.

"Chelly and me," he said finally in a gulping voice, "we go back a ways." He touched his lip with straight fingers, smearing blood.

"How far back?"

"Twenty-five years." The words came quick and quiet. "She and I were like, close."

"In Gatwick?"

"Yeah."

"You saying you and Chelly were lovers in Gatwick, twenty-five years ago?"

"Yeah."

"When she was fourteen and you were, what, twenty-one?"

"Something like that. Yeah. She used to hang out with me at a farm down from her parents' place."

"Karillian's farm."

"Yeah. You know about it, then."

"I know about it."

Jessup swallowed. He was getting his breath back.

"Chelly's folks didn't like Karillian. They didn't like any of the rest of us that hung out there, either. They always had the cops patrolling the road, paying us visits because they said we were too loud. Chief of police was a guy named Clapp. Always hassling us. His kid, Alden junior, had the hots for Chelly and was always trying to get her to go out with him. She wouldn't give him the time of day."

"Alden junior," I said.

"Yeah."

"How old was he?"

"Then? About fifteen or so. A real Nazi, just like his old man. Always shooting or lifting weights or showing off his pecs."

They've gone soft, I thought, the pecs. But it was starting to make a little sense to me. "Keep going," I said. "Tell me more."

"Chelly was Cheryl til she ran away once and joined me after I came out here. After college. I took her up to Canyon de Chelly and she fell in love with the ruins. After that, she was Chelly and anybody who called her otherwise could fuck off. She stayed with me about a week. But I wasn't looking for trouble. I brought her back. Her old man was so grateful he struck a deal with me. If I stayed away from his daughter, he'd buy me off, give me some dough to go live someplace else. I was never that close to Chelly to begin with. I mean, she was all right for laughs, we had some good times down at the farm. But she was a kid, y'know what I mean?"

"All too well."

"Mind if I sit up?"

"Be my guest."

Jessup sat up on his elbows and looked at the dust on his clothes. "I suppose I shouldn't have done it but I was broke. I took the money. Three grand it was. Moved out here permanent in seventy-one. Bought this little patch. Built the shack. Became a desert rat." He grinned at me. Or squinted to see if I was buying his story. "That's about it."

"So you're telling me you've had no contact with Chelly Killbride in twenty-five years."

"None. She doesn't even know where I live. None of 'em do—Chelly, her old man, her old lady. In fact, I'm surprised you found me."

"Yeah, well, that's my job."

"How'dja do it?"

"Trade secret," I said. "What were you doing back East this past year?"

He looked at me, a sorry dog caught in surprise. He flicked his eyes downward as if the answer to my question lay near his nose. "I always come back East for a little while every year."

"You were there from at least late last summer until less than a week ago. That's more than a little while, wouldn't you say?"

"Yeah, well, I fell into some good luck, I guess." He smiled to himself with a kind of lazy self-satisfaction I found annoying.

"Shondra Maine," I said.

Jessup's face twitched in temporary shock. "You talked to her, too?"

"Maybe."

He looked away. "Doesn't matter." And laughed to himself. "What a milk-chocolate bitch she is, huh?"

I looked at him a long moment.

"Was," I said.

Jessup looked at me.

"She's dead," I said.

Jessup kept looking at me. His eyes conveyed one emotion behind their yellow mask. It wasn't shock, grief, or compassion. It was fear.

"Somebody killed her last night in Connecticut. When I got near to where she was, they tried to kill me, too."

Jessup sat there on his elbows, barely breathing. The cords of his stubbled neck moved as he swallowed. His lips worked. When finally he said, "You're shittin' me, aren't you?" the stunned tone of his own voice convinced him otherwise.

"Who?" His face searched mine.

"You tell me."

"Honest truth. I got no idea."

I studied his face. He appeared not to.

"You know she turned tricks on the side?"

"You're sayin she was a hooker?"

"Jesus, man. What did you think she was? A Red Cross nurse?"

"No." An amazed grin spread across his yellow face. "She was loose, no doubt about it. But a hooker? Shit! She told me she was a model." He laughed at the apparent success of her deception.

"Shit!" he repeated, more nervous. Less amused.

"How'd the two of you meet?"

He turned his mind away from his own folly and looked at me.

"We met in Burlington at a bookstore. You know Burlington?"

"Yeah."

"You know Chassman and Bem? The poetry section. We met there. She came on to me like—like this . . . whirlwind."

"How'd she do that?"

"Aw, you know: 'You like poetry? I like poetry, too. You're a poet? I'm a model.' She said she was in catalogue fashion. Up from New York to take a break for the winter. We hit it off pretty quick."

The image of Pippa Locke slumped over her *latte* flashed in my mind. Pretty quick, indeed.

"Why do you think she came on to you so strong?"

Jessup lifted a hand. "I thought it was my poetry and my looks."

"She never told you she lived in Groton?"

"Where, Connecticut?"

"Yeah."

"No."

"Or that she worked at Foxwoods Casino selling drinks."

He laughed. "You're makin' this up, right?"

"I'm not. But she was obviously making up something to get close to you."

"You're losing me." But the mirth in his voice was hollow, as if inside he was navigating his own dark hell. Fear cascaded off his body like a bad odor.

"Does it cross your mind that Shondra may have wanted more than your poetry from you? That someone might have put her up to getting it?"

Jessup shook his head as if this was all too perplexing for him. "For what? I don't follow."

"Again, you tell me."

"I don't get what you're getting at."

"Look." He was making me angry. I put the knife near his face. He cowered again. I spoke quietly. "A woman's dead. She seduced you into becoming her lover, right?"

He thought about that and tipped his head to the side. A maybe.

"Her execution appears to be the work of professionals. Real wet jobbers. Now, either she had served her purpose to them and was therefore expendable, or she knew something—maybe even about you—that they didn't want her to know and they had to kill her. Which is it?"

Jessup's lips quivered. "You've lost me. I—honestly don't know what you're talking about. I—"

"Shondra got an ice pick in the skull. Right here." I tapped the back of his neck, making him flinch. "What do you suppose they're gonna do if they catch up with you? Slice off your dick, stick it in your mouth, and *then* kill you?"

"Maybe her going out with me and getting iced are unrelated," Jessup said. His arms were trembling. He sat up a little more. "Maybe this has got nothing to do with me."

"I don't think so. Shondra had something going with

Chelly. Somebody had to put them on to each other. You're the only common link."

"Wait, wait. I don't understand. You're saying I—"

"—Introduced the two of them. Somebody had to do it. Chelly and Shondra got along famously. There are pictures of them. The kind of pictures that might make a pair of blackmailers some decent money. Were you and Shondra trying to blackmail Chelly?"

Jessup was shaking his head violently. "You're making me crazy! I haven't seen Chelly in years. I don't know what you're talking about, blackmail. I wouldn't do that to Chelly anyway. Or anybody else. That's not my style."

"No? What is your style then? How do you live out here? What do you do for work if you don't blackmail former lovers?"

"I get jobs!" Jessup's face under the yellow sweat-streaks was slick with agitation. "I bounce around. A little of this, a little of that. Save up some money, fix my truck, travel, write my poems. What's wrong with that? Yeah, I was East last winter. Had me some good times. But this shit you're throwing at me about blackmailing Chelly—"

"If it wasn't blackmail, what caused you and Shondra to break up a week ago?"

For at least the second time Jessup seemed to regard me with the dread of a man discovering that his private life is public knowledge.

"Shondra and me had a fight." He gave his head a priggish twitch. "Over something inconsequential. But it was enough for both us to call it quits. So we split." He shut his eyes. Opened them.

"The fight had nothing to do with your maybe discovering that Shondra was getting it on with Chelly?"

"No!" Jessup closed his eyes again. "I don't know anything about that, I swear."

A coyote trotting beside the creek in the low scrub suddenly saw us and gave a little yelp and changed direction. It looked thin and unhealthy, like the yellow man sitting on the ground at my feet.

"Who do you know, criminal or otherwise, who might have wanted to see Shondra Maine killed?"

Jessup kept his eyes closed. "Nobody, man." He pressed his fingertips to his temples.

"Is there anything you know that might give the same people reason to want to kill you?"

"*No!*" He forced his eyes open. "Jesus! Are we through with the questions?"

"Just a couple more: What was going on at Armen Karillian's the night Jerry Leathers died?"

"Shit, what is this? *This Is Your Life?* Who the fuck are you? Ralph fucking Edwards?"

"Just give me the truth."

"Aw, man." Jessup sighed in alcoholic exhaustion. "Jerry Leathers was this slightly retarded kid who lived in town. He used to come around Armen's farm and hang out with us. Back then Armen was doing skag some nights, just a little. He wasn't hooked. Jerry Leathers saw him do up one night and copied him. The kid killed himself. He didn't know what he was doing."

"And you were there?"

"I was around. Upstairs. But I didn't see him do it because if I did I woulda stopped him. I told the U.S. Attorney this, in a sworn statement. Go look it up yourself. It was a goddamn accident."

"What about Spoonacre and Keel?"

"Aw, man. You know them, too?"

"I know everybody. What about 'em? Was either of them there that night?"

"I don't remember."

"Ehh . . ." I made to backhand him. He raised his hand to his face, flinching.

"Honest I don't."

"Come *on* . . . !"

I flicked a backhand across his head.

"All right!" He slowly uncoiled from his cringe. "Spoonacre may have been there." He ducked his head. "Like I say, I wasn't there! But it looked like John was maybe gonna be heading for some kind of accessory charge. Duncan, I'm not sure. The night Leathers died we were all doing different shit. Armen was doing horse. I was doing grass with Chelly. Duncan was tripping his brains out. Spoonacre, I'm not sure. He may not have been high on much of anything. But it was . . . weird. I came downstairs from being with Chelly—she was Cheryl still—and there was the Leathers kid, needle in his arm, froth on the mouth. I tried to resuscitate him. Mouth to mouth. No use. Boom. He was dead. Everybody else had split. I told Cheryl to get dressed and get the hell out of there. She did. Then I called the cops. They came. That was it."

"You didn't talk first to Spoonacre, Karillian, or Keel about what had happened?"

"No. They wandered back while the cops were there, but we didn't talk."

"And you didn't clean up the place before the cops arrived."

"That's the thing." Jessup looked at me. "It was already cleaned. I threw my shit down the toilet. But except for the works in the Leathers kid's arm, there wasn't nothing left in the house."

"How'd Karillian and the other two act when they came back to the house?"

"Surprised." Jessup smiled at the memory. "Like they couldn't believe their eyes. Like, 'How did this happen here, Officer?' " He made a square's daffy face by pushing out his upper lip and blinking. "It was the start of a long night."

"What happened?"

"Place got turned inside out. We were taken into town and held overnight and grilled by Clapp senior, which was illegal. The next day the state boys came in and the narco feds and the U.S. Attorney's office and the FBI and the ATF and the Treasury Department. And I thought we were fucked." He sighed. "But we weren't."

"You got off."

"Yeah, we got off. I don't know how, but the charges never came down and then once that was over I got out of there. Like I said, Chelly had been fun, but a little bit of the feds breathing down your neck goes a long way."

I gave him a little bit of breathing space before my next question.

"What happened to Karillian?"

He twisted his face in my direction, then he looked down at his dusty legs and sighed. "He split. I don't know where. One day he was at the farm, the next day he wasn't. He left after the Leathers kid died and before the air had cleared about our being charged with anything. Our theory—Spoonacre's, Keel's, and mine—was that he was afraid of being prosecuted. That they'd start investigating him and turn up God knows what else."

"Did he, like, drive off, flee on foot, get on a bus? What'd he do?"

"He couldn't drive. He'd lost his license years ago when he was out here, wandering around with Kerouac and Cassidy. We drove him everywhere—Spoonacre, Keel, and me. From Dartmouth up to the lake. His wife and kids rarely came up."

"Cora's the wife, right?"

"Right. She and Armen didn't get along too well."

"How so?"

"He just didn't help with the kids. You know. Poet off in his ivory tower."

I said I knew. But it was hard to picture Karillian penning his garbage in any place pure.

"They had how many kids?"

"Two. Mikah and Willow Jade. She was just a baby. Mikah was three."

"Did Karillian have any contact up in Gatwick with a Dartmouth professor named Kenneth Hewlitt?"

"Not that I know of."

"You remember Hewlitt."

"Yeah, sure. He taught English. Modern Brit lit or something, right?"

"Did Hewlitt or his wife ever come to Karillian's farm?"

Jessup rubbed his chin as if he was trying to remember. "I don't think so."

"Who had the summer houses south on the lake down from Karillian's?"

"I have no idea. The only house I cared about much was Cheryl's. Chelly's. And after a while I didn't dare go near there because her old man woulda had the shotgun out for me." He snorted at the memory.

Shadows were lengthening along the dry ground and

the creek was the color of ripe blueberries. I tossed Jessup's knife at his feet.

"One last question: What did you see in Armen Karillian?"

Jessup spoke with a kind of sententious reverence. His words surprised me.

"He was the gentlest man I ever knew. He showed me a different option from hewing to the middle-class dream. He was a lousy poet and a big bullshitter, but he was a very good man."

I nodded. Stood, took out my wallet. Dropped one of my cards on Jessup's lap. He picked it up.

"Watch your ass and call me if you need me," I said.

He mumbled something that was either "Thanks" or "Fat chance." I left.

I spent the night in Holbrook in a place called the Adobe Inn. I ordered the room service Mexican specialty and was in bed by ten o'clock mountain time. I was very tired. The next morning I drove to Albuquerque and took a noon plane back to New York. My car was where I had left it in the garage, and the gun was still under the spare tire. I watched my own ass. Nobody followed me. The driving was cool, fast, hard and dark up the New York Thruway. Black coffee kept me awake. The night sky through Addison county was as big as Arizona's.

At three in the morning I rolled into my driveway.

The men in the silver Olds were waiting for me.

25

THERE WERE THREE OF THEM: A BIG BLOND GUY SITTING
on the Olds's hood, a bald guy standing on the house deck,
and a third guy who came out from behind the trees on the
other side of the driveway and blocked me from behind.
All held substantial pistols, probably nines. They were
dressed in pleated slacks, long-tailed, short-sleeved polo
shirts, and white Air Jordan sneakers. They were big. The
blond was tall and thickset like a football player, the
baldie was short and squat and built like a big-time wrestler, and the guy who came out from behind the trees was
dark and medium height but packing muscle.

The blond guy pushed himself off the Olds and
started walking toward me, his gun aimed in two hands
toward my windshield. Baldie came one step behind him
toward my passenger door. Dark Hair closed in from the
left.

"Turn off the engine, step out of the car!" Blondie
flicked his gun in an exiting gesture.

I did as I was told.

The instant I was out of the car, Dark Hair was beside
me telling me to put my hands on my head and frisking me
for my gun.

"It's in the car. Right windbreaker pocket."

Blondie held me between his sights while Dark Hair
got the gun.

"Let me know if you need help with left and right," I
said.

"Shut up," Blondie said.

"Been waiting long?"

Blondie didn't speak. Dark Hair came out of the car with my pistol. His face was one of the ugliest I'd seen in many a year. A welted scar ran from his scalp and over the right side of his nose, down his mouth to his jaw. His teeth were snaggled and black around the edges. His ears and lower neck needed shaving. And his breath reeked. Pickled eggs and beer.

"I hope you handle a gun better than you do a chain saw," I said.

"I'm gonna be handlin' you better than both." He grinned. His voice was a mumbled history lesson in substance abuse.

"Where to, fellas? The Shed's closed at this hour."

Baldie told me to get moving and keep my mouth shut. Blondie flicked his head in the direction of the Olds. Dark Hair jammed his nine into the base of my spine. It was a Glock. It was the second time I'd been jammed in thirty-six hours. But I wasn't about to swat this one away. Not with two other Glocks aimed at my head.

They put me in the backseat of the Olds with Blondie on my left and Dark Hair on my right, their Glocks pressed between my pelvis and ribcage. Blondie was the biggest, youngest, and cleanest of the three. He wore a heavy gold bracelet on his thick football player's wrist and a gold chain with one of those broken coins whose other half was probably around the neck of a female Belorussian power lifter. His hair was short on the sidewalls, long on top, and a straight, long lock of it hung fetchingly off his forehead. He frowned the way guys with thick heads frown. Baldie, who had a Fu Manchu mustache and a size twenty-two collar, frowned, too. Dark Hair leered.

"Which one of you's the wet jobber?" I asked no one in particular when we were rolling. "Hold on, let me guess." I looked at Blondie. "You engaged Shondra in conversation on her passenger side." I smiled at Baldie's eyes looking back at me, dimly reflected through the rearview mirror. "You stayed in the car, 'cuz you're the driver, right?" Then I looked at Dark Hair. "That leaves you to work the ice pick. Tell me, what day-care center did they pull you out of?"

Dark Hair jammed his Glock hard against my ribs. I knew it was coming and braced. But it still hurt.

"You ain't gonna crack wise for very long, smart-ass."

"She talks tough," I said.

Blondie guffawed.

"You shut the fuck up!" Dark Hair snapped at Blondie. I looked at Blondie.

"Doesn't seem like your type," I said.

Blondie smirked but said nothing. Dark Hair's nostrils flared.

"Oh, man, you're gonna wish you never seen me . . ."

"I do already. So does your mother."

Dark Hair made to hit me with his gun. Blondie put his forearm in front of my face and stopped him. "No. You'll mess up the upholstery. We were told to wait."

"Back to your room," I said to Dark Hair.

"You shut up." Blondie poked me from his side.

"As you wish." I inclined my head. We fell silent.

They drove me across 104 and picked up I-89 in Georgia. We drove south until we came to exit 21, the Winooski exit, and took it into Winooski itself. It was four in the morning and Winooski, a former mill town whose mill was now a shopping center, was pretty dead. At the bridge over the Winooski River, we bore right on the Intervale Road and drove for a mile until we reached the top of the hill. We took the next right and dropped down off the hill a little ways. Then we took a left on a short dirt road that opened onto a hilly field. A blue Lexus was parked in the turnaround at the end of the field. Far beyond it, you could see the lights of North Avenue and the exit ramp for the connector and the lights defining the town of Colchester further north, across the big sweeps of marsh, woods, sandpits, and electrical plant. A quarter mile above us, from where we had just come down, the properties along the Intervale were light comercial and residential, but here, buffered from humanity by the steep slope of the hill, we were in a kind of wilderness, a lover's lane for thugs in posh cars.

The Olds stopped nose to nose with the Lexus, and

Baldie got out of the Olds. He walked over to the passenger door of the Lexus and opened it as Blondie opened his door and got out and Dark Hair jabbed me with the barrel of his Glock to follow. I did. When I was outside, Blondie told me to put my hands on my head. Then Baldie tucked his Glock in his pants, walked past us, and said he'd watch the road.

Like a war prisoner I was marched over to the Lexus. Sitting in the passenger seat, his bulk spilling beyond the door frame, his Gokey-booted feet swung to the ground, was Romeo "Bobby" Beaucharme.

"And good morning to you, Mr. Peter Boone," he said through his perpetual Cheshire-cat smile. He was wearing his trademark brown Stetson snap-brim hat and a nubby gold silk short-sleeved shirt and the biggest pair of triple-pleated brown linen summer pants I'd ever seen. In one thick paw was a Green Mountain Coffee Roasters travel mug, probably filled with Bailey's and one of Green Mountain's flavored coffees; in the other was a battery-powered Makita driver-drill with a wood-plug bit on the end of it. The wood-plug bit looked shiny and sharp.

"What gives, Beaucharme? I've got work to do."

"I know, I know, Peter Boone. I know you been workin'. I been wantin' to see you for the past two days, child, but you wasn't home. Busy Peter Boone. Where was you?" The grin was inquiring.

"Riding the Log Flume at Santa's Land."

"Naw!" Beaucharme hefted himself out of the Lexus and stood before me. He was shorter than me by about eight inches, broader by almost twenty. "You went off somewhere lookin' for that butt-wipe, Tom Jessup. Where is he, Peter Boone? The night is old and these big old bones want to get to bed, child."

"Can't say. Why'd you have to kill Shondra Maine and burn her out? She have something you don't want her to have?"

"Ooh!" Beaucharme puckered his lips and his brown eyes twinkled in the moonlight. "Now, who say I go and do a thin' like that? You say?"

"I can add."

"Ooh, yes. And from what I hear, Peter Boone, you

can also jump, can you not? A rat-a-tat-tat!" Beaucharme laughed. Dark Hair, standing behind me, chortled a cloud of egg breath into my neck. Blondie, to the other side of me, smirked and shifted his weight from foot to foot. The Boss had made a funny.

"Now, I don't have much time, Peter Boone, and jus' like you, I need to see Jessup. Now, you gonna cough him up for me or am I gonna hafta pluck the info outta you one plug at a time?" He held the driver drill in front of my face and revved it once so I could see its bit in action in the moonlight. Its battery was freshly powered.

"I take it you're awaiting my answer," I said.

"You have that right." Beaucharme nodded.

I looked at him. If he didn't get shot up by someone bigger in the game, then someday the coronary artery that girdled and nourished his thick, corrupt heart would clog completely with yellow fat; or a valve in the heart itself would clog and kill him. Beaucharme was a low-grade in-state, out-of-state sleaze-bag, a self-made land-rich millionaire with subcutaneous links to what the police speculated but couldn't prove was organized crime. In Burlington, Beaucharme operated a restaurant food distributorship, a garden supply warehouse, and a marina. In the rest of the state who knew? But there were state's attorneys and county prosecutors and plainclothes federal agencies that wanted to find out. So far they'd turned up nothing. To my knowledge from those offices, Beaucharme was no longer hot.

But he would die someday. He revved the drill in front of my face again. I really didn't care. On her death-bed my mother had said two things to me that I tried to remember when I got into situations like these. She said, "One aspect of life is suffering." And she said, "There is nothing to fear."

I looked at Beaucharme. He was grinning and trying to get a rise out of me. Blondie and Dark Hair had their guns pressed at my back.

"You gonna talk?" Beaucharme was still grinning but there was an impatient edge to his voice.

"I'm really not. If you're gonna kill me or disfigure me you might as well get on with it."

The grin congealed. Beaucharme's head flicked back. I felt the pressure against my ribs release and I heard Blondie and Dark Hair slip the guns into their pants. Then Dark Hair put a hand on my right bicep to yank it down and Blondie put a hand on my left, and at that moment I took the momentum their yanks gave me and drove my elbows into both their heads. I drove one kick into Beaucharme's balls and that was the end of him for a while, and then I spun right and caught Blondie with a hard chop to his neck that was enough to shut down his neurotransmitters for a moment. Dark Hair had to settle for a backhand to the throat from my left. It wasn't as strong as it could have been, but I followed with a straight-ahead dig of my stiffened fingers into his solar plexus, a grab of his greasy hair with both my hands, a knee to his face that probably broke his nose, then finished him off by clubbing straight down on his neck.

Blondie went for his Glock but I kicked it out of his hand as he drew it from his belt and took him down with a sweet combination of lefts and rights, the first a straight left that jerked his jaw sideways about an inch, the second a right cross that smashed his nose, the third and fourth both body punches to the gut. These guys were big, ugly, and strong but they weren't fighters. I finished Blondie with a right cross to the jaw. As he staggered backward, I plucked the Glock from the grass, took off the safety, and aimed it at Beaucharme and Dark Hair.

"Call these fuckers off." I was breathing hard.

Dark Hair was lying on his back holding his nose in both his hands. The light was not good but it was good enough that you could see the blood flowing freely down his face. I took his gun off of him and threw it down the hillside. Then I bent over Beaucharme and frisked him. He was unarmed.

"What do you want to see Jessup for?" I asked the fat man.

"I got prostitis," Beaucharme groaned. "Why the hell didja hafta kick me?"

"What do you want to see Jessup for?"

Beaucharme's eyes were squeezed shut. His hands were tightly clasped between his legs.

"Truce, okay? You got your reasons, I got mine."

"Yeah, but yours nearly got me killed."

"Let it go, Boone. We'll call it even right here. I'll get my answers somewhere else."

"That's what I'm afraid of."

"C'mon. You don't want me on your case. Besides, we weren't gonna kill you tonight. Lorch said not to."

"Lorch in on this?"

"No." Beaucharme pulled a hand from between his legs and held up a finger. "That he is not." He lowered the finger and sighed. "But he's lookin' out for ya. I think he likes ya."

"I'm flattered." (I wasn't. What next? Flowers from Joe Valachi?)

"This is a one-time offer, Boone. Good for this evening only. Do yourself a favor. Get off your current order of business up in Gatwick and go back to catching insurance cheats."

I waited.

"Or else what?" I asked.

Beaucharme sighed again, his pain subsiding.

"Or else it won't be the wood drill next time. And it won't be a lot of driving and a talk. Ya know what I'm sayin'?"

"Yeah, sure."

"We got a deal?"

"I really doubt it."

Beaucharme closed his eyes and emitted a long, tired sigh. "Lorch said you weren't soft. You want a ride anywhere?"

"Just a car. I'll drop it off downtown with the keys in it near City Hall."

"Go ahead. But you gotta call Carl off."

"How do I do that?"

"Just whistle. He'll come."

I whistled. I got into the Lexus, pulled it away from the Olds, and shone its lights down the dirt road. I set the emergency brake and kept the engine running. I went over to the Olds, took my gun off the passenger seat, and plucked the keys out of the ignition. A half minute later

Carl came up into the light. He had his gun drawn and he shielded his eyes with it.

"Tell him to put it down right there," I said to Beaucharme.

"Put it down, Carl. It's all right. Let him go."

Carl stood like a stunned deer in the headlights for a long time, but Beaucharme repeated the command. Carl put the gun in the road.

"Now walk over to the side toward the others," I said.

He did. I got into the car, locked the passenger door, released the emergency brake, put the car in drive and drove to where Carl had dropped the gun. I opened the door, picked it up in the dirt, and drove away. Before turning off the dirt road I tossed both Glocks and the car keys in the bushes.

I drove into town. It was five in the morning. A homeless man on a bench in the park behind City Hall was sitting up rubbing his face and yawning.

"You and me both, pardner."

I parked the car across from the Flynn Theatre and called Bellino from a pay phone in front of City Hall. The gardens in front of City Hall were fragrant with balsam chips. I breathed in their fragrance. Bellino answered after the third ring.

"Did I awaken you?" I said.

"I was meditating," Bellino said.

"What is it this week?"

"Kabbalah," he said in his flat voice. "Tree of Life. I'm opening my energy centers."

"Will there be ribbon-cutting ceremonies at any of them?"

"Just some heavy dignitaries. Angels, archangels, spirit guides. What's up? You still only call when you don't know which pitch to throw."

"I know which pitch to throw. I always know which pitch to throw."

"Like fun." Bellino's voice was like dry sand. "If it weren't for my signals you'd have no high school memories to be nostalgic about."

"If I didn't shake off your signals we'd never have won the state championship."

"That is bullshit, Boone, from yet another delusional prima donna pitcher."

"No, that is the truth, you self-aggrandizing grunt catcher."

"Temperamental know-it-all hot dog."

"Shit-for-brains Cro Magnon ball receiver."

"Grandstander."

"Simian."

"I've got a favor to ask," I said.

"You always got favors to ask. What is it this time? My manicotti recipe?"

"That too," I said. "No. I wondered if you could watch my back for a few days."

Bellino said nothing for a moment.

"Who is it?" His voice was flat and dry, fearless and alert. Any trace of joking was gone from it now.

"Three guys working for Romeo Beaucharme. After tonight, maybe more."

"Beaucharme, Jesus. What did you do? Fuck his sister?"

I outlined what was going on. Bellino listened. When I was through he said, "Biggest small-time back-country Canuck wise guy in the state and you go and stir him up."

"Wasn't intentional."

Bellino asked for descriptions of the three. I told him. Bellino grunted. In his capacity as a special investigator for National Life he had data on most of the illegal activity going on in the state. Most of the data he kept in his head. All of it helped make him the company's best investigator.

"The guy Carl is local," Bellino said. "Name's Carl Weingard. Been working for Beaucharme for years. The blond guy, I'm not sure. Could be new heat. The dark-haired guy sounds like this combo platter from Detroit Romey likes to bring in for special assignments, Jimmy Komykis. Jimmy Ice Pick. Arson, wet work, shakedowns, Jimmy's a wild one, a human Swiss Army knife."

I wiped my face with the palm of my hand.

"My guess is, he's the one who killed the woman down in Connecticut," I said.

"Back of the neck?"

"Yeah."

"That's Jimmy. If he finds this guy Jessup you're talking about, Jessup'll be dead, too."

I didn't say anything.

"You all right for a couple hours while I wait to call in and clear some time off with the company?"

"I'm all right," I said.

"They do anything to you?"

"No."

"You do anything to them?"

"A little."

Bellino grunted. He had taught me how to use karate and boxing to defend myself. He was very good at both. He had taught me well.

"I'll be around by nine," he said. "That soon enough?"

"Nine's perfect," I said. "Don't forget your energy centers."

We hung up. I made another call, this time to Western Union. EASTERN HEAVIES HUNTING YOU, my wire read. WHY? YOU TELL ME. YOU MIGHT THINK OF MOVING OUT FOR A WHILE. BOONE.

I was drunk on balsam. I squeezed and unsqueezed my fists to flex the ache out of them. It was a short message, only eighteen words, but you never knew. I dialed a cab. It came in two minutes. The cab ride from Burlington to my house cost me fifty bucks plus a tip, but I thought only of the wire, on its way to Arizona. Maybe it would do the trick, save a life; you never knew.

Words have power.

26

SIX HOURS LATER, I WAS SITTING IN THE LEATHER ARM-chair in Professor Kenneth Hewlitt's office watching the good professor sweat. It was a hot day, with still no sign of rain in sight, and he was sweating like a hog on an iron spit. Beads of sweat stood out on his grizzled pate, and sweat trickled down his neck and into his starched white collar. My unannounced visit wasn't making him any less sweaty.

"You lied to me," I said quietly. "You pretended to barely remember the name Gatwick Lake when in fact you owned a place up there."

Hewlitt was mopping his face with a linen handkerchief, pulling his Armani tortoiseshells off his face and wiping his eyes. "I'm sorry." He put the glasses back on. "I didn't think any of it was relevant to what you were asking about. Chelly's disappearance and so forth."

"None of it relevant," I said. "Armen Karillian's son burns down your lake house in '84 and you don't find that relevant . . ."

"Yes, well. It's an episode I suppose I've wanted to blot out."

"Why, pray tell?"

"I suppose it's because the whole business brings up, frankly, painful memories for me." He waved his hand around, would not look at me.

"I want to hear about the painful memories," I said. "Every one of 'em. And I don't want any more of your ivory tower bullshit."

"I wasn't trying to mislead you." Hewlitt spoke in a defeated voice.

"What were you trying to do?"

"As I say—" He twisted his neck in his collar. "I was just trying to ease my pain."

"Why did Mikah Karillian burn you out?"

"You'd have to ask him."

I stood up and reached across Hewlitt's desk and lifted him out of his seat by the front of his Turnbull & Asser shirt. It was white with wide pink stripes and white cuffs and collar. It went well with his cream-colored summer slacks. I did not care at all what it went well with.

"Listen, you sonovabitch," I said, drawing his face close to mine. "One woman's missing, another one's dead. You're gonna stop playing games with me or in fifteen seconds that elephant tusk's taking a ride up your ass."

"OK, OK!" Hewlitt fumbled his jostled glasses back against the bridge of his nose. "I'll talk. Please. That was just a figure of speech. Could you let go of my shirt? Please?"

I did and pushed him back in his chair. Hewlitt smoothed his damp shirt, squared the wings on his paisley bow tie.

"Where were we?" He gulped.

"Once again," I said. "Why did Mikah Karillian burn you out?"

Hewlitt took a breath and swallowed. "I'm not sure. It never came out in his trial. And he never took the stand."

"Nevertheless . . ."

"Nevertheless, I think he burned me out because"— Hewlitt looked around the room. —"because he thought I'd killed his father."

"He thinks you killed Armen Karillian . . ."

Hewlitt nodded.

"What would make him think that?"

Hewlitt sighed, fidgeted, saw that it was hopeless. "My wife had an affair with Karillian. That summer he disappeared. Our marriage went to hell after that. We didn't divorce right off, but we separated. The Karillian kid thinks I bore a grudge. I did, but not enough to kill off his old man. The kid wanted to burn me down in the house. But I wasn't there. I was out on the lake, fishing. A neighbor saw the flames and called the fire department. They found the kid in the woods with the rags and kerosene."

More arson. I nodded. "So at least one person—Mikah Karillian—thinks Armen didn't flee but was killed."

"At least one, yes, I guess."

"And what do you think?"

"I don't know. I know I didn't kill him."

"Why didn't you tell me that one of the reasons Karillian might've fled was that he was probably about to be charged in the overdose death of Jerry Leathers."

Hewlitt looked at me, startled, then contrite. "I thought I covered that with you when I said he might have been in hot water over something local up in Gatwick."

"Something local you knew all about."

"Something ugly I hadn't had to think about in twenty-five years, Mr. Boone."

"Think about it now," I said. "Did Karillian flee to escape prosecution over Jerry Leathers's death or did somebody like yourself, with a motive like yours, kill Karillian?"

"I don't know. I tell you I didn't kill anybody!"

"But you were around Gatwick at the time Karillian disappeared."

"Yes, I was around." Hewlitt's left eye twitched. His breathing was nervous and shallow.

"And your wife, too."

"Yes, Nadine was there."

"Where is she today?"

"Nadine? She lives in Seattle. If you wish to talk to her I can give you her address."

"Later." I watched his left eyelid sputter like a bulb on a weak circuit. "What do you remember about Karillian's disappearance?"

"What do I remember?" Hewlitt removed his glasses to rub his twitching eye. "I remember the hubbub over the Leathers boy's death. It was a big shock up there. Then about ten days later I remember Armen's wife, Cora, coming to my house with her children, asking where everybody was. It seems that not only Armen wasn't at the farm, but the others, what's their names, Spoonacre, Jessup, and Keel, weren't there either. Nobody knew where they'd gone. Then a week or so after that, Spoonacre, Jessup, and Keel came back, and any charges that had been considered against them were dropped."

"And Karillian by that time was gone."

"Yes."

"Did anyone look for him? Search for a body?"

"State police combed the farm, dragged the lakeshore, ran a sonar detector up and down the lake itself. Never found a sign of him. If I remember correctly, they put out an APB and got nowhere. That's when all the hagiography about his joining Ho Chi Minh or Fidel started up."

"When was the last time you saw Armen Karillian?"

"Me? Oh, Jesus." Hewlitt looked old, tired, defeated. "The last time I saw the bastard was about a week after the Leathers kid OD'd. It was nine o'clock at night and I was just walking back up to the house after an evening of fishing. I had caught a couple lakers and I was feeling pretty good. There was a garage in back of the house. It's still there—the fire never got it. I walked around behind it to get a board to clean the fish and there they were, Nadine and Karillian, naked as bluejays and going at it like a couple out of Hieronymous Bosch. I suppose I was too much of a gentleman to make a scene. I went into the house, shut the door, turned on the light and waited. When Nadine came in a half hour later I told her I wanted a divorce. That was it. That was the last time I saw Karillian."

"And you didn't kill him."

"No, I didn't. To be honest, I wouldn't have minded strangling both of them, but I didn't. Christ! Ask my ex."

"Maybe you waited until she wasn't a witness," I said.

"And maybe I didn't." The twitching eye undercut Hewlitt's effort at defiance. I gazed out the window. I could see Bellino, a tough, dark fireplug in black T-shirt and tight-fitting jeans, standing in front of Parkhurst, his thick arms folded across his thicker chest, his eyes scanning the streets for a silver Olds or a blue Lexus.

"Where's Taylor?" I turned to Hewlitt. "I'd like to ask her some questions."

"She's taken a few days off to visit friends in Boston. She said she'd be back in the office tomorrow. I take it you and she hit it off pretty well." I detected a look of lofty disapproval behind Hewlitt's twitching eye.

"You might say that." I stared him down. "She leave a number where she can be reached?"

"She didn't. Uh, look. Are we through? I'm not a daytime drinker but our conversation has given me a thirst for a Hanover Inn martini. With lunch, of course. You're welcome to join me."

I declined.

At the door Hewlitt had regained some of his patrician composure.

"I'm sorry I didn't level with you the first time," he said.

"So am I," I said. I took the moist material of his shirt into my fingers again. "But if you didn't level with me this time, chum, you're gonna be sorrier still."

I left him in the doorway wiping his face some more.

The outer office was filled with men and women in summer clothes. They were noisily jabbering in small groups about deconstructionism.

"Paging Dolph Schays!" I shouted above the din. "Dolph Schays?"

"Who is Dolph Schays?" a woman in a white pants suit asked me.

I looked at her. "Does anybody here know who Dolph Schays is?" I shouted.

The room went silent. Everyone blinked.

"Figures." I shook my head. And left the overheated room.

27

THE PHONE BOOK AT THE CONVENIENCE STORE ON THE hill above Gatwick had only one Leathers in it, Irwin, at 19 Lake Avenue. The address turned out to be not an avenue at all but a potholed single-lane road that ran along the southwest shore of the lake and petered out at the base of a granite cliff. There were oil storage tanks and a cable head-end station at the start of the road. The air shimmered hazily over the lake, and laundry hung dead on the clotheslines near the old winterized houses that in the twenties had been summer retreats for New York writers and editors. It was not hard to picture the summer people in their white clothes, in their Adirondack chairs on the little scraps of lawn that now were weed-grown, sipping their drinks and drawing succor from the old lake.

Nineteen Lake was a dilapidated clapboard house, two stories of unpainted dry rot and cracked window-panes on a crumbling brick foundation in a grove of old locust trees. There were seagulls on the sagging ridge of its roof and on a dumptruck-sized load of bottles and cans off the back door. There were old tires and washing machines in the silty mud under the trees. The gulls watched me with black judgmental eyes and did not budge when I walked up the spongy back steps. A breeze off the glassy waters of the lake carried the odor of gin, tuna fish, and gull guano.

I was getting tired again. When I turned around, I could see Bellino's black Bronco parked at the beginning of the road near the oil tanks. Once a backstop, always a backstop was one of several jokes between us.

I knocked on the back door.

From within I thought I heard a voice say something. The humidity made the day feel hotter than Arizona. I strained to listen through the door. The only sounds were the buzzings of flies around the pile of trash and the shrill calls of gulls on the roof.

I knocked again.

This time I heard a thump from within and a human moan. I opened the door. Inside, I was greeted by the sight of an old man sitting at a kitchen table with his head in his arms. The smell of gin intermingled with the odors of body sweat and old urine. A half-empty fifth bottle of Old Mr. Boston gin stood beside a jelly jar at the man's elbow. The jelly jar itself was nearly full. When I said "Hello," the head lifted and the eyelids slid back independent of each other, like the covers on two rolltop desks.

"Mr. Leathers?"

"Mmn."

The face was rounded, gray, and depressingly down-turned as if gravity and sadness controlled it completely. The bloodshot, drooping eyes looked not at me but at a space in middle distance between us. Looking at the thick, pelted, old shoulders draped in an old-fashioned strap undershirt, I thought of Artie Cole in his house at the other end of the lake. These men were like two drunken bookends. It was the material in between them that was giving me fits.

"Mr. Leathers, my name's Boone." I stood at the door and told him what I did. I told him who I was looking for. He shut his eyes.

"Cheryl," he said in a voice thick with alcohol.

"Your Jerry knew Cheryl, didn't he?" I tried to speak slowly and not to shout.

"What's that?"

I repeated the question. "Jerry knew Cheryl?"

"Oh, yes," the thick voice answered. "They were this close." He raised a tired hand and crossed his first two fingers. "Jerry loved. Cheryl. Cheryl. Was nice. To Jerry."

"Cheryl was nice to him."

"Yep." The broken man raised the jelly glass to his mouth and sloshed gin into it.

"What happened to Jerry, Mr. Leathers?"

"What happened?" The glass wobbled away from the mouth. "They killed him."

"Who killed him?"

"Cheryl's friends."

"But not Cheryl?"

"No. Cheryl loved Jerry."

"Which of Cheryl's friends killed him?"

The drooping eyes blinked and searched the table for the names.

"The hippie boys. Can't remember their names."

"Spoonacre? Jessup? Keel?"

"Not Jessup. His mother wouldn't abide it."

"His mother?"

"She worked up at Killbride's."

"She did?"

"Around then. Til she was fired." The old head bobbed on its soft shoulders.

"What about the other friends?"

"Keel." The tired lungs pushed the words out. "Spoonacre."

"Keel and Spoonacre? They killed Jerry?"

The tired head nodded almost imperceptibly.

"How do you know it was them?" I asked. "How do you know they killed him?"

The old head moved from side to side like an animated dinosaur's in a museum show. A sore on the corner of the mouth was the color of old hamburger. "Clapp said. Their prints were on. The needle."

"Chief Clapp said that?"

Again the head nodded. "Yep."

"Old Chief Clapp, right? Not the Clapp who's chief now?"

"Alden Clapp. Senior." The words squeezed out of the mouth in a tired groan.

"Chief Clapp found prints on the hypodermic syringe that killed Jerry. Is that what you're saying? And the prints were Spoonacre's and Keel's."

"Mmm . . ." Irwin Leathers rubbed his face with a thick, callused hand.

"What happened?" I said. "Why weren't Spoonacre and Keel arrested?"

The thick throat emitted a laugh like a death rattle. "Lack of evidence!" The voice said these words with the first shred of energy I had heard out of it. The energy conveyed emotions of cynicism and grief.

"I'm sorry," I said quietly. "I don't follow. What do you mean by lack of evidence?"

The big head bobbed on its thick soft neck and its lips blew out air in slow motion as if my question was elementary. "Clapp! Lost the needle!"

I shut the door behind me, drew a chair from the table and sat beside the stinking old man. "You're saying Chief Clapp Senior, who found prints on the hypodermic that killed your son, went and lost it?"

"That's what. I'm saying. That's what. He said."

It was my turn to rub my face and blink.

"The state police, the feds never got to see the needle?"

"Never got to." The old head shook sadly from side to side. "Clapp lost it. Month later, he died."

"How?"

"Heart attack, I think."

"Who became police chief after him?"

"Had three or four. Interim chiefs. Then when he was old enough. Clapp's kid took over."

"Alden Clapp junior," I said.

"Yep." The old man nodded. "Far as I'm concerned. He's a chip off the old block."

I looked around the kitchen. The sink was piled with dirty dishes and the countertops were littered with old gin bottles, stacks of mail, and clumps of cereal boxes. The linoleum floor, once white, was now as yellow as Irwin Leathers's teeth. The teeth were in a glass on the window shelf beside a rodent trap with a dessicated gray mouse under its wire bail.

"Mr. Leathers, why haven't you made more of a fuss about this?"

"Fuss? Fuss wouldn't bring. Jerry back. Would it?" He worked up a sly smile.

"Did either Clapp tell you not to make a fuss?"

The old head twitched and looked embarrassed suddenly. "Can't say. As they did."

"But you can't say as they didn't, either."

The head wouldn't answer.

"Has Cheryl been to see you lately, Mr. Leathers?"

The lips compressed in a saurian smile. "Couple weeks ago. Cheryl comes an' sees me. All the time."

"She does . . ."

"Mmn-hm!" The head nodded. "Cheryl's. A good one. So. Was Jerry. Over there." His neck twisted slowly, like an ancient turtle's. I looked behind him. On the back wall of the kitchen were framed photographs of a teenage boy. I got up and looked at them. There were about a half dozen. The boy was dark-haired and had the thick unfinished features characteristic of Down's syndrome patients. Jerry was beaming in all the photographs, a true love child. In one, wearing bell-bottom jeans and a tie-dyed T-shirt, he stood arm in arm with a teenage girl wearing blue eye shadow and an alarmingly short minidress. The girl looked like Chelly. Both she and Jerry were mugging for the camera like maniacs.

"Is this Cheryl?" I asked Irwin Leathers. But the father of the long-dead boy had passed out into drunken sleep.

Down at the oil tanks I told Bellino I wanted to go see the spot where Hewlitt's house had stood. Bellino listened to me without expression. He was wearing dark, Ray Charles-model sunglasses, and, as always, it was impossible to tell what was going on behind them. His forearm, bicep, and shoulder muscles bunched comfortably over the bottom of the window frame. His face behind the deep black of its perpetual five o'clock shadow was implacable.

"Sound OK to you?" I said.

"Lay on, Macduff," he said without emotion.

With windows up, I drove down the main street of Gatwick. I saw Bobby, the patrolman, walking into a pizza restaurant but he didn't see me. Bellino followed at a comfortable distance behind me. In the fifteen minutes it took to reach the intersection in front of the Karillian farmhouse I saw no suspicious vehicles or patrol cars. At the T near the lake, instead of turning right toward Arthur Cole's, I turned left and made my way up a steady rise toward the houses in the distance. There were two of them. As I climbed the rise I could see Bellino through my rearview, parking on the cement bridge that crossed the inlet to the lake. He'd look like a fisherman and have a clear view of traffic in all directions.

The houses at the top of the rise were vacant—summer houses that didn't appear to see much use. Their yards needed mowing and there were FOR SALE signs in front of both of them. As I passed the second one I realized that the light overhead had changed and now, in early afternoon, there might be a thunderstorm. Big thunderheads from the north end of the lake loomed behind an amphitheater of massing gray clouds. The surface chop of the lake far below refracted the grayness.

The road rambled a short ways down a hill and came out upon a turnaround surrounded by tall spruces. Off one side of the turnaround, through the trees, was a gravel driveway. I parked to one side of it, put my gun in its kidney holster under my shirt, stepped from the car, locked it, and walked in.

As the sky darkened, walking in under the dark trees was like entering an enchanted tunnel. The air was very still and suddenly cool. My footsteps crunched on the fine gray gravel. At the end of a hundred feet or so the trees ended and more light entered and the drive opened upon a big yard, its grass yellowed by drought, its neat perimeter defined by a thigh-high rock wall. The yard was very flat and dry, and there was an old white two-bay garage in the far distance of it. Behind the garage, thrusting jaggedly into the sky, was a fire-blackened brick chimney.

I walked to the garage. It was a vintage twenties one with six-over-six windows in the side walls, a pavilion roof, and doors that hinged vertically and opened away to the sides. Behind the garage, the proportions of the house were no longer discernible. The fire's remnants had been bulldozed into its cellar hole and earth had been smoothed over the remnants, leaving the chimney to appear like a naked brick trunk that had sprouted from the frizzled sod.

I peeked into the garage. Its right bay was vacant but the left held a car covered with a gray canvas tarp. It looked perfectly at home in the otherwise denuded space. I walked around the perimeter of the property and noted how it afforded good views of the lake between big old white pines and how you could look down the shore in either direction and not see any houses.

A rumble of thunder sounded in the distance over Jay. In the front left corner of the property, the rock wall opened to a long flight of flagstone steps descending to the lake. Flanking one side of the steps was a row of mature poplars. Though there was no wind to speak of, their leaves trembled in the gray air.

On the other side of the steps, a pole railing made of red cedars separated the steps from a steep gully. At the bottom of the gully a narrow brook, controlled by a pair of heavy sluice gates near the bottom of the steps, trickled away from the lake. The water in the brook was clear and tea-stained. The pebbles at its bottom seemed to undulate in the moving water.

I walked down the steps, thinking about Hewlitt walking down them that evening twenty-five years earlier and weighing what he had told me with everything else I knew. I felt I was trying to make an intuitive connection with Hewlitt's past. I thought it might help me understand everything else—even Jerry Leathers's death. I lost focus as the air stirred, the wind picked up from the north and I smelled the first drops of rain on the wind.

A crow, its tail feathers glistening in the gray light, was standing on the sandy strip of beach at the bottom of the steps. It was plucking at a clump of pink cloth. The cloth was a hair elastic known commonly, I believe, among women, as a scrunchy. As I approached, the crow dropped the object from its beak, made its harsh call, and flapped off. Then, as I looked at the big, cistern-sized space formed by the two heavy sluice gates near the bottom steps, something caught my eye that made my legs sag.

It was a face, submerged under roughly a foot of the sluice gates' six feet of water, and you knew before you even put your hand in the water and touched it that the face was dead. Its hair wavered in the mossy depths; its eyes, once alive to my own, evidenced longing and inwardness and regret.

The face in the water was Taylor Swimm's.

28

SHE LAY BETWEEN THE SLUICE GATES IN THE GRACEFUL arching posture of a high jumper frozen in midflight. The water between the gates suspended her like a specimen in amber. Her neck was stretched back and her legs were bent at the knees and her arms hung below her trunk in perfect stillness. I looked at her. Her mouth was partly open and the expression on her face reminded me of moments in our coupling. Experience had taught me not to get stuck in the carnality. Still, I ached inside at what I saw. A sudden sweep of wind shook the water's surface and made the body disappear in a shower of diamond lights. But it was only momentary.

I looked up and down the lake but nobody was on it that I could see and the beach was in a little cove that was snug and sheltered. I knelt and reached into the water and pulled the body up by the armpits. It was stiff, cold, and heavy with water and death. Water streamed out of the half-open mouth and out of the nostrils and the skin was clammy cold and rubbery and the face was blue and purple and grayish white. I braced my leg against a gatepost and tried tipping the rigid body forward. It wasn't easy. I heard snapping sounds in the hips. I twisted it enough sideways and leaned out over the water enough to see the long contusion on the back of the head. It was a long, narrow, ugly, bloody contusion made by something long and heavy and hard. It had split Taylor's scalp in the same way that my scalp had been split some days earlier, and its impact, I surmised, would have been enough to render her unconscious.

But not enough to kill her. Her killer had likely thrown her into the narrow sluiceway. She had been dead long enough for rigor mortis to have set in, but not so long for bloat to have begun and to have floated the body to the surface. So maybe a day then. Death did not come from the blow. Death had come from drowning. When I lowered the stiff body back toward the water I saw the blue bruise on the white, smooth sternum where the blouse button had ripped between the hard white breasts. It was the same blouse she had worn that night with me. It was the same shorts and sneakers. She was wearing no bra. The outline of the nipples looked no longer so delicious to me. It was only a guess and I was not one to be a good guesser right then, but I guessed that the killer had struck her from behind, then thrown her unconscious into the sluiceway. To have drowned her, he would have had to pin her underwater. How?

I lay the body gently back into the water and went to the cedar railing near the steps. The last rail, closest to the sluice gates, was dislodged, pinned at the ends by single nails barely driven into the tops of cedar posts. It was easy to imagine a killer wrenching the railing loose and using it as a pike to push the unconscious woman down, down, deep into six feet of water until her lungs filled.

The rail would explain the chest bruise. But it would not explain the murder itself, nor who the murderer was, nor what had brought Taylor Swimm to the charred remains of Kenneth Hewlitt's summer house in the first place.

I returned to the body. It had turned very slightly sideways underwater and I noticed the small black nylon carry bag still buckled around the hard white dead smooth waist. Reaching into the water, I touched the bag, which was at the hip, and felt the shape of a folded wallet inside. Carefully, I felt near the navel for the carry bag's quick-release clip, unsnapped it, and slid the carry bag free into my fingers.

I brought the carry bag out of the water. I walked behind one of the big pines alongshore and sat down against its trunk because my head had started to feel light. The wind had picked up and there were whitecaps far out

on the lake, and across the lake you could see fingers of
rain wetting the mountains.

The wallet I found inside the carry bag was a
woman's, an old, brown and very soft wallet, and although its leather was wet and dark on the outside, the
carry bag's water resistance and the wallet's own clasp had
prevented water from soaking its contents completely. In
fact, several of the cards and papers I found were mostly
dry. There were two twenties, a five, and four ones in the
bill section, three quarters, two dimes and two pennies in
the change pouch, and a variety of ID's and credit cards
under plastic. I looked at the cards. There was a Dartmouth part-time employee's ID with Taylor's picture on it
and the name TAYLOR ANNE SWIMM. There were Visa and
MasterCards made to TAYLOR A. SWIMM, each with expira-
tion dates within the year. And there were three or four
simple white embossed calling cards printed TAYLOR
SWIMM, with a post office box address in Hanover.

What threw me were the other pieces of identification.
Deeper into the plastic accordion-fold were Discover and
MasterCards in the name of W.J. GOLTZ. And in the name
of WILLOW JADE GOLTZ there was a Social Security card and
a very up-to-date Vermont driver's license.

As if it had come from someone else, I heard myself
groan.

Willow Jade Goltz's driver's license had Taylor
Swimm's picture on it.

I squeezed the license in my fingers. I stood and
stalked back to the body in the sluiceway. So that's it, I
said silently. You're Karillian's daughter. I looked at the
face on the license, so alive, and the face in the water, so
still and inward and lifeless.

"What were you doing here?" I shouted aloud. I was
suddenly very angry. I thought I could hear her voice in the
trees, straining to answer me. It was the wind.

"What was your game, Willow Goltz? Or Taylor
Swimm? Or whoever the hell you were?"

I slapped at the body with my hand, splashing myself
in the process. The wind picked up and the big drops of
rain that had been off in the distance started to land. The
water in the sluiceway darkened so suddenly that for a

moment the body of the beautiful woman it held seemed
to disappear in its darkness. But then the body came back
into view, like a hologram.

When it did I caught a glimpse of a peculiar object
shining at the bottom of the sluiceway. Or did I?

Several big raindrops fell into the sluiceway, shattering its surface, and then the rain came down hard. Zipping
the wallet back into the carry bag and hugging the carry
bag close to my chest, I stood over the sluiceway a minute.
Then I reached into the water one more time, leaned forward and pulled the dead woman's face toward mine, and
kissed the dead mouth. It was like nothing I had ever
kissed before. Rationalizing that the body was safest
where it lay, I lowered the head back into the water and
watched until it was again fully submerged. A great weight
pressed at my chest from inside. The rain was cold and
hard and soaked my shirt against my arms and back and
plastered the hair on my head. A bouquet of air bubbles
perhaps trapped in Willow/Taylor's clothes suddenly
erupted from the dark depths of the sluiceway. The rain
erased them.

"Not in vain!" The rain's urgent hiss on the lake
mimicked the dead woman's urgency in orgasm. Dazed, I
staggered back up the stone steps to the garage.

The lock on the left bay had been broken, and the car
under the gray dropcloth was Willow/Taylor's green
Volvo.

When I got back to Bellino, he said I didn't look too
hot and I told him I needed to make a phone call. At a
service station pay phone south of Gatwick I called my
friend Barry Files at state police/homicide and told him
about the body near the lake. He said I could fill him in
later. I told him he'd do well to keep Clapp out of the
loop, and he said he'd take the notion under advisement.

"I thought you and the girlfriend were taking the
summer off together," Files said.

"Yeah, well. Plans changed."

"You two haven't broken up now, have you?"

"Remains to be seen. But it's a possibility."

It must have been the way I said it because Files, nor-
mally quick with the needle, was silent for a while.

"I'm sorry," he said, finally.

"Don't be."

"Yeah, but I am anyway."

I told him to call me when he got back from the crime scene. We said our good-byes and I hung up the phone.

29

A CLOSER INSPECTION OF THE CONTENTS OF TAYLOR/ Willow's wallet revealed a name to me on the back of one of her calling cards. It was written in ballpoint in clear, firm block letters and underlined several times in slashing strokes. THE GREENTREE CORPORATION.

"Hey, Beleen! You know a business entity called the Greentree Corporation?"

Bellino was sitting in an Adirondack chair on my deck, a mug of freshly ground Colombia Supremo coffee in his thick paw, a nine-millimeter Weaver Nighthawk across his lap. The rain had stopped and Bellino was admiring a double rainbow in my front meadow. I was sitting at my dining room table with the contents of Taylor/ Willow's carry bag spread before me.

Bellino tilted his head back but did not turn around.

"The Greentree Corporation sounds like a place that sells condo units and homemade fudge. Never heard of it."

Neither had I. I had filled Bellino in on what I had seen at Hewlitt's property. I told him about Taylor's identity switch and how she had worked for Hewlitt. I did not tell him about my orgiastic night with her. The thought of that night put me in a deep funk. I tried not to think about it.

Bellino had listened quietly, his power palpable in its stillness.

"She might have been looking for something someone didn't want her to find," he said.

"Maybe." I thought about her apparent secretiveness

with Hewlitt, his telling me she was going to Boston, but then winding up dead at his place.

Hewlitt.

Now I tapped the edge of the calling card on the tabletop.

"What's the name of the guy who handles corporate stuff at the Secretary of State's office?" I shouted at Bellino again.

"Bernie Blodgett!" Bellino answered without hesitation. "Guy never thanked me for putting him on to a dummy corp down in Rutland last winter."

"He's a civil servant. Above the fray. I'm gonna give him a call. You want more coffee?"

"How 'bout the two Danishes I saw in the breadbox. You'll never eat 'em."

"I might eat 'em."

"Like fun. C'mon. It's the least you can do while I cover your ass."

He had a point.

"Nuked. No butter," he added.

I nuked and served him the Danishes. Then I put in my call to Blodgett. He was in and remembered me from a number of insurance-related cases I'd called him about. I asked him if he could tell me what the Greentree Corporation was. In his blandest of bureaucrat's voices he said he probably could.

"Let me pull it up on the computer."

Willow Jade Goltz at Kenneth Hewlitt's, I kept saying to myself. Doing what? Trying to succeed at what brother Mikah had botched?

Blodgett came back on the line.

"OK, it's up. What do you want to know?" he said.

"What've you got?" I took out my pen and notebook and waited.

"There's a lot!" Blodgett cleared his throat. "OK. Greentree Corporation is a closed corp based in Burlington. There's a P.O. address. You want it?"

I said I did. He gave it to me.

"Its officers and sole owners as far as I can see are John and Penelope Spoonacre . . ."

Spoonacre?

"Whose address," Blodgett continued, "is Champlain Valley Road down in Charlotte. There's a lot of DBA's."

"What's a DBA?" I hoped my voice wasn't conveying any of the surprise I felt. Spoonacre. Jesus.

"DBA means 'doing business as.' If a corporation is running other businesses under its aegis, it's required by the state to submit trade name registration forms for each one."

"I see."

"Greentree has at least ten listed here on screen one . . ." There came the sound of computer keys clacking over the wire. "Nine more on screen two."

"Hm." Interesting. Spoonacre overseeing so much. "What are they, the businesses?" I asked.

"Far as I can tell, they're all cash businesses," Blodgett said. "Reading at random, you've got Adventure Video, Scrub-a-Dub Wash Hut (I assume that's a laundromat), Jiffy Guy Carwash, Lakeland Cinema, Mack's Muffler, Simple Stop Gas, Wow Convenience. I've seen snappier names. You want me to go on?"

"No, that's OK. Where are these places located?"

Blodgett hummed one note as (I assumed) he scrolled down the screen.

"You've got a few down in Barre and Montpelier. But the preponderance are divided between Burlington and Gatwick."

"Gatwick?"

"Yeah, by the lake. I'd say Gatwick is nosing out Burlington for dominance . . . eight to six."

I stared at the July picture of cows in a field on the *Vermont Life* calendar hanging on my wall. Howcum, I wondered, there's never any cowshit in those pictures?

"Bernie, could you fax me a hard copy of that list? Like, today?"

"Sure. No problem."

He promised me the list in five minutes.

As we rang off, Bellino opened the sliding screen door and came back inside carrying his empty plate and mug and his gun. He looked like an ethnic freedom fighter or a tough version of Danny DeVito, if DeVito ever grew a foot and pumped iron.

"Where do you want these? You find anything?" he asked, chewing.

"Dishwasher. Blodgett's gonna fax me some dope on Greentree, but it's owned by our buddy, Spoonacre, and his wife, Penelope, with business interests up in Gatwick, among other places."

Bellino inclined his head. I had told him about Spoonacre and the other two Poetry Gang members.

"So the late daughter of the late poet Karillian had a late interest in Spoonacre's outside business interests."

"That's what it looks like."

Bellino ran his tongue noisily over his teeth to clean off the Danish. "What now, Sherlock?"

"I'll want to go back up to Gatwick tomorrow morning to check out some of Spoonacre's DBA's, but right now, while there's still daylight, I'd like to pay a visit to the address on Willow Goltz's license."

Bellino plucked the laminated card off the table.

"It's only got a post office box down in Landen."

"I know. But the P.O.'s in the general store, and if it's the same storekeeper who's been there when I've stopped through, he should talk."

Bellino nodded, flipped the card back on the table. Peered out the window at the vanishing rainbow.

"To what do you attribute our lack of thugee visitors today?" he said.

"They're probably still looking for their car keys," I said.

"You'd best beef up your firepower," Bellino said.

I showed him the Smith & Wesson nine under my shirt, the .22 Pocket Partner in my leg holster, and the Ithaca Stakeout in the door holster of my Saab.

"They loaded?" Bellino asked with vague menace.

"No. I thought I'd buy Greenie Stick'em Caps for 'em at the gyp joint near McDonald's. Of course they're loaded."

Bellino considered the weaponry. His upper lip twitched but he did not smile.

"You're beefed," he said.

30

LANDEN, VERMONT, POP. 631, IS A TINY VILLAGE SOUTH of Montpelier, near the eastern flank of the Northfield Mountains. On its lone main drag sits an ancient white United Methodist church with a flat wooden steeple and a peeling black clockface that never tells the right time, a two-room schoolhouse with a playground smaller than my side yard, a garage that specializes in the repair of Ski-Doo snowmobiles and Harley-Davidson motorcycles and a decrepit general store housing the village's post office and Tri-State Megabucks machine. Its valley location made Landen a boom market for satellite dishes. My boyhood recollection of it was of a village always in shadow. On those rare occasions nowadays when I fished the Dog, I passed through Landen, sometimes stopping at the general store for soda, coffee, or a road beer. The owner, a butcher, kept a meat counter in the back. The meat always looked bad. The canned goods featured brands I never saw anywhere else. The produce was always rotten. The cracker boxes had a film of dust on them. In the spring, night crawlers in a bucket shared space in the cooler with the beer and soggy sandwiches. I loved the place.

It was nearly six o'clock, closing time, when Bellino and I arrived in front of the Landen General Store in separate cars. In the store's little side lot Bellino backed his car next to mine so he could watch the road, and I locked my car's doors because of the shotgun, tapped my nose as I walked past Bellino, and went inside the store.

The post office window was closed for the day, and there was one woman at the counter, paying with food stamps for a quart of milk, a loaf of bread, and two cans of Dinty Moore beef stew. The woman wore flip-flops and a quilted pink bathrobe and she smelled bad. The grocer, in a white shirt, black necktie, and meat-stained white apron, had Brylcreemed brown hair and steel-rimmed glasses with very thick lenses. The lenses were light-sensitive or lightly tinted and gave him the air of an East European apparatchik. He was wrapping some slices of salami in thick butcher paper for the woman. He tied the package with string. String! The good old days.

When the woman was gone I approached the counter.

"Help you?"

I showed him my license. He barely glanced at it; instead, he peered at me through his secret agent glasses.

"I'm looking for a woman named Willow Goltz," I said.

"Doesn't live here anymore." He spoke with an unaffected Yankee twang that vaporized certain r's and whose tone was as tart as old cider.

"She had a post office box here, though, didn't she?"

"That's right. Used to live in the apartment across the street." He pointed out the store's big plate glass window to an old white triple-decker that sat out of the late afternoon heat under a pair of soaring maples.

"She from around here?"

"Not exactly. Her mother had a place here years ago. Just down the block."

"She still around, the mother?" I knew she wasn't.

"No." The grocer crooned and pushed his tongue against his mouth in the manner of the circumspect.

I waited for more. When nothing more was forthcoming, I said, "Where is she?"

"The mother?"

"Yeah."

"Dead." He looked up to gauge the impact of the word on me.

"How?"

The Yankee mouth sprang open like a whittled doll's before the words came out. "Suicide, they say."

I nodded. It squared with what Hewlitt had told me at our first meeting.

The grocer's face was cool and implacable. "Eup. Medical examiner's report said she shot herself with a pistol." He raised his eyebrows to let that one sink in, too. "Course, I was on the ambulance squad back then, and I can tell you firsthand it didn't look like no suicide to me."

We looked into each other's face. "It didn't."

"Nope."

"How's that?"

"Waal!" The face became quite animated. "Position of the body for one thing. Position of the gun for another. Gun's in the woman's right hand, entry wound's in the left temple. To pull the trigger she'd have to have been a carnival contortionist."

He demonstrated with his arm, orbiting it around his head.

"I see what you're saying."

"Plus, she left no suicide note, no provision for the two kids."

"Right. Willow has a brother, doesn't she?"

"Ye-ss! Moondog or Milksop or whatever his name was. Year older than the girl. Cute kids. Mother adored 'em. But she was a round heels, the mother."

"Was she?"

"Augh! Always a different man, every week. Sometimes not every week, sometimes every day."

"You remember any of the men who came through?"

"No, this was twenty-three, twenty-four years ago. Folks said she was the little victim whose husband skipped out on her, left her with the kids. Waal, she played that role like a cat in perpetual heat."

"What do you mean?"

"Waal, she never worked. I saw the boyfriends come in, buy her a week's groceries, buy the kids anything they wanted. Oh, yes, she knew how to string a man along. But work . . ." He shook his head and clucked his tongue.

"You don't remember any of the boyfriends."

"Not really. They came in all sizes and shapes. Slobs and gentlemen. Young and old. Married men and singles. She had 'em all."

"How long was she here before her death?"

The grocer sniffed. "Eighteen months? Maybe two years."

"And the kids were still little."

"When she died, the boy, MicMac, whatever his name was, couldn't have been more than four. The girl was what. Two or three?"

I pictured two little kids in a bare room minus their mother. Not a pretty sight.

"What happened to the kids after their mom died?"

"State took 'em. Mother left no will. There was no next of kin. Far as I know, state put 'em through foster homes and private orphanages until they were eighteen. I lost track of 'em until about a year ago. Then the girl come back, full of questions about her mother and how she died. Stayed a couple months across the street. Then moved out."

"She learn anything?"

"From me?"

"You or anybody else."

"I told her more or less what I've told you. It appeared to me she'd reached the same conclusion about her mother's death on her own."

"She leave a forwarding address?"

"Nope." The grocer began wiping down the counter, straightening the sundries clustered around the cash register. "She asked if she could keep her mailbox and pick up her mail here. I said fine. There's no law against keeping a P.O. address."

"She say anything about where she was going next or what she was doing?"

"Said she was gonna look for work someplace else, wasn't sure where, probably in the area, so it was more convenient for her to come back here for her mail until she got settled. That was six months ago. As far as I can tell she hasn't gotten settled yet."

"You seen her recently?"

He considered. "Couple weeks ago."

"You have any idea where she lived before she came here?"

The grocer thought for a moment. "No."

"What about the brother? I think his name was Mikah? What happened to him?"

The grocer snorted and spat into a trash barrel at his elbow. "He went to prison!"

I feigned surprise. "For what?"

"Arson! Burned somebody's summer place up on Gatwick Lake. Rumor round here at the time was, the place belonged to one of the mother's old lovers."

"A boyfriend of the mother owned the place that the son burned?"

"I wouldn't call him a boyfriend. More like a play-boy. Thought he was the cat's own ass in his little red MG." The grocer displayed long yellow teeth.

"So you remember the boyfriend then?"

"If it's the same one. He'd come off and on through here in his tailored clothes and little driving cap all the time the mother lived here. MG had the steering wheel on the right. He was real proud of that."

"You remember his name?"

"Nope."

"Was it Hewlitt?"

"Don't remember."

"You know where he lived? Worked?"

"Nope."

It didn't matter. I had a pretty good idea who the owner of the red MG was.

I thanked the grocer for his time. He said not to worry about it. I asked him if he had any theories about who might have killed the mother. He didn't. "Maybe the son was on to something," he said.

Outside in the parking lot, sitting in Bellino's car, I told him what the grocer had said.

"And Hewlitt still owns the cherry 'G," Bellino said. I nodded.

"This Hewlitt sounds like a slippery dick," Bellino said.

I didn't disagree. Bellino asked me what I wanted to do next.

"I want to go home, eat a hamburger and french fries with homemade chili sauce and fresh peas from the garden, drink beer and burp, go to bed before ten, and catch up on my sleep," I said.

"While I stay up all night and keep you alive . . ."

"We'll sleep in shifts," I said. "I sleep eight. You sleep two."

"Fuckin' A. I'd let you get killed before I agreed to a deal like that."

"Two hours. A floor and a blanket. It's the best I can do."

"Eat shit and die," Bellino said.

Throughout the drive home as the light dropped and washed the green landscape in gold, I thought about Willow/Taylor's mother and all those men. It made me think about my own amazing night with Willow/Taylor and how each of us that night had used each other. I felt bad about my behavior. I felt worse for the dead women.

Like mother, like daughter.

Sometimes it's in the genes.

31

BLODGETT'S FAX FROM THE SECRETARY OF STATE'S OFFICE
ran two pages and contained the names of nineteen businesses owned by the Greentree Corporation, John A.
Spoonacre, Esq., president. Four were in Barre, one in
Montpelier, six in Burlington, and eight in Gatwick.

The next morning, after a peaceful night of split
shifts, Bellino and I studied the list over a breakfast of
blueberry pancakes, real Vermont maple syrup, Canadian
bacon, scrambled eggs, orange juice, and coffee.

"Blodgett's right. They're all cash businesses," Bellino
said.

"Majority of them in Gatwick," I said.

"The businesses could be clean," Bellino said. "Or
they could not be."

"What I don't get is, if I was Spoonacre, why would I
be in a rush to establish businesses in a town where I'd had
a serious scrape with the law?"

"How long's Greentree been incorporated?" Bellino,
sitting across from me at my dining room table, tried to
read the first fax page upside down.

"Says here since 1974. That's the same year
Spoonacre graduated from Harvard Law."

"Ambitious little fuck to be setting up his own closed
corporation right out of law school."

"I wonder how many of these cash businesses he
bought at the time he incorporated," I said.

"One way to find out," Bellino said.

"You want to take a ride up to Gatwick with me in

the Batmobile? I'm persona non grata with the local police there."

"Does that mean I get to show my face in town and you don't?"

"Something like that. You could run a title search on a couple of these businesses while I scope 'em out through the Duck Blind."

"Does the refrigerator in that piece of shit still work?" Bellino asked.

"In the Batmobile? Absolutely. I'll stock it with whatever your little Neopolitan heart desires. You want lasagne, we'll get lasagne. You want *pasta e fagiole,* we'll get *pasta e fagiole.* Ditto Chianti classico and eggplant parmesan. For you, Ernie-o, the best."

Bellino rubbed his hand over his sharkskin jaw and feigned repugnance. "Cold lasagne in a stinking van with you," he muttered. "I must be fucking nuts."

We armed the Batmobile after breakfast. The Batmobile was my surveillance vehicle, a '79 blue Ford panel truck I had bought many years ago from a Red Sox hitting phenom turned bankrupt flash-in-the-pan has-been. It was nondescript on the outside, a stoic if slightly rusted survivor of many Vermont winters and many frame-rattling trips over washboarded back roads. Inside, though, in what I called the Duck Blind, I had equipped it with a Zeiss periscope mounted to a Sony 8 minicam that fed the Zeiss's reflections to one of two NEC color video monitors and a top-of-the-line Fisher tape machine. The Zeiss's two viewing ports gave me the freedom to do surveillance and record what I saw simultaneously. The monitor meant I could lock on a location and, if nothing was happening, read a book or pumice my nails and glance at the monitor from time to time until something did happen. With my own hands I had installed shag carpeting on the floor, a wall and a door between the Duck Blind and the driving compartment, a captain's chair at the periscope, a cushioned sleeping bench along the van's right wall, small, covered peepholes through all four walls, and pine storage cabinets, a nautical sink, and a minirefrigerator along the left. A dented aluminum thimble covered the top of the Zeiss where it stuck through the roof, shielding it from prying eyes. A couple of NRA decals and a BYE BYE BERNIE sticker on the back bumper completed the look. Now if I could only amortize the fucker.

We loaded the Batmobile with my Ithaca Stakeout and Smith & Wesson nine and Bellino's Weaver Nighthawk, his short-barreled Remington 870 twelve-gauge, and his Sig Sauer P-225 nine. At DJ's in Johnson we bought four ham-and-cheese grinders with the works, four liters of Pepsi, two liters of Mountain Dew, two bags of State Line potato chips, a six-pack of Otter Creek ale, two bags of Pepperidge Farm Nantucket chocolate chip cookies, a fistful of Slim Jims, and twenty-four pieces of Bazooka bubble gum.

Looking at the stuff arrayed across the counter Bellino growled, "What about lunch?"

We drove north for about a half hour through regions of marsh and softwood where the winters were typically harsh and the land was rolling. This was the northern end of the Vermont piedmont, where there were many ponds and streams and where the glaciers had scraped the land, leaving random mountains. Bellino drove, his eyes flicking back and forth between the road, the landscape, and the view from the side-view mirror. He talked little and his head barely moved. His hands on the wheel were thick and hard, the muscles across his chest and back rolling and solid.

Somewhere above Eden the cellular phone rang. It was Files from state police/homicide.

"You're on the road," he said.

"I'm on the road."

He got down to business quickly. "The woman's body was where you said we'd find her."

"Yeah."

"She was pretty beautiful."

"Yeah."

"I'm confused, Boone. You said the woman's name was Willow Goltz, right?"

"Right."

"Then why did we find registration in the Volvo's glove compartment to Willow Goltz but Visa bills and other mail addressed to someone named Taylor Swimm?"

"They're the same person."

"Huh?"

"Willow Goltz was using the name Taylor Swimm as an alias. Why, I'm not quite sure. I think it has something to do with her going undercover to investigate her mother's death."

I explained what the grocer had told me about Cora Goltz's "suicide." I could hear Files scribbling away as I talked. I did not mention Hewlitt by name but I did say that back in the early seventies, before she died, Cora Goltz had had a number of boyfriends.

"And you think this Willow Goltz thought one of the boyfriends murdered the mother?"

"There's a strong possibility. She sure seems to have gone to a lot of trouble to change her identity so she could poke around."

"This Willow Goltz have anything to do with what you're working on?"

I spoke carefully. "Indirectly. The spouse of my client had a literary research relationship with Willow Goltz in Hanover. Goltz, using the name Taylor Swimm, was working for a Dartmouth professor down there."

"Kenneth Hewlitt."

"Right."

"On whose property in Gatwick the dead woman was found."

"Right."

"What were you doing there, Boone?"

"The son of a literary figure my client's spouse admired apparently burned Hewlitt's house on Gatwick. The arsonist's name is Mikah Karillian. Hold on to your hat, but I have it on pretty good knowledge that Mikah Karillian is Willow Goltz's brother."

"Wait a minute, wait a minute. You're saying that the brother of the dead woman we found on Hewlitt's property burned down the house on that property?"

"In 1984," I said.

Files, on the other end of the line, was speechless for a moment. "Why?"

"You'd have to ask Mikah Karillian. Failing that, your next best bet is Hewlitt himself."

I could hear Files's careful, logical, analytical mind trying to wrap itself around everything I had said so far.

"Have you talked to Hewlitt?" he asked.

"In the context of searching for my client's spouse, yes."

"Who's your client?"

"As you know, I'm not at liberty to say."

"But if I talk to Hewlitt, he'll tell me anyway," Files said.

"You're probably right," I said.

"So who's your client?"

"A Gatwick resident named Arthur Cole." I did not tell Files that Cole was Win Killbride's son-in-law. "He'd like to keep the spouse's status quiet," I said.

"I got no problem with marital confidentiality," Files said. "You gonna be home later on?"

"Maybe. Maybe not. Try this number if you can't reach me there."

"Fine." Files paused. I braced. "One last question. You touch the body, Pete?"

"What?"

"You touch that body?"

I sighed. "Only to see if it was dead. And it was."

"Dead and murdered," Files said. "We can't find a wallet or an ID on the body."

"Maybe she wasn't carrying one."

"We're down here with a search warrant at Hewlitt's garage apartment where she lived and we can't find one here either."

I said nothing.

"You find a wallet on her, Pete?"

"Not that I can recall."

"You find an earring?"

"Negative."

"We found one at the bottom of the pool. Can't find the second on the dead woman."

I said nothing.

"You revise your recollection," Files growled, "give me a call."

When Files had rung off, Bellino looked over at me through his sunglasses.

"You know, stealing evidence from the crime scene is obstruction of justice," he said quietly.

I looked at him. "I know."

"It's a felony matter that could easily mean loss of one's P.I. license, a fat fine, and probably jail time."

"I know that, too."

Bellino nodded to himself, looked back at the road.

"You know the dead woman's carry bag and wallet?" he said.

"Yeah?"

"I think you should wipe 'em down and wrap 'em in one of the Glad bags back there in the Duck Blind and at the next roadside trash receptacle we encounter, I think you should chuck 'em."

"You do . . ."

Bellino nodded.

"Since when did you start getting paranoid?" I said.

"It's a selective kind of thing with me. Touching that bag this morning, I felt it giving off bad karma."

I said nothing.

"It'd be a chicken shit way to ruin one's career," Bellino added.

"You're probably right."

At a rest stop outside the little town of Lowell I had Bellino pull over. I wiped down everything in Willow/Taylor's wallet, the wallet itself, and the carry bag. I put the wallet's contents back in the wallet, put the wallet in the bag, and zipped it shut. Then I unzipped it and removed the Dartmouth picture ID made out to Taylor and the Vermont picture driver's license made out to Willow and the calling card with Greentree written on it.

Bellino observed me.

"I'm keeping these for now," I said.

Bellino's right shoulder shrugged indifferently.

I made sure there was no traffic coming in either direction before I stepped out of the van and dropped the knotted bag into the trash barrel. There was a very used and very messy disposable diaper in there. With a stick I flipped it open and slathered its contents on the bag, then left it lying there as a sort of excremental deterrent. I was gagging by the time I got the lid on.

Bellino quietly watched me as I got back in the van.

"You and this Goltz woman, you were close," he said in his dry voice. "Weren't you?"

I said nothing.

"Never mind. It was on your face yesterday. Boone, it's none of my business except—with everything else going on—you know, this missing woman, shooters coming after you and shit"—Bellino pushed the back of his forearm against my upper arm—"you'd best get over her."

"It's not a problem," I said.

"You sure, buddy?"

"I'm sure."

Bellino lifted his sunglasses and looked into my face. His eyes were green and as flat as a snake's. "Just remember, Boone, and I'm fucking serious about this: Suffering spoils the aim. And all suffering stems from desire."

"End quote, the Buddha," I said. "Satori."

Bellino snapped his fingers under my nose. His eyes blazed. "You better believe it."

32

THE GATWICK TOWN HALL WAS A STONE BUILDING ON Main Street in the center of town. There was a metered parking lot in back and from it I could see the Gatwick Police Station a half a block down. Bellino parked in an empty space a few rows away from the town hall, and I scuttled via the through door into the Duck Blind. Bellino took the list of Greentree businesses and put it in his leather briefcase.

"Who are you?" I asked.

"I haven't decided. I'm either me from National Life or Joe Blow developer looking for some easy targets."

"Don't be gone long."

"Don't eat my grinder."

He slammed the van door after himself and locked everything. Through the left-side peephole I watched him enter the back door of the town hall. From the right-side peephole I could watch the police station. To watch better I upped periscope and focused on the building and back lot. There wasn't much going on back there. Three road crewmen had a gravel spreader disassembled in front of the town garage and Bobby the cop was yakking with them. You saw the easy arrogance and thick-gutted swagger with which he talked to the road crew. I did not like him. I touched the sutures, now a prickly dried scab along the back of my head. I would have to go to Anny's and get them taken out soon. Or maybe Bellino could take them out. If Nan was here she would take them out but she's not here so stop thinking like that. I disliked Chief Alden Clapp, Jr., even more than Bobby. What he had done still angered me. The anger was like the slow burning in my brain of very thin crossed low-voltage wires.

I saw him, I saw the chief. In his dark green Pontiac civilian's car he pulled into the station's back lot and gestured Bobby over to the driver's window. They talked for a moment; then Bobby went around the car and opened the passenger door and got in, and the chief gunned the engine and the Pontiac slid out of the lot. It turned right, toward Main Street, and at the corner of Main it turned north in the direction of the lake.

Through the front-wall peephole I could see through the windshield toward one of the businesses I remembered on the Greentree list. It was called Action Arcade and it occupied a rear storefront behind Main Street. At ten o'clock in the morning Action Arcade wasn't seeing much action. But out of habit I watched it. At around 10:05 a jug-eared guy in a white short-sleeved shirt stepped out of the arcade and leaned against the doorway, smoking a cigarette. He took only a few puffs on it before tossing the cigarette on the pavement and crushing it out with his shoe. He looked both ways before casually turning and walking back inside. As soon as the door shut behind him a car pulled in front of the building. It was a late-model, mint blue BMW 520i and the driver was none other than John Spoonacre. He was wearing a summer-weight navy blue suit, a light blue Oxford cloth shirt, and a yellow necktie, and he stepped out of the car with the stricken alertness of a marked man soon expecting a bullet through the ribs. He looked around the lot, nervously pushing his tortoiseshells against his nose, and locked his car and strode nervously into Action Arcade.

Two minutes later a second car pulled into the lot next to Spoonacre's. It was Chief Clapp's Pontiac, and the chief, wearing a silk tweed blazer, tan slacks, and a crimson knit tie, casually emerged from it, toting a briefcase. Bobby slid into the driver's seat, the chief said a few words to him, and Bobby backed out and drove off. The chief strolled into the arcade, looking both ways and whistling.

I watched the arcade through the periscope. Twenty minutes went by. Nothing happened. At around ten-thirty, after having been in the town clerk's office for over a half hour, Bellino returned. His face looked cool and implacable.

"That place is a fucking Jurassic Park," he said, sitting in the driver's seat and speaking to me through the Blind door, which I opened a crack.

"You find anything?"

"Oh, yeah, I found something. But their filing system is a disaster. They keep index cards on every real estate transaction and supposedly file things chronologically in the deed books. But it's haphazard. The town clerk herself is this dinosaur who for all intents and purposes ought to be given a quill pen and a ticket to Tiny Tim's house."

I told him who I had seen walk into Action Arcade.

"That's interesting." For a moment Bellino seemed lost in his own thoughts.

"So what did you find?" I said.

Bellino shook his head to clear it. "I decided, since Spoonacre incorporated Greentree in '74, that the smart thing to do was start there. See if he made any of his Gatwick purchases that year."

"And?"

"Oh, yeah."

"How many?"

Bellino held up four fingers on each hand. "All eight of 'em."

"He bought eight businesses the year he graduated from Harvard Law."

Bellino nodded.

"I wonder if he's independently wealthy," I said.

"Doesn't have to be." Bellino sniffed.

"How so?"

"Well . . ." Bellino spoke slowly. "According to the deed books, our friend Spoonacre bought each of the eight properties here in Gatwick for, quote, 'a dollar and other considerations.' Unquote."

"Really?"

"Mm-hmm. Seller was this corporation called Roundstock. No other reference in the book. I called Blodgett to see what he had on Roundstock . . ."

"And?"

"He had nothing."

"Nothing?"

"Yeah, he figured it dissolved as corporations do. A long time ago."

"So Spoonacre buys properties here for a lousy eight bucks and the corporation that sells it to him disappears."

"That's the long and short of it," Bellino said.

"Chief Clapp appears to have some involvement in this," I said.

Bellino nodded. "What do you want to do?" His eyes flicked around the lot, looking for shooters.

"Spoonacre looked plenty nervous walking into the arcade. You want to wait here until he comes out?"

"Sure." Bellino shrugged. "This is as good a place as any to be ambushed."

We waited, me in the Duck Blind, Bellino in the driver's seat. It was a pleasant sunny day, not as hot as it had been in recent days and not as humid. Cars moved in and out of the back lot but none was a shooter's car and nobody bothered us. Nobody approached the Action Arcade either. At ten minutes to eleven, Spoonacre emerged from the building. His suit coat was on his shoulder and his light blue Oxford cloth shirt was dark with sweat. His face was pasty with shot nerves. He fumbled his car keys from his pants pocket and shakily unlocked the driver's door and climbed in behind the wheel. As he backed the BMW from its space, Chief Clapp strolled from the arcade and Bobby materialized out of nowhere with the green Pontiac.

"What do you want to do?" Bellino said.

"Tail Spoonacre," I said. "Be discreet about it."

"I'm always discreet."

Bellino picked up the BMW on Main Street and kept a safe distance behind it. He followed it south out of town and we didn't stop the tail for several miles until it became fairly clear that Spoonacre was heading back to Burlington.

"Another lead bites the dust," Bellino said.

I stuck my head out the door of the Duck Blind.

"Let's go back into town and look at the other businesses on Greentree's list. Even though it's not finding us the woman, it might still get us somewhere."

Bellino nodded. He started the engine and hung a neat, sharp U-turn back toward town.

For the remainder of the morning we looked at the businesses on Greentree's list. On Gatwick's Airport Road, a land of strip development and fast-food franchises, we passed the Jiffy Guy Carwash, the Lakeland Cinema, and the Gas 'n' Such gas station convenience store. Near one of the residential neighborhoods we saw the Scrub-a-Dub laundromat and the Gatwick Dry Cleaners. And on the main drag, besides Adventure Arcade, we found Adventure Video/Music and, next to it, Wow Convenience.

"American nomenclature at its best," Bellino said.

"Park over there." From behind the partly opened door I pointed to a parking lot beside a small Price Chopper store. It sat diagonally across from Wow Convenience and Adventure Video/Music and there were several good unmetered parking spots near the street that suited our stakeout purposes well. Bellino nosed into one that was away from the main flow of traffic and cut the engine. He slouched in the driver's seat and together we looked across the street at the two stores. Both were in an old red brick building that in its lifetime had doubtless seen other franchises and the glitz in their windows was in contrast to the building's superannuated gentility. Posters for *Pulp Fiction, Boxing Helena* and *Legends of the Fall* hung in one window of Adventure Video/Music. Blowups of CD covers by Phish, R.E.M., and Nine Inch Nails hung in the other. The windows of Wow Convenience were a snaggle of neon beer signs. In the little lake town the two stores were lively eyesores on a street of old buildings with quaint facades. You wanted to visit the stores yet you wished them poorly. People were using them both at the noon hour.

"I'm gonna go over and take a look at 'em," Bellino said. "You want anything?"

"No, I'm fine."

He left and locked me in and I shut and locked the door to the van's driving compartment and watched him through the periscope. Crossing the street, his movements were slow, smooth, and thick-muscled like a bear's and they reminded me of when he used to walk to the mound when I pitched—calm, smooth, and unfazed by anything happening around us.

He went into Wow Convenience first and a few minutes later he emerged, stood on the sidewalk to take in the noon traffic, then sauntered into Action Video/Music. He was gone for nine minutes and when he came back he was carrying two plastic video boxes and a plastic bag containing several CD's.

"What did you get?" I asked when he squeezed through the driving compartment into the Duck Blind.

"For you, *North by Northwest.* For me, *The Last Emperor.*"

"Had I known you were going to rent something I'd have made some requests."

"I have no desire to see *Aliens III,*" Bellino said.

"There's nothing to be afraid of. It's only a movie."

Bellino tossed the tapes on the counter and stretched out on the daybed. He took out the CD's: *Voodoo Lounge* by the Rolling Stones, *J Mood* by Wynton Marsalis, and *Shepherd Moon* by Enya.

"Enya?" I said, snatching the disk away from him.

"I like Enya," he said, snatching it back.

"Keep those off the expense account," I said.

Bellino flicked his chin with his fingers at me.

"Interesting shit over there," he said, looking at the register tape.

I waited.

"Both places offer discounts if you pay in cash," he said. "At Wow it's not much—like, four percent—but at Adventure Video/Music it's ten percent."

"Not bad," I said.

"The gross total with tax for the two video rentals and the three CD's came to forty-two dollars and sixty-one cents," Bellino said. "With my ten-percent discount I paid thirty-eight thirty-four. My savings on the merchandise exclusive of tax was four dollars and a dime. With the tax it was four dollars and twenty-seven cents." He turned the receipt over in his fingertips.

"So," I said, "they give a nice discount."

"Right." Bellino handed me the receipt. "Find it on the sales slip."

I looked for it. It wasn't there. I said as much.

"The girl at the register calculated the discount on a sheet of paper *after* she had rung up the full amount on the register," Bellino said.

I nodded. "You gave her thirty-eight thirty-four. She rang in forty-two sixty-one."

"Gives the management four dollars and twenty-seven cents to play around with," he said. "The place was doing a lively business when I was in there. They're open seven days a week from nine to nine. You figure, conservatively, a place like that is grossing a half million a year. Conservatively."

"Of which ten percent or fifty thousand bucks is ghost money," I said.

"It gives Spoonacre a nice little niche to process fifty thousand bucks from someplace else," Bellino said.

"If Greentree gives you nineteen niches to work with at a conservative average, say, of twenty-five thousand bucks a year . . ."

". . . That's four hundred seventy-five thousand dollars you could launder and not even raise an eyebrow," Bellino said.

"Spoonacre as a money launderer," I said, peering back into the periscope. "Taking meetings with the town's chief of police."

"You know something," Bellino said, "I'll bet it's more than four seventy-five a year. With some of those places he's got over in Burlington, I'll bet he could run a million bucks through his books and no one's the wiser."

"He'd be paying state and federal taxes on whatever he launders, though," I said.

"Yeah, but if he does it right, fabricates phony billings, pays his wife or whomever a consulting fee, he knocks his tax bill down, too. In any case he considers the tax a small price to pay for cleaning up black or dirty money."

"Or he's clean and we're blowin' smoke," I said.

"One way to start finding out," Bellino said.

"I'll take first shift," I said.

"You want to do lunch right off?" Bellino sat up and put the CD's on the floor.

"What've you got in mind?"

"Well, seeing as my schedule was thrown off this morning by being your bodyguard, I thought I'd meditate."

He looked calm and serious. I resisted a snappy putdown. Besides, I knew that a meditated Bellino was an effective Bellino. "Be my guest," I said.

I watched him take off his shoes and position himself on the daybed. With surprising flexibility for such a big man he drew his feet up and tucked them against his hips. He shook out his arms and rolled his shoulders and neck and placed his hands palms up on his knees and touched his index fingers to his thumbs. I watched him take three deep cleansing breaths and close his eyes. The lotus position. I had taught it to Bellino the year my wife died, the year I came back from India. His response to the lotus had surprised me. It was as if it unlocked something within him and sent him traveling in a new direction. Before I had shown him the lotus he was Belleen, my old catcher, my teammate, the power lifter, a grunt. But after he had tried it for a couple weeks he quietly became a student of religious truths. I would come upon him in his gym reading *The Perfection of Yoga* or *Sayings of the Buddha* or *The Tree of Life* or excerpts from the Bible or the Koran or whatever and he would lay the given book down and smile and not say anything about it. But I could see a difference in him. I could see it in the way he did things. He did things without fear or frustration. He did things with love. He did not remark on his transformation and he never preached. He did not espouse meditation or recommend that I do it. He did not push his beliefs on me nor did I seek them. He simply lived. And when I asked, just as simply, he showed up.

Now I let him do his meditation while I watched the storefronts through the periscope. There were twelve rechargable wet-cell batteries in a compartment below the taping system. I switched on the first pair and switched on the video monitor. I switched on the minicam and fiddled with its focus knob and the focus on the periscope. I pulled up an image on the monitor of both storefronts. I could see the curb, the sidewalk and both stores' front doors. I sat back in the captain's chair and watched. Customer traffic into both stores was moderate but steady. People came out of Wow Convenience with sandwiches, sodas, coffees, beer, and basic groceries; the traffic out of Adventure Video/Music was mostly rental tapes. Bellino came out of his trance after thirty minutes or so and we ate our grinders and chips, drank our Pepsis, and watched the monitor. When either of us needed to take a leak we used a small chemical pot in the van's back left corner. We whiled away the afternoon watching *North by Northwest* on the second monitor and playing chess on a magnetic board I kept in the van. Bellino beat me two games straight playing old Ruy Lopez and Paul Morphy openings. Outside, we could hear cars and people passing but nobody bothered us. We were invisible. The van became warm with our body heat and the electrical equipment's output. I switched on a small roof fan and cracked a roof vent and we suffered the wire heat and our body smells slightly less.

Evening came. Nothing odd had shown up across the street and we both knew we might be barking up the wrong tree and we certainly weren't any closer to finding Chelly but we stayed on. We knew we would stay to closing. We ate all the cookies in both bags, drank the Mountain Dews, and went after the Slim Jims, but agreed we would save the beers until after hours. We switched seats, urinated, stretched, read magazines, and talked in low whispers. As the evening wore on, kids in cars and motorcycles stopped at the stores for tapes and beer, and the lights went on in both storefronts and the picture on the monitor took on a shadowy, grainy quality that made what was going on across the street seem sordid and bleak. I could not put the search for Chelly out of my mind but in Bellino's company I was able to put aside the frustration I felt in not being able to find her and the sadness I felt in losing Willow/Taylor. Bellino was all business. Even when we were quiet or playing chess, he meant business, and the hours slipped by quickly, charged as they were with his purposefulness.

At nine o'clock, the front lights in both stores went out and the clerks in each came forward and locked the front doors. The cars and trucks that had been parked along the curb seemed to disappear all at once and the sidewalk, a moment ago the thoroughfare for a dozen or so kids, emptied completely.

"Gatwick shuts down pretty quick," murmured Bellino in his soft, sandpapery whisper.

"Too quick," I answered. "Look."

On the video monitor we saw a dark green Pontiac pull up to the curb and Alden Clapp, now in his shirt-sleeves but still out of uniform, emerged from it.

For whatever it was worth I switched the tape player on to RECORD. Hours earlier, I had put in a blank tape and cued it up.

Clapp was carrying a couple black deposit bags, and before he could even knock on Wow Convenience's door it was opened by the clerk. Through the window we could see Clapp at the front counter, opening the bag so that the clerk could put what looked like the day's cash and receipts into it. They seemed to speak only a few words to each other before Clapp closed the bag and strode out the door, walking the few steps to Adventure Video/Music. There, the scene repeated itself. Through the space between the two posters we saw Clapp himself clean out the register, then walk out of the front door, which the clerk locked after him.

"Spoonacre owns the stores and Clapp, the son of his nemesis, collects the receipts for them," Bellino whispered.

"I want to stay with Clapp," I said. "Can you drive?"

"Sure."

We stayed with Clapp as he collected receipts at every one of the other six businesses owned by Spoonacre. By nine forty-five his car was full of money and he was heading east out of town toward the Northeast Kingdom.

We tailed him. Bellino was a great tail artist and we kept far enough back that Clapp would suspect nothing. We drove on a highway called Route 111 and it was black, smooth, and curving in the night. Off to the right we knew we were passing Seymour Lake because we could see the lights of the houses and their reflection on the black water through the trees.

At the junction of 114 Clapp turned north, and we followed at a greater distance now because there were no other cars on the road and the countryside was dark and wooded and the road was twisting.

Five or six miles up Route 114, where the trees were very thick and close to the road, Clapp turned left. Bellino stopped the van on the highway shoulder to put more space between Clapp and us. Then he rolled ahead slowly until we came to the turn. It was a dirt road, a narrow, potholed, puddled road that climbed a hill through the dark trees. When we rolled down our windows and killed the van's engine we could hear the engine of Clapp's car pulling it up the hill. We waited until we could not quite hear it anymore. Then Bellino restarted the van and we crept up the hill. He kept it in first and went very, very slow. He used only the parking lights. The glow they cast on the road was weak and eerie.

33

IT FELT AS IF WE CLIMBED THE ROAD FOR HOURS BUT IN fact it was only about ten minutes. Trees overhung the road and the hill was dark and fissured from old rains and from time to time Bellino would stop the van, kill the lights, and we would listen. It was a warm dark night and the woods surrounding the road were alive with night sounds. In the distance we thought we could hear Alden Clapp's Pontiac but we couldn't be sure.

Bellino inched the van up the hill. From time to time I would glance over at him for any sign of emotion. But all I saw was the outline of the closely shaven head, the thick neck, and the calm face reading the narrow road with the aid of the yellow lights.

About a mile in, the road widened slightly and looked freshly drained and graveled. Sections of culvert pipe lay on one shoulder and a freshly cut drainage ditch bordered the other. Bellino went about a hundred yards up this new section, then switched off the lights and stopped the van. He killed the engine.

"Listen," he whispered.

We stuck our heads out the windows. At first I could hear only the steady chirp of marsh frogs, the distant wild hoot of an owl, the muffled *chirr* of katydids, the mechanistic click of locusts. They formed a soup of night sounds. But then, beneath those noises I heard the low sound of men's voices and suddenly the soft thud of a car door closing.

"Up the hill and around the bend," I whispered.

"I say we leave the van here and go up and have a look," Bellino said.

"What do you say we back it into a turnout so it's off the road in case Clapp comes down again?"

Bellino nodded. Without starting the engine he slipped the brake and backed the van down the hill. It was not as steep here as it was down below. The road ahead climbed and turned left but it did not climb too steeply and the van did not roll backwards too fast. The brakes squeaked softly as Bellino backed the van into a turnout below the drainage ditch and switched off the parking lights. He set the brake. We were tucked behind a shoulder off the curve. A car coming down off the hill would have a tough time seeing the van if it wasn't looking for us. Bellino took a deep breath.

"I think we should bring the guns," he said. "The guns and the Super-Eight."

"Once an insurance snoop, always an insurance snoop."

Bellino shrugged. "If there's anything worth recording up there, we don't need to waste time coming back here for the camera."

"You'd make a great mother-in-law."

We quietly got out of the van, pressed the doors closed, and opened the rear doors to get the guns and camera. I stood guard as Bellino smoothly thumbed seven twelve-gauge shells into his Remington Riot's cupboard and slipped a clip of fresh nine-millimeter hollows into his Nighthawk. He racked a shell into the Remington's firing chamber and slid an extra shell into its undertube. He put a handful of shotgun shells in his left front pocket and three more clips of nines in his right. As he stood guard I slid a clip of nines into my Smith & Wesson and thumbed eight shells into my Stakeout. I uncoupled the Sony from its periscope mount, loaded it with a fresh tape, and mounted a night-vision lens over its regular one.

"When did you go night vision?" Bellino whispered.

"Last year."

"You like it?"

"I don't know. I've never used it."

Bellino gave me a thumbs-up and his calm, inscrutible

smile. I slipped two clips and a few more shells into my pockets, we carefully closed and locked the van's rear doors, then strapped on our guns; I picked up the camera and we started up the hill. The gravel crunched softly under us and we walked on the balls of our feet. The road curved to the left and as our eyes adjusted to the darkness we could see how it climbed and we could follow its contours through the trees. The only thing that worried me about walking through the darkness was skunks. Their eyes made no glow and they did not scare. Bellino walked with both his guns at his shoulders and it made me think about their weight but I heard no sound of discomfort from him. He could heft nail kegs in each hand and not break a sweat.

"Here we go," he whispered.

Ahead of us, we could see lights poking between the dark trunks of thick pines. As we came around the bend and moved closer to them, we could see they came from a cabin. It was a new, clean, freshly built cabin with a tidy front porch and a roof tall enough for a loft. The lights were electric and now as you listened you could hear the muted hum of a generator coming from a shed under the trees a few yards away. Alden Clapp's Pontiac was parked near a small new garage. The garage was made of logs like the cabin's and both its sliding doors were closed tight.

"Place came from a kit," Bellino whispered.

"Come on. We'll look in the side windows."

We stayed low and kept close to the trees that fringed the road and made our way toward the windows to the left of the house. Sticks snapped and leaves rustled beneath our feet and we stayed together and moved slow and held our shotguns by their undertubes and watched the cabin for any signs of movement near the door. We could hear the men's voices more clearly now but not so clear that we could make out the words. Moving closer to the first side window we could see them moving around the front room. We stood behind trees less than thirty yards from the cabin and peered into that window, the sound of the generator louder now in the shed behind us, the light in the big front room warm and woody and dim in the summer night.

Three men in easy chairs were there in the big front

room. The first, Alden Clapp, sat in profile to the window, the black deposit bags in a loose pile at his feet. The second and third were guys I hadn't been introduced to by name, only by breath and jaws and noses and their Glocks pressed into my back.

The blond one had a black eye. The nose of the dark-haired one was taped with a shoehorn-shaped metal splint.

"They look familiar to you?" I whispered to Bellino.

"Dark-haired guy is Jimmy Komykis from Detroit. Jimmy Ice Pick. Blond guy I believe is Cary Singleton, one of Beaucharme's strong-arms from Albany."

"They're the guys who paid me a visit in the wee hours a couple nights ago."

"Are they." Bellino nodded. "Nice job on Jimmy's nose."

"Yeah, it was fun."

"Looks like Cary and Jimmy are doing business with the chief."

Doing business was one term for it. Another was laundering money. As we watched, the blond guy, Singleton, took stacks of paper cash from a black satchel at his feet and set them on a coffee table in front of him. Clapp opened one of the deposit bags, counted the cash in one of the stacks and slipped the stack into the bag. I set my Ithaca Stakeout on the dark ground, lifted the Sony Super 8 to my eye, turned it and the night lenses on, and began recording the scene unfolding before us. Clapp slid a single stack into each of the deposit bags, then gathered all of them up and walked them out of the cabin to his car. The Sony 8 purred softly against my face. The image through the night lens was like the images we received from Baghdad during the Gulf War—greenish gray and grainy but surprisingly clear. Clapp put the bags in his trunk and took from it a bottle and a six-pack. The beer was Budweiser; the bottle looked like a fifth of Bushmill's. When Clapp walked back into the cabin with the booze we could hear Komykis say in his slurred voice, "Now you're talkin'."

"You just get all that?" Bellino asked me.

"Think so."

"Juicy."

As we both watched and I continued to record, Clapp said something we couldn't hear. Komykis gestured behind him with his thumb and shrugged. Murmuring a few words at Komykis, Clapp set the bottle and six-pack down and looked at Singleton, who rose and led Clapp to a door at the back of the big room. Watching them was like watching the Green Mountain version of a scene from *Rear Window*. Light from the front room spilled into a room in the back as Singleton opened the door and he and the chief stepped inside. The window of this back room was much smaller than the window in the front but not so small that you couldn't see what was inside it when Singleton switched on its light. From where we stood we could see a bed with a figure sitting up in it. The figure was dark-haired, nude, female, gagged, and blindfolded, and handcuffs secured her to the frame of the metal bed. Even from thirty yards away and even though the blindfold covered the upper half of her face and a piece of duct tape covered her mouth, you could tell who it was by the fine nose and sinuous white body, and then her presence in that room made sudden, horrible, evil, gut-twisting sense.

The handcuffed figure on the bed was Chelly Kill-bride.

I nudged Bellino and nodded once.

"That her?" Bellino mouthed the words. I nodded again. Bellino moved close to me.

"What do you want to do?" Bellino breathed the words in my ear without moving his lips.

"First thing," I breathed back, "get a better shot of Clapp in that room with Chelly. Then get her the hell out of there."

"How you want to do that?"

"In a minute I'll check to see if there's a door around back. If there is, I go through the front door. You come in through the back. We tie the guys up with what we can find and skeedaddle."

"And if there is no back door?"

"We both go through the front and move fast so they can't use her as a shield." I took a deep breath. "Cover me."

I crept away from the tree I had been hiding behind

and, keeping low, moved carefully toward the cabin. The best way to move, I had learned, was low and quick and in a straight line. I kept the Sony running and aimed at the rear window. I reached the side wall and aimed the Sony over the rear window's sill. My shirt was soaked in sweat and my face was flushed. My heart was pounding and it was an effort not to gasp for breath.

But the Sony did its work. As I alternated watching through the viewfinder and taking my eye away to watch my back, Singleton filled a hypodermic syringe with something in a small clear vial, then tried to turn Chelly over on one hip. She resisted by thrashing her body sideways as much as she could and kicking blindly with her legs. Clapp silently gestured for the hypodermic. Singleton gave it to him, then lay sideways across Chelly, subduing her legs with one arm and turning her sideways with the other. Through her mouthpiece Chelly moaned. Clapp waited until Singleton had a vice grip on her, then poked the hypodermic into her hip. Chelly emitted a muffled roar. Clapp sent the dose home and extracted the needle. Singleton released Chelly. Both men watched her for a while. I kept the camera running. About a minute later you could see the dose start to work; Chelly's legs went slack, her head rolled once in a half-circle, then lolled to one side. Her wrists went limp in the cuffs. Singleton stepped forward and slapped her lightly on the cheek. When she didn't respond, Clapp drew a sheet over her body, covering her nudity. Both men left the room.

The moment the light went out there, I moved along the side wall and peeked around back. There was a door squarely in the middle of the back wall, with a breakable window in case Bellino had trouble bursting in. I crept near the trees along the back perimeter of the property and made my way quickly and silently back to him.

"There's a door. Let's go," I whispered.

"We better move quick," Bellino whispered back. "Clapp's getting ready to leave."

I spun around to see the chief in the front room, standing and talking to Komykis and Singleton. The two thugs were back in their easy chairs, pouring themselves big tots of whisky and cracking two beers.

"Here's how we do it," I whispered to Bellino. "You watch me go in. The second I'm there, you break for the back door, take it down any way you have to, but come up from the back and be careful to stay out of my line of fire. Whatever you do, protect the woman and don't let any of those stooges near her."

Bellino nodded. As we had done long ago after baseball games, we patted each other on the back of the head. I switched off the Sony, laid it on the ground, and picked up my Ithaca. Bellino took the safeties off his Nighthawk and Remington, and I circled along the woods' edge to the front of the cabin. I circled deep in the darkness so they couldn't see me and brought myself to the side of Clapp's car. Staying low, I worked my way around to the driver's door and noted its open window. Watching for any movement from the cabin, I raised myself from my crouch, put my arm through the window, and slipped the keys from the ignition. I squeezed them in my free hand and silently slid them into my pocket. Then, resuming my crouch, I slipped the safety off my Ithaca, took my Smith & Wesson out of its holster, undid its safety, quietly shucked it once to suck a cartridge into its chamber, and made my move.

I moved low and slow and quiet, staring with wide white open eyes at the screen door on the porch and feeling with the balls of my feet before putting my weight onto each forward step. There were exactly twenty steps to the first step of the front porch, and with each I got better at breathing in synch with each step and not letting my cuffs brush and not losing my balance though it was hard with guns in my hands and the scent of violence in the balmy night air.

I reached the first step. I had no way of knowing whether it would creak when I stepped on it and for that matter had no way of knowing if the screen door was locked or unlocked. Turning to peer into the darkness of the side yard I could see Bellino step from behind his tree and point once with his index finger toward the front door.

Go!

I took the front steps in two strides and was across the front porch and at the front door in two more.

Grabbing the door handle I pulled it gently once to see if it was unlocked and when I discovered it was I yanked it open and simultaneously bellowed like a man possessed: "Freeze!" Then I was in the hallway outside the big room and then I was in the room itself where I saw Clapp turn around and dive behind a chair, covering his head as he dove, and Komykis go into his pants and come up with a gun from under his shirt, and Singleton roll sideways off his chair and go for a gun under his belt, and the moment Komykis raised the Glock I shot him once with a blast from the Ithaca that blew his shirt up against his chin and blew a ragged dark hole in his chest the size of a basketball. Singleton came up from the roll with his Glock in both hands but before he could squeeze off a shot I fired once with the Smith & Wesson and hit him squarely between the eyes. Bone, blood, and brain sprayed the log wall behind him and his head snapped back with the impact of the shot. He fell forward on his face and the Glock fired a round when his hand hit the cabin floor. The bullet went into the floor.

Chief Clapp, meanwhile, was cowering on the floor, his hands on his head, his legs drawn upward in the fetal position. Bellino burst in from the back room. I shouted "It's OK!" and he lowered his guns and stepped over Singleton's body and kicked the Glock away. Singleton's legs were spazzing. Komykis's throat was making kitchen-drain sounds. Blood was burbling from his mouth. He looked pinned to death in the easy chair. His eyes were open wide and his body vibrated and then he went still. Singleton's legs stopped their spastic twitches. A dark pool of crimson blood widened beneath his face as if by magic. The back of his skull was ragged with splintered bone and bits of brain. A fistula of brain protruded from Singleton's blond, bloody hair. The air rang with the aftershock of the shots and hung heavy with the smell of gunpowder and blood.

"You OK?" Bellino spoke to me but we both kept our guns aimed at the chief. I nodded once. With surprising nimbleness, Bellino sidestepped to Komykis and kicked the Glock free of the dead man's hand.

"Get up," I said to Clapp.

"Don't shoot!" Clapp kept his hands over his head. I put the safety on on my pistol and tucked it into my pants. With one hand I lifted Clapp by the back of his shirt and rolled him back in his easy chair and punched him once hard across the side of his nose. It began to bleed. He put both hands to it and moaned and hunched forward. I set the shotgun aside and lifted him by the wrists and hit him once in the gut and once in the jaw and the neck. He fell back in the chair.

"Who kidnapped Chelly Killbride?" I leaned close to his bloody face.

"They did!" Clapp was gasping and his mouth was full of blood.

"Whose cabin's this?"

"Mine."

"So you're an accessory to kidnapping."

"It wasn't my idea!"

"Whose was it?"

Clapp was holding his face as if any moment it would fall onto his lap in pieces. "I can't say."

"Was it Beaucharme's?"

"If I tell you I'm a dead man!" His body was vibrating in terror.

"You're a dead man anyway."

"Don't kill me!" Clapp took his hands down and clasped his blood-smeared fingers in supplication. "Please! I got a wife and kids! Don't kill me I'll do anything don't kill me."

"Shut up!" I slapped him flat-handed across the face. He closed his eyes and began to cry. "Where are the keys to Chelly's cuffs?"

He pointed with a twitching finger to a clump of keys on his belt. I yanked them off and tossed them to Bellino. "Get her out of there," I said to him.

Bellino felt Komykis's neck for a pulse and tapped the dead man's eyeballs with his index finger. He felt Singleton's neck next. Komykis and Singleton weren't a problem anymore. Bellino disappeared into the back room.

"Where's her car?" I asked Clapp.

Through sobs he answered, "In the garage," then

added, "We weren't going to hurt her! No one was meant to get hurt!"

"Tell that to Shondra Maine," I said. "Tell that to Willow Goltz."

"The Goltz girl's death was a separate matter." Clapp gulped. "It had nothing to do with this."

"What did it have to do with?"

"I don't know. Just not this!" Clapp's eyes were closed and tears streamed down his face and neck.

"Did you kill Willow Goltz?"

"No!"

"Who you laundering money for? Beaucharme?"

"If I tell you I'll be killed!"

"Who holds the hypo that's blackmailing Spoonacre?"

"I don't know what you're talking about!"

"The needle that killed Jerry Leathers!"

"That's Dad's doing. Before he died. He gave it to Beaucharme."

"Why?"

"I don't know."

"Did Beaucharme have something on your father?"

"I don't know!" Clapp was hysterical.

"But he has something on you."

"I can't say!"

"Never mind. You put yourself into this hole, you can dig yourself out of it. I've got everything that was going on up here on videotape. Tomorrow you're gonna call a news conference in front of City Hall and you're gonna resign, you and that little lard-ass, Bobby. Of course, your ability to call the news conference will depend on what the state police will want to do with you, but before the day is out tomorrow, you're out as Gatwick's police chief. Got it?"

Clapp whimpered but nodded. Bellino walked back into the room, holding both sets of cuffs in one hand.

"She's really out cold," he said.

"No sweat." I kicked Clapp in the leg. "Get down on the floor. On your stomach."

"Don't shoot me! Naw! Please don't shoot me!" His face was a blubbering mask of blood and tears.

"Shut up! Get down there!"

I forced him facedown on the floor and gestured for Bellino to cuff him from behind. The cuffs made their crisp, authoritative clicking sound when Bellino clamped them down.

"I think we ought to attach him to something," Bellino said. "Slow him down a little bit more."

"You're right," I said. "If I was feeling really perverse I'd strip him naked and cuff him to the bed."

"Who'd want to see him naked," Bellino said.

We ended up uncuffing him, then recuffing him to a support post near the center of the room. His position afforded him a perfect view of the two dead bodies.

"Don't leave me here to look at 'em!" he pleaded.

"Close your eyes," Bellino said quietly.

I put the handcuff keys at Clapp's feet.

"If you're any good you'll be able to unlock 'em yourself."

"You're not gonna kill me?"

"Nope. But you're gonna resign. How you deal with the bodies is up to you and Beaucharme for now. Just remember: I've got a tape that links you to them and to Chelly's being forcibly held in this place against her will."

"What are you gonna do with it?" His voice was pure panic.

"I haven't decided yet. But you and Bobby resign tomorrow. Got that?"

The chief shuddered and nodded.

While Ernie got Chelly, I got her Land Rover out of the garage. It was covered with a blue plastic tarp and the silver Olds was in the other bay. The Land Rover had plenty of gas in it. I backed it out of the garage, turned it around so it faced down the road, then left it in PARK with the motor running and went back inside to help Bellino.

Chelly was asleep or unconscious on the bed and Bellino was looking through a closet.

"Can't find her clothes," he said.

"Don't worry about 'em," I said.

"You want to take any of the drugs?"

There were vials of sedatives, bottles of tranquilizers and alcohol, and packets of hypodermic syringes on the table near the bed.

"Just take one of each so we can see what they've been doping her up with."

Bellino had taken the blindfold off her eyes and the tape off her mouth. Now, as the two of us started to bundle her up in the sheet, her eyelids fluttered and she made a tired, moaning noise.

"Who are you?" she mumbled, barely opening her eyes.

"Friends," I said.

"Where am I?"

"A bad place," I said. "But we're leaving it. Right now."

"How'd I get here?" She groaned.

"That's one we'll worry about in due course," I said.

"I want to be safe." She began to cry.

"You are safe now," I said. "And we're going to another place where you'll be even safer."

"Good." She lapsed into sleep again.

I wrapped the sheet around her and picked her up in my arms.

"Let's go," I said to Bellino.

"Where to?" Bellino said.

There was only one place I could think of.

"McArrigal's," I said.

34

WE DROVE SOUTH ON THE DARK ROADS, BELLINO AT THE wheel of my van and me driving Chelly Killbride's Range Rover. Chelly lay asleep under the sheet in the back of the Range Rover, barely stirring even when we went over bumps, and dead asleep when we turned up John McArrigal's driveway. Bellino had called John on the van phone, asking if he would take in a few visitors. John must have agreed because when we arrived just after midnight, the porch lights were on and John and Anny were in the kitchen in their bathrobes waiting for us.

I asked Ernie to keep an eye on Chelly while I went into the house to explain things to John and Anny. I did not tell them what appeared to be going on up in Gatwick or where we had found Chelly. All I told them was she had been held against her will and repeatedly drugged for over a week and that Bellino and I had found her.

"Is this your bipolar case?" John asked me at the kitchen table.

I nodded. "She's pretty doped up." I unpocketed the glass vial we had taken from the cabin.

"Phenobarbital," John muttered. "Big enough dose to knock an average-sized adult out for hours."

"Where is she?" Anny asked. Her face showed a hardness I had seen in it other times.

"Bellino's with her in the car."

"We've got a bed made up for her in the downstairs guest room," John said. "Let's get her in here."

We walked out into the night coolness together, and when Anny saw Bellino leaning against Chelly's car, his arms folded and the hint of a smile on his face, she moved ahead of us and walked up to Bellino and hugged him.

"My baby, Belleen."

"Mama Anny." Bellino's thick arms encircled Anny's back and he put his nose down against her shoulder. Anny rubbed the back of his bristly head. She looked through the window of the Range Rover at the sleeping Chelly.

"Oh . . . baby." Anny's voice was a motherly groan.

"Can you get her out of there, Ernie?" I asked.

Bellino flicked a finger against his forehead. He lifted Chelly out of the car and carried her in his arms and Anny walked beside them, touching Chelly's cheeks and forehead with her strong slender nurse's hands and peeling Chelly's eyelids back and making clucking sounds all the way into the house.

We laid Chelly down on the bed and when we removed the sheet we had bundled her in and Anny saw Chelly was completely naked, she said, "Did her captors keep her that way?"

I nodded. "Cuffed, gagged, and blindfolded."

Anny's eyes narrowed and her jaw tightened. "They ought to be shot!"

Bellino and I exchanged glances but kept our mouths shut.

We got Chelly under the covers and John and Anny looked her over, took her pulse, and double-checked her other vital signs.

"Well, she's not in any physical danger from the Phenobarbital," John said. "But when she wakes up she's liable to be disoriented and could get panicked. One of us needs to stay up with her."

"I'll stay up with her," I said. "In the morning, if you don't mind another visitor, I'll call her husband, bring him over here. She shouldn't go back home until things are a little more stabilized over there. You have any problem with our camping out here for a couple days?"

"Not at all." John looked at Anny.

"Baby, you keep her here as long as she needs to stay." Anny looked fierce. I hugged her.

"We ought to have a doctor come check her out in the

morning," John said, looking down at Chelly. The light from a milk glass lamp cast a warm glow on his kind, tired face.

"Doctors still make house calls?" I said.

"I know one or two," John said.

"Can they be discreet?"

"Oh, yes." John laid a hand upon the sleeping face and gently stroked the cascading brown hair back from it.

Chelly slept until dawn. I was asleep, too, stretched out on a cushioned bedroom chaise. I awakened to the sounds of her stirring under the light covers.

Her voice was thick with sleep.

"Jesus, where am I?"

"You're at a safe place."

I moved a wooden chair near the head of the bed and sat beside her.

"Who are you?"

I told her. I told her about her husband hiring me to find her. She seemed to understand that.

"How did I wind up here?"

I explained in general terms. We both yawned at each other and rubbed the sleep out of our eyes.

"So you're my rescuer," she said.

"I guess I am," I said. "A friend and I."

She smiled at that. Her smile was uninhibited, almost wanton.

"Do you know who the men are who kidnapped you?"

"No."

"Do you remember how it happened?"

She clamped her eyes shut and made a small nod.

"It happened in Burlington. On Main Street in front of the Flynn Theatre." She spoke slowly. I gave her a glass of water to drink. She drank it all. "I had just parked there. I was going into the Flynn to buy tickets to a Joan Baez concert. I got into the lobby and a bald man came in after me and touched my arm and said, 'I think your car is being towed.' I turned around and said, 'What?' and he repeated it and took me by the elbow and walked me back through the lobby to my car. A man in coveralls was, like, leaning on the front of my car and, like, filling out a ticket, and he said if I didn't move my car immediately he'd have to tow it. He was, like, really ugly, with this awful scar down his nose.

"I didn't feel like arguing with him. I got in the car and just as I leaned forward to turn the ignition I felt this cloth go over my face with some kind of chemical on it and then I must have passed out because I don't remember anything until I was on a bed in some place with all my clothes off and this gag and blindfold on my face and my hands cuffed."

"Did you ever see your abductors' faces again?"

"No. They kept me blindfolded the whole time. They only undid my hands when they walked me to the bathroom but even then, when I used the toilet, they'd first handcuff me from behind and then leave me there for a little while. Then they'd be the ones . . . with the toilet paper . . . to . . ." She began to cry.

"It's OK." I patted her head, feeling my anger burn toward the dead men in the cabin. "You don't have to talk about it."

Chelly wept without shame. Outside, the sun rose through the big trees across the Connecticut River, sending long shafts of orange light through the polished bedroom window.

"I'm sorry." Chelly sniffed and gamely shook her head to bring herself back.

"Nothing to be sorry about." I hesitated before asking the next question. "What were you doing that day over in Burlington?"

"When I was kidnapped?"

"Yeah."

Lips parted, she knitted her eyebrows in concentration. "You know, I don't remember what I was doing over there."

"Were you looking for Tom Jessup?"

Chelly looked at me for a long moment. "Do you know Tom?" Her voice was tender and questioning.

"We've met," I said. "Were you looking for him?"

"I may have been . . ." She suddenly looked sweet and vulnerable and mystified all in a breath.

"Were you looking for him at the apartment on Pine Street where he was living?"

"I think so." She looked very sweetly puzzled.

"Why were you looking for Tom Jessup, Chelly?"

She breathed out softly. The breath punctuated her confusion. Her fatigue. She pressed her lips together like she was pressing on lipstick. Then she blurted, "I don't know!" and began crying again.

I reached for a towel on the table near the bed and dipped it in a pitcher of water there and wrung it out and rubbed her face gently with the cool towel.

"It's OK." I rubbed her face and eyes. "It's OK."

"That is what I was doing," she said between sobs. "Looking for Tom. But I can't remember *why* I was looking for him and . . . and . . . looking for him makes me *sad*!" She wept harder.

I stroked and rubbed her cheeks and eyes with the towel and she shook her head at whatever it was she couldn't remember or that made her sad.

When she had calmed somewhat, I spoke quietly.

"You didn't find him?"

"No."

"Did you find anybody else at Tom's apartment instead?"

Her eyes moved from mine like a guilty child's.

"Was it Shondra Maine?" I asked in what I hoped was my least threatening voice.

Chelly gave a small nod. "Yes. Shondra."

"Shondra took you in."

"Yes. Shondra was nice. She was nice to me." More inward nods.

"Did you see Shondra more than once, Chelly?"

"Yes." She was staring blankly ahead now, remembering. "More than once."

"And Shondra was always nice to you."

"Yes."

"But you never saw Tom . . ."

"No. I tried." She spread the fingers of one hand and twisted it in front of her. "But I never saw him."

"And Tom never tried to get in touch with you."

"No."

"And did you ever tell Shondra why you were looking for Tom?"

"Uhm." A dazed frown wrinkled her forehead as she sought to remember. "I must have."

"But you don't remember what you told her . . ."

"I must've been up." Chelly looked at me as if she had made a small discovery. "I get up and I say things and do things . . ."

I thought of the Polaroids I had taken from Shondra's bureau, now locked in my basement safe. Say things and do things. Yes.

"But you don't always remember everything you say or do."

"Not everything, I guess."

I gave her my most sympathetic nod. They were starting to make a little sense, the photos. What Shondra intended to do with them and why she was killed seemed clearer also.

"Does Tom Jessup know something you want to know?" I asked quietly. "Is that why you want to see him?"

The puzzled sad sweetness clouded her face again. "I don't know." The words came out as a bare, haunted whisper. "I don't know . . ." Her eyes went wet with tears.

A soft knock sounded on the bedroom door and Anny, dressed for the day in khaki shorts and a beautiful brown Phish T-shirt, stepped into the room.

"Good morning!" she said in a soft, singing voice. "How we doing?"

"We're doing."

I smiled at Anny. She kissed the side of my head.

"Good morning, Chelly. I'm Pete's friend, Anny."

Chelly stopped crying enough to say, "I'm getting your sheets all wet."

"Baby, that's what they there for." Anny moved in quickly and I gave her the towel and my place on the chair. In a way only she could do, she moistened the towel and wiped Chelly's face and hair and made deep humming sounds from her chest with every stroke.

I stood back and watched. I felt very tired, but glad

that Bellino and I had succeeded in what I'd been hired to do. As Anny tended to Chelly, John and Belleen came into the room. The look of pleasure on John's face when he saw Chelly awake was pure and uninhibited.

"Well, good morning, Chelly," he said, smiling broadly. "I'm Pete's friend, John McArrigal. I see you've met my wife, Anny."

Chelly smiled under the covers like a child who knows true security when she sees it.

"Thank you for putting me up," she said.

"The pleasure is all ours." John gave her a courtly incline of his head and his unaffected smile.

"You perhaps interested in a little breakfast?" Anny said to Chelly.

"I know I could handle some juice or something. I'm really thirsty." Shaking her head, Chelly smiled in wonderment.

"That's the stuff they've been giving you to knock you out that's making you thirsty," John told her. "Plus, I think you're probably not a little dehydrated."

"I'll get you some orange juice on ice." Anny rose from the chair and exited the room.

"How you feeling?" John asked Chelly in his gentle voice.

"I'm tired and a little verklempt."

"That's fair." John smiled. "After what you've been through it's perfectly reasonable."

"They never hurt me, but it still wasn't nice."

"Of course it wasn't. Listen, Chelly, I've called a colleague of mine, a doctor, and asked if she'd come over and check you out. Is that OK?"

"Sure." Chelly's voice was very quiet. "But I probably ought to have a bath or shower first. I'm pretty gross." She tried to laugh but it turned into tears. John sat in the chair next to her and laid his hand on her head and stroked her hair.

"Anny can get you into the shower in a minute. And I know she's got some clothes laid out for you. Pete thinks your husband ought to be brought over. I guess he's been pretty worried about you."

"Oh, Arthur!" Chelly closed her eyes and cried some more.

Anny came back into the bedroom carrying a tall glass of iced orange juice and a small bowl of sliced canteloupe on a wooden tray.

"Here we go."

Anny set the tray down on the bedside table and John gave her the chair. As Anny helped Chelly sit up in bed so she could drink the juice, John beckoned Bellino and me into the hall.

"She's pretty tender right now." John spoke in a low voice. "Dr. Slatkin's a shrink. I'll be interested in what she has to say. She may prescribe something to smooth the emotions. Or she may suggest a few days' observation."

I took this in. "Can she be discreet?"

"No question. Jane Slatkin's the best."

"It's mainly for Chelly's safety. There may still be some rats out there that'll want to bring her harm once they realize she's gone."

"I understand," John said. "You bringing the police in on this?"

"No," I said. "The family's asked for discretion."

John said he had no trouble with that.

"Belleen." I looked at Ernie. "How'd you like to pick up Chelly's husband in the van and bring him over here. I'll call to let him know you're coming, but stick him in the back so he doesn't see how you get here, and watch for tails."

Bellino responded with a double thumbs-up.

"What about you? What are you gonna do?" He looked at me with a flicker of concern for my safety.

"Me? I'm just going to do another round of house calls. See if I can't unravel one or two things."

"Hewlitt?" Bellino said.

"And a couple others," I said.

Bellino pursed his lips in thought.

"Watch yourself," he said in his dry voice.

Anny came out of the bedroom and frowned at us and shook her head. "She's one hurtin' pup," she muttered.

"Thank you for doing this," I said to her.

We could all see Chelly in the bed, gingerly biting down on a chunk of canteloupe.

"Not a problem." Anny looked at each of our faces. Then she looked at me. "Turn around." I did so. In an instant, the nurse's fingers were poking at my scalp.

"What did you do? Rub them sutures in Krazy Glue?"

"I've been waiting for you to come by and take them out."

"Well, they should have come out days ago. Come on in the kitchen before you grow skin over 'em and I gotta scalp 'em out."

"Not a pretty prospect," Bellino said.

"You stay out of this," I warned him.

"You want John and me to pin him down?" Bellino asked Anny.

"I know somebody's gonna hafta stuff a hankie in the boy's mouth or he'll squeal like a stuck pig."

"I will not!" I said.

"Yes, you will," Bellino said.

Later, at the kitchen table, feeling Anny clip each stitch, I weighed what I still had to do.

"Gotta make it safe for Chelly to go home," I said to Bellino.

He drank coffee and watched with sleepy eyes.

"Gotta break the spell," he said.

35

SEEING KENNETH HEWLITT WASN'T GOING TO BREAK THE
spell for Chelly or anyone, but maybe the good professor
would recommend a book for me to read and make the
trip to Hanover worth my while. I found him, appropri-
ately enough, waxing his right-hand-drive MG in the
driveway in front of his house. He was dressed in a polo
shirt, Bermuda shorts, and Timberland deck shoes, and
protecting his grizzled pate was a black wool designer
baseball cap with a sweatstained suede brim. He was not
smoking grass as Corky Gullet had been that fateful noon
seven days earlier, but gin fumes emanated from a sweating tumbler of clear liquid at his feet. It was not quite
noon. The spindle-shanked educationalist was starting
early.

When he saw me drive in, he did not smile or wave.
He just stood near the front fender, with one hand holding
the jar of paste wax, the other the chamois cloth, and
gaped like a J. Seward Johnson bronze depicting a blue-
blooded Lost Weekender.

"Hi, Ken, it's me again." I stepped out of John McArrigal's Subaru Legacy wagon.

"I've got nothing to say." Hewlitt backed off a step
and raised his hands as I walked up to him.

"Yes, you do." But I decided not to belt him.

"I can ask you to leave or call the Hanover police and
have you arrested for trespassing." He had the jar and rag
in front of his face, awaiting my first blow.

"And you can tell me all about you and Cora Goltz or

I can call my friend Barry Files of the Vermont State Police and he can sweat it out of you for me."

Hewlitt cocked his head sideways from behind his pathetic barrier.

"I'm not sure I follow," he said, immediately cowering in anticipation of a punch to the head.

I closed my eyes, sighing.

"You and Cora Goltz were lovers. Your wife, Nadine, and Cora's husband, Armen Karillian, were lovers also. I want to know if you and Cora were hot for each other the same time Nadine and Armen were, or before, or after, or what?"

Hewlitt tried to salvage his snobbish self-respect.

"I wish you wouldn't speak of Cora in those terms." He cleared his throat pompously. "Nadine either for that matter."

"Oh, my apologies." I spoke in a bored voice. "When were you lovers? During Nadine's and Armen's affair? Or after, to spite her?"

Hewlitt looked around helplessly, hating to be pinned down.

I waited as long as I could stand it.

"Do I have to phone the Vermont police?"

Hewlitt, fuming in defeat, sighed.

"All right, it was afterwards. All right? After the summer. After Karillian had taken off. Cora moved to . . . to—"

"Landen," I said, refreshing his memory.

"That's right, Landen." He looked away from me as if by doing so I might disappear.

I didn't.

"And . . . ?"

"And, as your prying mind would no doubt understand, it proved to be an easy matter for me to slip away from Nadine, tell her I had business in Burlington or something, and go see Cora. Nadine tried, after I discovered her with Karillian, to patch things up between us. But I was furious at her. Furious. So I gave her the proverbial back of my hand. Now, is that what you wanted to hear? Then, there you go, buddy. You heard it."

I watched him angrily put the chamois in the jar and

set both on the gravel near his feet. He picked up his gin glass and took a long pull from it. His throat pulsed as the alcohol went down.

"How long did the affair between you and Cora last?" I asked.

"How long?"

"Yeah. Did it last until she died or had you cut out by then?"

Hewlitt stared at me, pin-eyed. He was boiling. I didn't care.

"It lasted"— Hewlitt wavered before saying it —"until she died. I was due to see her the day they found her. The babysitter discovered her dead. The way we scheduled things, three days a week the babysitter would come an hour before I did and take the kids with her and then Cora and I would have from ten to three o'clock together. It went on like that for over a year and a half and I will tell you without shame it was good for both of us, Cora and me."

"I'm happy for you," I said. "Go on."

"That day as I approached the house I saw police cars and an ambulance in her driveway, so I kept driving. I never went in to see what was going on. But I knew it was over. The attendants were carrying in the stretcher and they weren't in a hurry.

"I read about it in the papers the next day, Cora's suicide." He shook his head. "I've never talked to anyone about this before."

We stood in silence for a while. A limp breeze from the river barely moved the high branches of the hemlocks. Hand on his hip, Hewlitt swigged morosely from his glass, a bug-jawed, superannuated Lothario.

"Some people don't think it was suicide," I said. "Some people think it was murder."

"I heard that, too." Hewlitt adjusted the Armanis on the bridge of his nose. "It might be true. It might not. If you're here to accuse me of murder, pal, you're barking up the wrong tree."

"It's one of the few trees I've got," I said.

Hewlitt took a deep gulp of the watery gin.

"Years after Cora died," he said gravely, "I learned

from her doctor she was susceptible to bouts of depression. I never saw it." He waved the glass around. "But maybe I wasn't looking for it."

"You think depression killed her?"

Hewlitt shrugged. "It's not impossible."

"What about Willow?" I looked him in the eye. "Or Taylor, if you prefer to call her that. Why do you think she entered your life?"

Hewlitt shook his head. "I don't know." He was grim to the point of looking remorseful. "When the police told me her real identity, it knocked me on my ass. I was dumbfounded. Still am." Up went the gin tumbler. Down again.

"Why was she here, really? Did you ever figure it out? What was she doing? What did you tell her?"

"That's just it. I didn't tell her anything. Whatever it was she was looking for—in her father's papers or by talking to people—whatever mystery she was trying to solve that drove her to work undercover, she was doing it on her own. I don't know if she ever knew about her mother and me. We never talked about it. And back when the affair was going on I saw Willow only once—she would've been two, at most three years old then."

"Not old enough to remember you," I said.

"I don't think so."

"Did Willow ever let on in any way what she was really up to?"

Hewlitt vigorously shook his head.

"She was a cool cookie," he muttered. "Never even gave me a hint that she wasn't what she said she was."

I waited.

"Which was . . . ?"

"Which was a twenty-six-year-old woman who had dabbled at a number of jobs and finally decided academics was what she wanted to do."

"The Beats."

"You bet." Hewlitt nodded emphatically. "And their spoor, like Karillian."

"Did you ever talk about Karillian with her, even just on literary terms?"

"Oh, sure. But Taylor—excuse me, Willow—learned early on that I wasn't much of a Karillian fan in the literary sense. So very quickly we stopped engaging in those kinds of discussions. It was more her just working on Karillian's papers. Disappearing for a while. Coming back. Working on 'em some more."

"Have you gone through the papers to see if there's anything in them she might have been looking for?"

Hewlitt shook his head with sullen impatience.

"It's dog shit—just a lot of Armen rantings. My take on what she was doing is she was learning about her father. She'd never known him. He disappeared when she was, what, two? So Dartmouth has his papers and she comes to Dartmouth."

"With an alias?" My voice was quiet.

Hewlitt raised both hands. "I'm not a detective. *You* are. You tell me why she was playing Taylor Swimm."

"Maybe I will someday. But for now, you tell me why she was murdered on your property."

"Look." Hewlitt bobbed and feinted in despair to demonstrate his openness toward me. "I've been over this a hundred times with Files and the rest of his cronies. I have no idea why she was there. I never told her about the property. She had to have learned about it from someone else. As for my whereabouts the day she was murdered, I was in my office in Sanborn House the whole time and you can fucking go and ask the goddamn department secretary!"

The veins bulged on his shorn temples. The lips on his lean mandibles twitched. I watched them twitch, glad they weren't mine.

"Who killed her, then?"

"I don't know!"

Hewlitt clutched his forehead and massaged it as if it were a cap that unscrewed.

"If I knew who killed her I'd have told the police." He was almost breaking. "She was obviously on to something—Willow, I mean. Either that, or the murder was something random or had to do with her past or—who the hell knows?"

"Her killer does," I said.

With Hewlitt's permission I asked to see Willow/ Taylor's living quarters. Hesitating slightly, he led me through the side door of the garage and up a set of carpeted steps to a studio apartment on the second floor. It was spare, dark, and hot in the apartment. There was a living area with a tiny kitchen to one side, a bathroom with a toilet, sink, and tub, and a bedroom with a double bed, closet, and chest of drawers.

I asked Hewlitt if I could poke around a little.

He shrugged. "Be my guest."

Unlike Shondra Maine, Willow/Taylor's bureau had only clothes in it and not very many of them at that. The closet held a few more—simple, functional wear that bespoke both impecunity and indifference to high fashion.

"Did the police take anything with them?" I asked.

Hewlitt shook his head.

"To my surprise, they didn't take anything. Nor for that matter did they stay up here very long."

I could picture Files impatiently jingling the change in his pocket as his minions combed the place for clues. After fifteen minutes of retracing their footsteps I concluded Files had reason to be impatient. There was nothing there. Only a framed photograph on the coffee table indicated Willow/Taylor's lost past. It was a black-and-white snapshot of what I assumed was the Karillian family when it had been whole. Armen, in T-shirt and khakis, was holding baby Willow; Cora, in a form-fitting plain black dress, had her arm around toddler Mikah, and none of the four was smiling. The kids looked pensive and both adults looked suspicious and tired. Willow had grown up to have her mother's beauty. Willow was in the morgue now.

Hewlitt, swigging gin behind me, cleared his throat.

"Cora kind of looks like her, doesn't she?" he said.

I nodded in agreement.

"I should've seen the resemblance," he continued. "But I never looked for it."

At the bottom of the apartment stairs, the Siamese, Pip Pirrip, was waiting for us with a dead baby robin in his jaws. When Hewlitt saw what the cat had done he hurled the remains of his drink at it. The cat dropped the bird and bolted.

"You fucking shit!" he shouted bitterly. "I'm gonna skin you someday!"

The cat, sensing an ultimate irresolution in its master, stopped midway on the lawn to wipe the gin from its face and whiskers.

From Hewlitt's I drove the hour to Burlington and parked on a side street a block down from 7 Pine. It was cooler than it had been for quite a while and the security kid at the desk remembered me. So did the plaid receptionist in Spoonacre's office. She said her boss was gone for the day and might not be in tomorrow either.

"Do you know where he's gone?" I asked.

The receptionist, wearing a tomato red suit, tapped the point of a Tiffany pen on a newspaper as she looked at me. The newspaper was opened to the word scramble.

"I think Mr. Spoonacre's in Gatwick."

"You think or you know?"

"I'm pretty sure."

"I'll bet you're right," I said.

Riding the elevator back down to the lobby, I thought of Spoonacre sweating and striding in Gatwick. Trying to stop the hemorrhaging. I'd attend to him later. For now, I still had one more afternoon call.

It was cool and quiet as I climbed the stairs to the offices of Pettigrew & Keel. When I slammed the main door after myself, a woman's anxious shout sounded from the back of the shadowy office.

"Duncan?"

Keel's wife, Hepzibah, burst from her office and froze when she saw who it was. She was dressed in a blue-and-white tentiform muumuu and Birkenstock sandals. Her streaked hair was a bird's nest and her eyes were black with fatigue.

She slapped her hand on her ample bosom.

"You gave me a fright. I thought for sure it was Duncan. I've been waiting for him for three days!"

"He's not around?"

"No." The shrew I had encountered on my first visit was gone, replaced by a meek, stout woman whose drooping face radiated vulnerability.

I walked around the front counter and approached her.

"He's been gone for three days," she continued.

"Didn't tell me where he was going. We have our differences, but it's not like Duncan to disappear like this."

"Have you phoned the police?"

"Yes."

"What are they doing?"

"They found his car . . ." Tears welled in Hepzibah Pettigrew's exhausted eyes. Her face, with its amplitude and close features, reminded me of a character's in a nursery rhyme.

"Where?" I asked quietly.

"At the Dartmouth Medical Center. Yesterday. He wasn't in it. I don't know how it wound up there!" She began sobbing softly.

"Do the police have any leads?"

She shook her head, sniffing. "No."

I looked at the design pit. It had been stripped. Where once there were six Macintosh 840's, now there were six empty workbenches and gaggles of surge protectors.

"What's the deal?" I gestured at the room. "You two getting out of greeting cards?"

Hepzibah shook her head again.

"We sold the computers. To raise capital. It's touch and go. We may be going under. Duncan said the day he left he might have a way to salvage everything."

"But he didn't say where he was going."

"No. Just that he wanted, in his words, 'to check out an option.' Whatever that meant. And that he'd be gone for the day. When he hadn't come home the day after that, I called the state police."

She produced a wad of tissue from a pocket on her muumuu and blew her nose.

"You're welcome to look in his office." She walked past me and opened its door. "I already have. The police haven't. I didn't find anything."

Neither did I. Duncan Keel's office remained curiously cryptic and spare, as if its desk, poster, synonym finder, and Meisterstück pen were the sole keys to his heart. Maybe they were.

Outside his office, in the design pit's empty gloom, I asked Hepzibah Pettigrew a final question.

"Has your husband ever talked to you in any way

about his Gatwick days with Armen Karillian and company?"

Grim anxiety seemed to have settled permanently on Hepzibah Pettigrew's pudding face.

"Only once." She twisted the tissue in her hand. "And then only elliptically. He said that that summer at Karillian's farmhouse had taught him just about everything he felt he would ever need to know about human nature, his own included." She paused. "He said he didn't like what he learned."

Fifteen minutes later, I found myself snagged in rush-hour traffic on Main Street, inching my way toward the interstate and the mountains beyond. It was a clear afternoon but the golden, sensual light pouring across Champlain to the west did nothing to illuminate the dark events of the past eight days. First Chelly gone. Now Keel. And Shondra dead. And Willow/Taylor. And a police chief and probably a lawyer horribly exposed.

I had to admit when it came to this case that, like Keel, I didn't like what I had learned either.

Keel checks out an option, disappears. His car is found in a hospital parking lot . . .

The long stream of cars began moving up the golden hill at a steadier speed. Behind me the sun, reflected in the rearview mirror, was blinding.

36

I WAS SITTING IN AN ADIRONDACK CHAIR ON THE MCARRI-
gals' back porch, reading the *Burlington Free Press*. Bellino was reclined on a cushioned teak deck chair, reading a
book titled *Active Meditation*. At the far end of the back
lawn I could see Arthur Cole doggedly pacing back and
forth, a pained sentry in a canvas corset. Bellino had
driven him over from his house the day before and his
reunion with Chelly, as John had told it, had been very
moving and emotional. The dinner that night had also
been emotional with many toasts to Ernie and me and a
certain number of protests from us that proved futile and
tears from Arthur and Chelly and looks of wonder from
Trey and Zach and warm smiles from John and Anny and
some laughter and more tears and from Chelly and Arthur
occasional tense stares of vacant pensiveness. No one
asked Ernie and me for details about the rescue and both
of us remained mum on the subject, but in private Cole
took me aside and told me how grateful he was and
pressed another whopper check on me. I signed it over to
Ernie.

At Jane Slatkin's suggestion, Chelly was off any kind
of medication for a while so that she could flush all traces
of the thugs' Phenobarbital from her system and also be
observed by John for signs of bipolarity. That was fine
with Chelly. That was also fine with Arthur so long as she
stayed under John's observation and he, Arthur, didn't
have to take responsibility for her treatment alone.

Neither Chelly nor Arthur seemed in any rush to go
home and that was fine with Ernie and me so that we

could satisfy ourselves that they would be safe once they got back there.

The day was hazy and humid again. Bellino, dressed in his usual black T-shirt and, today, dark green shorts, was sweating heavily in the shade. I, in an off-white short-sleeved bonefishing shirt and baggy blue shorts, wasn't doing much better.

"You see this?" I held up the front page of the second section for Bellino to read. The headline of the top story read RESIGNED GATWICK CHIEF AND PATROLMAN DEAD IN DOUBLE SUICIDE.

Bellino lay the open book on his stomach and folded his thick hands over it. His expression was imperturbable.

"What does it say?"

I read him the story. The long and short of it was that Clapp and Bobby had been found the previous afternoon on an anonymous tip in Clapp's cabin. They were stark naked and lying beside each other in a pool of blood, each with a bullet through the roof of his mouth and holding his own police revolver. A note found near the bodies and signed by both men communicated their undying love for each other. Authorities believed the suicides were linked to the men's resignations from the Gatwick police force, which, the article reported, had occurred earlier that same day.

"Quote: 'This is a tragedy of the first magnitude,' State Police Detective Barry Files said outside the cabin. 'These were two fine cops no matter what their personal situation might have been. I regret that that situation apparently led them to take their own lives together.' End quote."

I folded the paper and placed it underneath my chair. Bellino dog-eared the page he had been reading, closed the book, and placed it underneath his chaise. For a while we both watched Arthur Cole patrol the back lawn.

Finally, Bellino spoke without looking at me.

"Beaucharme?" he said in a quiet voice.

"Can't think of anybody else who'd be so tidy about it."

"He'd have had to clean up two bodies and a lot of blood first."

"Mm-hmm."

"Where do you suppose he put Jimmy Ice Pick and Cary Singleton?"

"I shudder to think. I honestly do."

Bellino was silent for a moment. We watched as several bumblebees scuttled over the tops of Anny's chive blossoms.

"Clapp could have gotten rid of the bodies himself," he said. "Before he called Beaucharme."

"He could have," I said. "Either way, Beaucharme wasn't going to be too happy with the developments."

"So Clapp was a dead duck."

"Very dead," I said.

"How do you feel about that?"

"I'm never crazy about people dying," I said. "Even people I dislike. On the other hand, if you don't let your cabin out to kidnappers you improve your chance of staying alive."

"Unless you feel you have no choice in the matter," Ernie said.

"There's that."

The barest flicker of a smile tightened Bellino's lips. He picked up his book and resumed reading. I reread the newspaper article carefully. A few minutes later I heard the screen door open; then Anny's hand was on my shoulder.

"You got a minute?" she asked in a quiet voice. "John's with Chelly. They'd like to see you."

She put her hand on Ernie's crewcut head. "You stay here, my Buddha. Mama Anny's gonna bring you a slice of strawberry-rhubarb pie and a cup of coffee."

I rose. "As always, he gets the better deal," I said.

"You get what you deserve," Bellino said.

I entered the house through the back door and walked through the kitchen and hallway to John's office in the house's farthest ell. The office door was opened halfway and I could see John sitting on a bentwood stool in the middle of the room. He beckoned me in and put an index finger to his lips. I pushed the door open a little further and stepped around it and into the room.

Near John, Chelly was lying back on a comfortable leather-covered reclining chair. Her eyes were closed and her legs were stretched in front of her and her arms rested comfortably on the chair's padded arms. She was wearing clothes that Arthur had brought over the day before: brown shorts, a yellow short-sleeved blouse, white crew socks, and expensive gray Mephisto walking shoes. Her hair was up. Her turquoise-and-feather earrings nearly touched her shoulders.

"Chelly, it's OK. It's our friend, Peter Boone." John spoke in a voice that I remembered him using when he hypnotized me after my wife was killed. It was a tranquil, soothing, poet's voice and it was clear from the way Chelly was breathing that the voice was having a strong effect on her. Her eyes were closed and her breathing was slow and deep.

John continued.

"Peter's going to sit with us while you get more and more relaxed. He's going to close the door and make sure nobody bothers you. He's here to protect you and help you relax."

John nodded for me to quietly close the door. I did so. John gestured for me to sit in his empty desk chair. I did. John's office was big, white, comfortable, and soothing, with many houseplants, a contemporary bleached oak desk, and a simple grouping of couch, recliner, armchair, and stool. Gauzy drapes in natural tones filtered the light through a big arched window. Braided rugs and muted oil paintings depicting Vermont landscapes through the seasons gave the room a New England finish. It was a welcoming room, a room without bias or judgment. John said it beat the confessional box by a country mile.

"You're very relaxed," John was saying to Chelly. "With each word I speak and each breath you take you are much more relaxed." He paused. "Are you relaxed?"

"Mmm." Chelly smiled and pressed her head back farther in her chair and breathed deeply.

John waited. After a while he stood up from the stool and retreated to the armchair across from the recliner.

"Chelly?"

"Mmm."

"You're in a very safe place where you can feel free to think and talk about anything you'd like. You know that."

"Mmm." Chelly nodded. Her eyes remained closed, her smile serene.

"And you can come to this room in your imagination whenever you need to, whenever you feel worried or threatened or unsafe or unsure, this room is here. And in it, in your imagination, you can find comfort and peace and safety and security. Do you understand?"

Eyes closed, Chelly nodded. She continued to smile.

"Remember how you said to me yesterday you sometimes felt unsure? Unsafe?"

"Mmm." A small frown formed above Chelly's closed eyes. Her smile disappeared.

"Well, you don't have to feel that way," John continued. "And if it's all right with you, like we talked about yesterday, I'd like to guide you back along your own personal time line to see what it is that might be upsetting you. To see if we can't help you feel more calm, more relaxed. Does that sound OK?"

"Mmm." Chelly nodded. The smile did not return.

"Then what I'm going to do is ask you to stand now and walk with me along your time line. And I'll be here every step of the way to protect you, and Peter is here and everything is OK and you're fine." He paused. "You want to stand now?"

"Mm-hmm."

"You can open your eyes."

Chelly opened them. She was still deep in the trance. John helped her tilt the recliner upright and took her hand and helped her stand. He guided her to an open space near the right-hand side of the room. He had Chelly stand on a painted white stripe that ran across the room.

"This is your own personal time line," he said quietly.

"Neat," Chelly murmured.

"Your past is to your left; your future is to your right."

With a slow turn of her head, Chelly looked left, then right.

"Would you like to go back a little into your past?" John asked.

Uncertainty clouded Chelly's drowsy face.

"I'm not sure," she said.

John moved close to her and took her hand.

"I'm right here with you. And Peter can stand on the other side of you if you'd like."

"Yes," Chelly said, a faint edge of dread in her slumbery voice.

John nodded to me and I stood and quietly took my place on the other side of Chelly and took her hand.

"Hi, Chelly. It's me."

She smiled to herself and lowered her head demurely. The grace of the gesture reminded me of the young Jacqueline Kennedy.

"Want to turn toward your past?" John said.

"Yugh!" Chelly jokingly contorted her face.

But she made the quarter turn with us and looked down the long white line. When John asked if she was ready and she nodded, the three of us started walking slowly into her past. It was like walking in a funeral or a very slow wedding procession. We would each step forward with one foot, then bring the other foot up next to it. With every two or three steps John would quietly call out an earlier age for Chelly.

"You're thirty-five now."

(Step. Pause. Slide. Pause. Like walking a patient who's just had a cast removed . . .)

"You're thirty now."

(Slide. Pause. Chelly wavering before taking the next step. Pause. Slide . . .)

"You're twenty-five now."

(Pause. Step. Pause. Slide. Pause. Both John and I watching Chelly's foot hesitate before moving forward.)

"You're twenty now."

Chelly trembled. I felt her hand squeeze mine hard.

"I'm getting nervous," she gasped. Her head went up like a drowning woman gulping for air.

"It's all right." John patted her hand. "Peter and I are with you."

(Pause. Slide. Pause. Step . . .)

"I'm definitely nervous!" Chelly cried.

"You're fifteen now . . ."

"Oh, my God! I'm scared!"

"You're all right!" John and I were suddenly having a

tough time holding her up. It was as if, by taking the next step, she feared she would fall into an abyss. She grabbed John by the shirt and would not let go of him.

"I'm scared! I'm scared! Oh, please don't make me walk there!—"

"We won't make you walk there." John's voice was warm and calm. "We won't make you walk there. It's all right."

"I won't step there! Don't make me do it!"

"We won't make you do it . . ."

"Don't make me go any farther!"

John was putting his arms around Chelly when she totally lost control. Her legs collapsed beneath her and John could not hold her up. I took hold of her under the arms and John held her face in his hands. Her legs flailed. John spoke loudly above her frightened screams.

"It's all right!" he shouted. "Chelly, we're stepping away from the time line. You're not fifteen. Look! We're stepping away."

I moved her off the white stripe and John got his desk chair and we sat Chelly on the chair a few feet off and away from her fifteenth year. She was trembling and sobbing quietly and John began talking to her in his firm, soothing voice.

"It's all right now. You're off the time line. Look. You're off the line."

Chelly looked at the line. Her eyes were big and very wet. Her jaw trembled and her arms were drawn against her body as if she was naked and cold and covering herself. John stroked her head and spoke comfortingly to her for a while. She was still in the trance. John's calm voice began to relax her somewhat.

"A question, Chelly. We're over here. Your time line is over there. Is there something terrible over there on your fifteenth year?"

Chelly stiffened and shook her head.

"Fourteenth and fifteenth." She swallowed, trembling.

"Your fourteenth and fifteenth years—they were both terrible?"

"Part of them!" Chelly's trembling hands were raised

an inch from her nose, as if in anticipation of her face shattering into tiny pieces.

"Did things happen back then that make you scared now when you think about them?"

John was squatted beside her. I brought him the bentwood stool and he sat. Chelly had her hands in front of her eyes and her head was turned toward John so she wouldn't have to look at the line. Through the gauze curtains covering the back window I could see Anny walking with Arthur Cole. She was throwing back her shoulders, tucking in her trim waist. Showing him how to walk.

John leaned closer to Chelly.

"What do you see that's so upsetting when you look over at your fourteenth and fifteenth years?" he asked quietly.

"They're awful!" Chelly sobbed.

"What do you see?"

"It's too terrible to look." She turned her head toward the stripe and spread her fingers slightly to peek through them. At the sight of the line she twisted her head away again.

"It's terrible to look at but you want to see it," John said.

"Yes," Chelly said. "But I'm scared."

John looked at her face as if he was looking at a powerful painting.

"You haven't looked back in over twenty-five years," he said. "Have you?"

"No," Chelly said.

"You know what I think?"

"What?" Chelly said.

"I think you're going to be less scared tomorrow and we'll be able to look at the events of your fourteenth and fifteenth years and you won't be afraid and we'll be able to find peace with those events so you can live a wonderful, healthy life. Does that sound OK for you, Chelly?"

"Mmm."

"You don't have to look back there anymore today. When I count to three your time line will be gone and all you'll see is an old white stripe on the office floor. I'm going to count to three now. One. Two. Three. The time line is gone and all that's left on the floor is that old white stripe. You can look at it."

Chelly lowered her hands from her eyes and turned her head and looked at the stripe on the floor.

John took his hand off her hair.

"It's just an old stripe," he told her.

After ten minutes of relaxing her and speaking affirmations to her (designed, I imagined, to strengthen her shaky self-esteem), John brought Chelly out of the trance.

When she opened her eyes, an astonished smile spread across her face.

"Whoa! Wait a minute! I was over there." She pointed at the recliner. "How'd I get over here?"

John rubbed her arm.

"You stood up and walked," he said.

"Does this mean I'm gonna start walking in my sleep?" Chelly pushed at her sagging hairdo.

"Oh! Did you want to become a sleepwalker?" John asked in mock confusion. He and Chelly shared a laugh.

"I feel as if I've been swimming in a river of calm," she said.

"That's a good way to look at it. And it's real. You have every reason to feel calm. You're going to feel anxious occasionally because you've been through a lot. But as time goes on you're going to feel more and more calm, and as we look at the things in your past that make you anxious or depressed or overly energized, and you gain *control* over those things and let them go, you'll feel calmer still."

"I feel like I'm swimming in gold," Chelly said. After a pause she looked at each of us. "I'd like to paint."

"We can get you paints," John said.

It was agreed Ernie and I would buy Chelly a set of watercolor materials after lunch.

When she had left John's office after kissing him and me on the cheek, John wiggled his eyebrows at me and shut the door.

"Wow," I said quietly.

"That is what you would call someone carrying around a traumatic event," John said.

" 'It's too terrible to look,' " I quoted. "Do you see a

connection between this traumatic event and what Arthur calls her manic depression?"

"Maybe." John rubbed his eyes and yawned powerfully. "My hunch is that if she is bipolar, it isn't systemic, it's psychological. Mind you, that's only a hunch. But if I'm right, then whatever happened to her back when she was fourteen has as much chance of being the triggering cause as anything else, including her recent abduction which may also trigger a bipolar episode down the road."

"So what do you do?" I watched John massage the back of his neck with his hand. For the first time that I could remember he looked truly tired.

"Do?" He took a deep breath. "Keep talking if she'll have it. Whatever her state of being these days, she doesn't need some trauma from her past clouding up an otherwise potentially happy existence."

We both turned toward the back window and watched Chelly cross the back lawn toward Anny and Arthur. When she neared them, they both extended an arm and drew her to them. Arthur laughed and Chelly kissed him on the cheek and Arthur threw his shoulders back to show Chelly the results of Anny's walking lesson.

"There's still love in that marriage," John said.

The noon light held the three figures in sharp relief against the dark trees far away.

"For better or worse," I said.

37

OVER THE NEXT FIVE DAYS JOHN CONTINUED THE LATE morning therapy sessions with Chelly. The day after that first one I waited around on the back porch and read the papers but John did not call for me after the first session and I took it as a good sign that my hand-holding services weren't required any longer and that John could handle Chelly alone. He did let me know that he felt she was making progress and that she had asked at the second session if what she said during the sessions could be kept between her and John.

"She says she feels self-conscious enough around all of us because of what she's been through," John said to me one afternoon when Bellino had taken everybody else grocery shopping. "She hopes you're not offended if she goes it alone in there."

"She's not alone. She's with you," I said. Then added, "Scary thought."

"I try not to think about it," John said. And smirked.

All of the adults, including Arthur, did secretly watch to see if Chelly showed any signs of mania. She did not. Nor to John did she seem any more depressed or emotional than anyone would be who had gone through a similar ordeal. "I'm not saying she isn't manic-depressive," John said to me one night. "And she is, as we speak, somewhat depressed. But I think there's a very good chance she might dance out of it. Anyway, she wants to keep the hypnosis sessions going."

"Good," I said.

"She's an interesting woman," John continued. "She

knows she's afraid of something, and yet she's not afraid about going back and trying to confront it."

I remembered John so many winters ago helping me confront my fears.

"She's got a good guide," I said.

Armed with a shopping list from Chelly I bought her a thirty-six-tube set of watercolor pigments, a dozen sable brushes of different thicknesses, a dozen black drawing pencils, a couple sets of plastic mixing cups, and many tablets of expensive textured paper. The days continued hot and damp, and in the hot, damp afternoons Chelly took the boys, Trey and Zach, for walks in the woods behind the house or along the river across the road, and they took the painting materials with them in two knapsacks, along with jars of water and paper towels and bottles of San Pellegrino water for Chelly and apple juice for the boys. Like a couple of paranoid Secret Service agents, Ernie and I trailed them from a distance, neither of us yet believing that Chelly was entirely safe.

It turned out—in my humble estimation anyway—that Chelly was a better watercolorist than she was an oil painter. Maybe it was because the medium of watercolors didn't allow her the same paint-hurling liberties that oils did, or maybe she was just intuitively good with them, but many of the watercolors she produced were actually nice to look at. They captured the tranquil, hazy, abundant essence of the landscapes around the house in a style that reminded me of old watercolors by Bonnard and J.M.W. Turner.

"These are gorgeous!" Anny said in the kitchen one afternoon when Chelly and the boys trouped back from one of their outings.

"You think so?" Chelly said, touching her throat.

"I know so," Annie said, looking at the paintings arrayed across the kitchen table. River scenes done in broad, transparent colors, they nicely evoked the Connecticut's lazy sinuosity.

"Look what we did!" Zach, the younger, fanned his watercolors atop Chelly's and Trey, the older and cooler, quietly followed suit. The boys' paintings were quick and luminous, playful and impressionistic.

"There's somethin' wrong," Anny said. "I don't see any space aliens or rockets from Mars here, Zach."

"Moh-mm! We're painting what we *see,* not what we *imagine!*" Zachery sighed, exasperated at his mother.

"Chelly taught us," Trey said, matter-of-factly. "Chelly's a good teacher."

Anny surveyed the riches her artists had brought her and beamed with fierce pride.

"She *is* a good teacher." Anny turned to Chelly. "Baby, you're good!"

Chelly blushed.

"Armen always used to tell me to paint from my imagination," she said. "For twenty-five years that's all I did. Now I only want to paint from life." Her expression went blank as if she was realizing something for the first time.

One morning, six days after we had found Chelly, Ernie and I were sitting with Anny at the picnic table under the maple, each of us armed with a pair of stubby forceps, attacking a mound of strawberries in a huge stainless steel bowl. Arthur Cole, as had become his habit after breakfast, was developing his newly discovered posture by walking John's fence line. Anny, watching him as her hands deftly plucked the tops off the bright fruit, clucked her tongue.

"You know, that man either oughta talk to John about getting in touch with one of our surgeon friends down in Boston," she said, "or he oughta do hypnosis therapy with John."

"Or both," I said. "But he's been told surgery wouldn't work."

"By who?" Anny said. "The same quack who says his wife is bipolar?"

After six days with Chelly, Anny had come to feel there was nothing much wrong with Chelly that John's mesmerism and a little R&R couldn't cure.

"The quack and the surgeon could be the same person," I said.

"All I know is, hypnosis and surgery are both a whole helluva lot better than blowin' out your liver on Russian gin!"

"Vodka," I said. "Yeah, he does put it down, doesn't he."

"Augh!" Anny rolled her eyes. "If that man finds one more excuse for sneakin' up to his room with a glass I'm gonna throw him out. I will. I will!"

"Oh, come on. You wouldn't do that."

"I'll help her," Ernie said in his flat voice.

We turned to see Ernie scrutinizing Cole with the same flat, uninflected gaze he turned on everything he encountered.

"I can respect a guy being in pain," he continued. "But I can tell you, as one who still feels the shreds of shrapnel in his legs and who also had shreds removed from his lower back, there are ways of overcoming pain. There are also ways of getting rid of it."

"Guzzlin' Stolichnaya ain't livin' with it," Anny said.

"Maybe you could have a little tête-à-tête with Arthur," I said to Anny.

"If Arthur don't stop his drinkin' he's gonna get a little hammer-à-tête," Anny said grimly.

Suddenly, a scream came from inside the house. It was high and sharp and came from John's office, and each of us stopped coring strawberries and looked up.

Another scream sounded from the office, followed by a loud wail and a low, sustained moan.

Anny's eyes narrowed.

"They're gettin' down to business in there," she whispered. Her jaw muscles worked.

Ernie's eyes actually widened.

"Do you think we should go—?"

"Shh!" Anny put up her hand and strained to listen for more sounds. From within John's office, the moaning sound was growing quieter and underneath it you could hear John's voice patiently murmuring, bringing his client back under control.

From out of the garage bay in the barn, Trey and Zachery, also wide-eyed, appeared.

"Mom?" It was Zach.

"It's OK, honey. It's just Daddy with Mrs. Killbride."

The two boys stood and looked at their mother as

another scream, less loud than the first, sounded from inside the house.

"Come on over, fellas." Ernie beckoned the boys with a world-weary shrug. The boys shuffled over to the table.

"Is she all right?" Zach said.

"She's all right," Anny said.

"That scream sounds really creepy," Trey said.

"Yes, but your dad's helping her." Ernie put a thick hand on Trey's shoulder. Both boys moved closer to the big man. From within the house the screams and moans diminished, John's murmuring voice took over, and finally none of us could hear anything.

"I think it's stopped," Zach said in a vaguely stunned voice.

"I think so," Anny said.

At that moment, Arthur Cole, in shorts and a green linen short-sleeved shirt, walked down from the hill behind the maple. His carriage, thanks to Anny's coaching, was ramrod straight. He was frowning.

"Did anybody hear that scream?" he asked all of us.

We nodded. He ventured up to the table and spoke tentatively.

"Your husband knows what he's doing, right?"

Anny closed her eyes and nodded again. When he saw we weren't going to comment he tried smoking us out.

"God, it was so terrifying, wasn't it?" His eyes came to rest on me.

"Yeah, it was," I said. "But John knows what he's doing."

Arthur Cole stood there listening like a sweet stray not quite believing its new family is real.

"It seems to have stopped," he said.

"Come have a strawberry and forget your woes," Anny said in her coy, soothing voice.

In the afternoon, when Chelly went off to the river with the boys for their painting lesson, and Arthur went upstairs for his postprandial nap, John took me out on the front porch. We sat on the front steps and kept an eye on Chelly and the boys down on the riverbank.

"I think we're making progress," John said to me quietly.

"She was making quite a racket in there this morning."

"That's part of the progress. Can I ask you a couple questions?"

"Fire away." I saw a trout rise far out in the middle of the river.

John produced a slip of paper from his shirt pocket and poked a pair of reading glasses on his nose.

"Who's—" He scanned the paper. "Who's Armen?" he said.

I looked over at him. He shrugged. "The name's come up a few times."

I told John all I knew about Armen Karillian. He listened, motionless, in silence as I spoke, but I watched his eyes move left and right as he mulled over my information.

"So what you're telling me is, his disappearance is a mystery," John said when I had finished.

"So I've been told."

John blinked and patted his compressed mouth with his fingertips. "What about Tom Jessup?"

I briefed him on everything I'd learned about Jessup. "He and Chelly were lovers, apparently, when Chelly was Cheryl and fourteen years old and Jessup was a twenty-year-old Dartmouth student."

"That's interesting," John said after a moment. "Did Chelly ever find Jessup on this last little adventure of hers?"

"No. At least that's what she told me. She did find somebody else in the process." Without getting into the gore I explained about Chelly's apparent fling with Shondra Maine and about the pictures I had obtained. "Shondra Maine's dead, either because she knew too much and had served her purpose with the thugs who kidnapped Chelly, or because she was planning on going into the blackmail business on her own and the thugs didn't want her free-lancing."

John looked energized. "She's mentioned Shondra Maine," he said.

"Under hypnosis?"

"Yeah. Up until now I haven't been able to make sense of the reference but you're burning off the fog."

"Happy to oblige." I hesitated. "Can I invade client confidentiality for a moment?"

John gave me a sweet smile.

"You can try . . ."

"Under hypnosis or otherwise, has she said anything to you about why she was looking for Tom Jessup?"

"No. And come to think about it, I haven't asked her."

I told John what had happened that first morning when I had tried asking her. "She couldn't remember why she was looking for him. Then she started crying."

"Maybe I can pop the question the next time she's under," John said.

Across the road, John and I could see Chelly and the boys, sitting in the shade of a river locust, their painting materials spread around them on the grass, the sound of Chelly's voice rising in a teacherly murmur above the sounds of birds and locusts. All three of the painters were wearing crumpled straw hats that Chelly had bought in town, and all three were quietly bent over their white tablets.

"Who needs Giverny when there's McArrigalland?" I said.

"She's a natural with them," John said in his quiet voice. "You know, I almost don't think she's bipolar and her problem, based on everything I've seen and heard so far, is definitely not systemic."

"Is that good?"

"It may mean that over the long haul she needn't be on any kind of drugs. In my book, not needing drugs is good."

"Amen," I said.

In the evenings after supper the household took on the atmosphere of a comfortable summer camp, with all of us returning to the big round dining room table after dishes were done to play summer camp games like poker, gin rummy, Russian bank, and canasta. We played for nickels or M&M's, and sometimes Chelly helped Zach because he didn't understand betting, and the two of them became known at the table as the Cardsharps because they won more pots than they lost and Trey, in frustration, repeatedly accused his younger sibling of cheating.

"We don't cheat," Chelly said, demonstrating that there was nothing up either hers or Zach's short sleeves.

"Zach cheats," Trey spoke with seasoned bitterness. "He cheats all the time. He's terrible!"

"You're just jealous that Chelly loves me and not you!" Zach shouted.

I thought Anny would fall off her chair. John covered his face with one hand, his shoulders shaking.

Chelly's composure was regal.

"I love you both," she said, bestowing kisses on both boys' foreheads.

"What about me?" Arthur said, perched on a kitchen stool across from her. He claimed the stool was more comfortable than a chair.

"You get yours later, sir." Chelly inclined her head.

We all howled.

38

I WISH I COULD SAY WE ALL LIVED HAPPILY EVER AFTER IN John's house—John, Anny, Trey, Zach, Arthur, Chelly, Ernie, and me. As it was, we all did pretty well for the short time we had together. We were a team. We were like my teammates and me on the Red Sox that golden summer when I came up, playing and rooming and traveling together, and living very much in our own mutually supportive, interdependent, sweet yet separate reality. The trouble with such an existence, I had learned, is no matter how hard you try to keep your reality separate, you can't prevent the rest of the world from invading it. The world will always find ways to remind you of its existence and your connection to it, and if you ignore it or try to push it away, it will push back and sometimes hurt or even crush you.

In my case the reminders from the outside world came in the form of two phone calls. The first happened eight days after Chelly's rescue. Bellino and I were walking up John's steep driveway, having just run six miles together along Route 5. The sun was low and orange over the Connecticut River and mist hung in the meadows along its banks because the night had been damp and cool. Between breaths, Bellino was telling me he was good for only a few more days' bodyguarding and then he had to go back to work.

"It's OK," I said. "I can look after Arthur and Chelly."

"Yes," Bellino said with great patience, "but who, my child, will look after you?"

"Don't you think our night at Clapp's cabin turned the heat down a tad?" I said.

"You have always been an optimist," Bellino said. "You will remain an optimist right up to the moment someone lifts a pistol behind you and shoots you in the back of the head."

"I can watch my back now."

"Not being so sure of that might help keep you alive," Bellino said in his gruff whisper.

I stopped and he kept walking up the driveway.

"Boone baby!" Anny called from the kitchen door. "Telephone!"

I jogged past Bellino and as I passed him I poked my finger in the back of his head.

"Bang!" I said. "And you call yourself a bodyguard?"

"I've spared you from violent types so far, have I not?"

I called over my shoulder. "Just barely."

Anny, making corn muffins at the stove, said I might want to take the call in the privacy of John's office. "It's Nan," she said, glancing at my face for some reaction.

The same thrill of anxiety I remembered from those times I was called on to pitch radiated through my body. I smiled at Anny. She patted me on the back. I walked with numbing legs and a hard-beating heart to John's office. I sat in his chair, lifted the receiver, and watched my finger waver as it tapped the console button for the house line.

"Hello?"

"Hi," said Nan. "How are you?"

"I'm fine," I said. "How are you?"

"Um. OK." Her voice sounded quiet and tentative. "I tried calling your house but your answering service said you weren't around. Also, that you haven't been picking up your messages."

"Yeah. I've been a little negligent these past few days."

"Well, I put two and two together and figured that if anybody knew where you were it was John and Anny."

"And here I am."

"And there you are. Are you, like, visiting them for a few days or something?"

"A little work, a little visiting. It's turning out to be a good way to catch up on my sleep."

"You sounded like you needed sleep the last time we talked."

"I did. Things got pretty busy for a while."

"And Anny says Bellino's staying there, too?"

"It's a regular old home week up here," I said. "You should join us."

"That's what I called about." There was a pause. I could sense Nan's steeling herself to say something she didn't want to say.

"I may be staying here a little bit longer than I expected," she said.

I nodded to myself.

"Michael?" I said quietly.

"Michael's not the issue," Nan said. The sigh that came next betrayed her shot nerves. "It's Mom." She hesitated. "There's a lump, a big one. More like a mass." She told me where. In and on both ovaries. She didn't have to tell me any more. I knew what it probably meant. "Her doctor's put her on to an oncologist who's very nice. The oncologist wants to run a bunch of tests, like, very soon."

"I'm sorry," I said.

"Thank you." Nan's voice was a whisper.

"How did the doctors discover . . ."

"Mom told me a few days ago she'd been in pain and feeling run-down. I'd been too busy running around to notice. Then when she told me, I noticed how gray she looked and she told me where it hurt and how much. I took her to the doctor's yesterday. Now she's on painkillers and tomorrow she sees the oncologist."

"Again, I'm sorry."

Nan was crying.

"It's all right. I'm OK." She spoke between sobs. "It's just we were having such a good time together."

"I know you were."

"Mom, your dogs, and me. We were having such a great fucking time. Oh, Boone! I feel so awful."

"I know you do."

"I read in this book about growths on the ovaries."

"Don't leap to conclusions before the tests are in," I said.

"I know. But do you know what it says about the percentages?"

I knew about the percentages.

"The percentages are bad, Boone."

"It might be something else," I said. But neither of us believed it.

Upstairs, I could hear Chelly reading *The Lion, the Witch, and the Wardrobe* to the boys. She had been reading it to them for the past three or four days. She had promised to read the entire Narnia series to them. She had them in the palm of her hand. One night at dinner she said it was hard to say who had it rougher—the characters in Narnia or the rest of us around here. Zach had said the Narnia characters, definitely. "Except on the nights Mom serves lima beans."

I wiped my face with my T-shirt to keep the sweat from dripping into my eyes.

"What can I do for you?" I asked Nan. "Right now, what can I do for you?"

"Will you let me keep your dogs a little while longer?"

"Of course," I said. "You don't even have to ask."

"Mom loves them, Boone. She calls them her guardian angels."

"That's perfect," I said.

"In the past couple years since my father died, Mom had kind of retreated from things."

"She hasn't sounded in retreat on the phone when I've talked to her," I said.

"It's because of the dogs, Boone. They take her out of herself. You should see the three of them on the rocks in front of the cove. It's like they were meant for each other."

"Maybe they were."

We fell silent for a while.

"Aw, shit!" Nan said. "Just when she was starting to have fun . . . !"

"Hey, kid, one day at a time," I said. "Like Anny always says, 'Don't rush the bridges.'"

I could hear her sniffing and blowing her nose.

"I come here to finish a book," she said. "I start an affair, my mother gets happy, and now this. It's like a punishment."

"It's not a punishment," I said.

"It feels like punishment," Nan said.

"It's not. It's just a condition, a bad condition like you said, but it's no cosmic retribution for anything."

"That's how it feels," she said.

"I know. All I can say is that's how it is, and I'm sorry you have to go through this right now."

I heard her take in a long breath. Then she exhaled.

"So am I."

"Hang on to the dogs. If they become a nuisance or you'd just like them taken away, give me a call and I'll come get them."

"Thanks." Her voice was quiet and small. "And . . . you can come down here anyway if you want. Just to visit?"

"I'd like that but I don't want to cramp your style."

"I'll tell you if you're cramping it," she said.

"Will you?"

"Yes."

"It's a deal. I'll talk to you when my schedule clears up."

I could hear her breathing in my ear and hear the squeak of her hand gripping the receiver.

"Boone?"

"Yeah?"

"I'm sorry if I hurt you."

"Don't be sorry," I said.

"Yeah, but I am."

"Give your mom a big hug for me."

"OK."

"And keep your chin up."

In the kitchen, Anny and Bellino were sitting at the table, drinking coffee and eating corn muffins. I touched Anny's face as I walked in and she turned and kissed my hand.

"How's Nan?" she said.

"Not so good." I explained the situation. Bellino's

face remained thoughtful. Anny's eyes narrowed as she sipped her coffee and listened.

When I was through, Bellino looked down at the table.

"That's a shame," he said in his sandy voice.

"They make an official diagnosis yet?" Anny asked.

"Not yet," I said.

Anny's jaw muscles worked.

"Then she mustn't rush the bridges," Anny said.

"Yeah, I quoted her that one."

"She mustn't." Anny held her head high and looked at me for a long time.

The rest of our breakfast together was quiet.

39

THE SECOND TELEPHONE CALL THAT SIGNALED THE reinvasion of outside life and the end of my bodyguarding holiday came the next morning at my house while I was watering my indoor plants. I had been away many days, and when I told Bellino I needed to go home and pick up fresh clothes and take care of a few other matters, he said, "Tell me about it," and volunteered to go with me just in case.

We left in the Batmobile right after breakfast, and before we left I quietly asked John to keep Chelly and Arthur out of sight.

"I could leave a gun with you," I said to John.

"I'm a pacifist," John said. "What would I do with a gun?"

"Use it to undermine your belief system and protect Chelly."

"Keep it," John said. His kind hazel eyes gazed into mine. "We're making progress, by the way. She's opening up, though she's still pretty murky about age fourteen."

"And all without the benefit of drugs," I said.

"And all without drugs." John nodded. "Though in her case the jury's still out on that one."

"She seems a lot stronger and calmer than when she first came here. Arthur says he's never seen her so mellow."

"The kids adore her." John smiled with paternal gratitude.

"One of life's bonuses. Speaking of which, Arthur

told me to tell you he wants to settle his bill with you for Chelly and for putting the two of them up here."

"Tell Arthur not to worry about it." John looked bored.

"Let him pay you. He can afford it. Plus, I think it helps him feel he's done the right thing in hiring all of us."

"He'll get my hourly rate. But as far as Chelly and his staying here, they're our guests, for God's sakes."

"Let 'em be paying guests."

"Are you kidding? Anny'd kill me if I took their money."

I thought about this.

"You're right," I said. "OK then. Fuck your hospitality. You're not getting a goddamn dime."

John tried getting me in a headlock. I picked his pocket. We skittered around on the driveway for a few seconds. When he released me I gave him back his wallet.

Later, in the van on the drive down to my house, Bellino asked me when I thought Chelly might be able to go home. I was driving; he was sitting in the passenger seat, his Nighthawk cradled in his lap, his eyes scanning the roads for suspicious vehicles.

"I don't know," I said.

"You think Beaucharme's got a new crew out looking for her?"

"I don't know about that either. In a way, I'm more interested in John making her safe from herself, if he can, than in us making her safe from Beaucharme."

"They're both dangers," Bellino said quietly.

"Yeah, but over the long haul she's gonna be a better person if she can get her head back in order."

"Head won't do her much good with a bullet in it," Bellino said.

"True enough. Let's let her get through the next couple days and then evaluate what we want to do about Beaucharme."

"We've got some leverage to do it with." Bellino pointed to the videotape. It was wrapped in bubble paper and duct tape and sitting in a canvas satchel between our seats. Bellino's receipt from Action Video was also in there, along with the list of businesses in Spoonacre's name.

I thought about Spoonacre fronting for Beaucharme's money-laundering and about Clapp serving as Beaucharme's part-time legman. Part of me wanted to go after both the hood and the lawyer. But another part of me said wait. For Chelly to catch up with her psyche?

The house was hot and stuffy, the plants wilted or shriveled. From my deck I looked down at my pond and saw the circles break its glassy surface.

"Brookies are hungry," I said to Bellino.

"You got any trout chow?" Bellino said.

"In the cupboard under the sink. There's a ten-pound bag of it."

Bellino took a stainless steel bowl from the stack nestled inside my KitchenAid mixer, filled the bowl with chow, and ambled along the path near the rock wall to the pond. He carried the bowl in one hand, the Nighthawk in the other. He looked like a character from a fishing show on ESPN. ("Whoo-wee, Larruh! Look how mah Nahthawk blew apart old mithta brook trow!")

I took a big copper watering can with a tapered spout from a storage closet in the back hall and filled it with water from the kitchen sink. The pipes thumped in the basement when I lifted the tap and the water came out in rusty spurts. Then the spurts cleared and the water flowed from the tap in a smooth, white, hissing column. I carried the can to the big selloum in the corner of the dining area and gave it a big drink. My wife and I had bought the selloum when we were first married and now it had a thick brown lower trunk where dead stems had broken off and deep roots and many twisted gray feelers. I wiped the dust off its broad leathery leaves, then carried the can to the ficus near the window and gave it the rest of the water. There was stickiness on several of the ficus's leaves and I wiped it off with a wet paper towel and searched the leaves and stems for scale. I found three small dry lumps of it. For the life of me I couldn't figure out where it came from. I got rid of scale whenever I saw it but more always came. I considered it another handmaiden of entropy.

I refilled the watering can and commenced watering

the smaller plants on a shelf under the front window. The lemon geranium in a big Mexican terra-cotta pot got only a small drink because the phone rang before I could finish watering it. Setting the can on the floor, I answered the phone on the third ring.

"This is the Southwestern Bell operator. I have a collect call for anyone from Tom. Will you pay for the call?"

"Who?"

"Tom. Will you pay for the call?"

"Sure." (What the hell.)

"Go ahead, please."

I heard an electronic click and the sound of breathing and then a voice pitched to a nervous tenor shouting, "Boone?"

"Yes. Who's this?"

"Boone, this is Tom Jessup."

"Jessup, where are you?"

"I'm at a pay phone near the bus station in Winslow. It's at the Easy Eight motel. I've been trying to reach you for the past two days. Where you been?"

"I've been away."

"I'm trying to get a bus to the airport in Albuquerque but there isn't one for another two hours. *I don't think I can hold out that long!*"

"What are you talking about? What happened to your truck?"

"They burned it, just like they burned my house and all of my stuff. But they didn't get me. I was down on the creek fishing. I saw them waiting for me back at the house. I hoofed it to here but I know they're looking for me 'cuz I saw them in town!"

"Who are they?" I said. But I already knew.

"A fat man, a bald man, two big men. Listen, Boone—" I could hear Jessup gulping for breath. "Did you get the package I sent you?"

"I don't know. I haven't checked my mailbox. When did you send it?"

"Yesterday afternoon. Express Mail. Thirteen dollars and fifty cents."

"I'll look for it. What's in it?"

"Can't say. Nope. Can't say. No, I can't. But you'll

figure it out. Now listen: Once you get it, don't lose it. And if anything happens to me . . ."

The voice slid away.

"Yes? Jessup, *you there?*"

It came back loud.

"If anything happens to me, call my mother in Lebanon, New Hampshire. Tell her I told you to call. She'll understand—"

"Jessup! What the hell's this about?"

The tone of pure terror in Jessup's voice sent electrical currents through my arms.

"I don't think I'm gonna make it, Boone!"

"Jessup! Why don't you go to the police?"

"I can't. They'll come after me and kill me!"

"They're already after you."

Silence.

"They're already after you!" I shouted angrily.

The voice came back in a nervous rush.

"Thanks for your telegram. I should've listened to it. I shouldn't have told Pippa where I lived. Did they get Pippa?"

"I don't know. What have they got on you, Jessup? What have you got on them?"

"What I've got's coming. I tried Keel and it didn't work. Take good care of it. Hey, wait a minute. What's this! Don't touch me. Can we talk? Hey, lookit! You've got the wrong guy! Hey, you've got the wrong guy! Ooup!—"

Sounds of a scuffle reverberated from the other end of the line. I could hear the strained sounds of a man being strangled.

"Jessup!" I bellowed into the receiver.

"Mommee!" The strained voice of Tom Jessup echoed from the other end of the line. "Mommy . . . !" The voice sounded farther away. "Mommy, they're killing me! Stop them! They're—killing me! Augh!" There came a brief, choked scream and then more scuffling sounds and then a series of three thumps like a foot kicking a wall, then the noise of a car and the receiver clattering.

"Jessup!" I shouted. "Jessup! You there?"

There came another series of short, quick clatters and

then there was silence and the sound of shuffling feet. I heard a brushing sound and a few more clatters and then a new voice came on the phone, a deeper voice speaking in dark, uninflected tones.

"Tom can't come to the phone right now. At the sound of the beep leave a message and he'll get back to you," the voice said. Then a low, sinister chuckle and a click. Silence. Then a dial tone.

"Jessup!" I rattled the tone button. "Jessup!" Blood pounded through my head.

In a frenzy I dialed Arizona information and got the number for the Winslow police. It took me four tries to slow down enough so I could dial it correctly. Bellino, carrying the empty bowl, walked into the house and observed me cursing as I failed the third try. He tilted his head at me.

"Jessup just called. I think somebody snuffed him while he was talking to me!"

"Who?" said Bellino.

"Beaucharme's new crew, I expect."

A woman's voice came on the line.

"Winslow Police Department."

"Yes, I'd like to report a possible murder."

"What is your name, sir, and where are you calling from?"

I told her. There was the usual frustrating rigamarole until I could make her understand that even though I was speaking to her from Vermont, the person being murdered was not.

"And where is the murder victim, sir?"

"In Winslow. He said he was calling me from a pay phone near the bus station at the Easy Eight motel."

"Do you know which pay phone at the Easy Eight sir?"

"No, I don't."

"Do you have an address for the Eight bus station?"

I thought my head was going to explode.

"No, I don't. The Winslow bus station! The Easy Eight motel. He was waiting for the bus to Albuquerque! Could you send someone over there to check?"

"In Albuquerque, sir?"

"No! To the bus station in Winslow where buses leave for Albuquerque. Can't you get it straight?"

"I'm doing the best that I can, sir."

We went over it all one more time and in the end she said she would call me back when she heard from the officer on the scene. I hung up the phone and explained to Bellino everything that had happened. His uptake was considerably quicker than the Winslow police dispatcher's.

"Beaucharme's got a crew working long distance," he said.

"And one Poetry Gang member bites the dust."

I went through the motions of calling the Southwest Bell operator and getting the number Jessup phoned from. She said it was listed as a pay phone near the Easy Eight Motel. I phoned the Winslow police dispatcher and told her the address. She said the Easy Eight was where the buses left from.

"Why didn't you say that before?"

"I thought you said the Easy Eight *near* the bus station," she said.

I sucked air to buy time to cool off. She said she'd call me. As soon as she rang off I phoned EMS in Burlington and asked for Pippa Locke. She wasn't in today. I told the guy who answered how urgent it was that I talk to her and after a half minute he reluctantly gave me her home number.

Pippa the Campa answered on the fourth ring.

"Pippa!" I wanted to shout *"You're alive!"* Instead I told her who I was. She remembered me. She was wary and businesslike.

"Has anybody since me contacted you asking for Tom Jessup's whereabouts?" I asked.

"Yes," said Pippa. "A cousin."

"A cousin?"

"Yes. He came into the store saying he was a cousin and Jessup had told him I'd know where he was."

"Did you tell him?"

"Yes."

"What did you tell him, Pippa?"

"I told him to check over on Pine Street at Shondra

Maine's apartment and if he wasn't there, he'd probably gone back to Arizona."

"You told him where in Arizona?"

"Yes. Why? Is there something wrong with that?"

"No. There's nothing wrong with that. What did the cousin look like?"

"He was short and bald and built like a wrestler."

"Did he have a mustache?"

"Yes. Like a Fu Manchu. Is there anything else? This is my day off and I've got a lot of things to do."

"There's nothing else, Pippa. Thanks for your time."

I barely had time to cradle the receiver before the telephone rang again. It was the Winslow police dispatcher saying that the investigating officer hadn't found anything of a suspicious nature at any of the phone booths near the Easy Eight.

"Are you sure you have the right location?" she asked.

"I'm pretty sure, yes." But it didn't matter. What mattered was what I had heard. The few seconds of terror in Jessups's voice before the voice was strangled.

The dispatcher said if her colleagues turned up anything relating to my call she would certainly get back to me. I asked her if any fires had been reported in the past few days near Clear Creek. I heard her working her computer keys.

"There was a fire at a Mr. Jessup's property," she said. "But apparently he had a burning permit."

"He did?"

"To burn an outbuilding." A short silence ensued. "That's funny." More computer-key tappings came over the telephone. "The fire marshal isn't issuing fire permits. Well, I wonder how—"

I left her to ponder the incendiery event at Jessup's. When I hung up, Bellino gave me his usual unexcited demeanor.

"You want to get Beaucharme now?" he asked quietly.

"In a second. Does the post office deliver Express Mail to rural routes?"

"Not unless Congress has doubled their pension."

I called my town's post office. There was an Express Mail package with an Arizona return address waiting for me at the window, I was told. I told the postmaster I'd be right down. I finished watering the plants, packed a few more changes of clothes in a duffel bag, and wrapped a few bottles of white wine for John and Anny from my wine closet in the clothes.

The post office in my town sat beside the Grand Union and the pharmacy, and the air was cold in there and the postmaster was friendly. He slid a big red-white-and-blue envelope over the counter and I signed the card for it and walked back out to the van where the air was hot.

Bellino watched me slit the envelope with my buck knife and draw out the contents and look through them. He looked through them with me. When we were through looking at them, Bellino said, "Let's worry about Beaucharme later."

Back at John's, the atmosphere inside the house was hushed yet electric. Anny put a finger to her lips when Bellino and I entered the kitchen, but we had heard the screaming long before I turned off the ignition and we were quiet together in the kitchen while Arthur, out in the yard, fretfully paced.

A half hour later John emerged from his office, his face haggard, his shirt dark with sweat. "I need your help. We've had a breakthrough," he said in a low voice.

"What is it? I'll do anything."

John rubbed his face with the palms of both hands. He looked exhausted.

"Hold on to your hat." He hesitated before plunging on. "Chelly wants to see her mother."

"That might not be a bad idea," I said.

"Quick," John said. "She wants to see her quick."

When I asked him why, John said that as her counselor he wasn't in a position to say.

"But based on everything I've heard from her in the past week," he said, "I think she should do it."

"All right," I said, thinking about Jessup's package. "But Bellino and I come, too."

"Fine," John said.

"Also," I said, "I don't think Claire Killbride should necessarily know in advance Chelly's going to see her."

"I agree," John said. "I think it should be a surprise."

We talked a little bit more about the meeting, but not too much. When we were finished talking, I said I would set it up.

40

THAT AFTERNOON, I PUT IN A CALL TO CLAIRE KILLBRIDE at her house on Gatwick Lake. After the phone had rung four times I considered hanging up but at the last moment somebody picked up the receiver.

It was Becky Lightfoot, the senior Killbrides' artist-in-residence.

"Oh, it's you," she said when I identified myself. Her voice became palpably cold. "What do you want?"

I told her. She sniffed.

"Mrs. Killbride is in New York City," she said. "Mr. Killbride is in Burlington on business."

"How long will Mrs. Killbride be in New York?" I said.

"For several days. She's overseeing the installation of her Picassos at the Guggenheim."

"Where is she staying? I'd like to get in touch with her."

"I'm not sure I should tell you that. This is a very important moment for Mrs. Killbride."

"It's about her daughter," I said.

"The missing one?" Becky Lightfoot sniffed.

"That's the only one she's got. I'm sure Mrs. Killbride would appreciate hearing what I've learned so far."

"Well, would you like to tell me? I'll of course pass on any message to her."

"I'd like to speak to her myself." I was firm. "It's rather urgent."

Becky Lightfoot's sigh was impatient.

"She's staying at the Carlyle. Room eight fourteen,"

she said. "If you call now you might reach her. I just rang off with her eight minutes ago."

"Thank you."

A sniff. "Good-bye."

She hung up on me before my own good-bye left my throat. I was using the phone in John and Anny's bedroom because John had a few afternoon clients in his office and the bedroom was the next quietest place in the house. On a cherry bureau across from the four-poster bed on which I was sitting I could see a small framed photograph of John, Anny, my wife, and me taken during batting practice behind the cage at Fenway Park. I was in uniform and had my arms across the shoulders of the three of them and my wife had her head nestled against my shoulder. The night the picture was taken I pitched a four-hitter against the Orioles. Two weeks later my wife was dead. In my first session with him after her death John said to me that loving and dying change everything. They had certainly changed everything for me.

Now, looking at the face of my wife in the photograph, I dialed Manhattan information for the number for the Carlyle Hotel, dialed it, got an English accent at the front desk, and asked it to ring Claire Killbride in 814. The phone rang twice and then Claire Killbride's cultivated voice was in my ear.

"Hello?"

"Mrs. Killbride?"

"Yes."

"This is Peter Boone, the investigator your son-in-law hired to find your daughter."

"Yes, I remember you. Have you found Cheryl? For that matter, have you heard from Arthur? Win and I have both stopped by to see him. He hasn't been home for days."

"I know where Arthur is," I said.

"Well, where is he?"

"I can't say," I said.

"Well, that's certainly a mysterious answer. Have you found Cheryl, Mr. Boone?"

"That's what I'm calling you about. I'd like to talk to you about Cheryl."

"Well, talk away, but I have to be going in five minutes. Perhaps you know, I'm in New York to oversee—"

"Yes, I know."

"—the installation of four of my Picassos at the Guggenheim and I'm very busy—"

"I'd like to talk with you in person," I said.

"Well, I'm afraid that will have to wait for three days when I'm back in Vermont."

"It can't wait. I can come to New York."

"Well, yes, I'm sure you can, but you see, I'm extremely busy and—"

"It'll only take a few minutes of your time, Mrs. Killbride."

"But—"

"And I promise you it is about your daughter. I'm sure you care about your daughter, don't you, Mrs. Killbride?"

"Of course I care about Cheryl. What do you take me for? A moral imbecile?"

"I don't take you for anything, Mrs. Killbride. I need to see you tomorrow. Say, at one o'clock. At whatever location in Manhattan you choose."

"Well, it'll have to be at the museum because we're doing the installation tomorrow." She cleared her throat impatiently. "Can't this wait seventy-two hours until I return home?"

"No, it can't," I said quietly. "And the Guggenheim at one tomorrow afternoon would be fine."

Coughing sharply, Claire Killbride succumbed to her irritability.

"Can't you tell me now what this is all about, Mr. Boone?"

"I can tell you tomorrow, Mrs. Killbride."

"Do you know where Cheryl is? Have you found her? Tell me, Mr. Boone. Tell me!"

"Tomorrow," I said. "Thank you for your time, Mrs. Killbride."

She started to squawk about how this was exactly the last thing she needed to be bothered with right now and wasn't I unprofessional not to state my business fully and couldn't I have picked a better time to call. I really didn't want to hear it. Before she could work up a full head of steam I did something that gave me surprising satisfaction.

I cut the connection.

41

THE NEXT MORNING, AFTER A LIGHT BREAKFAST, DURING which you could have sliced the tension around the table with a spoon, John, Chelly, Ernie and I piled into John's Subaru Legacy and drove the ninety miles to Burlington Airport. Ernie drove and I rode shotgun and John sat in back with Chelly, murmuring things to her that I couldn't hear and holding her hand and putting his head close to hers to hear her when she murmured things back to him. She was wearing a green-and-white shirtwaist dress of Anny's and a natural-colored short-sleeved linen jacket and her hair was pushed back with a black headband and for the first time since I had seen her she wasn't wearing her signature earrings. Her face was pale and devoid of makeup. The wadded tissue she carried fit her fist like a talismanic figurine.

I had told John and Anny about Jessup but we had not told Arthur or Chelly. John said Chelly's determination to see her mother was very strong and she had not backed down when I told her the meeting would take place in New York. In fact, she laughed when I told her we would see her mother at the Guggenheim.

"The Guggenheim," she said. "Surrounded by all her great artists."

"Is that OK?" I said.

She looked at me.

"OK?" she said. "Is the Guggenheim OK? It's perfect."

Now I looked back at her next to John and saw how he had his arm around her and how her eyes were closed

and her head was pressed against his chest. I gave him a
wink. He closed his eyes and opened them slowly and
smiled.

Early that morning, Arthur had taken me aside in the
living room and asked if there was anything he could do.

"You can take care of Anny and the boys," I said, and
hesitated before adding, "and maybe stay off the firewater
for today?"

He swallowed and I saw his lips work and his eyebrows lift.

"I hit it pretty hard, I guess, don't I?" he said.

"To tell you the God's honest truth, Art, yes, you do."

He bobbed his head in acknowledgment.

"Anny says I've got a habit as bad as any junkie's."

"Maybe not as expensive," I said.

He didn't laugh.

"I'd like to kick it," he said. His eyes filled. "Y'know?
Fuck the pain. I'd like to kill the booze demons!"

I put my arm on his shoulder. He turned his head into
my shirt and started sobbing into it.

"It's not impossible," I said. "Not to give him more to
do, but I think John could help you."

Regaining his composure, Arthur drew away from
me. "I've talked to him. He says I should have a go at
some of his surgeon pals in Boston."

"It's worth checking out."

"I haven't tried Boston," Arthur said. "I've tried New
York."

"I'm sure John could help you beat the potato juice.
Hell, he helped me once when I was going down the
tubes."

"He helped you?" Arthur look at me, surprised.

"Sure. John helps everybody in distress."

Arthur scuffed his toe against the braids of the living
room rug. He was barefoot, in his usual shorts, and his
feet were wide and hairy. "You know, with guys like John
who help people, I always wonder, who helps them?"

"I know what you mean," I said.

"Y'know?" Arthur Cole's eyes were shiny. "Who
helps the helpers?"

At the airport, Bellino dropped the rest of us at the

curb and dumped the car in the parking lot behind the Hertz rentals. The morning was cool and overcast, and a thick layer of clouds partially obscured the mountains to the east and west. I bought four one-day round-trip plane tickets at the Delta Express counter and I paid for them with my credit card and put them all in the pocket of my blazer. I next checked my Smith & Wesson nine with the woman at the counter and it was very involved because of terrorist fears, but in the end, the gun, which was unloaded, was wrapped in one piece of bubble paper, its cartridge clips in another, because I had a carry permit for New York and I had phoned the counter earlier. Bellino did not have a carry permit, so therefore he was not bringing a gun with him to New York, but Bellino had martial skills and against a gunman at close range, he still had an advantage.

After I got the tickets, Bellino stood guard in the hall while Chelly used the women's bathroom and John and I bought mints and newspapers for the flight. It was not very crowded in the waiting lounge. When we passed through the metal detector and took seats against the wall, Chelly clutched John's hand, closed her eyes, and began to tremble.

"It's all right," John said. "You're doing magnificently."

"I want to do this. It's the most important thing I've ever done, but I get so scared . . . !"

"There's really nothing to be scared of," John told her. "You visualized all of this with me yesterday. And now you're here and you're living it. You're living the visualization. You can do this. Or you don't have to if you don't want to do it."

"No, I want to." Chelly sat up straight and wiped her eyes with her fingertips. "You don't have to worry about me. I want to."

"We're not worried about you," John said.

"No," said Bellino, leaning forward in his chair. "You're a rock, Chelly."

Chelly touched Ernie's face.

"Oh, I love you," she said, frowning at him. "And I love you, John, and I love you, Peter Boone."

"We love you, Chelly," John said very quietly.

He and Bellino held each of her hands.

After a while Bellino turned and looked at me.

"Now I know I have a heart, because it's breaking," he said.

I patted him on the spot Chelly had kissed.

"I don't think so," I said. "In your case it's probably just gas."

42

THE SOLOMON R. GUGGENHEIM MUSEUM SITS ACROSS FROM Central Park East on a paved scrap of earth between Eighty-eighth and Eighty-ninth Streets. My wife used to drag me there when we came to New York, and I came to enjoy its quarter-mile-plus ramp and six smooth concrete spirals and most but not all of its exhibits, though I had not been back since my wife's death and if it weren't for the errand that brought me there now, I would probably not have stepped foot in the place again.

Our cab from LaGuardia dropped the four of us at the main entrance on Fifth Avenue, and I tried the front door, which was locked. Behind me, John had his arm around Chelly who was rubbing her forehead, and Ernie was scanning the sidewalks for trouble. I pounded my fist hard on the glass door, and a guard in a blue blazer and gray slacks came to it and waved his palm sideways, parallel to the ground.

"We're closed!" He mouthed the words silently.

I pointed at my watch.

"I have an appointment!" I shouted. "One o'clock!" It was two minutes to the hour.

The guard opened the door about a foot but blocked the opening with his body.

"Yes?" he said in a Spanish-tinged tenor.

I told him my name. "I have a one o'clock appointment here with Claire Killbride. She's overseeing the installation of four of her paintings. She's in the museum somewhere."

The guard narrowed his eyes at me. Then he looked at a sheet of paper on a clipboard he carried under his arm.

"Hole onna momen," he said.

He closed the door and signaled a colleague in the foyer. The colleague lifted a walkie-talkie to his mouth and began talking into it. I turned and looked at John, whose eyes were blinking and moving around a great deal.

"Shouldn't be a problem," I said.

Chelly's eyes were closed and she was taking deep breaths.

"It won't be much longer," John whispered into her ear.

A long minute passed. Then the guard reappeared and opened the door. With a brusque wave, he started to beckon us inside, then lifted his hand in front of my face.

"Whoa-whoa! Way-way. You all gone see Meez Keel-bride?" he said.

"They're all with me, yes," I said.

The guard eyed the four of us with suspicion. But he swung the door open wide.

"Tay de elebator tooa lef. Top ram."

We did as we were told, but not before we paused at the edge of the foyer to take in the openness and the sky-light and the smooth, ribbony cream-colored spirals form-ing a tranquil basin six bands high. Chelly looked at the space and swallowed. Her eyes went blank.

"Oh, boy," she breathed nervously.

John still had his arm around her.

"C'mon, kiddo. You can do it."

"Nothing to worry about," Ernie said. "We're right beside you."

As we walked across the bottom of the main gallery, I looked up and saw the head of Claire Killbride some six stories above us, moving upward along the top spiral and peering down at us with cool disapproval. The head disap-peared.

We rode the elevator silently to the top floor. Just before the door opened, John said to Chelly, "All you've got to say to her is what you said to me. That's all you've got to do. We're right here with you. We'll all hear how she responds."

When the doors opened we had to step around a workman in blue coveralls who was opening a big wooden crate with a pry bar. He was dark-haired and muscular and his back was to us and the crate was mounted on a dolly. Elsewhere along the ramp you could see two or three other workers muscling crates on other dollies. Many of the big compartments along the circular outside walls were draped in tan muslin, and where there were no drapes you could see blank walls or Picassos in heavy, gilded frames leaning against the walls, waiting to be hung. From below rose the sounds of workers calling to one another over the random sounds of hammering, crate-moving, and drilling. The gallery was like a human hive.

"I feel like I'm inside a Häagen-Dazs container," Bellino muttered to me.

"You wish," I said.

As we approached the top of the ramp, a muslin curtain covering the third compartment moved. Suddenly, Claire Killbride swept out grandly from behind it. She was wearing a long-sleeved black silk dress, high heels, and a moderate-size Gucci bag with a long chain strap. Her silver hair was permed to perfection, her eyes glittered, and her cool patrician smile widened when she looked past Bellino and me and spotted Chelly.

"Cheryl, Cheryl!" She opened her arms and moved swiftly past us and embraced Chelly. "They've found you. Where were you? Darling! Win and I were so worried."

"I'm sure you were, Mother." Chelly did not reciprocate the woman's embrace.

"But let me look at you. Oh, what a surprise, Cheryl!" She held Chelly before her at arm's length. "You look tired, dear!"

"Perhaps I am, Mother."

"When Mr. Boone said he wanted to see me, I had no idea—!" She looked at John, Ernie, and me. "This is a wonderful surprise. Augh!" She slapped her hand against the base of her throat and fluttered her eyes. "Where did you find her?" she asked me. "Or did you come home on your own as I predicted you would?" She looked as if any moment she would affectionately chuck her daughter's chin.

"I found her in a cabin," I said. "She was being held there against her will. That's not what we came to talk about, though. John?"

John stepped forward and inclined his head toward Claire Killbride.

"Mrs. Killbride. I'm John McArrigal, Cheryl's, uh, Chelly's therapist. I'm a licensed psychologist practicing in Vermont. Chelly and I have been talking together for over a week now, and Chelly indicated to me recently that she needs desperately to speak to you, to confront you with some matters that, frankly, have been locked up within her for quite some time. In the past eight or ten days, at first under hypnosis and then without it, she's been able to unlock those old memories. They've been pretty scary for her. But, as I'm sure you know, your daughter's a tough egg."

"Yes, I know." Claire Killbride smiled loftily.

"She'd like to talk to you, in front of us. She has things she needs to say to you."

"Does she?" Claire Killbride cocked an eyebrow coolly.

"Yes, she does. We both felt the need was urgent enough that we came all this way to see you," John said.

"Yes, in the midst of what I would describe as one of the three or four most important days of my life." Claire Killbride looked around at the Guggenheim like a diva surveying La Scala.

"This is an important day for Chelly as well, Mrs. Killbride." John spoke quietly.

For a moment Claire Killbride acted speechless.

"Well, I don't know whether to be flattered or put out." She flashed her blinding smile. "I am of course thrilled that Cheryl is safe and sound but now I am being asked to endure what?—let me guess—a litany of her old grievances so that she can what? Heal herself?"

"They aren't old grievances," Chelly said softly.

"What? What was that, Cheryl?" Her mother spoke sharply.

"They aren't old grievances." Chelly spoke somewhat louder.

We all stopped talking and stepped to the outside of

the ramp to let the worker from the elevator pass. He had his shoulder against the crate and his dark hair hung in his eyes. He rolled the dolly to the first display compartment and pulled it behind its muslin curtain. A moment later we could hear him working on the crate some more with his pry bar.

"If they're not old grievances," Claire Killbride said with aplomb, "then what are they?"

Chelly took a deep, shaky breath.

"Questions. Comments. Observations," she said.

"What kinds of questions?" Claire Killbride cocked her head. Her gray eyes danced behind a patronizing smile.

"Like—what did you do with my baby?" Chelly asked with a great rush of breath.

"Baby?" Claire Killbride's smile turned quizzical. "What baby?"

I looked at John. He closed his eyes and nodded at me.

"The baby I delivered in our house, the house you and Dad gave Artie and me. I'd just turned fifteen years old. I had the baby in yours and Dad's bedroom, the bedroom Artie and I use now. Your doctor gave me a shot. I was big when I went to sleep. But when I woke up I had a bandage on my tummy and I wasn't big anymore. I was small. Shall I show you the scar?"

She started to unbutton her dress at the waist. John stopped her.

"I don't know what you're talking about." Claire Killbride's smile was confused.

"I had a baby, Mother! I carried it to term. Your doctor gave me a C-section. I can remember now, thanks to John, what it was like when the baby came out. It was all bloody and mucousy! The doctor slapped its bottom and made it cry and wrapped it in a blanket and handed it to you. You took it out of the room. I remember that now. What did you do with it?"

"I didn't do anything!" Claire Killbride shouted. "This is all a fantasy! I won't have this, Cheryl. I'm warning you!"

"You'd have made me have an abortion but I didn't show for a long time and then it was too late to have one!"

"This is nonsense!" Claire Killbride huffed.

"You thought the father was Armen Karillian because you knew he'd been fucking me!"

"How on earth would I ever know a thing like that?"

"Because you caught him fucking me under a canoe down by the lake. And you shot him because you were jealous because he had just been upstairs in your bedroom, fucking *you*!"

The air up there on the top spiral seemed suddenly charged with electrons. Claire Killbride slapped her hand on her forehead and declared, "Well, now I've heard everything!"

"No, you haven't." Chelly kept right on going. "You remember how you came upon us and rolled the canoe away from us and you and I struggled with the gun? All these years you had me thinking I was the one who pulled the trigger on Armen. I felt I had to repay him for his life somehow. That's why I wanted to write his biography. But you're the one who should be writing it. *You* pulled the trigger. You shoved me aside. Armen pulled his pants up and ran into the lake and tripped. And you ran up to him and you shot him twice in the back. You were so angry you jumped on his back and held him underwater til he drowned. I *saw you*!"

"I never did any of that in my life," Claire Killbride said. "Armen Karillian fled the state and probably the country because Armen Karillian killed the Leathers boy with heroin."

"You and Dad threatened me after that and made me not remember," Chelly said tearfully.

"Poppycock!" Claire Killbride looked archly at John. "Are you her doctor now? Have you put these fantasies into Cheryl's head? I know how you people work, preying on weak minds. I shall see to it you are disbarred, or whatever it is they do to doctors. I am going to sue you for everything you are worth for filling my daughter's head with this—this *garbage*!"

John said nothing.

"Tom Jessup didn't think it was garbage," I said.

"I beg your pardon?" She glowered at me.

"I don't think it's garbage, either," I said. "The night

Karillian was shot, Jessup was approaching the oak grove for his own liaison with Chelly. He ran to the lake and wrestled the gun from you seconds after the shooting. He never saw you pull the trigger but he heard the shots. And you and your husband never refused the yearly payments to him when he started blackmailing you."

Claire Killbride squinted. "What yearly payments are you speaking of?"

"The ones that rose in thousand-dollar increments from three thousand dollars when he first brought Chelly back from Arizona to twenty-seven thousand dollars this year. He sent me a photocopy of his original letter to you, dated 1970. He also sent me copies of the receipts, all twenty-five of them, one for each year. Apparently, he'd come back East every year just to collect his money in person, then head back to Arizona where nobody knew he lived. Your husband and he met in Burlington, in the park behind City Hall. Jessup would wait on a park bench. Your husband would walk by, offer him the newspaper he was carrying. Inside the newspaper was the cash wrapped in a receipt. 'As per our agreement,' the receipt said."

"This is ridiculous!" Claire Killbride spluttered. "All your accusations are absurd. Besides not shooting him, I never had sexual relations with that low-life Karillian." Her face was a taut mask.

"Yes, you did," I said. "Karillian kept a journal of his last summer on Gatwick Lake. In it, he brags about his sexual prowess. He speaks of the women he bedded that summer in code: salt and carbon. Salt is sodium chloride. NaCl. Carbon is C. Nadine, Claire, and Chelly. I read excerpts at Dartmouth College. I know Karillian was having an affair with Nadine Hewlitt. Her ex-husband told me he came upon them coupling. Jessup's written testimony and Chelly's recollections support your motive for killing Karillian. He was having sex with your teenage daughter. And you were jealous as well as outraged. Shall I go on, Mrs. Killbride, or do you want to state things for yourself?"

"Everything you're saying is a complete fabrication," Claire Killbride said. But the arrogant expression on her face was shriveling.

"I have reason to believe that either you or some of Bobby Beaucharme's henchmen also killed Karillian's wife, Cora Goltz, back in '72 when she began to investigate her husband's disappearance on her own. Whoever killed her tried to make it look like suicide but it wasn't. Whoever killed her, in effect, put the two Karillian children, Mikah and Willow Jane, in an orphanage.

"Both children have been seeking to avenge their parents' deaths ever since. Mikah burned down Hewlitt's house, thinking Hewlitt had done the killing. But he was wrong and he went to jail for it. Willow took a more deliberate approach. She changed her identity. Called herself Taylor Swimm and slowly put the pieces together by going through her father's papers."

"And talking to me," Chelly said quietly. "Though I didn't realize at the time what she was doing."

"Willow Goltz as Taylor Swimm paid you a visit about a week ago. Was it to accuse you?"

Claire Killbride, in consternation, shook her head.

"Whatever her reasons, you convinced her to go with you to Hewlitt's property and there you killed her, using— what? A rock to strike her in the back of the head, and one of the cedar railings leading down to the lake in order to drown her between the sluice gates? Need evidence? The state police found a peculiar shiny object at the bottom of the sluice gates. I'll wager anything it's one of your earrings."

Claire Killbride's face was ashen. Her eyes were like her daughter's, big and round.

"What do all of you want from me?" She stepped back from us. "Do you think I'm going to walk out of here and go quietly to prison after being submitted to this . . . this *star-chamber*?"

"We don't expect anything, Mrs. Killbride," I said.

"I only came here to tell you what I remember," Chelly told her mother. "To confront you with the fact that I know you killed Armen Karillian. And . . . *and*— to ask you *please* to tell me where my baby is!"

"I have no idea where that filthy baby is!" Claire Killbride snapped. But then realizing what she had said, she tried to recover. "Besides, who would want to bring a child fathered by that loathesome Karillian into the world?"

"Armen wasn't the father!" Chelly cried. "Tom is!"

"The housekeeper's riffraff son!" Claire Killbride sneered. "Perfect."

"You and Dad told me the baby was born dead," Chelly said. "But I heard it and saw it with my own eyes before you drugged me again and told me lies that it had died. I know it didn't die. I heard it cry. It was *beautiful*! I heard you take the baby to a man in the hall. You said, 'It's yours,' and he said, 'Thank you' and you said, 'Now go!' "

"—Cheryl, I never—"

"I want my baby! I want to know where it went. That's why I got crazy and started looking for Tom, figuring he'd know 'cuz he's the father. He got me pregnant at Canyon de Chelly. That baby was beautiful. It was my one great work of art! All my painting and sculpture is crap compared to that baby. This has all been locked up inside of me for twenty-five years, Mother—twenty-five years! But now it's not locked up. John helped me unlock it. And you've got to tell me where the baby is, Mother, you've got to tell me!"

"Guard!" Claire Killbride called in her stentorian, aristocratic voice. A guard in a blue blazer by the topmost elevator bank looked across the empty space that separated him from us and raised his hand.

He pointed at himself.

"I need you!" Claire Killbride shouted with angry authority. "Quickly!"

"Don't do this, Mother." Chelly, crying softly, shook her head.

"I need you!" Claire Killbride roared to the guard over her daughter's sobs.

From every level of the main gallery, workers and security people peered upward toward the topmost spiral. Claire Killbride, calm and regal, stepped toward the hip-high rail and looked down at them.

"It's all right!" She waved. "We're all right up here!"

"Please don't do this, Mother."

The guard moved up the ramp like a cross-country

skier doing dryland training. He pushed past us to answer Claire Killbride's call.

"Guard, these people do not belong here and they are harassing me," Claire Killbride told him.

"Mother, don't."

"Will you please escort them from the building at once!"

She turned and strode back to the curtained compartment from which she had first emerged and disappeared behind her muslin barrier.

The guard, who was black, extended his arms the way guards do when they want to keep fans off a basketball court.

"OK, folks," he said, "you heard the lady. Let's go."

"Mother!" Chelly called toward the curtain.

"It's all right." John took Chelly's arm and started to move her away. "Let's not break the law ourselves."

"But she didn't tell me where my baby is!" Chelly's face was bone white.

"C'mon, Chelly." Bellino put his arm around her. "You did great. Let's not blow it now."

"But she didn't tell me!—"

"She will," John said. We moved down the ramp. I walked behind Chelly and from time to time looked back at the guard, who continued to keep his arms extended and made sure we kept moving along.

"Nice day," I said to him.

The guard said nothing. He was big and young but had already perfected that look of weary neutrality that seemed to be a guard's essential job skill.

We made our way to the elevator. Chelly said, "I desperately need to use the bathroom."

"We aren't here to make trouble," I told the guard.

He pointed around the elevator bank. "Rest room's over there."

Time is a funny thing. An event may seem to happen in slow motion though in fact it happens in seconds and is over before you know it or can say it or can scream. The event that happened as John, Ernie, and I stood at the elevator bank was like that. Funny with time. I'm not sure today which friend it was who nudged me, but I do remember the nudge and then the shouts from the topmost spiral and then spinning around and seeing the dark-haired workman pushing Claire Killbride against the rail. And then his shouts came above her screams: "You killed my father! You killed my mother and my sister!" And then he was lifting her up, up over his head and flinging her off the topmost spiral, though he had not anticipated her agility or the strength of her Gucci bag's strap. In her desperate effort to save herself, she had somehow looped the strap around her killer's neck. When he flung her into space he was yanked with her over the edge and the two, in terror—murderer and orphan—rode the space together to their deaths, broke their necks together at the bottom of the central void.

John and Ernie did what they could to keep Chelly from seeing what happened. But long before I reached the two bodies and the rattlesnake tattoo confirmed for me who Claire Killbride's clean-shaven killer was, I heard the screams.

Above me, from the spirals, the workers gaped down at the broken bodies. The screams continued for quite some time.

43

THE HOMICIDE DETECTIVES INVESTIGATING THE DEATHS OF Claire Killbride and Mikah Karillian were, to everyone's surprise, a married couple. The Hunnicuts, Ron and Kate. He was fortyish, tall, priestly. She was somewhat younger, a dead ringer for any of a number of dark-haired, haven't-been-seen-in-a-while film actresses. Both were quiet, patient, pleasant, and thorough. They also showed unusual tact as they questioned Chelly. In an administrator's basement office away from the nightmarish bustle of ambulance gurneys, popping strobe lights, yellow police tapes, chalk outlines, and static-clogged walkie-talkies, they asked us questions. There was a trompe l'oeil painting of a hen on the administrator's office wall. When the Hunnicutts were through with us, we were ushered by a uniformed patrolman to a side door on Eighty-eighth Street. Ron Hunnicutt's business card was in my breast pocket. His wife told John and me they would doubtless be back in touch.

It was nearly six o'clock when we stepped outside the Guggenheim; the sky above its creamy facade boiled with poisonous clouds. John proposed that we all return to Vermont immediately. I seconded the motion. Some time in the next day and a half an autopsy would be performed on Claire Killbride's broken body at the city medical examiner's office on Thirtieth Street and First Avenue. The gloomy business of shipping the body back to Gatwick afterwards would be handled by a funeral home I called in Montpelier. I'd have left the job of funeral arrangements to Win Killbride but the Hunnicutts couldn't reach him.

Nobody at his home or his gravel-business office knew where he was.

It was a hard trip back to John's place. Chelly cried almost continuously through the cab ride and flight to Burlington, and the few other plane passengers, businesspeople mostly, gave her extremely long looks. When we landed, a guy in a plastic raincoat patted her back as he passed her seat.

"You take care of yourself now," he said.

I had seen John in action many times before, but during that long drive his solace was transcendent. We all fed off of his tranquility. I did not think that Chelly could pass the night without some kind of pharmaceutical crutch but John talked her into a deep hypnosis shortly before we reached his place. When she stepped from the car she was heavy-hearted but somehow radiant in her grief.

After Anny gave Chelly a small bowl of chicken barley stew and she had eaten what she could, John put Chelly to bed. Then Arthur, Anny, Ernie, and I sat at the kitchen table and I told Arthur everything that had happened at the Guggenheim and why. Nodding and shaking his head, he took it all in. It began to rain and the steady sound of it on the roof seemed to have a quieting effect on all of us.

"Now I understand," he said.

"What do you understand?" I asked.

"Now I understand the kind of hold Chelly's parents have had on her. All these years. Since even before we were married. She'd tell me how crazy her mother made her. I'd tell her, 'Then let's move.' 'Oh, no. We can't do that,' she'd say. 'We can't do that.' "

"Maybe you can now," I said.

The next morning I left Chelly and Arthur in the others' care and drove the forty miles into Gatwick. It was a fresh, late July morning, and the streets looked bright and swept after a night of moderate rain. I drove up along the eastern shore of the lake, intending to visit Win Killbride's house, but when I saw his silver Corvette and Spoonacre's mint blue BMW parked in Arthur's driveway, I stopped there.

Ten days' worth of newspapers spilled onto the front

step when I opened the screen door. The front door was locked. Retracing my route around back, I came upon an empty shotgun cartridge box lying on the side lawn. I picked it up. It was dry and new. In the newly mown grass I could see a trail of footprints that disappeared behind the house.

The footprints stopped at the white gravel path that led to the cabin. I knew they would lead there. I walked parallel to the path so they couldn't hear my footsteps, but when I reached the edge of the oaks I saw they were waiting for me. Win Killbride was waiting for me. John Spoonacre was seated on the reproduction park bench in the middle of the grove and Win Killbride was beside him, pressing the end of a shotgun against the lawyer's neck.

"Stop him, Boone. He's gonna kill me!" John Spoonacre cried.

"You shut up!" Win Killbride jabbed him with the shotgun barrel.

"Don't do it," I said to Win Killbride.

"If you're carrying a weapon, you can lay it on the ground right now," Win Killbride growled.

"I take it Manhattan Homicide reached you," I said.

"On the ground, Boone. Right now."

I was wearing my nine tucked in my jeans underneath the tails of my khaki shirt. I looked hard at Killbride. He was puffy faced and red eyed. His thick arms looked like oak limbs steadying the shotgun and he stared at me with sullen dread.

I held up both hands.

"I'll disarm," I told him. "But you've got to promise me not to pull those triggers."

"I'm not promising anything!"

"Suit yourself. But it's over. You've got to know that."

"I know I told you to lay down your gun!" The voice was gruff and wild. It was useless to argue.

I kept my hands up and told Killbride I was going to take my gun out. I lifted it by its stock between my thumb and index finger, made sure the safety was on, and tossed it away from me. Striking the green turf it made a light thump.

"This is the wrong drill," I said, coming closer.

"Shut up!" The command lacked backbone.

"Win, we know Claire killed Karillian," I said. "We also know she killed Karillian's daughter. We *also* know that Beaucharme's boys kidnapped Chelly for two reasons: one, so they could somehow buy time to get the murder weapon back from Jessup and eliminate him as a blackmail threat; and two, so they could protect Beaucharme's money-laundering operations in Gatwick and elsewhere. Chelly had you and Claire worried. You were afraid she was starting to remember too much. Over the past year or so her mania had started to take focus: Find Jessup. So Beaucharme hired Shondra Maine to get to Jessup first, to get the murder weapon back. But she failed and was murdered when she started getting blackmail ideas herself. You feared everything was coming back to Chelly. But Chelly only wanted to know where her baby was. If you had told her she might have stopped there."

"But she didn't stop," Win Killbride said. "And Claire is dead."

"Thanks to Mikah Karillian," I said. "Not Chelly."

"The New York cops told me she confronted Claire in front of Mikah Karillian. If he hadn't overheard Cheryl's accusations he wouldn't have killed Claire."

"I doubt that," I said. "I think he was there to kill her whether Chelly showed up or not."

Win Killbride turned his eyes away from mine. He understood the score.

"Let me ask Spoonacre a question," I said. "Do you know what we're talking about?"

Spoonacre moved his eyes toward Killbride for permission to speak. Killbride nodded.

"All too well," Spoonacre said.

"Jessup told you about Claire murdering Karillian?"

Spoonacre nodded. "The day after it happened."

"But the Killbrides bought your silence."

"In a manner of speaking," Spoonacre said. "Mine and Duncan Keel's."

"We didn't buy your silence," Killbride growled at Spoonacre.

"No," I said. "Beaucharme did it for you. He's really

the one who took over." I looked at Win Killbride.
"What's the connection between you two in the first
place?"

"We went to high school together," Killbride said.
"He nearly drowned in this lake. In '46, after the war. I
saved his life."

"So, like in the fairy tales, in return for saving the
monster's life, you were granted three wishes."

"He told me, anytime I needed a favor he'd do it,"
Killbride answered glumly.

"So when your wife killed Karillian, you felt you
needed one," I said.

Killbride's head was slumped on his thick, rucked
neck.

"Yeah. I guess you could say, by then Bobby
Beaucharme was into that kind of help."

"So let me guess. He came and disposed of the body."

"He took it away. Said not to worry. Then, after the
police searches were done, he showed me how to dump it
in the lake."

"Did you dump it?"

He nodded.

"Wrapped in camouflage netting with lead weights all
around it. In about a hundred feet of water. Out there."
He pointed toward the lake. "Right in the middle. About
the same place I saved Beaucharme's life years before." He
chuckled without mirth.

"And then to buy Spoonacre's and Keel's silence,
Beaucharme got Clapp senior to lose the needle that killed
Jerry Leathers," I said.

"Yeah." Killbride nodded. He cradled the shotgun in
one arm and dug a cigarette from his shirt pocket. He lit it
with the old Zippo lighter.

"Only Beaucharme never does favors for nothing," I
said. "Payment for his corpse-moving service was you
handing over nineteen of your commercial buildings so he
could launder dirty money. He had Spoonacre on a short
leash with the needle. So why not make him the proprietor
of those buildings?"

"Oh, it was worse than that," Killbride said, smoking. "He had me put this asshole through law school!"

A sour smile spread across Spoonacre's lips.

"All to keep Claire from going to jail," I said.

"It was her money." Killbride blew out smoke. "We all stood to lose if she went."

I looked at Spoonacre. "What did Keel get for keeping his mouth shut?" I said.

Spoonacre shrugged and looked embarrassed. Killbride threw out an arm.

"Keel got to live his life," he said. "He was free to write his shitty little verses on birthday cards."

"He got immunity," Spoonacre added.

"But no money," I said.

"No." The two conspirators looked at each other.

I nodded. Cool breezes from the lake blew through the oaks. Their leaves rustling sounded like a waterfall. I pressed on.

"What did Beaucharme have on Clapp senior so that he could get him to lose the needle?"

Killbride exploded in tired laughter.

"Beaucharme owned Clapp senior," he said. "He practically *installed* the poor bastard as police chief. Back in '54. A long time back, over in Plattsburgh, Beaucharme helped him beat a morals charge by paying off the boy's family."

"*Boy's* family," I said.

Killbride nodded. "Beaucharme brought Clapp here, dusted him off, got him a job on the police force. Pulled some strings. Eventually got him the chief's job."

"Handy having a chief in your back pocket," I said.

"That it is." Killbride smoked, impassive.

"Seems to me, with Claire dead, you don't owe Beaucharme anything," I said.

"Maybe I don't," Killbride said.

"From where I stand, agreeing to testify against him makes a lot more sense than murdering Spoonacre."

Killbride smiled sadly to himself. All the fight was drained from him now.

"It was supposed to be beautiful," Killbride said. "After we cut the deal. Wouldn't turn to shit's what Bobby said."

"Prosecutors cut deals, too," I said. "Better deals than Beaucharme ever cut for you."

Killbride said nothing, only smoked. But then he moved the shotgun away from Spoonacre's face.

"What about me?" Spoonacre said. Droplets of sweat bathed his face and neck.

"If Win doesn't kill you Beaucharme will," I said. "You're both in a good position to cut prosecutor's deals."

Spoonacre slumped forward, his hands clasped between his knees. He already looked convicted.

"I didn't mean to kill the Leathers kid," he said. "Keel and me, we were screwing around with Armen's works. It was an accident."

"I'm sure it was," I said.

"I'd like to square it up." Spoonacre looked at me.

Nobody spoke for a while.

"I'd like to make a phone call to the state police," I said. "I'd like to help both of you square it up. Can I do that?"

Spoonacre unclasped his hands and turned them upward. It was OK with him. Killbride examined the engraving on his shotgun's side plates. He reset the safety and laid the gun on the grove's earthen floor.

"Go ahead," he said.

I picked my gun up off the grass and walked to where Win Killbride was sitting. I picked up his shotgun.

"One more question," I said. "I need to know: What *did* you and Claire do with Chelly's baby twenty-five years ago?"

Win Killbride took one more long draw from the cigarette, then flicked it from his fingers. It landed in the grass, sending slow ribbons of smoke into the cool air.

"It was part of the package for ridding us of Karillian," he said.

"Don't tell me." My guts congealed on his next words.

"Yeah," Win Killbride said. "Beaucharme got the baby."

44

LONG BEFORE FILES AND TWO OTHER PLAINCLOTHES COPS
reached Arthur Cole's, I decided to hit the road and follow
a lingering lead. Route 10 was still heavy with vacation
traffic, and the lineman's directions were still good. On the
road to Lon Jessup's trailer, dirty-faced children in ragged
clothes stared at me with blank suspicion. One of them
yelled at me as I passed.

"Hey, you! Hey, you!"

This time, parked beside the scabrous Dodge was a
trim green Chevrolet pickup sporting Vermont plates. On
its seat I noticed a neatly folded copy of the *New York
Times* Metro section. "Double Deaths at Guggenheim"
read the headline below the fold. The OXYGEN IN USE sign
had been removed from the trailer's screen door. All that
remained of it were two pieces of strapping tape. Hearing
voices inside, I knocked hard on the metal lintel and held
my breath. The breeze wafted septic stenches into my face.

The voices stopped. The sound of shuffling feet whispered across the trailer floor. The old woman, Jessup's
mother, magically materialized behind the screen.

"Oh, it's you."

I was standing with my hand shading my eyes from
the noon sun. Despite the stench I was trying to grin.

"I was in the neighborhood and thought I'd drop by,"
I said. "Do you mind if I come in?"

"Who is it, Hattie?" A man's voice inside the trailer
spoke sharply. It was not Lon Jessup's voice.

"I'm not in a good way right now," Hattie Jessup
said. "I lost Lon ten days ago—"

"I'm sorry to hear that."

"Well, he was very sick. But like the doctor said, the good thing is he isn't suffering anymore."

"I'm sure you're right."

She wasn't listening.

"Now I'm worried about Tommy. Some policeman in Arizona wired me, sayin' they'd found some of Tommy's belongings in a river."

"That's what I came to talk to you about."

"Is it?"

I nodded. "May I come in?"

"Who is it?" the voice said again.

Hattie Jessup turned away from the doorway. "It's a guy from the College."

She opened the door and I stepped inside. Sitting on a couch in the space once occupied by Lon Jessup's hospital bed was a familiar face. I'm not sure which of us was more surprised. I smiled.

"Hello, Kerr," I said.

The bitter old man looked at me, pin-eyed.

"What are you doin here?"

"Maybe I should ask you the same question."

Jessup's mother stepped between us and gave Kerr a brusque look. "You two know each other?"

Kerr looked at me with undisguised contempt.

"This is the private investigator, Boone, the one's been makin' trouble up at the Killbrides."

"He told me he was with alumni affairs." Jessup's mother eyed me with faint alarm.

"In a way I am," I said. "I'm a Dartmouth alum. But Kerr's right. I'm also a private eye."

"Well, I'll be!" The woman moved a little closer to Kerr. She looked me up and down. "What do you want, comin' into my home like that?"

"The first time I wanted to find your son so I might get a lead on a missing woman. This time it's something else."

"What would that be?" Hattie Jessup touched the moles at the base of her neck and glanced sideways at Kerr. His face was a bag of simmering venom.

"You didn't tell me when I mentioned her name that

you knew Chelly Killbride." I looked at her alarmed blue eyes.

"That's because you didn't ask," she said, pouting.

"No. It's because you're a good actress, Mrs. Jessup. You slapped your hands together when I said Chelly's name as if the name came out of the blue for you. When in fact you worked summers in the Killbride household."

"I'd never heard Chelly. The name Cheryl I would've remembered."

"And Chelly or Cheryl would've introduced herself so you would've remembered her in person. In case you couldn't tell who she was after twenty-five years. She had nothing to hide."

"Well, neither do I!" Hattie Jessup puffed her cheeks and threw back her shoulders.

"Yes, you do," I said. "You've been helping Tom blackmail Win Killbride for twenty-five years."

Hattie Jessup's mouth dropped open in a slack oval. "Why would I want to do a thing like that?"

"Because when Tom told you about Claire Killbride shooting Armen Karillian, you saw an opportunity for revenge, with Tom as your front. He had the murder weapon. It was his pistol to begin with. Claire Killbride had stolen it from Tom's room at Karillian's farm when she went down there once, looking for Cheryl. You made Tom give you the gun. You put him up to it."

"He's talkin' a lot of crazy nonsense!" Kerr shouted from the couch. "I'm callin' the sheriff."

"You can't from here," I said. "Remember? No phone. I assume you had to drive over here to feed her updates on my investigation. But that was OK, given your relationship to each other."

"What relation's that?" Kerr snarled, disgusted.

I hesitated before saying it.

"Lovers?" I held my breath. It was hard to think of two septuagenarians as such, but then their romance had happened twenty-five years earlier. "You and Hattie had an affair that summer Karillian was killed. Claire Killbride fired Hattie on some minor infraction. But deep down the two of you know why she did it. She'd caught you together in her house. She wanted to wreck your relationship. She wanted to fire you, Kerr, but Win intervened. You two and Tommy were furious over the firing. Then Claire shot Karillian and, as they say, the tables were turned."

Kerr sneered disgustedly and waved his arm in the air. "I've smelled manure before but never as rich as your crap!"

"It isn't crap." I looked at Hattie. "It's all in the note Tom wrote me before he died."

Hattie clutched her throat. "Tommy's dead?"

"You know he is. You know the thugs at your door were here to shut him down."

Her breathing grew labored; she plopped back on the couch beside Kerr. But her eyes were dry and worried, not grief-struck. Her look was turned inward on itself.

"The note was Tommy's confession to me. He knew he was going to die. He asked me to hand the blackmail receipts over to you and for you to destroy them. But I can't do that now."

"You can't?" Hattie Jessup's eyes were big with fear.

"No." I shook my head. "Not until you give me the gun that shot Armen Karillian. And not until you tell me what you did with Duncan Keel."

"Who?" Hattie and Kerr leaned forward. Both sets of suspicious old eyes were grim with fear.

"You know Keel. Both of you know Keel. His car was found a week ago in the Dartmouth Medical Center parking lot, but he wasn't in it. He knew about Tommy's blackmail. But he was being blackmailed himself. By the Killbrides. Over Jerry Leathers's death. All these years he's known Tommy's been collecting money from Killbride. How much, he probably didn't know. But when his card business went bad he knew where to come. He came here. He was desperate. He wanted in. He wanted money. Fast. I'm guessing you didn't give him any."

"I wouldn't give that little pipsqueak a dime!"

"Hattie!" Kerr tried to hush her.

"Did Keel ever find the gun? With the weapon that killed Karillian he thought he'd be in business. Did he get it?"

"Don't talk, Hattie!" Kerr grabbed her doughy arm. His face was flushed with alarm.

"There's one way to find out." I strode from the living room.

"Wait!" Hattie cried, but I ignored her.

It was only six strides down the short dark hall and into the cluttered guest bedroom. I dropped to my hands and knees and touched the box still under the daybed. I drew it out. The snapping turtle shells clattered in their tissue just as they had weeks earlier. Flinging aside the box's lid, I tried to open the lid of Tom's wooden shop-class box but it was padlocked. With one downward thrust of my right elbow, I smashed the lid's glass; the impact jostled the varnished carapace beneath it. When I moved aside the carapace, I found the gun. It was wrapped in a plastic bag, just as Jessup's note had said it would be.

I did not have time to lift the bag before Hattie Jessup entered the room and came at me with a fistful of sharp points. She chopped down with them toward my neck but I caught her arm. Her face was a mask of evil, spiteful rage. Inches from my face I saw what the points were— Lon's needles. With enough morphine in them to stun a horse.

I chopped down hard on her wrist. From the spiteful mouth came a piteous wail. The needles exploded from her hand, clattering across the floor like tiny missiles.

I heard Kerr coming before I saw him and then he was in the room, a meat cleaver in his hand and a look to kill on his mean, bitter face. As he came forward I flung Hattie at him, buying enough time for myself to spring backwards and stand. Hattie was on her back, screaming, and Kerr hacked down at me with the cleaver but I caught his arm and squeezed it like I'd squeezed his lover's. His yellow teeth bared, his sour breath panting in my face, he released his grip on the cleaver in a few long seconds.

"Where's Keel?" I asked.

"Out back. She put him there. It was her doing. I opposed it."

"Blackmailing Killbride was all your idea!" Hattie shrieked from the floor.

"Killing Keel wasn't!"

"If I'd not listened to you twenty-five years ago,

Tommy'd still be alive!" She broke down sobbing. There was nothing more to say.

I took the wrapped gun from the turtle shell and walked out the trailer into the yard. There was a stand of red sumac out back and a narrow path through it led downhill to a little pond. Brush fringed its abandoned shores and the pond itself was shallow with sediment. Dragging the small body of a greeting-card manufacturer down the weed-grown track would have been difficult for a woman in her seventies; difficult, but not impossible.

Through the shallow water you could see the sunken body in its burlap sack and you could see where the snapping turtles had made headway. When the police divers pulled it out you felt yourself go hollow. Where Duncan Keel had had a face, a large snapping turtle sat. It hissed when the divers tried to touch it.

45

ALMOST SIX WEEKS TO THE DAY DUNCAN KEEL'S BODY WAS recovered, I found myself at last in a place I had yearned for all summer. The Lamoille River flows below a granite ledge not far from my house, and the ledge shades the pools and eddies formed by its fallen rocks. Accessible from the highway, it was a favorite fishing spot for fly casters and worm-flingers alike, though now, in early September, few anglers came there. On this cool early evening, I worked an elk-hair caddis twelve off the riffles and reveled at having the stretch to myself.

I had found Chelly's missing child, a daughter, after applying a little pressure on Beaucharme, who, from a holding cell in St. Johnsbury, faced the prospect of life in a federal jail. It developed that he had given the baby to a U.S. senator from a southern coastal state. The senator, a blowhard and an image-conscious scandal-phobe, quickly acquiesced to a meeting between the adopted woman and Chelly. In fact, he thanked me for the opportunity to put his daughter's inquiries about her birth mother to rest.

The meeting took place on a sweltering day in August, in a ballet loft in south Philadelphia. The daughter, now twenty-four years old, taught classes to inner city kids as an antidote, she told us, to her father's racism. John, Chelly, Anny, Arthur, and I all peered through the loft door's wire-reinforced window as the daughter led a class of little black girls in blue leotards through a rigorous hour of *pliés, sautés* and *ronds de jambe en l'air.*

The woman looked like Chelly's taller younger sister.

When she came out to greet us in her black leotard she went right to her mother.

"Hi," she said in a tidewater accent. "You must be Chelly. I'm Miranda. Long time no see!" Both women squealed, welcoming each other's open arms. The rest of us grinned like fools as the reunited women hugged each other.

Chelly had grown strong in John's care. Off drugs of any kind for two months now, she was a changed woman, in Arthur's estimation. Perhaps it wasn't just hypnosis therapy that had transformed her, he confided one day in John and me.

"Strike me down for saying it, but her mother's death might be the best thing that ever happened to Chelly."

Chelly's decisiveness supported Arthur's view. Her father's ruin had not stopped her from putting the lakeside house up for sale the week after his, Beaucharme's, and Spoonacre's arrests. Anny joked that Chelly and Arthur just wanted to move in with her and John. But when the house sold a week after that, Chelly made a startling announcement.

"Artie and I are moving to New York City," she told all of us over dinner at my place.

"New York City?" Anny shouted. "*New York City!* Child, what you gonna do in New York City?"

Chelly looked at Arthur. He squeezed her hand. She turned back to Anny. "Artie's going to try to get his back fixed. And I'm going back to school so I can teach. And we're going to adopt!"

She put her fingers over her mouth and lowered her head.

"Well, well," John said. "The plot thickens."

"But I'll miss you, Chelly," Zach said.

"Well, I'll come back!" Chelly raised her head and wiped her eyes with the heels of her hands.

John's orthopedic friends in Boston had examined Arthur closely and finally referred him to a colleague he had overlooked in New York. The prognosis: without surgery, a lifetime of constant pain for Arthur. With surgery (on the tendons and lower discs), a sixty-percent chance of significant improvement.

"Not the best odds," Arthur told John and me.

"But sixty percent better than the status quo," John said.

Arthur had started to attend A.A. meetings and was scheduled for surgery in early October.

To date, Tom Jessup's body had not been found. But Armen Karillian's had been salvaged by divers with the help of Win Killbride's directions. Viewing the poet's skeleton in the state morgue, I thought about the horrifying effect his life and death had had on so many others. Break the spell, Bellino had said. The case had been an ugly fairy tale. It seemed now, at last, the spell had truly been broken.

I felt a twitch and the line tugged taut. I raised the rod tip and reeled in a twelve-inch brown. A minute later I had released it. A minute after that, I waded ashore.

Climbing the riprap from the river, I did not look up until I was nearly at the guard rail. In the parking area Nan and the dogs were sitting in her Blazer.

She opened the door and the dogs bounded out and tore around the Blazer to me. They nipped at my calves; Yeats leapt into my arms and Kai followed suit, licking my jawbones. I carried them around to Nan who was sitting at the wheel. She rolled down the window and smiled at me.

"Hello," she said.

"Hello. You're back."

"Yeah. For just a little while."

"How's your mom?"

"She's dying."

I nodded.

"I'm sorry," I said.

"Yeah," she said. "So am I."

"How's Michael?" I said after a decent interval.

"Moved to London!" She laughed. Then when she had quieted: "It stopped working a while ago."

I set the dogs down. I opened my hands. "Win some, lose some."

She shook her head.

"I'm sorry what I put you through," she said.

"No blame." I clapped my hands.

"I brought the dogs back because I'm not sure how long I'm going to be down there and I didn't want you to be without them."

"They can also be a nuisance," I said.

"They were never that."

I looked beyond her at the river flowing smoothly over the rocks, braided corrugations of browns, creams, blues, and whites. The riffles in the glowing evening were smooth and glowed white. I was frightened to ask the next question.

"How little a while are you going to be here?"

"A couple days. To check on the house and gather a few things to bring back to Connecticut."

She looked at me. "How 'bout you? You busy these days?"

"Just came off a case. This is the first time I've fished all summer."

"Any luck?"

"A small brown. But I wasn't working very hard."

She smiled. "I miss it."

"I've missed it, too. Maybe tomorrow night if you're not busy we could go fishing together."

"I'd like that."

"And, if you're not busy now, would you like to have dinner with me?"

"After I dumped you, you want to have dinner with me?"

"You didn't dump anybody. You did what you had to."

"Yeah, well. It must've felt like abandonment."

I thought of Taylor and felt a pang.

"Believe me, for a moment I abandoned you, too."

She smiled. "Your place?"

"Sure. If you don't mind omelettes and a salad. I need to go shopping."

"I don't mind at all."

"You want me to take the dogs?" I asked.

"For old time's sake I'd like to take them," she said.

"Fine."

I opened the doors and the dogs scrambled back into her car. When I looked into Nan's face I saw it had been stamped by what lay ahead. Sooner or later it stamped everyone. It was what made everything matter.

"I'm sorry," I said again.

"Don't be." Her smile would always transcend it. "You lead now," she said. "We'll follow you back."